Ransome's Honor

KAYE DACUS

HARVEST HOUSE PUBLISHERS

EUGENE, OREGON

Verses marked NASB are taken from the New American Standard Bible®, © 1960, 1962, 1963, 1968, 1971, 1972, 1973, 1975, 1977, 1995 by The Lockman Foundation. Used by permission. (www.Lockman.org)

The author is represented by MacGregor Literary.

This is a work of fiction. Names, characters, places, and incidents are products of the author's imagination or are used fictitiously. Any resemblance to actual persons, living or dead, or to events or locales, is entirely coincidental.

Cover by Left Coast Design, Portland, Oregon

Cover photo © Richard Jenkins

RANSOME'S HONOR
Copyright © 2009 by Kaye Dacus
Published by Harvest House Publishers
Eugene, Oregon 97402
www.harvesthousepublishers.com

Library of Congress Cataloging-in-Publication Data

Dacus, Kaye
Ransome's honor / Kaye Dacus.
    p. cm.—(The Ransome trilogy ; bk. 1)
ISBN 978-0-7369-2753-6 (pbk.)
1. Ship captains—Fiction. 2. Single women—Fiction. 3. Arranged marriage—Fiction. 4.
Married people—Fiction. 5. Portsmouth (England)—Fiction. I. Title.
PS3604.A25R36 2009
813'.6—dc22

                                                     2009004876

Printed in the United States of America

                09 10 11 12 13 14 15 16 17 / DP-NI / 10 9 8 7 6 5 4 3

To Jacob, Benjamin, Jordan, Michaela, Caleb, and Josh.

Delight yourself in the Lord, and He will
give you the desires of your heart.

PSALM 37:4

ACKNOWLEDGMENTS

Most sincere thanks to all the critique partners who helped me with the nuances and details over the years; to my agent, Chip MacGregor, for believing in me; to Kim Moore, Gene Skinner, and everyone else at Harvest House, for helping this story weigh anchor and forge ahead at full sail; to Ronie Kendig, for being William and Julia's biggest cheerleader and making me believe in this story even when it seemed like nothing would ever come of it; and to my family, especially my parents, without whom I couldn't have done this. And finally, all praise and glory to God for making my dreams come true.

Portsmouth, England
September 1802

J ulia, do stop fidgeting. One would think this evening were about you, not in honor of your father."

Seventeen-year-old Julia Witherington immediately stilled her hands and clasped them in her lap. "I am sorry, Mama. I am excited for Papa to be announced for the first time as Sir Edward, and you as Lady Witherington."

In the dim light of the carriage, the new crest on her father's Royal Navy coat vied for attention with the gold braid and sparkling epaulets indicating his rank of captain. If the war had lasted a few months longer, his posting to admiral would have been confirmed.

But if the Peace of Amiens had not come when it did, Julia would still be on the sugar plantation in Jamaica, not on her way to a ball in Portsmouth. A ball at which she expected something momentous to occur. Something she'd dreamed of for the past seven years.

Julia twisted the fabric of her glove around her left thumb. They'd been in London this fortnight past for her father to receive his knighthood. "You are certain all of your former officers will be in attendance, Papa?" She pressed her cheek to the carriage window as the assembly hall came into view.

"Aye, Julia, as I have already confirmed twice. Why do you have so much interest in former officers of the *Indomitable?*"

She turned to gape at him, surprised. Was he merely pretending not to know? What else could his private conference with Lieutenant William Ransome have been about this afternoon? "I know I was only ten years old when you took us to Jamaica on the *Indy,* but even after seven years, I well remember how kind the officers—and midshipmen—were to me and Michael." Her voice cracked on her brother's name, and as always, she sent up a quick prayer that somehow, somewhere, he was still alive. After two years, her heart still refused to believe him dead. *Lost at sea* simply meant lost. Not necessarily dead.

Mama gave her a reassuring smile. Thank goodness Mama did not keep her emotions hidden the way Papa did. But Julia had no cause to worry about her father's dismissive attitude. William Ransome was one of her father's favorite young officers, given the frequency with which his name appeared in her father's letters. Papa had no doubt approved the match and given William his blessing.

The carriage rattled to a stop on the cobblestone drive of the assembly hall. Julia's heart felt fit to burst through her stays. Tonight. She was certain. Tonight William would make his intentions known, and tomorrow the paper would carry the news of their engagement.

Walking sedately behind her parents and waiting to be announced proved a Herculean task, but Julia managed it—and she also managed not to look about the crowd with too much eagerness. William would come to her; she need not seek him out.

After the applause died away at her parents' introduction, she followed them into the press of well-wishers. She jumped when a hand slipped through the crook of her elbow.

Susan Barstow, her closest acquaintance in Portsmouth, beamed up at Julia, blue eyes twinkling. "I am so happy you've returned, Julia. Portsmouth has been a positive bore without you. Later, you must tell me all about London. But first...I shall set your mind at ease and tell you he is here. He and my dear Collin have vanished into the card room with many of the other officers; but now your father is here, they should reappear because the dancing will start soon."

Even as Susan spoke, several young men in Royal Navy uniforms entered from a side door. Taller by several inches than Susan, Julia stood on her toes. There—speaking to her father. Julia moved through the forest of people to rejoin her parents, Susan trying to keep up with her.

She arrived just in time. Tall and slender, his brown hair falling onto his forehead in loose curls, Lieutenant William Ransome straightened from bowing in greeting to her mother. His vivid blue eyes, pale yet impossibly fathomless, met Julia's. Anticipation of the event she foresaw this evening heated her cheeks. She controlled the size of her smile with enormous effort and bent her knees in a curtsey.

"Good evening, Lieutenant Ransome."

"Good evening, Miss Witherington." His baritone voice tickled her ears. "If you are not already engaged, might I request the honor of the first two dances?"

"I am not engaged. I would be honored." She settled her hand atop his proffered arm. Turning to walk with him, she caught the dimple in her mother's cheek, even as Lady Witherington curtseyed to a baron's wife. Yes, Mama also suspected what this evening would bring.

Throughout the first dance, Julia could hardly keep her eyes off William. Even though his uniform coat showed a bit of wear at cuffs and collar, to her, he was the most resplendent officer in the hall. The intensity of his gaze outshone even the admirals' uniforms.

As they awaited their turn to join in the complex figures of the allemande, Julia could not ignore the voices around her. The matrons made no attempt to hide their questioning of why someone of *Sir* Edward's importance and wealth would allow his daughter to waste her affections on an officer who sent all his earnings home to support his family, an officer who depended on the charity of his friends to stay in Portsmouth, an officer who was clearly courting Julia for her thirty-thousand-pound dowry.

If William heard the malicious rumors, his face betrayed no reaction. Finally, he and Julia joined hands and took their part in the dance.

"You realize, Lieutenant," Julia whispered, "that everyone will think you are not enjoying our dance if you continue on with so grave a countenance."

The left side of his mouth twitched, and some of the tightness around his eyes eased. "And we would not want to be the subject of any gossip, would we, Miss Witherington?"

Ah. Now he seemed more himself. "You have yet to tell me how you kept yourself occupied while we were in London."

"I mostly spent my time at the dockyard, trying to be useful."

Her sympathy went out to him. To her mother's dismay, Julia had not only involved herself in the running of the sugar plantation over the last several years, she had taken on the role of mistress, working with the steward and the foreman to manage the day-to-day operation. If someone were to tell her she would no longer be responsible for Tierra Dulce, that all her responsibility would be given to someone else, she would run quite mad with boredom.

"Is there any possibility of getting another ship? I am certain if there is anything my father can do..."

William's dark brows flattened into a straight line, once again obscuring his thoughts. "Not unless he goes out and attacks a French ship and restarts the war. The peacetime navy has no need for as many lieutenants as are currently made, and those with seniority get ships." His expression eased slightly. "Your father has assured me he will see me assigned to a ship as soon as a posting is available."

The music ended; William offered Julia his arm. "Will you take a turn about the garden with me? It grows quite warm in here."

Julia took several calming breaths, trying to still her racing pulse. She nodded and took his arm. On the way to the doors, she spied Susan—who was taking her position for the next dance opposite William's closest friend, Collin Yates. Susan's eyes widened when she saw Julia on William's arm. Julia nodded, and Susan bounced on her toes and clapped her hands.

The evening's entertainment had just started, so the garden was nearly deserted. William kept to the path, his stride slow but purposeful. Accustomed to his long silences, Julia took the time to calm herself so she could answer him in as dignified a manner as possible. She did not want to annoy him with an emotional outburst when he put the question to her.

He stopped at an ornate wooden bench within full sight of the path. "Shall we sit a moment?"

The early autumn air wrapped them in a warm cocoon while the remnants of the sunset bathed the garden in a lavender glow. She perched on the edge of the bench, trying to appear composed.

Instead of taking a seat beside her, William clasped his hands behind his back and paced a circle around her, much as a captain would tread the deck of his ship. Fingers twined tightly together, Julia watched and waited. After several minutes, he paused, half turned away from her.

"Miss Witherington, I—Did you have a pleasant sojourn in London?"

"London? Yes. I enjoyed seeing my father honored with a knighthood." She bit the insides of her cheek to keep from smiling over his choice to ease into conversation first.

"And do you know when you will return to Jamaica?"

"Not until the spring. Father wants to take no risk of hurricanes or storms on our return voyage."

A slight breeze ruffled William's dark curls. "I see."

What, precisely, did he see? Anxiety began to nibble at Julia's excitement. She wished he would just get on with it. This time, William's silence became unbearable after a few moments.

"Susan Barstow wrote to me in London to announce her engagement to Lieutenant Yates." And Julia very much wanted to walk back into the assembly room and share similar news with her friend.

"Collin is the second son of an earl with a large inheritance. He can marry as he wills. He is not dependent upon patronage and promotion to make his way in this world."

"There are other ways to gain fortune." Julia cleared the nervousness from her throat. "Marriage, for example."

Even in profile, it was obvious that William struggled with his thoughts. "It has been my experience that men who marry to gain wealth are rarely happy with their choice." He rounded the bench again and paused in front of her, his pale blue eyes troubled, indecisive.

"Not all marriages made for financial security can be bad. Not when there is affection before the marriage takes place." Heat rushed into her cheeks at her bold declaration of her feelings for him.

Her statement seemed to have no effect on his discomfort. His jaw flexed as if he were grinding whatever words he was not saying between his teeth.

She harkened back to the malicious things the women inside had said about her and William. How could she tell him she loved him all the more for sending his pay home to support his mother and sister, when he had not yet declared his love for her?

William sat beside her for the briefest of moments and then sprang to his feet and ran his fingers through his hair. "I cannot...No. It is better for a man to do what he must, to work hard to gain promotion through honorable service—to do what is necessary to gain patronage without sacrificing one's very soul."

Julia's heart, which had been near to floating all evening, sank like a hulled ship. "Then you...you are not...you would not consider..."

He turned, expression inscrutable in the shadows. "Come. I must return you to your parents. I would not wish to offend your father on this of all nights."

Forlorn numbness settled into Julia's limbs. Somehow, she managed to rise from the bench and accompany William into the hall. She kept her gaze directed forward, unwilling to witness everyone staring at her, knowing her humiliation would be obvious to all.

Though it seemed impossible, Julia soon stood beside her mother, watching William Ransome bow and walk away. He disappeared into the card room, followed shortly by Collin Yates.

Much to Julia's chagrin, Susan tugged at her sleeve.

"So?" Susan whispered. "Is it settled?"

All the pieces of Julia's broken heart lodged in her throat. She blinked against welling tears. "It is settled. William does not want to marry me."

"What? No, it cannot be!"

Several matrons nearby turned at Susan's outcry. Julia snapped open her fan and tried to stop the conflagration in her face.

Susan took Julia's arm and led her out of the hall onto the front steps. "Tell me what happened."

Before she could censor her words, Julia told her acquaintance everything—every word, every gesture—that had passed in the garden. Mercifully, her eyes stayed dry, and her voice cracked only a few times during the recitation.

Susan shook her head. "This cannot be right. If he did decide not to propose tonight, it is only because he has not yet secured your father's approbation."

"Then why were they closeted together for more than an hour this afternoon?" Julia sank onto the top step, heedless of soiling her white gown.

"William wants to marry you. I have never been more certain of anything in my life. Even my dear Collin said so when he saw you going into the garden." Susan reached her hand down to Julia. "Get up. I will not allow you to sit here and sulk when we both know that Lieutenant Ransome is in love with you and wants to marry you." She saw to the task of brushing the back of Julia's gown.

"He said that a man should do whatever he could, whatever is necessary, to gain promotion and patronage. You don't think he—"

"Do not even finish your thought. Except for my Collin, there is no man I have ever met more honorable than William Ransome. He would not toy with your affections just to get closer to your father."

Julia wanted to believe her friend, but icy shards of doubt prickled along her skin. She followed Susan back inside.

"I will speak with Collin, and he will speak with William." Susan squeezed Julia's hand and disappeared into the crowd.

"Julia—you look pale." Mama touched her gloved hand to Julia's cheek. "Is it a headache?"

Though nearly complete opposites in temperament, one thing Julia did share with her mother was their penchant for sick headaches during times of strain or worry. She closed her eyes and leaned her cheek into her mother's palm.

"Oh, my dear, why did not you say so sooner? We shall send for the carriage to take you back home immediately."

Never in her life had Julia chosen the coward's way out. But she could not stay, could not risk coming face-to-face with William again.

Once home, she dismissed her maid, needing quiet to try to sort through her thoughts. After disrobing, she left the white gown, the one she'd been so anxious for William to see her in, crumpled on the floor. With her dressing gown wrapped around her, she sank into the cushions on the window seat and stared at the sky.

Two years ago, she lost her twin brother at sea. Tonight, she lost William. What else would God take away from her?

※ ※ ※

In the morning, Julia dug into the deep drawer at the bottom of the wardrobe and pulled out a plain muslin work-dress. The yellow color reminded her of the hot Jamaican sun, something that usually brought her joy. Now everything seemed devoid of meaning or importance. Everything but Tierra Dulce. The plantation. Her home for the past seven years. The one place where she knew what to expect from everyone around her.

She needed to go home. There she would be happy again. There she would put behind her this trip to England and all the trappings of society her mother had wanted her to experience. There she would forget she ever harbored a dream of becoming William Ransome's wife.

Her mother must have believed her still feeling poorly, as a maid arrived with a breakfast tray shortly after ten o'clock. Though the food held no interest, Julia's stomach growled. She ate the toast and strawberry preserves and then returned to the window—just in time to see Susan Barstow turn into the front walk.

Knowing the butler would not admit any callers at such an early hour, Julia went down to meet her and lead her back to her room.

"Did you sleep at all last night?" Susan asked, divesting herself of her hat and gloves.

"Very little."

"I am sorry for that." Susan wandered to the window and then to the fireplace, finally perching on the edge of the chaise flanking it.

"Susan, what are you keeping from me?"

"I had a note from Collin first thing…" Susan took great interest in twining and untwining the end of her sash around her fingers.

Julia wanted to shake the diminutive blonde. "Yes? What did his note say?"

"Lieutenant Ransome left for Gateacre early this morning." The words rushed out, barely above a whisper.

Julia wrapped her arms around her aching stomach and leaned against the window frame. "To Gateacre? But when will he return?"

Susan rushed to Julia, putting her arm around Julia's waist. "He told Collin he does not expect to return unless he is recalled for duty."

William's words in the garden reverberated in Julia's head. What little hope she'd managed to cling to through the night shattered.

"He…he never intended to propose to me."

"You cannot know that—"

"Yes, I can. He as much as confessed it to me. He said he was only interested in patronage and promotion to make his fortune, not marriage." Julia moaned, tears pricking her eyes. "He courted me only to grow closer to my father. My father must have promised him yesterday some kind of position or that he will see William well-placed as soon as he can. That must be what happened. Why else would William have left today?"

Susan stepped back and planted her fists on her narrow hips. "I refuse to believe William Ransome would do that."

Julia uncrossed her arms and smoothed the front of her gown, swallowing back the bleak disappointment of shattered dreams. "I believe it. And I will never forgive William Ransome. Never."

Chapter One

Portsmouth, England
July 18, 1814

William Ransome pulled the collar of his oilskin higher, trying to stop the rain from dribbling down the back of his neck. He checked the address once more and then tucked the slip of paper safely into his pocket.

He took the four steps up to the front door of the townhouse in two strides and knocked. The rain intensified, the afternoon sky growing prematurely dark. After a minute or two, William raised his hand to knock again, but the door swung open to reveal a warm light.

A wizened man in standard black livery eyed William, bushy white brows rising in interest at William's hat, bearing the gold braid and black cockade of his rank. "Good evening, Captain. How may I assist you?"

"Good evening. Is this the home of Captain Collin Yates?"

The butler smiled but then frowned. "Yes, sir, it is. However, I'm sorry to say Captain Yates is at sea, sir."

"Is Mrs. Yates home?"

"Yes, sir. Please come in."

"Thank you." William stepped into the black-and-white tiled entry, water forming a puddle under him as it ran from his outer garments.

"May I tell Mrs. Yates who is calling?" The butler reached for William's soaked hat and coat.

"Captain William Ransome."

A glimmer of recognition sparkled in the butler's hazy blue eyes. In the dim light of the hall, he appeared even older than William originally thought. "The Captain William Ransome who is the master's oldest and closest friend?"

William nodded. "You must be Fawkes. Collin always said he would have you with him one day."

"The earl put up quite a fight, sir, but the lad needed me more." Fawkes shuffled toward the stairs and waved for William to join him. "Mrs. Yates is in the sitting room. I'm certain she will be pleased to see you."

William turned his attention to his uniform—checking it for lint, straightening the jacket with a swift tug at the waist—and followed the butler up the stairs.

Fawkes knocked on the double doors leading to a room at the back of the house. A soft, muffled voice invited entry. The butler motioned toward the door. It took a moment for William to understand the man was not going to announce him, but rather allow him to surprise Susan. He turned the knob and slowly pushed the door open.

Susan Yates sat on a settee with her back to him. "What is it, Fawkes—?" She turned to look over her shoulder and let out a strangled cry. "William!"

He met her halfway around the sofa and accepted her hands in greeting. "Susan. You're looking well."

Her reddish-blonde curls bounced as she looked him over. "I did not expect you until tomorrow!" She pulled him farther into the room. "So—tell me everything. When did you arrive? Why has it been two months since your last proper letter?" Susan sounded more like the girl of fifteen he'd met a dozen years ago than the long-married wife of his best friend. "Can you stay for dinner?"

"We docked late yesterday. I spent the whole of today at the port Admiralty, else I would have been here earlier. And I am sorry to disappoint you, but I cannot stay long." He sat in an overstuffed chair and started to relax for the first time in weeks. "Where is Collin? Last I heard, he returned home more than a month ago."

Susan retrieved an extra cup and saucer from the sideboard and poured steaming black coffee into it. "The admiral asked for men to sail south to ferry troops home, and naturally my dear Collin volunteered—anything to be at sea. He is supposed to be back within the week." She handed him the cup. "Now, on to your news."

"No news, in all honesty. I've been doing the same thing Collin has—returning soldiers and sailors home. I only received orders to Portsmouth a week ago—thus the reason I sent the note express, rather than a full letter."

"But you're here now. For how long?"

"Five weeks. I've received a new assignment for *Alexandra*."

"What will you do until your new duty begins?"

"My crew and I are on leave for three weeks." And it could not have come at a better time. After two years away from home, his crew needed some time apart from each other.

"Are you going to travel north to see your family?"

"At the same time I sent the express to you announcing my return to Portsmouth, I sent word to my mother telling her of my sojourn here. When I arrived ashore earlier today, I received a letter that she and Charlotte will arrive next Tuesday."

"How lovely. Of course, you will all stay with us. No—I will brook no opposition. We have three empty bedchambers. I could not abide the thought of your staying at an inn when you could be with us."

"I thank you, and on behalf of my mother and sister."

"Think nothing of it. But you were telling me of your assignment. Your crew is not to be decommissioned?" Susan asked.

"No. I believe Admiral Witherington understands my desire to keep my crew together. They have been with me for two years and need no training."

"Understands?" Susan let out a soft laugh. "Was it not he who taught you the importance of an experienced crew?"

William sipped the coffee—not nearly as strong as his steward made it, but it served to rid him of the remaining chill from the rain.

"Yes, I suppose Collin and I did learn that from him…along with everything else we know about commanding a ship."

Susan sighed. "I wish you could stay so that I could get out of my engagement for the evening. Card parties have become all the fashion lately, but I have no skill for any of the games. If it weren't for Julia, I would probably decline every invitation."

"Julia—not Julia Witherington?" William set his cup down on the reading table beside him. He'd heard she had returned to Portsmouth following her mother's death, but he'd hoped to avoid her.

"Yes. She returned to England about eight months ago and has become the darling of Portsmouth society, even if they do whisper about her being a 'right old maid' behind her back. Although recently, Julia's presence always means Lady Pembroke—her aunt—is also in attendance." The tone of Susan's voice and wrinkling of her small nose left no doubt as to her feelings toward the aunt.

"Does Admiral Witherington attend many functions?"

"About half those his daughter does. Julia says she would attend fewer if she thought her aunt would allow. I have told her many times she should exert her position as a woman of independent means; after all, she is almost thir—of course it is not proper to reveal a woman's age." Susan blushed. "But Julia refuses to cross the old dragon."

"So you have renewed your acquaintance with Miss Witherington, then?" The thought of Miss Julia Witherington captured William's curiosity. He had not seen her since the Peace of Amiens twelve years ago…and the memory of his behavior toward her flooded him with guilt. His own flattered pride was to blame for leading her, and the rest of Portsmouth, to believe he would propose marriage. And for leading him to go so far as to speak to Sir Edward of the possibility.

"Julia and I have kept up a steady correspondence since she returned to Jamaica." The slight narrowing of Susan's blue eyes proved she remembered his actions of a dozen years ago all too well. "She was very hurt, William. She believes the attentions you paid her then were because you wished nothing more than to draw closer to her father."

William rose, clasped his hands behind his back, and crossed to the floor-to-ceiling window beside the crackling fireplace. His reflection wavered against the darkness outside as the rain ran in rivulets down the paned glass. "I did not mean to mislead her. I thought she understood why I, a poor lieutenant with seeming no potential for future fortune, could not make her an offer."

"Oh, William, she would have accepted your proposal despite your situation. And her father would have supported the marriage. You are his favorite—or so my dear Collin complains all the time." Silence fell and Susan's teasing smile faltered a bit. "She tells the most fascinating tales of life in Jamaica—she runs her father's sugar plantation there. Collin cannot keep up with her in discussions of politics. She knows everything about the Royal Navy—but of course she would, as the daughter of an admiral."

A high-pitched voice reciting ships' ratings rang in William's memory, and he couldn't suppress a slight smile. Julia Witherington had known more about the navy at age ten than most lifelong sailors.

"William?"

"My apologies, Susan." He snapped out of his reverie and returned to his seat. "Did Collin ever tell you how competitive we were? Always trying to out-do the other in our studies or in our duty assignments." He recalled a few incidents for his best friend's wife, much safer mooring than thinking about the young beauty with the cascade of coppery hair he hadn't been able to forget since the first time he met her, almost twenty years ago.

❧❧❧

Julia Witherington lifted her head and rubbed the back of her neck. The columns of numbers in the ledgers weren't adding properly, which made no sense.

An unmistakable sound clattered below; Julia crossed to the windows. A figure in a dark cloak and high-domed hat edged in gold stepped out of the carriage at the gate and into the rain-drenched front garden. Her mood brightened; she smoothed her gray muslin gown and stretched away the stiffness of inactivity.

She did not hear any movement across the hall. Slipping into her father's dressing room, she found the valet asleep on the stool beside the wardrobe. She rapped on the mahogany paneled door of the tall cabinet.

The young man rubbed his eyes and then leapt to his feet. "Miss Witherington?"

She adopted a soft but authoritative tone. "The admiral's home, Jim."

He rushed to see to his duty, just as Julia had seen sailors do at the least word from her father. Admiral Sir Edward Witherington's position demanded obedience, but his character earned his men's respect. The valet grabbed his master's housecoat and dry shoes. He tripped twice in his haste before tossing the hem of the dressing gown over his shoulder.

She smothered a smile and followed him down the marble staircase at a more sedate pace. The young man had yet to learn her father's gentle nature.

Admiral Sir Edward Witherington submitted himself to his valet's ministrations, a scowl etching his still-handsome face, broken only by the wink he gave Julia. She returned the gesture with a smile, though with some effort to stifle the yawn that wanted to escape.

He reached toward her. "You look tired. Did you rest at all today?"

She placed her hand in his. "The plantation's books arrived from Jamaica in this morning's post. I've spent most of the day trying to keep my head above the flotsam of numbers."

Sir Edward's chuckle rumbled in his chest as he kissed her forehead. He turned to the butler, who hovered nearby. "Creighton, inform cook we will be one more for dinner tonight."

"Aye, sir," the former sailor answered, a furrow between his dark brows.

That her father had invited one of his friends from the port Admiralty came as no surprise. Julia started toward the study, ready for the best time of the day—when she had her father to herself.

"Is that in addition to the extra place Lady Pembroke asked to have set?" Creighton asked.

Julia stopped and turned. "My aunt asked…?" She bit off the rest of the question. The butler did not need to be drawn into the discord between Julia and her aunt.

The admiral looked equally consternated. "I quite imagine she has somebody else entirely in mind, as I have not communicated my invitation with my sister-in-law. So I suppose we will have two guests for dinner this evening. Come, Julia."

Once in her father's study, Julia settled into her favorite winged armchair. A cheery fire danced on the hearth, fighting off the rainy day's chill. Flickering light trickled across the volumes lining the walls, books primarily about history and naval warfare. She alone knew where he hid the novels.

He dropped a packet of correspondence on his desk, drawing her attention. She wondered if she should share her concern over the seeming inaccuracy of the plantation's ledgers with her father. But a relaxed haziness started to settle over her mind, and the stiffness of hours spent hunched over the plantation's books began to ease. Perhaps the new steward's accounting methods were different from her own. No need to raise an alarm until she looked at them again with a clearer mind.

She loved this time alone with her father in the evenings, hearing of his duties, of the officers, politicians, and government officials he dealt with on a daily basis while deciding which ships to decommission and which to keep in service.

The sound of a door and footsteps in the hallway roused her. "Papa, how long will Lady Pembroke stay?"

Sir Edward crossed to the fireplace and stoked it with the poker. "You wish your aunt to leave? I do not like the thought of you without a female companion. You spend so much time on your own as it is."

"I do not mean to sound ungrateful. I appreciate the fact that Aunt Augusta has offered her services to me, that she wants to…help me secure my status in Portsmouth society." Julia stared at her twined fingers in her lap.

"It seems to have worked. Every day when I come home, there are more calling cards and invitations on the receiving table than I can count." Going around behind his desk, he opened one of the cabinets and withdrew a small, ironbound chest. With an ornate brass key, he unlocked it, placed his coin purse inside, secured it again, and put it away.

"Yes. I have met so many people since she came to stay three months ago. And I am grateful to her for that. But she is so…" Julia struggled for words that would not cast aspersions.

The admiral's forehead creased deeply when he raised his brows. "She is what?"

"She is…so different from Mama."

"As she was your mother's sister by marriage only, that is to be expected."

Julia nodded. To say anything more would be to sound plaintive, and she did not want to spoil whatever time her father could spare for her with complaints about his sister-in-law, who had been kind enough to come stay.

Sir Edward sat at his desk, slipped on a pair of spectacles, and fingered through the stack of correspondence from the day's post. He grunted and tossed the letters back on the desk.

"What is it, Papa?"

He rubbed his chin. "It has been nearly a year…yet every night, I look through the post hoping to see something addressed in your mother's hand."

Sorrow wrapped its cold fingers around Julia's throat. "I started writing a letter to her today, forgetting she is not just back home in Jamaica."

"Are you sorry I asked you to return to England?"

"No…" *And yes.* She did not want her father to think her ungrateful for all he had done for her. "I miss home, but I am happy to have had this time with you—to see you and be able to talk with you daily." Memories slipped in with the warmth of the Jamaica sun. "On Tuesdays and Fridays, when Jeremiah would leave Tierra Dulce and go into town for the post, as soon as I saw the wagon return, I would run down the road to meet him—praying for a letter from you."

His worried expression eased. "You looked forward to my missives filled with nothing more than life aboard ship and the accomplishments of those under my command?"

"Yes. I loved feeling as if I were there with you, walking *Indomitable*'s decks once again."

His sea-green eyes faded into nostalgia. "Ah, the good old *Indy*." His gaze refocused and snapped to Julia. "That reminds me. An old friend made berth in Spithead yesterday. Captain William Ransome."

Julia bit back sharp words. William Ransome—the man she'd sworn she'd never forgive. The man whose name she'd grown to despise from its frequent mention in her father's letters. He had always reported on William Ransome's triumphs and promotions, even after William disappointed all Julia's hopes twelve years ago. He wrote of William as if William had been born to him, seeming to forget his own son, lost at sea.

Her stomach clenched at the idea of seeing William Ransome again. "He's here, in Portsmouth?"

"Aye. But not for long. He came back at my request to receive new orders."

"And where are you sending him, now that we're at peace with France?" *Please, Lord, let it be some distant port.*

Sir Edward smiled. "His ship is to be in drydock several weeks. Once repairs are finished, he will make sail for Jamaica."

Julia's heart surged and then dropped. "Jamaica?" Home. She was ready to go back, to sink her bare toes into the hot sand on the beach, to see all her friends.

"Ransome will escort a supply convoy to Kingston. Then he will take on his new assignment: to hunt for pirates and privateers—and if the American war continues much longer, possibly for blockade-runners trying to escape through the Gulf of Mexico. He'll weigh anchor in five weeks, barring foul weather."

Five weeks was no time at all. Julia relaxed a bit—but she started at the thump of a knock on the front door below.

"Ah, that must be him now." Sir Edward glanced at his pocket watch. "Though he is half an hour early."

"Him?"

"Aye. Did not I tell you? Captain Ransome is joining us for dinner."

Chapter Two

Sir Drake Pembroke followed the Witheringtons' butler upstairs to the drawing room. Upon being announced, Drake stalked past the underling with an insolent tone into the richly appointed room, but he stopped after a few paces.

Lady Augusta Pembroke did not rise from the settee at the other end of the room, nor did she look up from her needlework. His mother's dark hair framed her face in tight curls, the rest of it drawn up in the back and covered with a white mobcap.

"Have you an explanation for why you are in Portsmouth instead of London, where I sent you?"

Drake's stomach cramped with anxiety. "London was…everyone has left Town for the country. There was no point in continuing the expense of the stay."

"What of Miss Harworth?"

"Circumstances…beyond my control…before I could propose marriage, her mother removed her to Oxfordshire to stay with family there."

His mother laid her sewing in her lap and pressed two bony fingers to her left temple. "I thought I told you to be cautious—to take every care to ensure no one in London discovered our circumstances." Each word, carved out of her soft voice by her sharp enunciation, reached Drake clearly across the distance. "The Harworth girl's legacy would have covered all of your debts, as well as the lien on Marchwood. How could you let her slip through your fingers like that? I spent more than a year working on the mother, befriending that insipid woman. For what? For you."

Drake flinched, though she never raised her voice. "I do not know...I never told her..."

"Never mind. I have a new plan. Come, sit. We have little time before the others join us." She waved him over to join her. "But Drake, I must have your word, your solemn oath, that you will do nothing to jeopardize this. No paramours, no gambling."

He stopped midway down into the chair. "No gambling?" He sat and pulled the chair closer to her. "But..." He implored her with his eyes.

"Oh, all right. Cards only. Nothing else. And no more borrowing money. I have a little set by. I can pay for two servants—no, just two—a man and woman of all works. The Witheringtons believe Pembroke Hall is being gutted and refit, else I would have had to go live in the gloomy old place myself weeks ago. The last of the riding horses from Marchwood is here—I had to terminate as many of the staff there as I could. You may have the beast for your transportation."

The panic Drake had lived with for the past fortnight evaporated. Staying one step ahead of the debt collectors had worn on him—he'd actually plucked a gray hair from his eyebrow this morning. "So tell me of your new plan."

She looked around the grand room. "What think you of Admiral Witherington's house?"

"I am sitting in a room that looks like the furnishings could pay off several of my debts. Naturally, I like it. I wish our houses were so richly appointed."

A smile deepened the creases beside her thin lips. "This is my plan."

He waited, but she said no more. "What?"

"This—this house, the money that bought and furnished it, dear boy."

He frowned. "Have you...you aren't...Mother—not you and—and—and the admiral?"

Lady Pembroke's mouth dropped open into a horrified *O*. "No, indeed! I cannot believe you would think such." She leaned forward and clasped his arm. "I mean you…and Miss Julia Witherington."

He inhaled when he should have swallowed and coughed so hard tears came to his eyes. "Me?" he croaked. "And the admiral's old-maid daughter?" He shook his head and glanced around for something to ease his throat. A sideboard holding several glittering crystal decanters beckoned from near the enormous fireplace. He shot from his chair like arrow to target. The first burning gulp of brandy returned his senses. His hands stilled, his stomach and mind settled.

Leaning his shoulder against the mantel, he turned to face his mother. "I apologize, ma'am. Pray, do continue."

She closed the distance separating them. "Miss Julia Witherington, as you so aptly pointed out, is a spinster. At nine-and-twenty, she is no yearling filly out for her first Season. However, she is not unattractive, though a bit wide through the hips. That makes it less likely she'd die in childbirth, more's the pity."

"Mother, really." He did not want to be saddled with a wife, but he did not wish the girl harm.

"You have not yet met—well…the point is that she has a thirty-thousand-pound legacy. I know, not quite so grand as Miss Harworth's fifty; however, it is enough to cover the mortgage on Marchwood. And her father has always been very generous with her pin money. I suspect he gives her fifty to one hundred pounds each month, so I should be surprised if she does not have a large bank account of her own."

"Paying for the mortgage would be a good start, but I do not see how marrying her for the thirty thousand will be beneficial in the long term."

"She stands to inherit all of her father's properties and fortune."

Drake stared at his mother, poured another drink, swallowed it in one gulp, and stared at her again. "Properties?"

"This house, some little farm in the north part of the country, and one of the largest, most lucrative sugar plantations in the West Indies."

Drake tried to imagine the pecuniary value of all his mother listed. The sums were too vast for his mind to grasp. "How? Why is the fortune not going to the nearest male relative?"

"Unlike the Pembroke baronetcy and estate, Sir Edward's fortune is his own, gained through his deeds at sea and the astonishingly wise investment in the sugar plantation. He can leave it to whom he pleases. It pleases him, apparently, to leave it all in the hands of his daughter." She raised one meager, dark brow. "Which will be of great benefit to you."

"What do I need to do?"

Lady Pembroke smiled. "I am still thinking over the details. But I do know you only have a short amount of time."

"Why?"

"Because her father wrote the terms of the legacy such that if Julia is not married by her thirtieth birthday, she receives the money in her own right. I have heard her talking about giving most of it to the fund for those slovenly sailors' families down near the docks." She reached over and took his hand in hers. "Your need is greater than theirs, my dear. And after all, her mother was a Pembroke by birth—why should not her money go to rebuilding the Pembroke family fortune?"

"How long until her birthday?"

"Six weeks. So there is no time to waste."

 catca

Julia ran her hands down the skirt of the blue silk she'd hurriedly changed into so she looked presentable for dinner with outsiders. Her emotions swung between anger at her father for inviting William Ransome for dinner and fear that she would be unable to hide the hurt that still clung to her like barnacles on the bottom of a ship. At least she knew from her father's letters that William had never married. Could he possibly, after all this time, regret...?

She stopped the unbeneficial line of thought and grasped the doorknob, reminding herself she'd sworn never to forgive him. Steeling her spine and trying to appear as though the memories did not affect her, Julia entered the drawing room.

Her heart rattled in a staccato tattoo at the sight of the man standing near the fireplace, his back to her. Black ribbon secured the queue of black hair at the nape of his neck. She didn't remember William's hair being quite so dark.

Taking a deep breath, she continued toward them, drawing her aunt's attention and interrupting whatever it was Lady Pembroke was saying.

"Ah, Julia dear, do come in. I am so pleased to finally have the opportunity to introduce my son, Sir Drake Pembroke, baronet." The man at the fireplace turned, revealing a handsome if somewhat haughty face.

Shocked relief nearly knocked Julia off balance. She recovered and curtseyed before her cousin came out of his bow. "Sir Drake, your mother has spoken of you often."

"Miss Witherington, I find my mother has not been quite forthcoming in her letters. I expected to find my cousin a handsome creature, yet I see before me a radiant young woman whom none in London can rival."

The calculated falsehood in his words nearly made her laugh. "Sir, you flatter me."

Aunt Augusta's tightened lips indicated she, too, found the compliment empty and unnecessary. "As soon as the admiral joins us, we can repair down to dinner."

A spasm of nerves churned Julia's stomach. "My father has also invited a guest for dinner—" The brass knocker on the front door sounded again. *Dear Lord, please let me make it through this night without embarrassing myself by becoming violently ill.*

She clasped her hands at her waist, pressing the nail of her thumb into the opposite palm to keep them from trembling.

Footsteps on the stairs—Creighton leading William Ransome closer. In a brief moment, the man on whom Julia's girlhood dreams had centered would once again be in the same room with her.

"Ransome!" Her father's voice reverberated through the sitting room doors. "Good of you to be punctual."

William's deep tones carried, though his words did not. Like an iceberg in the middle of the Caribbean, Julia's tight hold on her emotions began rapidly melting.

The bright brass buttons and gold braid adorning the two officers' coats gleamed and glittered in the candlelight.

The intensity in William's blue eyes pierced her, even from across the large room. Though he was more weather-worn, the years had been kind to him. He moved with the confidence of an experienced captain instead of the more submissive scurry of a lieutenant.

Not wanting to see William's scrutiny of herself, Julia affixed her gaze on her father.

Lady Pembroke introduced Sir Drake to the admiral, and each greeted the other with civility, though neither appeared impressed.

"Lady Pembroke, Sir Drake, may I present William Ransome, captain of His Majesty's Ship *Alexandra*."

Julia stood still as a Grecian statue as bows were performed. She clamped the tip of her tongue between her teeth and drew in a deep breath to try to abate a wave of light-headedness.

"And I am certain you recall my daughter, Julia."

Again, William's blue eyes seemed to burn into her own. She managed a semblance of a curtsey.

"Miss Witherington."

"Captain Ransome."

"Now we are all here, shall we go down to dinner?" Lady Pembroke took her son's arm and started toward the door.

"By all means. I shall go ahead and inform Creighton we are ready." Admiral Witherington charted a course for the door. "Ransome, you will be so kind as to lend your arm to Julia?"

"Aye, aye, sir."

Aye, aye, sir, as if responding to his superior's order, not as if he were about to perform a duty out of pleasure.

Thankful for the layers of separation her glove and his sleeve provided,

Julia rested her hand as lightly as possible atop his arm. At least, when side-by-side, she did not have to try so hard to avoid his gaze.

They followed Sir Drake and Aunt Augusta, who whispered to her son all the way to the dining room. Halfway down the stairs, Drake glanced over his shoulder and gave Julia a smile that sent a cold chill down her spine. Though handsome, his slightly hooked nose and thick, dark brows that hooded his eyes gave him an air of menace.

William cleared his throat. "Are you finding Portsmouth to your liking, Miss Witherington?"

"Inasmuch as it is not Jamaica, I find that there are enough diversions to keep me entertained. And, of course, Susan Yates is nearby." She glanced up at him and caught the slightest hint of a smile at the corner of his mouth.

"I called on Mrs. Yates this afternoon. She asked me to pass along a message to you." His upturned lips now twitched.

"Yes?"

His eyes flickered toward the ceiling before he spoke. "She asked me to convey her disappointment that you will not be at Lady Fairfax's party this evening, and to tell you she will be thinking of an apt punishment for abandoning her in such a manner."

Julia did something she'd been certain she could not do in William Ransome's presence: she laughed. "I fear I shall be paying that punishment for some time to come. Thank you for serving as messenger."

He paused two steps from the bottom and turned to look at her. Julia's heart nearly stopped—her breathing did.

"Miss Witherington, I—"

"Come, you two, no dawdling." Augusta Pembroke's shrill voice severed the tension between Julia and William.

He pressed his lips into a thin line and led Julia into the dining room.

Julia dropped her hand from William's arm and walked to her regular seat at her father's right hand. Sir Drake held the chair for her, his eyes glittering like onyx. Though she dreaded conversation with William, she discovered she would much rather sit beside him—whom she knew and resented—than her cousin, whose very presence made her feel like she was covered with sand fleas.

The admiral prayed, asking God's blessing on the food, the guests present, and the Royal Navy. "Eat hearty, Ransome. You won't find a better cook than our Mrs. Stooksbury. Whatever happened with your man—Doughty, wasn't it?"

"Dawling. Still with me, sir."

"Have his skills improved since last I visited?"

"No, sir, though he does try hard." William loaded his plate with roasted vegetables.

"Perhaps this furlough will give you a chance to find a new steward. I cannot have one of my very best wasting away for want of proper care."

Julia cringed inwardly. *One of my very best* indeed. She knew what her father meant. *The man who has replaced my son in my affections.* Her appetite vanished, and she studied her father from the corner of her eye. How could he carry on like this with William when he knew full well of William's treatment of her last time they were all together?

"Miss Witherington?"

At her elbow, Sir Drake offered the platter of mackerel. She nodded, and he served a small portion for her.

"I hope you have settled in well and are finding England to your liking, cousin." He served sweetbread and vegetables onto her plate without a glance at her.

"It is much colder here than what I am accustomed to, Sir Drake."

"Cold?" His condescension slipped into a derisive chuckle. "Just a few days of rain to break the heat of the summer. Nothing to regard."

"In Jamaica—"

"Once you have been in England for a while," Drake spoke over her as if she hadn't said anything, "you will come to appreciate the variety of weather. Besides, we are quite temperate down here in the south. Up in Scotland, even now there are places still covered in snow. Though I cannot imagine why you would ever travel to such a heathen place as that."

"She could possibly pay a visit to your Aunt Hedwig," Lady Pembroke said, "as you did last year, son."

"I do suppose the part of Scotland Lady MacDougall lives in is a somewhat better clime and landscape than some places in England, like the northwestern shore." Drake leaned closer to Julia as if to share a secret. "I had the misfortune of staying a fortnight just outside Liverpool and found it to be the most dreadfully dull spot in England."

Julia glanced across the table at William, curious to see his reaction to Drake's words. If she hadn't known him as well as she did, the suddenly precise movement of lowering his fork to rest on the edge of his plate wouldn't have meant anything to her. The lines around his icy-blue eyes became more pronounced.

"It is farming country, so perhaps not to your liking." William's clipped words betrayed little of his native regional accent. "The Ransome family has lived in that part of the country for many generations."

Lady Pembroke, seated beside him, gave William a pitying look. "Then you must resent the fact that the Royal Navy has kept you from it."

"A man of honor never resents doing his sacred duty." Sir Edward's voice took on a hard edge. One thing Lady Pembroke had not learned in her three months in the Witherington household was to hold her tongue when it came to her disapproval of the Royal Navy.

Julia dropped her gaze to her plate to hide the smile trying to overtake her lips. If her aunt continued making snide comments like that about the navy, perhaps Julia would be free from her sooner rather than later.

❧❧❧

William resented aristocrats who felt they had the right to belittle anyone not fortunate enough to have been born with a title. At least the admiral had not changed since receiving his knighthood.

"Oh, Sir Edward," Lady Pembroke's coy tone rasped across William's skin like splintered wood. "You know I had no intention of insulting Captain Rutherford's honor."

"Ransome, m'lady," William corrected her. Unbidden, he looked across the table. The slight smile playing around Julia's mouth added fuel to the building fire of annoyance inside him. She had just cause to carry hard feelings toward him, but she did not have to take such obvious pleasure in her aunt's disparaging remarks.

Julia's mirth vanished, however, when Sir Drake leaned closer to her, his arm brushing hers, to insist she take a serving of asparagus. William almost smiled before he could stop himself. One thing he would never forget about Julia: she hated asparagus.

When Julia didn't respond to Pembroke's overbearing attempts to engage her in intimate conversation, the baronet returned his attention across the table. "What will you do to keep yourself occupied now we're at peace with France, Captain Ransome?"

William forced a polite expression. "I am blessed to remain captain of *Alexandra*."

"But the war is over these three months. How has your ship been put to use?" The tone of contempt in Lady Pembroke's voice was punctuated by Admiral Witherington's fork hitting his plate with an unusually hard *clank*.

William cleared his throat. "We've seen mostly home service since the Peace."

"In other words, they've all but recommissioned your boat as a cargo transport." Pembroke's expression came close to a sneer.

William called upon years of experience at hiding his reactions to keep the baronet from seeing his anger. "As a ship of the Royal Navy, we see to whatever duty the Admiralty requires of us."

Julia coughed lightly, looking at her father with concern. Indeed, the admiral's face showed signs of his rising temper. "You came to Portsmouth to receive new orders, did you not, Captain?" she asked in a rush when Sir Edward opened his mouth to speak.

William grasped Julia's purpose, also wanting to allay an explosion of temper by his superior officer. "Aye—yes, Miss Witherington.

Tonight, I shall inform my crew they will be dismissed tomorrow for a few weeks' home leave, but we shall weigh anchor at the end of August."

"And I hear you've seen much action during the war." Julia glanced at her father, worry still shading her green eyes when she returned her gaze to William. "Could we trouble you for an anecdote?"

William did not find speaking of his own exploits enjoyable, but a soft huff from Lady Pembroke decided him.

"Yes, Ransome. Tell them of your first command on *Hope*." But Admiral Witherington didn't give William a chance to draw a breath, much less begin the story. "Ransome here had just taken command of the *Hope*, a thirty-eight gun frigate, his first assignment as Post Captain, and sailed to the East Indies.

"He ran up on *Adamant*, a seventy-four gunner, just off the coast of Circas." The admiral's eyes gleamed as he warmed to his topic. "*Adamant* had come under bombardment by a French privateer and was hulled, burning, and sinking fast. Ransome made all sail to intercept, got the weather gauge of them, and commenced firing." Admiral Witherington regaled them with details of the engagement William could hardly remember.

William kept his attention trained on his commander, embarrassed by the knowledge that those outside of the Royal Navy took no interest in such recitations.

The dishes rattled when Sir Edward brought his palm down on the table in an enthusiastic punctuation to the story. "Not only did Ransome's gun crews stave off heavier cannon from the French, he captured the privateer and launched boats to pick up survivors from *Adamant*."

Heat itched under William's collar. "The French ship had taken damage from *Adamant*'s guns. And we did not come away unscathed, Admiral. *Hope* took heavy damage during the rescue attempt. We barely made it back to Madras, and the poor girl was scrapped for salvage."

Julia frowned and leaned forward. "A thirty-eight, fully crewed holds how many? Three hundred?"

"I had two hundred seventy-five souls aboard the *Hope* when we left port." William raised his eyebrows, encouraging her to continue.

For the first time since he'd seen her in the drawing room, Julia's air of aloofness vanished. "A seventy-four, like the *Adamant,* holds up to six hundred forty, not including the Marine contingent. Your ship wouldn't hold that number of men, even standing shoulder to shoulder."

He nodded, impressed but not surprised that she would so quickly be able to calculate the ships' capacities. "Yes, nearly nine hundred on a frigate would be nigh impossible. But Miss Witherington, keep in mind *Adamant* had been under bombardment all morning." Remembrance of the tragedy nearly locked his voice in his throat. "We only rescued eighty-three."

She closed her eyes briefly and shook her head. "I'm so sorry."

"God protected us long enough to keep those men safe and return them home to their families. My family was one of those blessed. My youngest brother, Philip, served on the *Adamant* as third lieutenant."

Pain flickered through Julia's green eyes before the guarded expression returned. William wished he could recall his comment—as it had only served to remind Julia of the loss of her own brother at sea.

"Ah. I see." Pembroke jerked as a footman accidentally brushed his arm while refilling his wine. "You stayed to mount a rescue attempt not from some altruistic reason like the fraternity of naval officers or Christian duty. You stayed only to try to rescue your brother."

Julia gasped and glanced at her cousin. At the head of the table, Sir Edward slowly rose, his face a mottled purple. "Do you dare impugn the reputation of one of the most highly decorated captains in the Royal Navy, sir?"

"Father, please. I am certain Sir Drake meant no harm." Julia clasped her father's arm.

Sir Drake inclined his head. "No, I meant no insult, Sir Edward." Although the words came out of Pembroke's mouth, his amused tone belied them. "No insult at all, Captain Ransome."

"Come, Julia, we should leave the men to their port and talk."

Lady Pembroke stood before William realized her intention and rose as well.

Julia's eyes flickered between her father and Sir Drake a moment.

"Actually," Sir Drake tossed his napkin on the table and moved languidly to his feet, "though I know it is quite rude of me to do so, I must take my leave. There is much work to be done at Pembroke Hall to make it habitable. Sir Edward, Miss Witherington," he bowed toward them, "thank you for your hospitality." Joining his mother at the door of the room, Pembroke turned and made the barest nod toward William. "Captain Ransome."

William mimicked the action. "Sir Drake."

As soon as the door closed behind the Pembrokes, Julia turned to face William. "Captain Ransome, I sincerely apologize for my relations' comments. They have not been in the habit of keeping company with naval families."

He wondered if the excuse sounded as empty to her as it did to him. "You are not to be held responsible for the words or actions of others, Miss Witherington."

"If you think you can bear Lady Pembroke's presence again, Ransome," the admiral said, "I would like to invite you to a dinner party here to celebrate your return and your successes in the war—Julia my dear, do you think we can have one planned by next Thursday?"

The openness in Julia's expression vanished faster than he could blink. "Yes, Papa. I will see to it."

The admiral picked up Julia's hand and kissed the back of it. "Invite Captain Yates and his wife as well. His successes should also be celebrated."

William's gut wrenched at the wary look in Julia's eyes. A dinner in his honor was not to her liking, apparently. "Sir, while I am honored to be so singled out by you, I must tell you that my mother and sister are expected in town early next week, so I will want to spend what time I can with them."

Sir Edward clapped William's shoulder. "Bring them along. It has been too many years since I have seen Mrs. Ransome. Your sister was hardly walking, if I recall correctly. I will brook no opposition, Captain. Do not force me to make it an order."

Though the admiral's tone had gone gruff, his stance rigid, teasing humor still danced in the superior officer's eyes.

William could do nothing but capitulate. "Thank you, sir."

"Good." Admiral Witherington leaned over and kissed the top of Julia's head. "My dear, if you would be willing to forgive our rudeness as easily as Pembroke's, I'll have Elton take me down to the docks with Ransome so we can have a few words about his orders."

"I do need to get back to the ledgers." She rose and followed them out into the foyer. "Good evening, Captain Ransome."

He bade her farewell and did his best not to watch her as she climbed the stairs. All of the qualities he'd first seen in her as a child and later as a debutante of seventeen had matured into the kind of woman any naval officer would dream of for his lifelong companion.

And she could have been his, but for appeasing his sense of honor. His vow to never burden himself with a wife doused him in coldness more frigid than the North Sea in January.

Chapter Three

All throughout Spithead harbor, eight bells clanged from every ship, marking midnight and the beginning of the middle watch. From the deck of the large, dark ship looming like a mountain above, a voice rang out, demanding the identity of the small vessel approaching.

William cupped his hands beside his mouth. "Captain William Ransome for the *Alexandra.*"

The familiar face of the fourth lieutenant, illuminated by a lantern, appeared over the gunwale balustrade. "Welcome back, Captain."

William paid the boys who'd rowed him out and then climbed up the accommodation ladder in *Alexandra's* side. Once he was on deck, Lieutenant Eastwick saluted by touching the fore point of his hat.

William returned the gesture and turned to the midshipman holding the lantern. "Pass word for Lieutenant Cochrane to join me in my cabin."

"Aye, aye, Captain." The teen scrambled to obey.

"Carry on, Lieutenant Eastwick."

The man eight years William's junior bade him goodnight, unable to keep a tone of disappointment out of his voice. William had no doubt that in his day-long absence, the crew had entertained themselves with wild speculations of what orders he was receiving. That not all of the lieutenants were on deck awaiting his arrival came as a mild surprise.

William walked through the vacant wheelhouse and entered the doors beyond into the dining cabin. The long table surrounded by ten tall-back wooden chairs served as dining table and workspace. He rounded the table to starboard and passed through the day-cabin and into the small chamber behind containing his hammock, desk, sea chest, and washstand—in addition to the large twelve-pound cannon square in the middle, reminding him at all times he made his home on a ship of war. After every action *Alexandra* took part in, his chamber smelled of burned gunpowder for days.

The main cabin door opened, and Dawling entered. "Welcome back, sir. I trust your visit to the port Admiralty went well."

William shrugged out of his sodden raincoat and tossed it toward his steward. "As well as could be expected."

A brisk knock sounded. William nodded, and Dawling admitted the first lieutenant.

William returned to the dining cabin. "That's all for now, Dawling."

The steward knuckled his forehead in salute and latched the door behind himself. Cochrane reported on the crew's activity since William's departure at eleven that morning. While Cochrane gave his report, William stood behind the head chair at the table, forcing himself to concentrate through his fatigue. When Cochrane finished, William unclasped his hands from behind him and rested them on the chair's high back.

His first officer—and friend—fidgeted with his coat cuffs and chewed the corner of his mouth. William held back a smile. After two long years at sea, everyone was eager for home leave, but most aboard worried they had come back to Portsmouth to be decommissioned. The thought that William could have entered port with Julia eagerly waiting for him, as the wives and sweethearts of many of his crew were even now waiting, gave him pause; but he brushed it aside in frustration and returned his thoughts to *Alexandra*'s new orders.

"I spoke at length with Admiral Sir Edward Witherington this afternoon." William's struggle against his inner turmoil made his voice sterner than he'd intended. But being the practical joker among the officers, Cochrane deserved to squirm a bit. "Tomorrow morning, I would like you to call the entire crew to order at four bells in the morning watch. I know six o'clock is two hours early, but we only have until noon to clear everything and all personnel from the ship."

Cochrane swallowed hard. "Aye, aye, sir."

"Dawling!" William called, and as expected, the door opened immediately.

"Aye, sir?"

"Go to the wardroom and inform the officers—not just the lieutenants, but the warrant officers and captain of the marines also—they are to assemble here in five minutes. Full dress is not necessary. Let Lieutenant Eastwick know as well—the midshipman of the watch can relieve him."

Dawling saluted and let the door slam behind him as he hurried away.

William sat at the head of the table and started looking through the pile of correspondence that had arrived in his absence.

"You're going to make me wait for the others, aren't you?" Cochrane paced the other end of the long, narrow room.

William looked at him over the top of a letter from a former commander. "Why shouldn't I? You might as well have a seat, Ned."

"Just tell me!" Cochrane grabbed the back of the chair nearest him and shook it as if it were his adversary. "Are we being turned out or not?"

The muscles in William's cheeks ached with the effort to hold back his smile. He skimmed through a few more letters. "May I remind you, Mr. Cochrane, at this moment, I am still captain of this ship and your superior officer. You might try to remember that fact when addressing me."

Cochrane flopped into one of the chairs with a sigh. Within the time frame, the other officers entered, each in varying states of dress, most in their shirtsleeves, a few with trousers and uniform coats hastily pulled on.

Once assured all were present, William dismissed Dawling and rose, clasping his hands behind his back.

"I know every man aboard is anxious to hear what orders Admiral

Witherington has for us." He paused and looked around the room at each of his officers. "The entire crew must vacate by noon tomorrow. All personal belongings left behind will become the salvage of the dockyard crew."

The officers shifted and murmured at the word *salvage,* and William had never seen a darker scowl on Cochrane's face. William schooled his own expression before continuing. "*Alexandra* will be turned over to the dockmaster at noon tomorrow and—"

"Not decommissioned!"

"Sir! Turned over?"

"They canna' scrap her, sir!"

"She's still a sound ship, even if she is patched up, sir!"

"Did you tell the Admiral—"

"Silence." William barely had to raise his voice for the assemblage to come back to order. "As I was saying, *Alexandra* will be given over to the dockmaster tomorrow…for a complete refitting in preparation for our next assignment."

A quiver of excitement ran around the room like a storm swell, but this time they waited for William to finish.

"The crew and officers are, as of noon tomorrow, at liberty. Officers will report back to me at the Admiralty on eleventh August; crew are to report back two days later. We will have less than a fortnight to fit up and supply her before we weigh anchor twenty-sixth August."

Exclamations of relief and gratitude filled the room, and the atmosphere changed from tense to celebratory. Above the noise, Cochrane made himself heard. "Where will we be going, sir?"

"Gentlemen, the war with America continues, and more ships are needed to patrol the Caribbean and the Gulf of Mexico for blockade-runners." Now William let his smile show.

The men exclaimed over their good luck of spending the winter in the balmy climate most of them had only heard about.

"Sir, some o' the men who came to us pressed two years ago—wha' if they don't come back from leave?" the boatswain asked.

"Matthews, any man of the crew who decides he does not want to sign on for our new assignment may stay behind. Replacements will be easy to find. I have ten requests for positions here," William held up the stack of letters, "from highly qualified sailors and officers desperate for a ship."

Every officer in the crowded dining cabin eyed the pages, smiles dimming.

"Lieutenant Eastwick, you may return to the deck and tell the crew currently on watch. Lieutenant Cochrane, rouse the petty officers to pass the orders to them and have them wake the sailors at six o'clock. Master Ingleby, the midshipmen are yours for the telling. If there are no further questions…?"

To a man, everyone murmured, "No sir."

"Dismissed. I have some packing to do." William joined their laughter and called for Dawling.

The burly sailor pushed his way into the cabin through the outflow of officers. "Should I wake Cook, sir? He'll need extra help packing up his pots and pans, and the purser—well, he were here, weren't he?"

William really should say something to Dawling about listening at the door, but as the steward wasn't prone to gossip…he watched the younger man bustle around both cabins, mumbling about the work needing doing before vacating tomorrow.

Dawling had been an ordinary seaman until William's previous steward had been killed in an action off the coast of Spain about a year ago. Experienced stewards weren't to be had, and every other skilled member of his crew had been needed where he was, so William took a volunteer.

Now would be an opportune time to find one of those many experienced men with no current employment, as Admiral Witherington had suggested. What would it be like to again have a steward who did not have to constantly be reminded of his duties? If he could find another place for Dawling—if perhaps one of the petty officers' mates did not come back…but Dawling had put forth a colossal effort to learn the job and had become a decent steward—nothing like the experienced servants of which his friends could boast, but competent.

William crossed to his desk and began to sort through the neat stacks of papers atop it. Much of it he would need in the next week as he finalized his logs and reported on his ship's activities. He had not given a full accounting in two years, so the task daunted him.

Dawling grew quiet, and William turned to see if he'd left the cabin. The steward stood in the door between the day-cabin and sleeping quarters, worrying one of the brass buttons on his uniform coat.

"What is it, Dawling?"

"Well, sir…it's just that…you see…" Dawling's gaze never lifted from the floor.

"Spit it out, man. You know you can tell me anything."

"Aye, sir." Dawling cleared his throat. "Sir, could I…what I mean to say is…would you…?"

William crossed his arms and raised his eyebrows.

Dawling released his breath in a low growl. "You see, sir, the truth is…I've nowhere to go on land. That's why I came to the navy as a lad—no family, no home. So what I want to ask is if you might take me with you."

Very few things in life could surprise William. No words immediately came to mind.

"I mean," Dawling quickly added, "I'll work—work as your valet or in the kitchen or wherever I can be of use, sir. But I can't afford to stay in a hotel or boarding house for three weeks, sir."

Dawling, working as his valet? William nearly laughed at the image. He had accepted Susan Yates's invitation to stay until *Alexandra* was habitable once again. Perhaps experience working with her well-trained household staff would be helpful. William could well afford to cover the extra expense to Collin and Susan's household, and maybe Fawkes could be convinced to take Dawling under his care and train the man in the areas where he most lacked grace, tact, and diplomacy.

"Very well. If you would like, I could use a valet."

❧

Gateacre, England

Charlotte Ransome flinched, her quill scraping a black mark across the parchment. The soft knock came again before the door opened.

Face illuminated by the candle she carried, Charlotte's mother needed no words to express her displeasure. "Do you know how late it is?"

She glanced at the porcelain clock she'd painted at school two years ago and grimaced. Half past midnight. "No—I did not realize…"

"When I awoke and saw the light—I thought you fell asleep with a candle still burning. What are you doing?"

"Just finishing a letter." Charlotte slid the written sheets under a blank one.

Mrs. Ransome's pale brows lifted. "You danced for hours and then came home and sat up later writing a letter? You remember the hired driver is to arrive at dawn?"

"Yes, Mama. I remember."

"And you could not wait to write your letter until after we are underway?"

"I…I could not sleep, so I thought I would finish it tonight." Charlotte moved so the light of the candle on her desk did not shine so directly on her face. Her mother was too perceptive by far.

Mama sighed—a sound Charlotte was all too familiar with. "We have a long, arduous journey ahead of us. I hope you do not become ill from fatiguing yourself before we even begin."

Charlotte laughed. "We shall be sitting in a coach for three days. I believe I will have time to rest."

"Very well. I expect you to be ready when the driver arrives. William is paying quite a handsome sum for us to have private conveyance. I do not wish to increase the cost by any delays."

"Yes, Mama."

Her mother's face eased. "I do not mean to be ill-tempered. I simply worry about traveling so far on our own."

Charlotte rushed to her mother and hugged her. "There is nothing to fear. Between your prayers and the protection of a private carriage, we shall arrive in Portsmouth safely."

Mama chuckled and embraced her tightly before looking pointedly at the open valise on the chest at the end of Charlotte's bed. "Complete your packing and get some sleep. We shall have a light breakfast before we go."

"Yes, Mama." Charlotte closed the door behind her mother. At her desk, she quickly scrawled the last lines of the letter, wrote the direction on the outside, and sealed it with yellow wax. Now it was finished, she had no idea when she might be able to post it.

She pulled a few things out of her valise, hid the letter in the folds of a petticoat, and returned to her packing.

Her stomach gave a leap. On Tuesday, they would arrive in Portsmouth. *Portsmouth!* Long had Charlotte desired to see the south part of the country, especially the city her brothers mentioned often. Hopefully she would be able to visit the dockyard, to see the place where the fleet was mustered to defend King and country. She hoped William would finally take them aboard his ship.

Her excitement changed to anxiety at the thought of her eldest brother. She had received letters regularly from William—and sent twice as many in return—but she'd seen him only once since childhood, two years ago for a very brief visit. So much had happened in her life since then.

She cast a glance at her trunk: packed, locked, ready to be carried downstairs by the coachman in the morning. The muslin-wrapped bundle buried at the bottom burned her conscience. If her brother, or worse yet her mother, ever discovered its existence and learned what it contained, she would lose their good opinion forever. Charlotte had to keep her secret without compounding her guilt by lying to her family.

This journey had given her the seeds for a plan. Now she needed to determine how to put the plan into action.

❦

Yesterday's rain had given way to sunlight that now streamed in through Julia's bedroom windows. The small clock on the mantel chimed eleven times. In two hours, her aunt would be receiving callers. When she did, she expected Julia's attendance. Where could Julia go to avoid sitting in the front parlor with her aunt all day?

Susan. Of course. She would call upon her friend and receive her punishment for not attending Lady Fairfax's card party yestereve.

After sending word for the carriage to be brought around, she dressed appropriately for morning calls—not wanting word to get back to Aunt Augusta she'd again been seen making calls in a work-dress.

A quarter hour later, her father's driver, Elton, handed Julia down from the barouche, escorted her to the front door of the Yateses' townhouse, and knocked for her. "Shall I wait for you, miss?"

"Let me find out if she is in."

After a few moments, just as Elton raised his hand to knock again, the door swung open to reveal Fawkes, impeccably dressed as always. "Good morning, Miss Witherington. Please, do come in."

"Thank you." She turned to Elton. "Return for me at two o'clock, please."

"No need, miss. Our driver can see you home when you're ready," Fawkes offered.

She argued, but to no avail. She sent Elton home and then followed the butler into the tiled foyer.

"The missus is upstairs in the sitting room." Fawkes motioned toward the stairs. "I apologize for not escorting you, miss, but..." he patted his left leg.

"No, no. I can find my way." Climbing up and down the several flights of stairs in the townhouse must be hard on the elderly man's joints. She ascended with ease. The double doors near the first floor landing stood open, and Julia could hear Susan humming. She knocked on one of the open doors. "Susan?"

"Julia! What a pleasant surprise." Susan Yates crossed the room and hugged her. "I'm so glad you came by. Can you stay for a while?"

"All day if you can bear my presence so long." Julia rested her hands on the shorter woman's shoulders and held her at arms' length. "I have come to receive my punishment."

Susan's tinkling laugh reminded Julia of why she enjoyed the younger woman's company so much. Regardless of the worries or troubles Julia carried, only a few moments in Susan's presence made them all disappear.

"I shall have to think of something appropriate to the level of the offense. Come in and sit down. I've bought a new hat for church tomorrow, but I think it needs something."

Julia shook her head at the mountain of ribbons and silk flowers piled on the low table in front of the gold and ivory striped settee. The new hat turned out to be a straw bonnet with a wide brim lined in blue silk that would frame Susan's cherubic face and emphasize her azure eyes.

"Lady Dalrymple asked particularly after you last night. She feared you must be gravely ill to miss one of Lady Fairfax's card parties." Susan rolled her eyes.

"I shall call on her tomorrow to reassure her of my robust health." Julia ran her fingers over the smooth, cool surface of a satin ribbon.

Susan launched into the gossip of new romances between young couples formed because of Lady Dalrymple's "shrewdness in arranging the tables." Apparently at least one engagement had been entered into in the last few months because of the dowager viscountess—or at least, she liked to brag so. "She was so disappointed you were not there last night. She was certain you and Sir someone-or-another would make a great match."

"Yes, she and my aunt are probably planning it together. Both of them would like nothing better than to see me married to some Englishman and settled on an estate in the country with a townhouse in London."

"Now, Julia," Susan chided.

"I know. But if I'm going to marry an Englishman, 'twill be one who will let me go home—back to Jamaica."

"Such as an officer in the Royal Navy?" Susan caught her bottom lip in her perfect, pearly teeth.

So, they'd come to that subject already. "You, more than anyone else, know my feelings about William Ransome."

"Julia, it was twelve years ago. You were only seventeen, he only twenty-two. He felt he still had to make his way in the world before he would be worthy to ask for your hand."

"Then why did he not renew his addresses once he began to gain fortune? When he was promoted to post captain? Because his true intention was never toward me, but to ingratiate himself to my father. Otherwise, he'd have answered my letter and explained himself." Julia pressed her fist to her mouth, mortified she had let the words slip out.

Susan's smile vanished immediately. "You...you wrote to him? After he went to Gateacre? You never told me."

Julia took control of her roiling emotions with one deep breath. "No doubt he, like me, was ready to move on, to forget that a simple flirtation was misinterpreted by everyone but him." She patted Susan's hand in reassurance. "Tierra Dulce is my true love; a husband, merely a complication. If I ever marry, I want to make a good choice, but falling in love does not figure into my plans."

"Why have you hardened your heart so to love? I do not wish to tell you what you have doubtless heard many times over...but when you fall in love with the man God has created for you, it's as if you've found a missing part of yourself. Until you meet him, you may never know something is missing."

"And then the woman must give up everything, must sacrifice her own wishes and desires to do the bidding of her husband, whether it is what she wants or not." Julia's throat grew tighter with each passing moment; deep breathing was not going to keep her tears at bay long.

"What makes you think so? Yes, many women *choose* to give up their own desires to fulfill their husbands' dreams. But just as many husbands make sacrifices to give their wives the desires of their hearts."

Julia tried to laugh, but it came out as a high-pitched rasp. "Perhaps Collin does for you. But I know of no others."

"Who—?"

"My father." Julia leapt to her feet and crossed to the window beside the fireplace. She folded her arms and glared out over Susan's beautiful back garden. "My mother pined for him, hoping he would send for her and bring her back to England. She dwindled away to a ghost of herself because she loved him so much. And he...the Royal Navy has always been his first love."

She turned, blinking away gathering moisture. "And you—what about all of these months, these years you've lived in terror, not knowing if Collin was dead or alive? You cannot tell me there haven't been times you wished you had never fallen in love."

Sorrow clouded Susan's sapphire eyes. "I will admit to a moment's regret now and again at having fallen in love *with a sailor,* but never have I regretted loving Collin. Even the worst pain I have felt at suffering miscarriage after miscarriage, the worst fear I have endured of not knowing if Collin would come home, has been better than never having loved at all."

Immediately contrite, Julia fell to her knees beside the settee and took Susan's hands in her own. "I am sorry. I did not mean—please forgive me. I know love has brought you joy. But it has brought me only pain. Everyone I have loved—my brother, my mother, William— I have lost. I do not see the purpose of willfully subjecting myself to that kind of pain again."

Susan's mouth tilted up even as her lips trembled. "Loving does mean loss. But would you give up the joy of the time you did have with your mother and brother to avoid the pain of separation?"

Julia sat back on her heels. Give up her mother? Michael? "If I admit you might have a point, will you lord it over me for the rest of my life?"

"Most likely."

She moved back to her seat on the settee. "Tell me all about the matches Lady Dalrymple said she made last night."

Julia's lap became a repository for the ribbons and flowers Susan rejected as she merrily repeated the viscountess's stories of matches made and broken, some all in the course of the evening.

Susan Yates fascinated Julia. Susan enjoyed talking about anything—

Collin said she talked just to hear the sound of her own voice—and required nothing but an occasional one- or two-word response from Julia to know she was still listening. Half the time, Julia wasn't sure what Susan was saying.

In many ways—from her seemingly constant good humor, to her forgetfulness, to her love of talking—Susan reminded Julia of Michael. If they'd had a sister—

A knock on the front door interrupted her musings. Now seated on the floor beside the low coffee table, the only notice Susan took was to say, "I wonder who that might be," and then continue with her story.

Brisk footsteps sounded on the stairs, yet Susan talked on, tossing more ribbons and flowers at Julia. With her back to the open doors, Julia could hear but not see the guest enter the room.

Susan finally looked up and then scrambled to her feet. "Gracious! Is it past two already?" In response, the grandfather clock chimed once for half-past.

Julia shoved the pile of accoutrements from her lap onto the settee and stood to greet her friend's guest properly. Framed in the doorway stood William Ransome, his crisp indigo uniform showing his strong-but-slim build to perfection. His dark hair curled a bit over the high collar, and the skin around his eyes crinkled when he smiled. Her heart thudded traitorously.

Susan's eyes sparkled when she looked from Julia to William. "Miss Julia Witherington, I believe you know Captain William Ransome."

If being forced to spend time with William was Susan's idea of an *appropriate* punishment for missing the card party last night, Julia did not want to know what Susan would do to her if she ever did something truly awful.

Chapter Four

William's stomach lurched—just as it did when his ship dropped into a trough in a storm-tossed sea. Julia's emerald green eyes widened, and her cheeks lost their color. He squelched the desire to cross the room and draw her into his arms, to beg her forgiveness for walking away from her twelve years ago. He had not slept last night, his thoughts entangled with comparisons of Julia Witherington as he'd seen her at dinner and the memory he'd carried tucked away in his heart for so many years. Though he'd thought it improbable, she was even more beautiful now than she had been at seventeen.

Susan cleared her throat, and he remembered himself and bowed. "Miss Witherington."

She came up out of a stiff curtsey. "Captain Ransome. I had not known you were expected, or I would have timed my call so as not to intrude—"

"Don't be a goose, Julia." Susan waved her hands for both of them to sit. "William has come to stay a few weeks until his ship is repaired." She pulled the bell cord by the door. "William, did Fawkes show you to your room?"

He dragged his gaze away from the pink ribbon Miss Witherington rolled around her long, slender fingers. "No. He suggested I see you first."

Susan hooked her arm through his. "Come then, I will show you. Julia, we shall return shortly." The housekeeper stepped into the room. "Ah, Agatha. Have Cook send up tea, please."

"I..." Julia looked from Susan to William and back to Susan. "Come, William."

He followed his best friend's wife out of the room and retrieved his small valise from the floor just outside the door.

"Imagine my surprise," Susan looked over her shoulder, preceding him up the stairs, "when dear Julia arrived for a visit on the same day I expected you to come stay."

The image of Julia's green eyes, full of pained displeasure, floated in his mind. "Susan, you know Miss Witherington does not welcome my presence."

Susan's laughter—so different than that of his men—jarred him. "Nonsense. She is as happy as I to greet an old friend." She stopped at the last door on the back side of the house. "Here is your room. I expect to see you in no less than twenty minutes." She wagged her finger at him.

He opened his mouth to disagree with her on Julia's happiness to see him, but the words stuck in his throat when he entered the luxurious bedroom. The heavy wood furniture—from the carved canopy supported by pillar-like bedposts to the wardrobe with a sparkling mirror in the door—was fancier than the finest inn William had ever stayed at.

"Twenty minutes." Susan flitted away.

It was just his luck Julia Witherington had chosen to call on Susan Yates today. And with the discomfort she'd shown last night and just now at his presence, he couldn't imagine why his innards—and good sense—mutinied at the thought of being near her.

If he had not written his mother and asked her to meet him in Portsmouth for a visit, he could have escaped north to Gateacre.

He sank onto a chaise that flanked the Grecian fireplace. "Lord, give me strength to overcome any lingering romantic thoughts of Julia Witherington. Make me forget I once planned to marry her."

᷈᷈᷈᷈᷈

Julia ceased pacing when Susan reappeared. "Really, I should leave. You must have much you wish to discuss with Captain Ransome—"

"Hush. I will hear nothing more on the subject. You must accustom yourself to his presence, as you will not be able to avoid him for the next three weeks."

Julia glared at her friend through narrowed eyes. "I hope you are not forcing us together in hopes William will renew his addresses to me."

Susan blinked, affecting an innocent expression. "I would never dream of something so conniving." At another knock on the front door, she slipped out of the room to stand at the head of the stairs, where she could hear the mumble of voices below. She nodded and then returned to the sitting room. "Admiral Hinds's wife has come to call. This is turning into a party."

Some of Julia's anxiety abated. Mrs. Hinds probably did not know Captain Ransome and could therefore be counted upon to carry the conversation.

The small, dark-haired woman entered and greeted Susan and Julia as old friends. The remainder of Julia's worries melted away under the two officers' wives' discussion of mutual acquaintances and the latest meeting of the Naval Family Aid Society, which Julia had not attended due to accompanying her aunt on calls.

Captain Ransome appeared in the doorway and cleared his throat. Julia tried to calm her heart, tried to ignore the fact the man was more handsome than his gold-adorned uniform, tried to stop herself from admiring the way the indigo of his uniform contrasted with the light blue of his eyes.

Susan finished introducing Captain Ransome and Mrs. Hinds, and they all regained their seats—Captain Ransome sitting in the armchair beside Mrs. Hinds, Julia with Susan on the settee.

"I heard you speaking of the Naval Family Aid Society." Captain Ransome looked from Susan to Mrs. Hinds. "I would like to make a donation if you could direct me to the treasurer."

Both women turned to look at Julia.

Her cheeks flamed. "I am the treasurer, Captain."

His eyes held hers a moment, inscrutable. "I understood you had not been in Portsmouth long, Miss Witherington."

"Nearly nine months."

"Miss Witherington wanted to participate, but because her father—" Susan gave Julia an apologetic glance—"because the admiral must carry out his orders of decommissioning the fleet, none of the families would accept the charity if they knew of her involvement."

"She has a finesse with numbers the rest of us lacked," Mrs. Hinds added. "Got us out of a pinch we did not even know we were in."

Julia focused on the pattern of tiny flowers in the fabric of her skirt and prayed for a change of subject.

"Julia has been able to acquire more donations for the fund in the last six months than we've had in the last two years." Susan beamed at her like a proud parent.

She would not have been surprised if flames burst from her cheeks.

Mrs. Hinds must have realized her discomfort. "Captain, what part of England do you call home?"

"Gateacre—a small farming town near Liverpool."

"We made berth in Liverpool harbor many times when I traveled with my husband during his captaincy…"

The admiral's wife kept the conversation going with stories of her travels around the world with her husband.

Julia found her gaze straying to William time and again. His eyes occasionally flickered her direction. Each time, she immediately turned toward Susan or Mrs. Hinds. He bore little resemblance to the fifteen-year-old midshipman who had not only concealed his knowledge of her true identity under her brother's clothes but had been kind and helpful as she'd climbed the rope shrouds to the foremast top several times. Even as a girl of only ten, she had recognized the strong features in his face—broad forehead, dark brows, square jaw—that would mature into the commanding presence he now possessed.

Coldness crept into Julia's spirit. This man seated across the low table had courted her not for her wealth, but for promotion, for her father's attention and patronage. He'd succeeded in gaining the admiral's affections—replacing her brother in her father's heart—but she refused to allow William Ransome the opportunity to hurt her again.

༺༻

Charlotte awoke with a start as the carriage rattled over yet another hole in the road. With eagerness, she'd arisen before dawn and had been downstairs, waiting for her mother before the driver arrived, as promised. Now, after more than eight hours of bumping, swaying, clattering, and rattling, Charlotte wondered why she'd ever imagined this journey to be glamorous. If only William had arranged for them to take the trip by sea—though that would have taken much longer—she could have been watching, studying, learning.

Mama sat across from her, calmly stitching away, embroidering tiny silk flowers onto the edge of a gossamer wrap for Charlotte. How her mother had the patience to do such intricate work...Charlotte sighed and took up the book splayed open on her lap. She'd never had the patience for sewing of any kind—she'd much rather be reading or out and about with Philip. Well, before he left for sea when Charlotte was seven. After that, it had just been her and Mama. Her three brothers, but William especially, had done their best to fill the void left by their father's death in a far-distant port mere months after Charlotte's birth. Her mother said they spoiled her.

She glanced down at *System of Universal Signals by Day and Night*, which Philip had studied but left behind in his bedroom before signing on as a midshipman ten years ago. She'd read it so often in the intervening time, she knew all of the flags individually as well as all of the signals they could possibly be combined to create. When they stopped for the night, she would exchange this book for the tome *Sermons on the Character and Professional Duties of Seamen*. If only her mother did not object to Charlotte's reading novels, she would be able to read that new one she'd picked up just the other day...what was it called? *Proud* and something? Something and *Preconception?* Both words started with *P*; that was all she could remember. But the same nameless lady had also written another book Charlotte had enjoyed.

The three volumes of the new novel were slim enough...perhaps she could conceal them inside *Sermons* and have something enjoyable to read after all.

ᜀᜀᜀᜀᜀᜀ

"I really must be going." Mrs. Hinds stood and began to slip on her gloves. "Admiral Hinds will have expected me hours ago. I do not usually make calls on Saturday, but as he had to be at the port Admiralty all day today, I could see no point in sitting at home alone when I could just walk up the street to see you."

"I'm so pleased you came, Mrs. Hinds." Susan reached out and clasped the other woman's hand. "And you know you are welcome anytime you wish to pay a call."

Julia got to her feet. "Yes, I should return home as well. My father and aunt will be expecting me for dinner."

Susan rested her hand on Julia's arm when Julia would have walked past her.

William adjusted his uniform coat with a tug at the waist. "Mrs. Hinds, may I have the honor of walking you home?"

The woman only a few years older than Julia and Susan beamed at him like a debutante. "Of course, Captain. It will allow me to introduce you to my husband." She took his proffered arm, and with polite farewells, the admiral's wife and William departed.

Susan kept hold of Julia's arm until they heard the front door close. She pulled Julia back down onto the settee. "See, that wasn't nearly as difficult as you imagined, was it?"

"The only thing I can say that was good about this afternoon is that it seems Mrs. Hinds has not heard the story about how I managed to run off the most eligible lieutenant in the Royal Navy twelve years ago and am now paying for it with my continued spinsterhood."

Susan's pale brows pinched in a frown. "Where have you heard such talk?"

"I did not hear it myself, but my cook reported she heard it at market this morning." Julia stood and wandered the length of the room, running her fingertips along the chair rail.

"Then it is even more important that you are able to greet him with indifference and allow no one to see that his presence in Portsmouth affects you in the least." Susan swiveled in her seat as Julia paced around behind the settee. "And perhaps, if you can put your lingering anger aside, you might find that the years have changed you both for the better—"

Julia stopped and pressed her fingers to her hot cheeks. "Susan, please. Do not ask me for more than I can give."

"Of course," Susan rushed to agree. "I would never imagine to tell you what you should think. I had just hoped…" She crossed the parlor to pull the bell cord.

"You had just hoped to see me married to your husband's dearest friend in the world."

The Yateses' carriage was ready for Julia before William returned.

"Please do not be angry with me, Julia." Susan held her hands out to Julia. "I cannot bear to part with you if you think ill of anything I said or intended today."

"Never fear." She took Susan's hands and squeezed them. "I am incapable of staying angry with you. I shall see you tomorrow morning at church." She allowed the driver to assist her up into the barouche.

"I will be wearing my new bonnet, thanks to you. You must be sure to observe it from a distance so you can tell me if it is becoming or not."

Down the road, Julia saw a flicker and recognized it as the sunset flashing off the gold braid on a navy captain's uniform. "Farewell, my friend."

The carriage rolled away just as William Ransome stopped beside Susan and offered his arm to escort her inside. Julia sank back against the soft leather seat.

William Ransome was more handsome than Julia had ever imagined him—and she had imagined him quite a lot over the years,
reading about him in her father's letters, in spite of the vow she'd made
to never forgive him.

The solicitude he had shown toward Mrs. Hinds and Susan, his
stated desire to help those families struggling to feed themselves due
to husbands and sons being turned out from the Royal Navy, made
the long-held resentment she'd nurtured for half her life chafe like
roughly woven wool.

Chapter Five

The dockyard bustled with sudden activity when a ship in the distance furled its sails and dropped anchor. Julia raised up on her toes, looking above the swirling mass of people to find the dockmaster she had spoken with earlier. The seaman—whose weather-beaten complexion resembled the hull of a ship covered in barnacles—saw her and moved in her direction.

"Master O'Reilley—do you know which ship has just put in?"

"Yes, miss. She be the *Audacious,* sixty-four."

Susan grabbed Julia's forearm, beaming. "It's his ship—Collin's ship! He's here."

"Ye be Mrs. Captain Yates, then?" the dockmaster turned his sharp gaze on Susan.

"Yes, I be Mrs. Captain Yates." Susan arched a saucy brow.

"And ye be?" He turned to Julia.

"Julia Witherington."

"Admiral Sir Edward Witherington's daughter? Come with me."

Julia grabbed Susan's hand as the dockmaster disappeared into the crowd. After avoiding several crates and cargo nets, they climbed a set of stone stairs to an elevated rampart overlooking the quay. The marine guard at the top of the steps nodded at Master O'Reilley and let them pass with no objection.

"Here. This be the best place for ladies to wait for the captain's return. If ye need aught, be sure to send for me."

"Thank you, Master O'Reilley."

The man scuttled off to his work. Julia perched on the low stone wall.

"I am so happy you agreed to come, Julia. The dockmaster would not have afforded *me* such a courtesy." Susan paced a small circuit, her hands fluttering with anxious energy.

"I think they would have."

"If only William had not been called in to the port Admiralty this morning…" Susan stopped and looked at Julia, a glimmer in her eyes.

The embarrassment and discomfort of their surprise meeting Saturday still simmered in Julia's stomach. Avoiding him at church yesterday had been easy enough. She'd only had to stay in the company of her aunt, who never deigned to speak to any naval officer or officer's wife unless under extreme social duress. As they'd exited St. Thomas's, Susan had found Julia and invited her to come along this morning to greet Collin.

Julia cleared her throat. "I am certain—"

"Oh, look—the ship's boats are being lowered."

Saved from having to speak of William, Julia stood and clamped her hand to the brim of her bonnet as a strong gust of wind whipped her face.

"You know it will be a while yet before Collin can disembark."

Susan fluttered her hand. "Oh, yes. I know. I have met him here many times."

As each boat left *Audacious* and rowed toward the docks, Susan announced it with unbridled glee. Launches from other ships brought in crates of all shapes and sizes. If they were in Jamaica, the market near the dockyard in Kingston would be ablaze with colors and music and the voices of vendors as they hawked their wares. The sultry air would be heavy with exotic smells of cinnamon and coconut, the rich smoke of pork and goat cooked over large fires.

"Why did you sigh?" Susan sank onto the embrasure beside her.

"Did I?" Julia came back to the dank-smelling, gray-and-blue present. "I was thinking of Jamaica."

Susan's smile dimmed. "Every time you say 'Jamaica,' I can see you miss it just a little more."

"Just as you would miss England should you be gone from these shores nearly a year. I want to go back..."

"And yet?"

Julia gazed out over the harbor, amusement tickling her insides. "How well you have come to know me. I want to go home, yet I do not want to leave my father. I have spent so much of my life away from him, but at least I had my mother."

"With no family remaining in Jamaica, what is it that calls you back there?"

"Oh, I have family there."

Susan's expression showed her shock. "But I thought...your father...?"

"My Jamaican family are not related to me by blood; however, they are my family nonetheless. They are the people who helped raise me when my mother was too ill, who taught me how to run the plantation, who supported and loved me when my mother died. Who want me to come home."

"You mean...you mean the..." Susan leaned forward and dropped her voice to a whisper. "*Slaves?*"

An old ember Julia thought had long since died away flamed back to life. "They are not slaves." She kept her voice even. "Not anymore. They were when we arrived. One of our tutors read transcripts of William Wilberforce's speeches. Michael and I came to understand how wrong holding other people as slaves was. We petitioned my father; for nearly a year, we worked on a financial plan to show him how freeing the slaves could make Tierra Dulce the most prosperous sugar plantation in the Caribbean. We believed it was the strength of our arguments, the brilliance of our plan that swayed him to our side. I have since learned he did not hold with slavery either and had been trying to devise a plan to do exactly what two fourteen-year-olds showed him could be accomplished."

"And did they—the ones who had been slaves—did they all stay?"

"Yes. All of the original families are still living on the plantation."

"Families?"

The zeal of Julia's antislavery passion faded into compassion for her friend, who was trying to understand. "Slaves on a plantation marry. They have children. Many of them are torn apart. When we freed our slaves, several had wives or husbands on neighboring plantations—my father purchased them and set them free to live and work at Tierra Dulce for a fair wage. It created animosity from some of our neighbors; some mocked my father for taking such a radical step. But when our fields produced more cane, when our workers generated more sugar, when our sugar brought in a higher price, it silenced most of them."

"I never knew..." The graveness in Susan's expression ill-suited her. Slowly, a smile crept back into her expression. "My aunt was a great admirer of Mr. Wilberforce. She took me to see him many times when I was a young girl, too young to understand the importance of the cause for which he fought so valiantly."

"Beg pardon, Mrs. Captain." Master O'Reilley's breaths came in puffs as he topped the steps to the rampart. "Thought ye'd like t'know, Cap'n Yates just departed *Audacious*. If ye both would like t'follow me, I'll take ye to meet him."

Susan fairly skipped down the steps behind the dockmaster, who parted the crowds and navigated a safe path to the head of the quay where the boats from *Audacious* had been putting in for the past hour. Collin had only been gone a month, but tears glittered on Susan's cheeks. Julia renewed her resolve that she would never put herself in such a position by falling in love.

"Wait here, missus, an' the cap'n'll be sure to spot ye right off."

O'Reilley joined the sailors and dockhands scurrying about as the large boat rowed in. The epaulets on Collin's shoulders identified him before the transport was close enough to clearly distinguish his face.

Susan gripped Julia's arm with both hands, excited as a child about to receive a treat. "Doesn't he look wonderful?"

Captain Yates shaded his eyes, his hand under the fore point of his hat, and scanned the yard until his gaze came to rest on Susan.

He lifted his hand in a wave. Susan released one hand from Julia's arm and waved emphatically in return. He turned to speak to one of his sailors—most likely his steward to see about having his dunnage delivered to the house—spoke to the two lieutenants still remaining, and parted company with his men.

Susan's grip became painful, but Julia didn't mind. Collin took the stone steps up to their level two at a time and rushed to his wife, pulling her into an embrace with such enthusiasm, his hat was knocked to the ground. Susan's would have been, too, had it not been for the wide blue ribbon tying it under her chin.

Laughing, Julia stooped to retrieve Collin's hat—anything to avert her gaze from her friends' enthusiastic greeting.

Collin accepted his hat and pressed Julia's hand in greeting. "Miss Witherington. What a pleasure to see you. I hope Susan has not been running you to distraction these last weeks."

"Not quite to distraction, no, Captain Yates," Julia teased.

He opened his mouth to say more but then looked over Julia's shoulder, and an expression of great surprise overtook his features. "Ransome! Bless me." Collin disentangled himself from his wife and stepped beyond Julia.

She turned in time to see the two captains embrace, pounding each other's back.

"Yates! Oh, it does me good to see you again." William Ransome stepped back and held Collin's shoulders, examining him. "Two years! And as I expected, you have not changed one bit."

Susan hooked her arm through Julia's, a contented smile glowing on her countenance. "Are not they the handsomest men of the Royal Navy?"

Julia gazed at the two men, trying to be objective. Quite opposite in appearance—Captain Ransome with his dark hair and light blue eyes, tall and trim; Captain Yates, shorter and broader, with blond hair nearly bleached white by the sun in stark contrast to his dark brown eyes—the two men did justice to their uniforms and would not be out of place in the most fashionable of receiving rooms.

"Aye, they cut fine figures," she admitted, albeit grudgingly.

Another uniformed figure caught her eye. Her father strode with purpose toward the two captains who, concerned only with their own conversation, had not yet noticed his presence.

Sir Edward came to a stop just beyond the two friends and cleared his throat.

Captains Ransome and Yates both snapped to attention and saluted, grasping the fore point of their hats. "Admiral Witherington, sir."

"As you were, men," Sir Edward snapped, returning their salute. "Captain Yates, am I to presume you have nothing of significance to tell me since you have not seen fit to report in? Ship in port for nigh on three hours, and as yet not a peep from her captain."

Collin's ruddy cheeks blanched pale. "Admiral Witherington, sir, I had to oversee the dismissal of my crew, the transport of the soldiers to shore—"

Her father's expression broke into a broad smile; he clasped the younger man's shoulder. "I'll expect to see you in my office at four bells in the forenoon watch tomorrow." He stepped forward. "Mrs. Yates, a great pleasure to see you again."

Susan returned his bow with a curtsey and a luminescent smile. "Thank you, Sir Edward." To see her husband singled out by an admiral was an honor of which few captains' wives could boast.

The admiral's smile widened. "I do believe lunch is in order. There is an inn just across from the port Admiralty where I believe we shall be able to find a table at this hour. Mrs. Yates, Julia, we would be honored by your attendance."

"How delightful!" Susan took her husband's arm and led him toward the carriage. William bowed to Julia and her father and then turned to follow the Yateses.

Julia took her father's arm.

"I do not know if I have ever met two finer men in my life." Sir Edward patted Julia's hand as they strolled up the rampart. "Nor finer officers. I would not be surprised to see both raised to the rank of commodore before year's end."

"Shall they see enough action, what with the war ended, to gain promotion?"

Her father grunted—whether a laugh or a growl, she couldn't be certain—and squeezed her hand. "They have both seen enough action already. I've only to find squadrons in need of commanders to be able to sign their orders. Although Ransome may be readier than Yates. In fact, if a certain commodore can be convinced to resign his commission and retire to the country estate he just purchased, I can sign Ransome's orders before he departs for the Caribbean."

Julia's stomach clenched as her father confirmed her greatest fear: he would take William Ransome in hand as his heir apparent for all of Portsmouth to see, as most of the Royal Navy already assumed the man to be. She suppressed the sound of frustration building in the back of her throat. She and she alone was heir to Tierra Dulce. No man, not even the *fine* Captain William Ransome, would take that away from her.

෭෬෨෩

Though Julia had arrived with Susan, to allow the Yateses a few minutes' privacy, Admiral Witherington suggested Julia ride along with him and William to the inn. William stood back as the admiral handed his daughter up into the open-topped carriage.

Seeing father and daughter together sealed the image of Miss Julia Witherington William had formed after their first meeting four days ago. The years had been kind upon her countenance; indeed, she could pass for a woman in only her second or third Season. However, her reserved demeanor, her serious expression broken only by a few smiles at Susan Yates, proved she had lost the spirit he'd seen in her as a young woman. Guilt prickled at him, wondering if the change could be marked by his cowardice in walking away from her instead of explaining why he could not ask her to marry him.

"Ransome, what think you of Parliament's refusal to revoke the income tax?"

William did not miss the wink Sir Edward gave his daughter and wondered at the man for introducing a topic so highly unsuitable for mixed company. "I believe, sir, a revocation of the income tax would be a relief to many of the sailors and soldiers returning from the war and being turned out on land on half-pay."

Across the carriage from him, Miss Witherington's brows knit together. "Do not you think though, Captain Ransome, the revenues from the taxes could better be used to stimulate economic growth—to create jobs for those men now without employment?"

The admiral *harumphed* but continued to smile at her. "There are few in the Royal Navy who would agree with you, my dear."

"You have spoken only to those who are still employed, sir." Her eyes sparkled and her full lips turned up. "Were you to inquire of those officers and sailors now wondering how to put the next meal on their tables whether they would like the creation of more jobs, they perhaps would agree with me—hardship in the short term to bring about greater good in the future."

The admiral nudged William's elbow with his own. "My dear Julia, were the circumstances reversed—if, instead of record high prices for sugar we currently enjoy, we could not sell it for enough to pay for shipping it to England, and yet Parliament refused to lower the tariff, would you not argue in favor of lowering the tariff?"

"Nay, Papa." A mischievous smile lighted her face, recalling to William the memory of the girl he'd known. "I would argue in favor of selling our sugar elsewhere."

"You see, Ransome? Wise as a serpent, and harmless as a dove, as a woman should be."

Miss Witherington reached up a gloved hand to push back the curls blowing into her face, bringing attention to her burning cheeks, her downcast eyes, and the disappearance of her smile. William had thought the words, quoted from Scripture, to be complimentary. Why should she have a negative reaction to them?

The barouche rolled to a stop in front of the Whitestone Inn. Admiral Witherington descended first and was immediately hailed by two admirals leaving the establishment. William stepped down and then turned and offered his hand to Miss Witherington.

"Ah, Captain Ransome, Miss Witherington." The shorter of the two admirals stepped forward. William did not like the suspicious gleam in the superior officer's eyes as he looked pointedly at Julia's hand, held loosely in William's.

As soon as both her feet were on the cobblestone, Miss Witherington moved toward the inn, putting her father between them. But William was certain that rumors of a sighting of him and Julia Witherington together would soon be making the rounds at the dockyard.

He forced his attention back to the admiral and Collin, consternated he had given so much attention and thought to discerning Julia Witherington's countenance and behavior. He had been back in Portsmouth less than a week and was already well aware of the rumors and speculation running rampant among the officers concerning himself and Miss Witherington and what supposedly happened between them twelve years ago.

William shook his head and returned his attention to his companions. He'd let the gossipmongers get to him.

"Ransome, why so silent?" Admiral Witherington's booming voice broke through William's thoughts. "You've yet to tell us of your capture of the French man-o'-war off the coast of Brest this winter. Quite the tidy sum when that prize paid out."

William allowed his superior to cajole the story out of him. The harrowing experience of almost losing his own ship before the heated battle turned in his favor still awakened him in the middle of the night in a cold sweat.

William kept his gaze on Sir Edward. "If it had not been for the superior skills of my officers—especially my sailing master—all would have been lost. The French ship had the weather gauge on us—they were bearing down with all guns run out. But my sailing master has a nose for the wind...swears he can smell when it shifts. He called for us to tack and beat to starboard, even though the wind came from the southeast."

Admiral Witherington shook his head in disbelief. "To go into the prevailing wind. Unthinkable."

Julia leaned forward, her brow furrowed.

William ignored the sensation of pleasure at having her hanging on his every word. "But he was right, sir. By the time *Alexandra* came about, the wind had shifted to the north. We were run out on both sides, they just on the larboard. We had them at sixes and sevens, and before they could recover, we had downed their mainmast and one of the sharpshooters had felled their captain."

"But if your master had been wrong—" Julia's cheeks reddened. "You must have implicit trust in your crew."

The softness in her wide green eyes quelled the resentment that rose at her questioning his decision. "It was a dangerous move, to be sure. And had my crew been less experienced, had we not been together for more than two years, I might not have listened. But experience has taught me to listen to my men."

Collin thumped his shoulder. "A good crew is a reflection of their captain."

"Well said, Yates!" Sir Edward slapped his open palm on the table.

Heat climbed the back of William's neck at the compliment, and he was grateful the admiral turned his attention to Collin.

Across the table, Susan cut her eyes toward Julia and then gave William a sly smile. He bit the inside of his cheek and pressed his lips together to maintain a pleasant demeanor. He had to live with Collin and Susan the next three weeks until *Alexandra* came out of dry dock. The last thing he needed was Susan trying to turn the clock back twelve years and make William regret his decision not to marry Julia more than he already did.

Chapter Six

D id you enjoy London, Sir Drake?"

"Oh, very much, my lady." Drake turned on all of his charm for the dowager viscountess. Mother said she would be important to have on their side.

"In what part of Town is your home?" Lady Dalrymple smiled as she pinned him with her mismatched brown and blue eyes.

"We are not fortunate enough—yet—to have a house in London," his mother hastened to explain. "Drake took a house near Harley Street." *Near* did not quite describe the distance between his somewhat shabby quarters and the most fashionable addresses in London. "He was received by all the best families."

Lady Dalrymple paid little attention to Drake's mother. "Did you meet, by chance, Lord Winston Everingham?"

His stomach curdled. He had met the Count of Southey, his paramour's husband. "Yes, my lady."

"And how fares my cousin?"

His insides knotted. Had Margaret, in her anger over discovering Drake's intention to marry the Harworth heiress, told anyone of their affair? "He is well, as far as I know. I met him only twice, at the theatre and at a ball."

The dowager viscountess pressed her lips together and nodded. "I must remember to write him a letter soon. I've not yet met his new wife, and I hear she is quite beautiful."

"As a man offering his opinion on the beauty of another man's wife, may I say what you have heard is correct. She is a beauty, in her way."

"Speaking of beauties, have you made the acquaintance of your cousin Julia yet? Since she arrived this past winter, she has created quite the stir among the eligible young men and officers."

Drake shifted in his seat, grateful for the change of subject. "I had the pleasure of dining with her last week. And I understand there is a concert tonight at which we shall be in company together again."

"Oh, those dreaded concerts. I never have had any appreciation for music—especially Italian arias sung by screeching sopranos. Speaking of dinner with Julia, I understand we are all to dine together with them Thursday evening."

Beside him, his mother blanched. "You are attending? Wh—what a pleasure that will be. But you do understand, my lady, that most of the people in attendance will be of the Royal Navy—all, in fact, excepting Drake and me?"

"Naturally—and that is why I am looking forward to it so much." Lady Dalrymple's mismatched eyes danced, though Drake could not imagine why.

"We shall look forward to your company." His mother showed all of her teeth when she smiled, looking something like a snarling animal.

Lady Dalrymple looked beyond Drake's shoulder. "Yes? What is it?"

The butler stood in the doorway of the ostentatious sitting room. "I do apologize, my lady, but Baroness Fairfax has arrived."

"Ah, good. Please show her in."

Drake stood and bowed as his mother curtsied in greeting to Lady Fairfax, a portly, silly-looking woman.

"I see we have nearly overstayed our welcome." His mother grabbed his elbow in a painful grip. "We shall take our leave of you."

"I shall see you both on Thursday." Lady Dalrymple inclined her head toward them. "You must tell me more of your thoughts on your cousin then, Sir Drake."

They exchanged farewells and showed themselves out of the room. Drake followed his mother downstairs and out to their ancient coach. He handed her up and then climbed in, closing the door behind him. The enclosed conveyance trapped the stifling summer air. He longed to strip down to his elegant linen shirt—well, it had been elegant a few years ago. But propriety, always propriety.

Augusta snapped open her fan and waved it vigorously before her flushed face. "You must be cautious—Jane Dalrymple is cunning. She might know more about your connection with Lady Everingham than she revealed. It is vital you stay in her good graces. She is the highest ranking woman in Portsmouth, and she quite dotes upon Julia."

"Yes, I picked up on that. And you need not remind me of my duty. I understood it the first several times you explained it on the trip here."

"Do not get saucy with me, boy."

"Yes, Mother."

"Now, tonight at the concert, be sure to arrive early. The admiral will keep Julia surrounded by naval officers. If you are to have any chance of gaining her affection, you must be at her side from the moment she walks in the door."

"Yes, Mother."

"You must ingratiate yourself with her quickly. I know you are capable of making her madly in love with you by the concert's end. But she does like to have her say-so about anything that comes into her mind. Do *not* talk to her of fashion or London—she despises those topics."

"Yes, Mother."

"Lavish attention on her—I think she will respond well to it, as she has had little experience with a real gentleman paying his addresses to her."

Drake wished the narrow carriage windows opened wider so he could stick his head out into the wind. Sweat trickled down his spine and the sides of his face. "Yes, Mother."

"And above all—do not mention her financial situation. She has complained on many occasions of the young men who court her, trying to gain her wealth."

He let out a rueful laugh. "Is not that what I am doing?"

"Yes. But what she does not know will make your task easier."

His *task*. When had wooing a wealthy woman become a task rather than an enjoyable pursuit? Well, if he was not going to enjoy the pursuit of Miss Julia Witherington, perhaps he could quietly find someone else who could make his confinement here as pleasant as possible.

Suddenly, tonight's gathering of what was considered society in Portsmouth did not seem quite so unpalatable.

∞≈∞

The quiet of the ride home began to ease the tension from Julia's shoulders. She had not missed the implication of Admiral Glover's amused wink at her when William assisted her from the carriage. Now with Collin home, perhaps he and William would occupy each other's time until William's departure in August, allowing her to spend time with Susan without the worry of running into him at their house.

Creighton opened the front door and took her gloves and hat before suggesting she take her rest and tea in the back parlor.

"Have tea sent to my room, please." She started up the stairs. "I must finish auditing the Tierra Dulce account books."

"Very good, miss. What time shall I send Nancy to you?"

She stopped at the first landing. "For what?"

"To help you prepare for dinner."

"I do not need help dressing for a family dinner, thank you, Creighton."

"No, miss, nor would I suggest such a thing. However, you may want assistance preparing for the concert afterward."

Julia groaned. She'd forgotten they were expected at the assembly hall for a concert tonight. "Best send her to me an hour before dinner, then." She trudged up the two flights of stairs to her room and threw open the large windows as soon as she entered to try to clear the stuffiness. Portsmouth had finally attained a respectable level of warmth, making the breeze off the harbor necessary.

She released her hair from the pins and let it tumble freely down to her waist. Standing in the window, the sun beaming down on her face, she massaged her scalp and finger-combed the tangles away.

In the front garden of the house across the lane, a young girl sat under a rose bower, poking away at a piece of needlework, her governess sitting nearby reading. Julia sighed. What kind of life did the child have to look forward to? Attending concerts, card parties, balls, dinners. Pretending interest in suitors pursuing her for her money. Hoping for a kind husband with whom she might have a good marriage.

The girl looked up and waved. Julia smiled and waved in return. The governess gave Julia an appraising look and spoke to the child, and then both disappeared into the house. Yes, best not let the mite look upon the spinster too long for fear her condition may be catching.

The young miss might not have much to look forward to, but Julia had a plantation to oversee. She crossed to her desk and opened the ledger, but the numbers swam before her eyes.

A housemaid entered with the tea tray, set it on the table near the fireplace, curtseyed, and left as silently as she entered. Julia left the desk to pour a cup and found she did not want to return to the ledger. Instead, she picked up the novel she had borrowed from her father's library and returned to the window seat.

Try as she might to concentrate on the story, the words slipped by unnoticed while thoughts of a certain naval captain plagued her.

She thrust the book aside and returned to the ledger. When she added the numbers in a column incorrectly three times, she finally forced herself to concentrate. She couldn't allow Tierra Dulce to develop financial problems simply because she could not discipline her thoughts.

The fourth time she added the numbers, she came up with the same total as before. Something was off, and it was not simply a difference in bookkeeping methods. With renewed interest in the ledgers, she delved into the entries, trying to find out where the error lay.

Nancy tapped on the door and entered. Julia looked at her and then at the clock. "Goodness, I did not realize how the time had slipped away from me." With regret, she set aside her work and moved to her dressing table. "I believe I would like to wear my hair down tonight."

Horror rounded the maid's mouth. "Oh, no. I cannot allow you to do that, miss. Lady Pembroke—"

Julia patted Nancy's hand that grasped the silver brush with white-knuckle intensity. "I will contend with my aunt. Have no fear—I will not let it reflect poorly on your performance." From her jewelry box, Julia withdrew a pair of carved mahogany combs decorated with scroll-work in mother-of-pearl. With dexterity born from years of experience, Julia swept the sides of her hair back and secured it with the combs. The wood was nearly the same color as her hair, but the opalescent, inlaid shell sparkled. A few shorter wisps of hair lay in loose spirals by her temples and ears.

Although Nancy suggested one of Julia's white dresses, Julia went down to dinner in a green silk organza. When she reached the first floor landing, her father exited his study.

"You look lovely, my dear." He escorted her down to the ground floor, where Julia had the pleasure of receiving Creighton's approving expression as he opened the dining room door for them. Footsteps on the stairs followed by a sharp intake of breath behind them made Julia turn.

Her aunt's thin, dark brows pulled together, wrinkling her pale forehead. "I do not believe you should go out in public with your hair unbound like a schoolgirl."

"If I cannot wear my hair however I like, I shan't go." Julia took her seat, not in the least ashamed of acting like the child her aunt accused her of resembling.

Lady Pembroke sputtered, color rising in her face.

Sir Edward squeezed Julia's shoulder. "My dear Lady Pembroke, is it more important for Julia to attend the concert or that she wear her hair a certain way?"

"She will be the laughingstock of all Portsmouth society, such as it is. The gossip of how she defies convention and goes her own way will ruin her reputation."

Mirth bubbled up in Julia and escaped as a laugh. "I believe, Aunt, my reputation as a 'right old spinster' will remain intact whether I wear my hair up or down."

Chapter Seven

Drake adjusted his gloves, trying to twist the middle finger of the left hand to hide a small burn hole. The five hundred pounds his mother had lent him "for housekeeping" had not stretched far beyond a cook-housekeeper and a manservant—and the stake for the game in which he planned to participate after this evening's entertainment.

The crowd milling in the vestibule outside the concert room of the assembly hall represented the highest echelon of Portsmouth society. Oh, how Lady Everingham would laugh at the pretensions of these people—"rustics," she would call them. Young dandies migrated about the room like bees, stopping to drink in the beauty of each successive blossoming female face—not nearly as adept at the art of flirting as those who grew up in the ballrooms and card rooms of Almack's.

Admiral Sir Edward, Miss Julia Witherington, and Lady Pembroke were announced. Rather than go to them immediately, Drake stood back and observed. He was not overly anxious to see his future wife up close again so soon, and he needed to know his competition and Miss Witherington's reaction to them. Several older couples—most likely the admiral's colleagues—approached and spoke to the Witheringtons, blocking his view of Julia.

When the crowd around them parted, Drake drew in a sharp breath. A gown of pale green that would not be out of place at St. James's flowed and draped the figure of a Greek goddess. Her long russet hair, unfashionably loose around her shoulders and in a cascade of plump curls to her waist, framed a face tolerable enough to see across the breakfast table each morning. Although small, her mouth was well shaped. But the square set of her jaw and somewhat stubbornly pointed chin kept her from being a true beauty.

He took several steps forward but then stopped. Why would a woman with wealth and tolerable looks such as hers remain unmarried at her age? He wanted to believe his mother's explanation that Miss Witherington had lived too sheltered a life in the West Indies and that Lady Witherington had protected her daughter by not allowing Julia to degrade the family by marrying someone in Jamaica.

He steeled his will. No matter the reason for her marital status, he would and must court her.

Flicking a piece of lint off the lapel of his black tailcoat, he started across the room, nodding at several women who gave him interestedly curious glances. Whispers followed in his wake.

"Drake, there you are!" His mother shot him a heated glance and then turned to the two she'd arrived with. "Sir Edward, Julia, you remember my son, Sir Drake Pembroke."

Admiral Witherington regarded him with an appraising gaze as he returned Drake's bow. As Miss Julia rose from her curtsey, Drake had a hard time coaxing his gaze away from the lace fitted into the low, square neckline of Julia's gown, which did little to conceal her pleasingly ample endowment.

"I hoped I might have the honor of sitting beside you during the concert, Miss Witherington. I am fluent in Italian and could translate the lyrics for you." He gave her a smile no woman had ever been able to resist.

Her full lips tilted up slightly—he wouldn't call it a smile, though. "Though I do not speak Italian, I am fluent in Spanish and picked up a little French as a girl. So I can make sense of the Italian lyrics."

He took a bold risk, lifting her hand and placing it in the crook of his elbow. "Then you must sit beside me, Cousin, and we shall compare our understanding of the words to see if you are correct."

"Ransome!" Sir Edward's voice made Julia jump, and she pulled her hand away from Drake's arm.

Drake ground his teeth. Could he ever have an evening in Julia Witherington's presence without that man around?

"Good to see you here, lad. Enjoying society while you can?" The admiral shook hands with the man, whose black suit and white waist-coat and cravat could not hide his military bearing.

"Aye, sir."

Drake bowed and couldn't help but notice the stiffness of Miss Witherington's posture and her averted gaze as she made curtsey to the captain. Before any conversation could be entered into, the doors to the concert room opened.

"Miss Witherington, shall we?" Drake extended his arm to his cousin.

Her gaze dropped to his arm as if considering its worth, and then under her long, dark lashes, she glanced toward Ransome. She looked up at Drake with a slight smile and rested her hand on top of his arm with a feather-light touch. "Yes, Sir Drake. Lead on."

⁂

William accepted Admiral Witherington's invitation to sit with him and ended up directly behind Julia and her cousin. For someone who seemed concerned with the niceties and fashions of society, Pembroke's long queue of black hair made William wonder just how socially astute the baronet was. After all, not even the oldest of the admirals—men famous for resisting change—wore their hair long anymore. And his cologne! In the two years William had been gone from England, the fashion of bathing often rather than wearing heavy scents to disguise body odor had caught on—but apparently not with everyone.

The featured soloist, a plump soprano with tall ostrich feathers stuck in her auburn hair, held the room in her command with the strength, range, and beauty of her voice. Though he thought her an adequate singer, William's attention strayed time and again to the curtain of mahogany hair hanging before him and the mother-of-pearl decorations glimmering in the candlelight. With each new song, Pembroke leaned closer to Julia and whispered a rough translation of the Italian lyrics. Even with William's limited knowledge of the tongue, he comprehended the meaning of the text better than Pembroke. Each time the man leaned toward Julia, her back stiffened, and she leaned farther away until she had moved several inches down the bench.

William wondered at himself for being pleased at her reaction to her escort. He had no right to jealousy; he'd lost that privilege long ago. But something about Pembroke—something other than his boorish behavior at dinner last week—unsettled William's gullet. Perhaps it was the way the man's eyes continually strayed to her chest. Or it may have been the overly pleased look in Lady Pembroke's eyes at the pair of them. If a man had looked at Charlotte the way Pembroke did with Julia, William would have called him out. Yes, the man's impertinence bothered William most. William had lost a suitor's right to take exception to Pembroke, but the admiral had become like a father to William, and that made Julia like a sister, did it not? As such, he could allow himself to be concerned on her behalf.

The first intermission brought agreeable relief. He assumed the music to be excellent, but it far exceeded his taste. The mixed voices of his crew singing hymns on Sunday mornings—from the soprano of the young boys to the deep bass of the saltiest of old seamen—with hearts and voices lifted to God in praise and thanksgiving was the most beautiful music of all.

He rose to stretch his legs and be introduced by Admiral Witherington to several other men of the navy, standing where he could see Julia from the corner of his eye. Lady Pembroke swept her son away to introduce him among her circle, leaving her niece seated alone on the bench.

Julia raised her hands and rubbed her temples, eyes closed, her brows drawn together in a pained expression.

"Gentlemen, please excuse me for a moment." Admiral Witherington bowed away and returned to his daughter. She immediately dropped her hands to her lap when her father sat beside her. A whispered conversation ensued, the admiral's brow furrowed in concern.

His daughter sat straighter and shook her head several times at what he said to her. William couldn't see her expression or make out her words, but after a moment of the admiral's listening to her, she leaned over and kissed his cheek.

Never, since the few months following his own father's death, had William missed him as much as he did now, witnessing the tender gesture from daughter to father.

"She is a lovely young woman, is she not?" A female voice whispered to starboard.

William turned. "Good evening, Mrs. Hinds."

"Captain, may I take your arm to my husband across the room?" She rested her hand on the arm he immediately offered, and they walked at her sedate pace through the crowded hall.

"I have heard the rumors of an engagement expected between you and Miss Witherington when you were younger that never came about." She gave his arm a gentle squeeze. "I am a great crusader for people marrying for love rather than for duty or money. Since you did not marry, I assume there was no love between you."

A bit taken aback by the lady's blunt comment, William searched for an appropriate answer. "I respect Miss Witherington and have no wish to further any rumors—"

"Nor am I insinuating either of you have done anything to bring about this gossip—other than just being who you are. As the daughter of a prominent and popular officer, she was bound to be thrust into the fore of the rumor mill for which the naval community is famous. As the favorite of said prominent officer, it is only natural your name should be linked with hers."

William strolled along beside her in silence, not sure where her thoughts led.

Mrs. Hinds stopped and turned to face him, her hand still grasping his arm. "All I am suggesting, Captain Ransome, is that you do not let the murmurings of the gossipmongers lead you to an action— or an inaction—that will make both you and Miss Witherington unhappy in the future."

Before he could answer, she left him, breaking her way through the crowd like HMS *Victory* through the French line at Trafalgar. He made his way back to the concert room, speaking only when spoken to, pondering Mrs. Hinds's words. *Action* or *inaction* that would make both of them unhappy? Leave it to a woman to be cryptic rather than straightforward.

The second set continued much as the first. The warmth in the room increased, and Julia attempted to cool herself with a fan that had some design painted in shades of green. She kept it flying fast, so William could not make out the image.

At the next intermission, she rose from her seat almost before the final note finished. "Please excuse me," she said to Pembroke, who stood beside her. She dipped her knees slightly before fleeing the room. And William could not blame her. The increasing warmth in the room served only to intensify the strength of Pembroke's cologne. William returned the baronet's brief nod and escaped to the hall himself.

Though accustomed to living aboard a ship carrying more than seven hundred men, the press of people in the hot room disagreed with him. He found the door that led to the balcony where several others had sought a breath of somewhat cooler air. He strolled the length of it, as he would the deck of *Alexandra,* hands clasped behind his back.

He was nearly to the end when he saw her. Pressed against the wall, deep in the shadows, was the unmistakable form of Miss Julia Witherington. The decorations in her hair and gold embroidery in her dress caught the light coming from a nearby open door. Her right hand rubbed her temple and forehead, and her left arm wrapped around her middle. William had seen that look aboard ship too many times not to recognize it.

He stepped closer and cleared his throat, then grimaced when she startled. "I apologize for disturbing you, Miss Witherington. But is there something I can get for you? A glass of wine to settle your stomach?"

She turned toward him, her face nearly the same pale green of her dress. "Thank you, Captain, no. I am well enough." Her eyes shifted to look beyond him toward the door halfway down the balcony.

He followed her gaze and saw Sir Drake Pembroke come out, lighting a cigar. William scowled. A gentleman did not smoke in the presence of ladies, and several still milled about.

William turned and offered his arm. "May I escort you back in?"

Indecision warred in her pale countenance. He thought he knew some of what gave her pause—the gossip her appearance on his arm in a social gathering would stir. But Sir Drake's turning and coming in their direction seemed to help with the decision.

"Yes, Captain Ransome. If you would be so kind as to let me take your arm to my father, I would be grateful." She rested her hand atop his arm, but then her grip tightened as she swayed against him, her eyes squeezed tightly closed.

ರೂಲಿಶಾ

Julia held her breath as a wave of nausea passed through her. The evening had started out well enough, but as soon as the concert began, the left side of her head started to throb, first at the temple, then shooting back behind her ear—the way her most incapacitating headaches started. Sitting beside Sir Drake had been no help either, with his overwhelming pungency. Even now, the thought of his cologne churned her stomach.

She swallowed hard. She should have let her father take her home an hour ago as he had suggested. If Elton drove her home now, he would be back in time to retrieve her father and aunt at the end of the concert.

"Are you certain there is nothing I can get for you, Miss Witherington?"

Why did William Ransome have to be so considerate? In this moment, she could almost forgive the man helping her navigate the clusters of preening, gawking, whispering ladies and gentlemen. Oh, but the stories that would be told of her tonight. Taking the arm of one man—a baronet and her cousin, no less—into the concert room, sitting beside him all evening, and then to all appearances, taking the air with Captain William Ransome, the man all of Portsmouth knew had not wanted to marry her.

She squinted against the dim light of the hall, the pain in her head making any illumination horrendous. The noise generated by so many people thundered in her ears, pulsating in time with the thrumming agony. She squeezed Captain Ransome's arm again, pausing in her steps as another wave of queasiness nearly overwhelmed her. A chilled sweat covered her body in the pressing heat of the room.

Where was her father? She took as deep a breath as she could against the stays of her corset and risked a glance up at William Ransome. Something about the expression of concern on his face brought back a memory of him as a midshipman. Her mother had been the one with a sick headache that time—compounded by seasickness from a storm tossing the ship about—and Julia had gone on deck in search of the surgeon. But as soon as she had stepped out of the cabin, the ship careened wildly, throwing her from her feet. Had it not been for Midshipman Ransome's quickness in catching her, she most likely would have been severely injured or even flung overboard. Michael, though, had not been so fortunate. But he'd considered the deep scar across his forehead from the loose block-and-tackle that knocked him unconscious a mark of distinction.

She stole another look at William, unable to suppress a surge of gratitude toward him. Finally, she heard her father's booming voice and was able to quicken her step to reach him.

He excused himself from his colleagues and took Julia's free arm. "My dear daughter." He kissed her forehead, and she leaned into his strength. "Come, I will take you home. Ransome, thank you for your consideration of Julia."

William bowed to them before she remembered to release her grip on his arm.

"Yes, thank you, Captain Ransome." Her head spun, so she settled for a slight bend of her knees and bowing her head instead of attempting a full curtsey.

Ransome seemed not to be offended as he took his leave. Julia quickly turned her gaze to the floor to keep from watching him walk away. Even with as horrid as she felt, she couldn't help noticing the way his hair in the back curled just a bit on his collar. Gratitude thumped in rhythm with the pounding of her headache. As much as she wanted to despise the man, every time she saw him, she became less and less able to hold on to the animosity she'd nurtured over the years.

Her father asked one liveried footman to deliver a message to Lady Pembroke as to their absence, and another to send for his barouche.

"Nay, Papa. You should stay. I am well enough to travel home alone. Elton will see no harm comes to me, and then Creighton and Nancy will take care of me once I arrive home. Aunt Augusta will be furious if both of us leave."

She could see clearly written in his expression that he did not want to stay for the last hour of the concert. Finally, he kissed the top of her head. "You are correct, as always. I shall stay if you are certain."

"I am certain, Papa."

He squeezed her hand. "Very well then."

They stood in silence a moment, Julia leaning again into his strength as she would against the thick trunk of a palm tree.

"What think you of your cousin Sir Drake?" Sir Edward's green eyes twinkled.

"He seems to have inherited the Pembroke countenance."

"Always the lady, aye? Diplomatic even when too ill to stand on her own feet."

The Witherington carriage rolled to a stop, and Julia took the steps carefully as the very ground below her seemed to shift to and fro. "Nay, just too ill to vent my spleen when others may be listening." She kissed her father's cheek and let him hand her up. "But in spite of my diplomacy, do not enter upon any marriage contracts with him without consulting me, please."

His booming laugh startled the horses, jolting the carriage and unsettling Julia's stomach again. He latched the door. "I will be highly upset if you rise apurpose to breakfast with me early in the morning."

"I plan to stay in bed as long as this headache remains, sir, have no fear."

He knocked twice on the frame. "Take her home, Elton." He waved as the coach rolled away.

Home. That was a place Elton and the horses could not take her. She closed her eyes against threatening tears. Going home meant leaving her father. Until he decided to leave the Royal Navy, he would stay in England. But having Aunt Augusta living with them for the past three months had shown Julia she would never be happy here. Jamaica was where she belonged. But she had no way to get there.

William Ransome.

Her eyes popped open. William would be sailing for Jamaica in four weeks' time. Regardless of whether she could forgive him for breaking her heart, she would be on that ship.

Chapter Eight

Collin, dressed in uniform, greeted William when he walked into the dining room at eight o'clock, serving kippers, ham, and sausage from the sideboard onto a plate.

"What's this?" William picked up a handwritten note from his place at the table.

"Dawling mentioned to Fawkes you are in need of a tailor." Collin carried his mound of food to the table. "Sturgess is fast and not overly expensive if you're just looking for pieces to tide you over until you weigh anchor. Susan wants me to go into High Street with her this morning to look at some furniture for the front parlor—she thinks it requires new fitting up. Rubbish if you ask me. We can drop you by the shop and pick you up when we're finished. It will not take long."

William had forgotten how talkative Collin was in the mornings. As Collin talked on, William examined the slightly frayed sleeve of his blue coat. Though Dawling's presumption irritated him, maybe new clothes were in order, even though as he hated to waste the money on them. He'd already received cards from several prominent members of Portsmouth society. At least his black evening attire, which he'd worn last night, was serviceable. And he suspected his dress uniform was receiving daily attention from Dawling's lint brush in preparation for Thursday's dinner at Admiral Witherington's.

He filled his plate from the sideboard and accepted the *Naval Gazette* from Collin, who disappeared behind the Portsmouth newspaper. The *Gazette* proved too depressing to read. What had once been a vital source of information on promotions, battles, and ship deployments was now filled with the lists of ships decommissioned and advertisements from men looking for placement on any ship that would have them.

Susan swept into the room, very pretty in a pale blue gown. Her blonde hair flowed loose in the back with a pink ribbon around the crown.

"I do not understand how you navy men can eat so early in the morning." She took two pieces of toast, which she spread generously with marmalade, and ate them with gusto. "It really is uncivilized to breakfast before ten o'clock."

Collin looked over the top of his paper, went back to reading, and then lowered it again. "Is this a new fashion that has taken hold in my absence?" He reached across the corner of the table and touched her hair.

"From what I heard the maids gossiping about this morning, wearing one's hair loose is the very latest. At least, that's what Cook heard at market this morning." Susan fixed her gaze on William. "Is it true? Did Julia actually wear her hair unbound?"

William remembered the way the long dark hair framed Miss Witherington's face, making her look as young as a debutante. "Aye, Susan, she did."

"My dear," Collin gave a melodramatic sigh and took up the paper again, "one person's actions do not make a fashion."

"You just wait and see if everyone does not think Julia a first-rater. If we do not see at least ten women with their hair unbound this morning, I will…" She looked around the breakfast room as if searching for something.

"You will what?" Collin challenged, face still hidden.

"I'll throw that yellow hat of mine you hate so much into the harbor."

Collin looked at her over a lowered corner of the paper, one eyebrow quirked. "You so believe everyone will follow Miss Witherington's lead that you are willing to get rid of your favorite hat to prove your point?"

Susan nodded. "I do. Now, if you are finished eating, we really should leave so we can accomplish all our errands before you have to report in to see Admiral Witherington."

Her husband stood, leaned over, kissed her on the cheek, and knuckled his forehead like a common sailor. "Aye, aye, Cap'n." He left the room.

Susan sipped her coffee. "William, do not look at me like that. I've not gone mad. But like our dear Julia, I get so tired of pins sticking into my head all day long."

William held his hands out in front of him in a defensive gesture. "I said naught. I claim no knowledge of women's fashions." He looked down at his coat and then rose as she did. "But you do seem assured it will catch on simply because Miss Witherington did it last evening."

Susan laughed and took William's proffered arm. "Not assured, but hopeful."

"But you said…" He frowned, looking down into her dancing blue eyes.

"What Collin doesn't know—and what you are not allowed to tell him—is that I do not care two figs about that yellow hat. I wear it only because he hates it so."

Shaking his head, not understanding why a woman would purposely taunt her husband, he escorted her into the front hall. There, he took his civilian hat from Dawling but waved off the seeming ever-present lint brush. The annihilation of lint from all William's clothing seemed one of the stewarding duties Dawling considered of supreme importance.

Collin's barouche carried them along at a fair clip toward the heart of the city. From under the brim of the bonnet in question—a contraption in straw lined with bright yellow silk and decorated with all manner of flowers and ribbons—Susan kept up a running commentary on all the gossip she'd heard about last evening's concert from *dear* Julia's unbound hair to her green gown. William kept his opinion to himself, but Julia's gown had been rather a relief to the eye in a room full of women dressed in white.

"And I understand, Collin, that Miss Julia Witherington was seen taking in the evening air on the balcony with a rather well-known and distinguished sea captain." Susan smiled at her husband before turning her amused gaze on William. "Is that so, William? Did you happen to take a stroll with Julia?"

William gave her the best smile he could muster. "Sorry to disappoint you, but I did not, as you put it, take a stroll with Miss Witherington. I happened upon her when I stepped out on the balcony for a breath. She was not feeling well, so I offered her the support of my arm to her father. That is all. I would have done the same for you had you been in the same situation." He turned his gaze to the passing buildings to avoid Susan's speculative gaze.

As they entered High Street, Susan began to look eagerly around them. "Look, there, in front of the post office—two young women with their hair loose. And there—"

William looked about as well, but his interest was in seeing the cut and color of the clothing worn by the men out and about. Wearing his uniform would be much easier. But regulations dictated that uniforms were to be worn for official business or functions only.

The carriage pulled up in front of Sturgess & Sons, and William alighted to the street.

"We'll return for you in about an hour." Collin touched the fore point of his high-domed hat, and William returned the salute.

He turned to enter the shop and inclined his head in greeting of the young dandy just coming out the door. Feigning enthusiasm he did not feel, he sailed into uncharted waters.

❧

Drake shrugged into his burgundy coat. "Please have the finished articles sent round to my townhouse."

Sturgess, while not the most renowned tailor in Portsmouth, did have a way with the cut of a garment that pleased Drake—and fit within the budget of last night's winnings. He made his mark in the book, promising his payment at the end of the month.

Sturgess stepped away from the high counter toward the door. "Ah, Captain Ransome. Please, do, come in."

Drake kept his growl of frustration inside. Was there no escaping the man? The sight of him today after his interference with Julia last night was almost more than Drake could bear. Had Ransome merely been performing a favor for the admiral, or was the man a rival for the attentions of the wealthiest unmarried woman in Portsmouth? If the gossip he'd heard at the club last night held any truth, Ransome bore watching. Most held that the captain and Miss Witherington were altar-bound, having been promised to each other for years.

But if that were so, why hadn't they married before now—or why hadn't their impending nuptials been announced already? He couldn't forget that Miss Witherington had seemed uncomfortable when the captain arrived last night and had willingly accepted Drake's escort into the concert room. Perhaps, as per the usual, the gossip was wrong.

However, he needed to know for certain. Stepping forward, he placed himself in the naval officer's path. Both inclined their heads in greeting.

"Captain William Ransome, is it not?"

Ransome looked no more pleased about the encounter than Drake. "Ah, yes, Sir Drake Pembroke."

"Did you enjoy the concert last evening?" Drake despised small talk with other men, but the niceties of society would not allow him to be blunt and ask the captain's intentions toward a certain not-so-young lady.

"Aye—yes. And you?"

"I enjoyed the first two sets immensely. I am only sorry my dear cousin fell ill and had to depart early. She seemed to be enjoying the music so."

Ransome's face remained an inscrutable mask. "Indeed."

Irksome man. "Are you to be long in Portsmouth, Captain?"

"Nay, little more than a month."

A smile tried to tug at the corners of Drake's mouth, but he resisted the urge. Banns had to be posted three weeks before a marriage could take place—unless a special license were obtained—so if no announcement came within the next week or two, Julia's fortune was Drake's for the taking. "Well, I am certain you will find many more amusements to fill your time." Drake settled his tall hat on his head. "Good day."

Ransome gave a curt nod.

Drake stepped out onto the walkway, pausing to give his eyes time to adjust to the morning's brightness. Perhaps he'd best call on his mother today to inquire after his *dear cousin*'s health.

Strolling down High Street, he returned nods of several young—probably married—women. Until he had secured an engagement with Miss Witherington, any thoughts of finding agreeable companionship must wait. Portsmouth, for all its pretensions of grandeur and elegance, was still little more than a country town where discretion would be nearly impossible. Once married and assured of an heir on the way, he would send Julia to Marchwood Hall and hie himself off to London to enjoy all that city had to offer someone with nearly unlimited financial resources. And he would renew his flirtation with Lady Margaret Everingham. The grandeur of Margaret's wealth and her social connections were worth forgiving her jealous gossiping.

Espying a jeweler on the opposite side of the street, he cut through the busy traffic and slipped in. A small trinket sent with a discretely worded note would bring her to contrition, especially once he shared his ideas for what he planned to do with the Witherington wealth.

"Why, my dear son!"

He flinched and turned. "Mother." He swept off his hat and bowed. "What a pleasure to see you. I had planned to call upon you later to inquire after Miss Witherington's health."

"Naturally. And I shall still expect you to do so." Augusta swept past him but then stopped and laid her hand on his arm. "If you come around three o'clock, she should feel up to receiving you." She winked and exited the shop.

Drake let his smile fade as the door clicked shut behind his mother. What would he do with Mother once he secured Julia Witherington's inheritance? His mother had made it clear she gained no pleasure in sharing the same home with her niece. He knew she desired to return Marchwood to its former glory and live there like a queen.

He browsed selections of jewelry for a half hour, interrupted by his inability to solve the problem of where to put his mother and Julia after the wedding. Finally, he settled on a pair of intricately etched silver hair combs. Margaret might be able to help him devise a plan—especially once he convinced her it would be in her best interest to ensure neither his mother nor Julia could interfere with Drake's activities once the marriage license was signed.

He might just be magnanimous and allow Julia to return to Jamaica after she produced his heir.

Chapter Nine

That is the eighth time you have looked at your watch in the past fifteen minutes."

William tucked the watch back into his waistcoat pocket at Susan's comment but stopped his pacing only to look out each of the windows overlooking the street. Mental images of a hired coach capsized on the side of the road quickened his heart.

What had he been thinking, to ask his mother and sister to take such a perilous journey on their own? "I should ride out and trace the route they were supposed to take."

Susan reached the parlor door before he did, closed it, and held on to the knob with her hands behind her back. "William, be reasonable. There are any number of logical explanations for why they are late."

"They were supposed to be delivered here at half-past twelve. It is now nearly one o'clock. They could have met with an accident—they could have been set upon by highwaymen—"

Susan burst into laughter. "Highwaymen?"

He glowered at her, ready to lift her out of his way.

She sighed. "Where will you go to look for them? Will you recognize the coach should you pass it? Do you plan to ride all the way to Gateacre if you do not see them on the road? And what should I tell them when they arrive twenty minutes after you ride out?"

His frustration needed venting, yet he could think of no outlet appropriate in present company. He stalked back to the windows and took up his pacing again, stopping abruptly before the one that had a view of the harbor.

He clasped his hands behind his back, set his feet shoulder-width apart, and let all emotion drain from him. He imagined the rhythm of the waves, and after a few moments, he could almost feel the floor beneath his feet rolling in time. His mother's and sister's lives were in God's hands, and all he could do was trust God for their safety. He affixed his eyes on the gleaming waters in the distance and entered the quiet place in his spirit where the Scriptures and prayers he had learned by rote dwelled. As gentle as waves on a sandy beach, a need for prayer washed over him.

O Eternal Lord God, who alone spreads out the heavens, receive into thy almighty and most gracious protection my mother and sister. Preserve them from the dangers of travel, and deliver them safely here with a thankful remembrance of thy mercies to praise and glorify thy holy name; through Jesus Christ our Lord. Amen.

An insistent tugging at his sleeve brought him back to the parlor.

"William—is that the coach? There. I believe—it is slowing." Susan patted his forearm. "They're here. We must go down to greet them."

Glorious anticipation swelled in his chest, and he turned and followed Susan downstairs.

Fawkes slowly rose from his chair beside the receiving table. "Shall I send for young Dawling to help with the baggage, sir?"

"Yes, please." William kept his demeanor in check, curbing the desire to throw comportment to the wind and run out to the street to ensure his mother and sister were indeed well and safe.

He joined Susan at the door as the coach rolled to a stop. Smoothing his lapels, William reached the street just as the footman opened the carriage door. With a deep breath, he leaned his head into the cab.

Although her age showed in the lines around her mouth and eyes, his mother sparkled with energy and vitality. And beside her sat Charlotte, no longer the young girl he'd last seen but a stunning woman of seventeen.

The smile beaming on his mother's face transported William into the past when, as a lad, his only goal each day had been to earn his mother's words of commendation. As the firstborn, he'd taken very seriously his responsibility as man of the house during his father's extended absences at sea.

He assisted his mother first. Once she reached the ground, she hugged him tightly and then raised a hand to caress his face. "William. Oh, how like your father you look."

Warmth filled him. "I am happy to see you, Mother. And Charlotte." He kissed her forehead after he helped her down. "I hardly recognized you."

Mrs. Ransome laughed. "Hardly recognized? With her dark hair and blue eyes just like yours?"

Charlotte's fair cheeks flushed scarlet. "Two years is too long, William. You must come home more often."

He offered his arms to escort them into the townhouse. "I would make berth in Liverpool often if I could. However, I must go where the Admiralty orders. Fortunately for me, I have a good correspondent who keeps me informed of all news from home." He smiled down at Charlotte.

She blushed yet deeper, and he caught a glimpse of the young girl he'd known in the expression.

· "Mrs. Ransome, Miss Ransome." Susan reached out toward them. "I cannot tell you how delighted I am to welcome you."

His mother released his arm and took Susan's hand. "Mrs. Yates, it is lovely to see you again. I hope our arrival is of no inconvenience to you."

"Not at all, ma'am! I have driven your son to distraction all morning with my eagerness for your company." She hooked her arm through Mrs. Ransome's. "Come. I will show you to your rooms so you can freshen up and rest before tea."

The three women disappeared inside, William following in their wake.

❦

Charlotte tried not to gawk as she climbed the stairs. Though the townhouse wasn't much to look at outside, inside, it exceeded what Charlotte imagined the grandest houses in London looked like: gleaming dark wood, gilt-framed portraits, thick Aubusson carpets, sparkling crystal wall sconces...

"Here is your room, Miss Ransome. I hope you find it to your liking."

Susan Yates opened a door near the end of the hall, stepped aside, and motioned Charlotte to enter.

The room was as delicate and frothy as Susan Yates herself—with surprising bursts of color scattered throughout. Ethereal white lace formed a canopy over the bed. Charlotte reached out to touch the exotic blue silk panels of the changing screen in the corner.

"Collin brought all of these back from China just a few years after we were married." Susan ran her hand over a length of red silk draped over a white chaise. "I could never bear to have any of the pieces cut up, and I thought they looked nice with all the white in here."

"They are exquisite." Charlotte tried to imagine the market in China where Captain Yates had purchased these fabrics...though she was certain her imagination could not do justice to the colors, smells, and sounds of a foreign port.

"Beg pardon, Missus. Miss."

Charlotte turned toward the door—and gasped. Her trunk balanced on one shoulder, her valise tucked under his other arm, the man entering the room looked unlike any household servant she'd ever seen—burly and scarred, his dark hair a wild tangle about his head.

"Ah, yes, Dawling. Please put Miss Charlotte's things there." Susan indicated a spot between the dressing screen and wash stand.

A tap on the door drew their attention from Dawling. William looked in. "Do you have everything you need, Charlotte?"

She'd forgotten how intense his eyes were. He had inherited their mother's ability to be able to look through a person's outside right to what they were thinking. "Yes, I believe I shall be quite comfortable."

"If you find you are in need of anything, please send for Dawling to fetch it for you."

"Oh, William, I already told you, there's no need to make extra work for your steward." Susan waved her hands to shoo him out of the room and then turned back to Charlotte. "Ella will act as your lady's maid while you're here. She can get you anything you need."

Shocked not only to see a woman confident enough to dismiss her brother but also at the fact that he actually moved into the corridor, Charlotte could only nod. Dawling knuckled his forehead and bowed out of the room.

Knuckled his forehead? Suddenly, the rough appearance made sense. Dawling was William's steward aboard *Alexandra*. Amusement trickled through her. If Dawling was at all talkative, Charlotte might just discover she needed him to fetch quite a few things for her. She could learn much from him.

"Tea will be served in about half an hour." Susan softly closed the door behind her, leaving Charlotte alone.

A breath of air stirred the curtains, inviting her toward them. She pushed the lace aside and stepped out onto the narrow balcony. Shading her eyes, she glanced to her right, up the row of townhouses on the opposite side of the street. So different from the view of rolling pastureland from her bedroom in Gateacre. She scanned to her left and saw the reflection of sun on water and the unmistakable spikes of ship masts.

Excitement danced a reel in her stomach. So close to her goal. Yet she must proceed with caution, lest someone uncover her plan and keep her from it.

A giggly housemaid came up with water for washing and assisted Charlotte into her pink gown. The girl seemed to be enjoying her time away from her other duties, so Charlotte allowed her to brush out and re-pin her hair.

She met her mother on the landing. Mama touched the curls beside Charlotte's ear. "Very nice."

"Yes, I thought she did an excellent job." She restrained her pace down the stairs to her mother's. They glimpsed two maids entering a door with trays laden with tea service and food, and followed them in.

"Miss Ransome, do come sit beside me." Susan patted the seat of the settee and then turned her attention to pouring tea.

William left his place standing beside the fireplace and sat in an armchair beside their mother. Nervousness disquieted Charlotte's stomach. William's expression was so stern and forbidding. After two years, he looked exactly as she remembered—except last time he had smiled at her often. How could this be the same man who had sent her drawings of sea creatures and birds when she was a girl and then answered her letters as she'd grown up? Where was the gentle humor, the compassion his words had conveyed?

In Susan Yates's company, no one had to struggle for conversation—it was rather like being a passenger in a runaway carriage. Even Mama, always calm and collected in company, seemed rattled by the whirlwind chatter.

"Day after tomorrow we are all to attend a formal dinner at the home of Admiral Sir Edward Witherington. Then next week, there is the ball at the home of Baron Fairfax. The Baroness extended a most gracious invitation to both of you when she learned you would be arriving in time for it."

Charlotte sneaked a glance at her brother. Was he truly so respected—and wealthy—that he counted aristocracy among his acquaintance? Excitement over the prospect of a formal dinner and a ball in the company such as Portsmouth afforded stole through her but just as quickly receded. She had no gown appropriate for such events, and the one person she would wish to dance with was on the far side of the Atlantic trying to make his fortune the hard way. Guilt over the idea of dancing with other men without his knowledge chased away all pleasant thoughts of the ball. She would go—she could think of no excuse that would not be a blatant lie—but she would not enjoy herself.

"Miss Ransome is somewhat smaller than I," Mrs. Yates was saying. "But I have just the gown to mark her coming out in Portsmouth society at the Witheringtons' dinner. I shall brook no argument, Mrs. Ransome. We will visit my dressmaker tomorrow morning, and she shall alter it to fit our beautiful debutante. By my seventeenth birthday, I had been married nearly a year, and my husband had been sent to sea the month after our wedding." Her eyes sparkled with irresistible humor. "But that did not stop me from dancing every dance at every ball—Collin, my dear, you are home!" With a laugh, Mrs. Yates rose and greeted the brawny blond man with a kiss on the cheek.

William performed the introductions—although their mother greeted Captain Yates like a long-lost son. Charlotte had a vague recollection of the fair-haired, freckle-faced young man who had come for a visit twelve years ago during the Peace of Amiens. She remembered mostly the funny faces he made and the acrobatics he performed to make her laugh.

Listening to William, Collin, and Susan tell stories about each other made Charlotte a little jealous. These two people—strangers—knew her eldest brother better than she did.

She shoved the envy aside. If her plan worked, she would have plenty of time to spend getting to know her brother better. And she could use that time to work her way so much into his affections that he would not deny her anything...not even her choice of husband.

Chapter Ten

Julia trimmed her quill and reread what she had written to the Tierra Dulce steward so far, mostly questions about certain entries in the copies of the ledgers and the numbers that did not add up. She finished the letter and then wrote another to the plantation's foreman, Jeremiah. She trusted no one else but Jeremiah to look after the plantation's interests in her absence, but she suspected the steward she'd been forced to hire in a rush before leaving for England would not respect Jeremiah or his position due to his African heritage.

When Julia was halfway through copying out the questions for Jeremiah to ask the steward on her behalf, Creighton knocked and entered on her entreaty.

"Beg pardon, miss, but Lady Pembroke requests your presence in the parlor."

"A caller?"

"Yes, miss."

"Cannot you tell her that I am in my room resting?"

"I tried, miss, but she saw you enter the library."

Reluctantly, Julia corked the ink bottle and laid aside her writing materials. She checked her appearance in the small gilt mirror over the fireplace. The pale gray muslin dress seemed as limp and tired as she felt. She smoothed her hair back to the thick coil of braid and, with a fortifying breath, crossed the wide hallway to the front parlor. The door stood open; Julia smothered a groan when she recognized the queue of black hair on the man who sat across from her aunt.

"Julia, dear, come in and greet your cousin." Lady Pembroke rose. "He has come especially to inquire after your health."

Sir Drake Pembroke's movement as he stood was languid, slow— almost slothful. Julia forced a neutral expression as she entered the room. She paused to answer Sir Drake's bow with a curtsey before stopping at the armchair beside her aunt's. Not every man could move with the crisp quickness and precision of a naval officer. Such a pity.

"Thank you for your kind concern, Sir Drake. My strength returns by the hour." Julia sat only after her aunt did so.

As Sir Drake moved to sit, a faint whiff of the cologne he'd been doused in at the concert two nights ago reached Julia's nose. Her head pounded in response. Could it be? Could the fragrance he wore have felled her?

"I called yesterday but was told you were too ill to receive visitors. I am so pleased to see you have regained your…color." Sir Drake's voice went a bit weak at the end of his statement.

Julia knew she looked anything but robust, but she smiled her thanks at the flattery.

"I was just telling Mother of my recent sojourn in Scotland visiting our aunt, Lady MacDougall."

A cold shiver trickled down Julia's spine. She had never had the misfortune to meet her mother's Aunt Hedwig, but she had heard about the baroness's philosophies of how ladies should behave from her earliest memories.

"Do you know Lady MacDougall, Miss Witherington?" he asked.

"Only by reputation."

Lady Pembroke cleared her throat, indicating her displeasure with Julia's response. "I thought we might visit Aunt Hedwig this autumn, when the weather is more pleasant for traveling. I am most anxious for Julia and our aunt to become better acquainted."

This was news to Julia. Of course, she would be back in Jamaica before autumn, so she gave the scheme no further thought. The conversation turned from Aunt Hedwig's late husband's estate in Scotland to London, and Julia clamped her lips together over a threatening yawn while Sir Drake droned on about what he had seen and done while in Town for part of the Season. Her mind drifted back to her unfinished letter, and she thought of a few more questions for Jeremiah to put to the steward. Only by extreme force of will did she remain seated, feigning interest in Sir Drake's pompous, self-gratulating anecdotes.

After what seemed like a great while—but only ten minutes by the grandfather clock in the corner—the unmistakable sounds of her father's homecoming reached the parlor. Julia strained to hear his movements, hoping he would come rescue her. After a few moments, the house once again fell still, and she returned to mentally composing the letter to Jeremiah.

The parlor door swung open and her father—still in full admiral regalia—marched in. Julia stood, relief flooding her.

Sir Drake popped up from his chair. So he *could* move with something more akin to snap and attention than she'd first thought. "Sir Edward. I am so pleased. I was uncertain I would have the honor of seeing you today."

Admiral Witherington wore a slightly disdainful expression. "Pembroke." He gave the baronet a quick visual inspection before inclining his head slightly. Much of the insipidness drained from Sir Drake's stance at the admiral's cold greeting.

Julia's legs twitched with the desire to cross the room to him.

"Daughter, I would see you in my study."

"Sir Edward." Lady Pembroke's voice had a shrill edge to it. "Perhaps you could take your tea with us before Sir Drake leaves, and speak with Julia later."

Julia cringed.

Her father made no movement, but a definitive sharpness overtook his gaze. "Thank you, madam, but I fear this is an urgent matter of business which cannot be delayed." He extended his hand. "Come, Julia."

Eyes trained on her father, Julia willingly obeyed. He clamped his hand around her elbow and led her from the room, securing the door behind them.

Crossing the hall, Julia whispered, "Aunt Augusta will be cross—we did not bid Sir Drake farewell."

He raised his brows and glanced over his shoulder at the closed door. "He is her son, is he not? Can she not bid him farewell for us?" He frowned. "I do not like her countermanding my request in front of a guest, though."

"Papa." She rested her hands flat against the braid-covered lapels of his coat. "My aunt meant only to be polite by asking you to stay." She kept her voice low so as not to carry.

He kissed her forehead, put his arm around her waist, and led her into the library, where a maid was setting up a tea tray. He dismissed the girl and closed the door behind her.

"Your defense of your aunt is admirable, if undeserved, my dear." He shrugged out of his coat, draped it across the back of a sofa, and sank into a plush leather chair.

Julia perched on the edge of the more delicate carved armchair beside the table and began to prepare her father's tea. "She wants nothing more than for you to become enamored of Sir Drake Pembroke."

He grunted. "She wastes her time, then."

"Papa," Julia chided, handing him his cup. "We know too little of him to judge for favor or ill."

He turned a surprised expression toward her. "How can you say so? Was not his impertinent behavior toward you at the concert enough to form an opinion of him? Had you but said the word, I would have had him flogged round the fleet—yes, in full presence of all assembled."

Julia tingled with pleasure at the compliment to herself implied in her father's words. "Thank you, Papa."

"I do not trust the man—but then, I learned long ago not to trust Pembrokes from the way they treated your mother. Thank God you take after me. Though, in some ways, you are much like your mother—she somehow managed to escape becoming like the rest of her family." He reached for a sandwich. "I believe your brother may have had more of the Pembroke constitution. He was a good boy, and I was prodigiously proud of him; but I think his lack of ambition for advancement in the navy may have come from the Pembroke blood."

Julia's innards froze solid. "I do not understand how you can say such a thing, sir. I have read to you from his letters where he expressed his greatest desire to please you and find patronage and move up the ranks."

"Now, now, Julia. Do not let my comments upset you so. I meant no offense, I assure you. Your loyalty to your brother does you credit. But you must admit to the differences in your temperament and disposition, for all that you were twins. Your quickness with books and learning, your head for numbers and business…Are not you the one who convinced me—and many of our neighbors—of the economic benefits of freeing our slaves and hiring them on at fair wages? Of making Jeremiah the foreman? And all when you were yet a girl of fourteen."

"It was Michael's idea. His plan—all except for the calculations of profit." Her throat clogged thinking of her twin's compassionate heart. Compassion was a more admirable trait than cleverness with numbers. If they continued speaking of Michael, she would only become upset with her father. "For what 'urgent business' did you want to see me, Papa?"

"What? Oh, did not you recognize it as a ruse to grant you escape from a situation you had no desire to be in?"

She swallowed the remainder of her tea, along with the emotion clogging her throat. "I did not want to assume of your intentions."

"I saw the letters to Jeremiah and the steward. If you finish them tonight, I will send them out on the supply ship that sails early tomorrow morning."

Ah, yes, the letters. Julia retrieved the papers, quill, and ink, and finished the missive to Jeremiah while her father read his correspondence.

Both looked up at a rap on the door.

"Enter." Sir Edward removed his spectacles as Creighton entered.

"Admiral Sir Edward, sir, there is a messenger from the port Admiralty downstairs with a message for you."

"See him in, please, Creighton."

Julia left her writing table and crossed to help her father into his uniform coat and then straighten the red sash across his chest.

"Thank you, my dear." He squeezed her shoulders.

"Should I go?"

"I see no reason."

Creighton returned with a man with a lieutenant's epaulette on his right shoulder, hat tucked under his arm.

Sir Edward stood before his desk, hands clasped behind his back, looking more imposing than she'd ever seen him. "Report."

"Sir—this arrived for you after you left." The young man handed over a letter. "I've been told to await your response, sir." His Adam's apple bobbled as he swallowed, his eyes not quite meeting the admiral's.

"Very well. Please, have a seat." Sir Edward motioned the officer to one of the chairs flanking his desk.

Julia returned to the smaller writing table in the corner and tried to put her attention back on her own letter, but her gaze kept drifting to her father. He perched his spectacles on his nose and sank into his large chair to read the missive. After a few moments, he took up pen and parchment and scratched out a brief note.

Within ten minutes of his arrival, the lieutenant departed with Sir Edward's response. Julia rolled the tip of her quill between finger and thumb.

Sir Edward removed his glasses and rubbed his forehead. "I've been summoned to the Admiralty in London. I am to depart at dawn Friday morning with Admiral Hinds."

"For how long?" She wiped the ink from her fingers and moved to the chair the lieutenant vacated.

"A month, possibly as long as six weeks. They are in need of admirals to adjudicate courts-martial."

Julia clasped her hands together in her lap, anxiety contorting her insides. "I see."

"I would offer to take you with me, but I am informed that we shall be quartered at the Admiralty so there will be no undue influence upon us by family members or interested parties in the cases." He tapped his spectacles against his chin. "Your aunt is here, so you will not be left alone. For all that I do not trust her, at least she will see to it that you are well chaperoned and no harm will come to you. I know you are capable of looking after yourself—that you took care of your mother for years while running the plantation almost single-handedly. But your aunt knows the ways of society better than you do. She can continue to help you take your place here. Follow her lead—she will not lead you astray."

But her father was supposed to be here—to buffer her from her aunt's attempts to push Sir Drake upon her. "Yes, Papa."

"And the timing is not all bad—at least I shall not miss our dinner party."

"No, not the dinner party." But he would, once again, miss celebrating her birthday because duty called him away.

"And I am certain that the Yateses and Ransome can be counted upon should you need anything."

"Of course."

"In fact, I believe I shall ask Ransome to watch over you. His mother and sister will be most helpful to him and to you in that task, I believe. I am certain Mrs. Ransome will be most anxious to be of service to you, as her husband was to me for so long."

"I will be honored to make Mrs. Ransome's acquaintance." Was this an attempt to subtly push Julia and William together? "But you need not ask Captain Ransome—"

"Nonsense. He will be glad to do it."

She was about to protest again when she remembered that William Ransome was to sail for Jamaica before the end of August. If she wanted passage aboard his ship, she needed to start trying to ingratiate herself to him. "Very well. I shall be grateful for his watchcare."

After all, turnabout was fair play.

Chapter Eleven

William stood at the drawing room window, looking over the back garden. He turned when Collin and Susan entered, Susan dressed in a white gown that made her look ghostly pale with her fair skin and light hair.

On Susan's heels came Charlotte. William couldn't believe his eyes at the woman standing before him. The pale pink gown and her hair were trimmed with pearls and roses, and she looked like royalty—and like she needed something to cover up with, as the lace inset at the low neckline did not do the job adequately.

His mother swept in behind them. "Mrs. Yates, your dressmaker is a wonder."

"Charlotte has such a fine figure, it would be hard for her not to look good in anything." She patted the blushing debutante's cheek. "Shall we go then?"

William kept his less-than-favorable comment about the indecency of the gown behind his teeth and followed Collin and the women downstairs.

"I am certain," Susan said, taking her wrap from the ancient butler, "that no women of the party this evening can boast of not just one but two of the most handsome men in the Royal Navy as their escorts."

"Yes, my dear," Collin helped her with the shawl, "I believe you are correct."

Susan continued her gay chatter all the way to the Witheringtons' home, enumerating the guests and what she knew to expect at table, from what "dear Julia" had told her. His mother and Charlotte seemed like mutes beside her.

How did Collin put up with the continual talking? William loved Susan like a sister, but staying under the same roof with the woman had, in just a matter of a few days, made him wonder at his friend's forbearance. From the benign expression on Collin's face, his friend didn't seem to mind the pointless prattle.

The barouche stopped before a large white house, where they were greeted at the front door by a butler with the snap and bearing that marked him formerly of the navy. After being divested of hats and shawls, they were shown upstairs, where several other uniformed men and white-gowned women milled about, accompanied by loud voices and feminine laughter—real laughter, not the simper usually heard in society.

The butler announced them from the door, creating a stir as Admirals Witherington and Hinds turned to greet them.

William bowed to his host. "Admiral Sir Edward Witherington, I am certain you remember my mother, Mrs. Maria Ransome."

"Mrs. Ransome, what a great honor it is to welcome you into my home." Admiral Witherington took Mrs. Ransome's gloved hand and brushed the knuckles with his lips.

"And this is my sister, Miss Charlotte Ransome."

The admiral's eyes crinkled in the same indulgent smile William had only seen Sir Edward give Julia. "Miss Ransome, you are a most welcomed addition to our number—and to Portsmouth at large."

Charlotte turned as pink as the roses in her dark hair. "Thank you, Sir Edward."

Admiral Witherington's attention caught on something over Charlotte's shoulder. William turned to see who approached aft, and his breath caught. Julia Witherington was the very image of an Athenian statue—but not of cold white stone. Her gown looked as if it had been made of liquid bronze, hair done up with gold ribbon woven throughout the mass, while several mahogany curls bounced around her shoulders.

Regret lapped at his soul like waves against the hull of his ship. She could have been his wife—*should* have been his wife—if only he'd not been such a coward.

Admiral Witherington made the introductions between Julia, Charlotte, and Mrs. Ransome.

Julia's smile flickered in her emerald eyes. "Mrs. Ransome, Miss Ransome, welcome to our home. I cannot tell you how pleased I am to make your acquaintance." She turned to William; her cheeks reddened, and she dropped her gaze as she inclined her head. "Captain Ransome."

Dawling had tied his neckcloth too tight tonight. And had a hot draft just flowed into the room? "Miss Witherington."

She turned to greet Collin and Susan—but he caught her steal a glance at him. He stopped the smile wanting to bloom, admonishing himself for behaving like a schoolboy, and turned his attention to the other officers.

A few moments later, Julia joined them. "Captain Mason, I wondered if I might ask you to escort Mrs. Ransome down to dinner this evening."

The man who'd served as Admiral Witherington's first officer for years smiled at Julia. "It would be my great pleasure."

"Captain Ransome," her green eyes seemed depthless in the glow of dozens of candles, "If you could lend your arm to your sister?"

He inclined his head. "Of course."

A hint of dimple appeared in her left cheek. "Thank you."

"Admiral Thomas Glover," the butler announced.

"Ah! Now the party's all here." Admiral Witherington greeted the other admiral and performed the necessary introductions.

"Well, then, I suppose Creighton will announce dinner any time." Admiral Witherington patted his slim stomach and winked at his daughter. "I've been smelling the wonderful aromas from the kitchen all afternoon."

"Papa, we are waiting on one more guest to arrive," Julia said softly. The sound of the door and voices in the hall did not bring relief to her countenance; rather, her brows pinched a little tighter together.

When the parlor doors opened, William understood.

"Sir Drake Pembroke," Creighton announced.

This roused Lady Pembroke and her companion, who both rose and crossed the room to greet him. Julia and Admiral Witherington excused themselves to greet this guest, and William tried to keep his attention on the story Mason was telling about his last voyage, but he was having too hard a time trying to watch Julia's interaction with her cousin. Was it William's imagination, or did all the vivacity and sparkle she'd shown since his arrival vanish when she greeted the baronet?

A few moments later, Julia eased around the room, unobtrusively arranging the couples. Charlotte, still looking flushed and excited, came and took his arm.

"Enjoying yourself?" he asked, happy he could provide her with an experience like this.

"Oh, immensely. Thank you, William, for seeing that we were invited. I've never seen a house like this before. And Miss Withering-ton...her gown..." Charlotte's raptures continued as they took their place in the order of precedence—just before Collin and Susan, who brought up the rear.

William's focus strayed beyond the two couples ahead of him to the reddish-brown curls that skimmed Julia's skin as she took the stairs on Admiral Glover's arm. The curve of her shoulder up to the column of her neck reminded him of the refined lines of the bow of a man-o'-war—

He trimmed sail and reversed course. Every time he was near this woman he devolved into a blithering idiot with no thought but her pleasing appearance in his head. Where was the famed Ransome discipline?

They entered the dining room, passing Lady Pembroke, who was being seated at the foot of the table by Sir Drake. He could not help but contrast Julia's behavior toward their guests with her aunt's. Her aunt had shown no pleasure in anyone's company but her son's and Lady Dalrymple's, whereas Julia seemed truly happy to have everyone here—with the exception, perhaps, of Sir Drake.

He smiled at that thought.

Glancing at the name cards, William was pleased to see he was to be seated between Susan—who sat at Admiral Witherington's left hand—and Mrs. Hinds, with Captain Mason on her other side. Julia held the seat of honor across the table from them at her father's right hand, with Collin beside her. William could not have asked for a better arrangement.

To his right, Susan talked with animation—about what, William had no idea—but as long as he feigned interest and reached for whatever dish she wished to sample next, she seemed content. At his left, Mrs. Hinds spoke to Captain Mason, their tones low.

"William?"

He turned at a nudge on his right elbow. Susan looked up at him in question. "I do apologize, Mrs. Yates."

She smiled at him, showing the dimples in her round cheeks. "So formal—I know, I know, 'in public' and all that rot." She dabbed her mouth with the white napkin. "I asked if you had already engaged someone for the first dance at the Fairfaxes' ball next week."

"In the few days I have been ashore, I have been nearly all day at the port Admiralty or in your company. Whom, pray tell, might I have asked?" The thought of spending an evening in a public place surrounded by young women trying to snare rich husbands—and even worse, their mothers—sent a chill down his spine.

"Cheeky! Did not any lady catch your fancy at the concert?" Susan's eyes flickered to Julia.

He bit the inside of his cheek to keep from showing his frustration at Susan's continual implications.

Admiral Witherington turned his attention to Susan and William. "I spoke with Lord Fairfax yesterday, and he assured me your presence is much anticipated. And you will have little chance at such amusements, once you've put out to sea. Do not deny all the young ladies of Portsmouth the pleasure of partnering you for a dance or two."

William kept his groan inside, but only with great effort. "Of course, Sir Edward." He couldn't help from looking across the table at Julia, but her attention was on something Collin was saying in low tones.

Conversation lingered on the ball for longer than William would have cared, but he noticed Julia did not join in Mrs. Hinds's and Susan's animated anticipation of the event. In fact, the more they discussed it, the less amused Julia seemed. Only when she shot a furtive look toward the opposite end of the table did William understand why Julia might not look forward to the ball. If the baronet's behavior toward her at the concert was any indication, she was right to worry about how he might behave toward her if they danced. He hoped for her sake the scandalous new dance gaining popularity on the Continent—the waltz—had not gained acceptance here.

The subject waned, and Mason mentioned a recent trip to the Caribbean, resupplying ships participating in the blockade of American ports in the Gulf of Mexico.

"And had you the opportunity to stop in Jamaica, Captain Mason?" Julia asked, leaning forward, interest illuminating her features.

"Alas, no, Miss Witherington, and I would have dearly loved to see Kingston again. We spent quite a happy fortnight there, did we not, Ransome? Yates?"

What William remembered most about his only visit to Jamaica was his disappointment at finding a very European city where he had expected grass-thatched huts and natives in animal skins. Collin had laughed at him and accused him of reading too many fantastic stories of the wilds of the West.

"Do you expect the American war will continue much longer?" Julia asked. "Now that the War Department and the Admiralty can commit more men to fight in North America?"

"It is hard to tell," Mason answered. "I spoke to only a handful of officers. They have quelled American privateers for the most part, but they are not at the forefront of the fighting—most of that is farther north."

Julia nodded, her brow furrowed. "I deplore the idea of war, however it has decreased the competition for Tierra Dulce from sugar coming out of New Orleans. But it has also made us a target of pirates more often, as there are fewer merchant ships coming out of the Caribbean."

"Pirates?" Collin asked. "I thought we had cleared those scoundrels out ages ago."

"For the most part, yes." Admiral Witherington signaled the butler to have footmen clear the dishes from the first course and begin laying out the second. "But there are a few that remain thorns in our side. There is one in particular…" He gave William a quick glance.

Part of the orders the admiral had given William this afternoon—the part he was not to share with any of his crew until their arrival in western waters—was the list of pirates he was commissioned to hunt down and bring to justice by any means necessary. He would inform Collin tonight when they could go over their orders and list in detail.

"Yes. Shaw, as he has fashioned himself." Julia's voice held a mixture of disdain and anger. "He has been haunting the waters of the Caribbean the past fifteen or twenty years. And he seems to know our harvest and shipping schedules intimately."

"He's no Morgan or Teach, nor has he caused the Royal Navy as much grief as Jean Lafitte seems intent to cause." Admiral Witherington passed a dish of plovers' eggs in aspic jelly to Susan.

William joined happily in the abuse anyone wanted to parcel out on the heads of pirates and foreign privateers, and the conversation continued until the dessert course was served. The atmosphere at the table reminded William more and more of the camaraderie found aboard a fellow officer's ship rather than a formal dinner.

A distant clock chimed nine o'clock. Julia invited the ladies to join her upstairs for coffee and tea. William stood and assisted Susan with her chair. Before Julia departed, Admiral Witherington had a whispered conversation with his daughter and then sent her on her way. Footmen cleared the dishes with quiet efficiency, and the butler saw to the service of port and Madeira.

Once each of the seven men in the room received their full measure, Admiral Witherington raised his goblet. "Gentlemen. To King George."

William raised his glass and voiced the Loyal Toast.

"To our ships at sea," Admiral Hinds toasted—the standard Monday toast. But along with the rest, William raised his glass.

"To our men," Admiral Glover added the Tuesday toast, and William smiled. Each day had its own traditional dinner toast, and as they'd all been off their ships a while, a week's worth of toasts seemed in order, though he did limit himself to small sips of the potent wine.

Mason smiled and said, "To ourselves, because no one else is likely to bother."

William took his turn, combining the Thursday and Friday toasts. "To bloody wars, willing foes, and sea room."

The toasting paused as the butler refilled several glasses.

Which left the Saturday toast for Collin. "To wives and sweethearts." He raised his glass.

"May they never meet," the other officers at the table intoned in good humor.

Admiral Witherington raised his goblet once more for the final and somber Sunday toast. "To absent friends."

"Absent friends," William repeated along with the others, his mind straying to those men he knew he'd never see again this side of heaven, praying some had finally made peace with God before their untimely deaths.

"Sir Drake, had you any service in the war?" Admiral Glover asked.

The dandy baronet seemed to startle out of a reverie—as if he'd allowed his mind to wander during the toasting. "No, Cap—Admiral. My father, General Sir Walter Pembroke, had been about to purchase a commission for me in one of his regiments, but he died before the commission was finalized. As I inherited the title upon his death, the family felt it imperative that I remain in England to oversee the farms and mills."

Admiral Witherington's face seemed carved from stone. "And how fare the Pembroke mills and farms?"

Curiosity piqued by Sir Edward's sardonic undertone, William turned to look down the table at the baronet.

Pembroke cleared his throat and took a drink from his nearly empty goblet. "Like many businesses, we suffer from a dearth of able workers, as many of our men were abducted and pressed into naval service."

Sir Edward's left brow raised—never a good sign. "I am certain had the press-gangs known the men worked for such an important enterprise, they would have left them alone. After all, with the Royal Navy fighting two wars simultaneously, having the extra men brought to our ships was quite a luxury, I assure you."

William reached for his goblet, still more than half full, and relaxed in his chair. Unbeknownst to the baronet, Sir Edward had just run out his guns and was waiting for the right moment to sound the attack. William made himself comfortable and waited for the next broadside.

A vein on Pembroke's forehead pulsed. "You must admit, Sir Edward, that businesses such as those owned by the Pembroke family—farms which raise pigs and sheep, and textile mills that produce woolen fabric—are of vital importance to the survival of this country. One might say as important as the army or the navy."

Admiral Witherington's complexion darkened ominously.

"Do you mean to tell me, sir," Admiral Glover jumped in, face pinched in a scowl, his Scottish brogue a little more obvious than usual, "that you would compare a paltry farming enterprise with the national importance of the armed forces of His Royal Majesty King George?"

William assiduously avoided eye contact with Collin—he did not want to interrupt this entertainment by bursting out in laughter.

"A paltry farming enterprise?" Sir Drake slammed his glass down on the table. "I will have you know that the Pembroke mills and farms provided woolen cloth to scores of highly regarded retailers throughout the south of England for generations, that they employed hundreds of people who would otherwise have been in the workhouse."

Sir Edward's lips twitched. "Yet you have shut down or sold off many of these mills, as they were of such vital national importance."

Pembroke drained his glass and snapped his fingers for the nearest footman to refill it. William made a mental note to keep his eye on the blackguard when they joined the ladies upstairs in a little while.

"Perhaps," Admiral Hinds interjected, "now that the war is over, those whose fortunes have taken a turn for the worse might see their business once again on the upturn."

Sir Edward looked as if he wished to spend more time baiting the baronet, but after working his jaw a few moments as if chewing on the decision, he left off and asked Mason to share about some of his most recent travels.

Turning to look at Mason, William could easily see Pembroke near the opposite end of the table, eyes narrowed, staring into his wineglass. William might have missed out on his one chance to make Julia his wife, but he would never forgive himself if he stood by and watched her marry Drake Pembroke.

Chapter Twelve

Charlotte couldn't stop staring at the opulence surrounding her. Admiral Witherington's home must surely rival King George's grandest palace.

"Miss Ransome. I feel I've yet to have a chance to speak with you this evening." Glowing like a flame in her bronze gown, Julia Witherington joined Charlotte at the bust of Lord Admiral Horatio Nelson.

"I cannot express my gratitude at being included in the invitation, Miss Witherington. I had no idea upon leaving Gateacre I would be dining in such grand style two days after my arrival."

Julia smiled. Of course her teeth were perfect—everything about her was. Except for the faint freckles across her nose. "Have you seen any of Portsmouth yet?"

"No—well, we did go through part of High Street to see Susan's— Mrs. Yates's dressmaker."

"I am certain you will find much to occupy you during your visit. I shall make the formal invitation to your mother, but I can tell you that I do plan to have you both out for tea one day next week. I can take you all over the house and grounds then." She patted Lord Nelson's head. "And if you are interested in naval history, I will even show you my father's study. He engaged an artist from Switzerland to paint his ship before it was decommissioned. The portrait hangs above the fireplace."

Charlotte's breath hitched with excitement. "And are you interested in naval history?"

"Through my father and brother, the Royal Navy has dominated my life—though perhaps not so much as yours, as I have spent more than half my years away from England." Miss Witherington glanced around. "Come, I must see to the service of coffee and tea. Please keep me company?"

Charlotte gladly fell in step with her hostess. "I did not know you also have a brother in the navy. Has he paid off, or is he still on active duty?"

Miss Witherington's humor dimmed. "My brother was lost at sea almost fifteen years ago."

"I am so sorry—"

"Do not fret." She patted Charlotte's arm. "I have reconciled myself to it."

They joined the rest of the women at the other end of the room. Once all the ladies had their cups, they drifted off to the grouping of chairs and sofas near the enormous fireplace.

Charlotte helped herself to tea, while Miss Witherington poured coffee.

"Who was that man at dinner—the one not in uniform?" Charlotte stirred in milk and sugar.

"Sir Drake Pembroke—my cousin." Her left brow raised. "Why?"

"Oh, I…" Charlotte's skin crawled at the memory of Sir Drake Pembroke's gaze raking over her time and again while they dined.

Miss Witherington moved closer. "I shall introduce you if you like. But I should warn you—the baronet is not the kind of man of whom your brother would approve."

⊰⊱

There had to be an easier way to obtain thirty thousand pounds.

Never before had Drake been so keen to leave a social gathering. He had come at his mother's invitation, hoping to enjoy a little society and a lot of Miss Julia's company. What he'd gotten was the society of his mother and Lady Dalrymple and the company of six sailors intent on attacking and belittling anyone not of their kind. However, the beautiful Miss Ransome might prove to be the diversion he was looking for here in Portsmouth if she followed through on the promises she'd made with her glowing blue eyes at dinner.

Julia stood at the table serving coffee and tea to the officers, her smile brightening her face and making her almost pretty. Her gown had no doubt cost more than Drake had lost at the Long Rooms last night, and she was the only woman in the room—aside from perhaps Lady Dalrymple—who could wear it without looking gaudy. The others were too pale, too plain, or too severe.

He supposed for those occasions when he needed a respectable wife on his arm, Miss Julia Witherington would fit the bill. He conjured his most seductive smile as the crowd of men around her dispersed. He finally stood face-to-face with her. Her green eyes dropped to the cup in his hands, but not before her smile faded.

"Miss Witherington, I have hardly seen you this evening. So when my mother requested I retrieve a refill of her tea, I felt myself the most fortunate man in the world."

She did not blush. She did not dip her head in embarrassment. She did not simper and try to cull more compliments. Her expression remained neutral as she reached for Lady Pembroke's cup and refilled it. "May I offer you tea or coffee, Sir Drake?"

Coldness settled in Drake's belly. No woman had ever been able to withstand his charms. "Which do you prefer?"

"The coffee is from Jamaica, so I must recommend it."

"Then by all means…" He nodded at the coffeepot.

Her movements were not rushed, but efficient and graceful as she served the steaming coffee and handed it to him.

"Thank you. May I request the honor of your joining us by the fireplace?"

"I—"

"Miss Witherington, you must come settle a dispute." Mrs. Yates approached and clasped Julia's elbow. "Oh, I beg your pardon, Sir Drake, but I have need of Julia for a moment."

Julia inclined her head at Drake. "Please excuse me." She allowed the other woman to drag her away to the opposite side of the room where her father, Ransome, and the other two captains stood near the large window.

In none of their previous encounters had Drake seen Julia interact with such animated friendliness as she did tonight.

He made his way back across the large sitting room to where his mother sat watching those nearest her with an imperious glare. Julia definitely was not his first choice of wife. But he'd run out of time. He needed her money, and he needed it soon. Letters from two creditors had arrived today. If two of them had tracked him to Portsmouth, the others would soon know his whereabouts as well. Published banns of his impending marriage to a proven heiress would hold them off.

He took the seat Lady Pembroke indicated in the small cluster of chairs, putting him between herself and Lady Dalrymple. Although the dowager viscountess could become an ally, he read his mother's scowls well enough to know that she put up with the aristocrat only because of her title and money.

Across the encircled seating area was the girl he'd sat beside at dinner. She did not enter much into the conversation, but her beauty recommended her to his attention. Rumors circulated about Portsmouth of William Ransome's wealth—and that he had two brothers equally rich. What, if any, legacy might they have settled upon their sister?

He looked at Julia again and resigned himself. In life, as with cards, he must place his bet where he had his best chance of the highest winnings. Although this technique had lost him considerable amounts of money, laying everything on the line for a promising hand had, upon occasion, won him some magnificent sums. Of Julia, Lady Everingham, or Miss Ransome, Julia would prove his best bet—his mother would see to it.

❧❧❧

Julia kept a piece of her attention on Sir Drake, mindful of his location should she have need of escape once more. Susan had played her role to perfection, rescuing Julia almost before necessary.

She returned to the serving table—and nearly walked straight into William Ransome. Her chest vibrated from the pounding of her heart. "Oh, I do beg your pardon."

"No apologies necessary." The gentleness in his expression drove away her concerns about Sir Drake.

Julia tried to smother her reaction to him. The last thing she needed was to let herself rekindle fondness for him. "I am so happy your mother and sister are here. I have quite enjoyed getting to know Miss Ransome better."

The corners of his eyes crinkled with his smile. "She was beside herself when she learned of the invitation."

Had she truly looked at this man since his return to Portsmouth? Or had something changed in him since his family's arrival? She could not define it, but somehow—whether in the expression in his sky-blue eyes or the soft smile that seemed to come so easily to his broad mouth tonight—she was seeing a different William Ransome than the man she'd greeted with forced indifference in Susan's parlor little more than a week ago.

"The coffee—it is from Jamaica?"

His question jerked her from her thoughts; he'd picked up the coffee-pot and was pouring his own. What must he think of his hostess? "Yes. From a neighbor's plantation. I understand from my father you are sailing to Jamaica soon."

He sipped the coffee. "Yes. Captain Yates and I will be escorting a supply convoy."

"Captain Yates is going too?" She looked beyond William to where Collin stood with her father and the other officers. "Does Susan know?"

"He only learned of his orders two days ago." He gazed past her shoulder, and she turned to see Susan gesturing with her hands as she spoke with Mrs. Hinds and Miss Ransome. "But I do not think he has told her yet."

"She will be disappointed he is not to stay in England longer. But such is the life of a navy officer's wife."

At William's silence, she turned her attention back to him—and heat crept into her cheeks at the intensity in his light eyes.

Mason's loud laughter behind him seemed to startle William from his thoughts. "Will you stay in England long?"

Julia let out a deep breath and shook her head. "I hope to return to Jamaica before the year is out, truth be told. Although now that Papa has no ship of his own, finding a captain willing to take on a female passenger is difficult—and Papa does not want me traveling on a merchant ship."

"I understand his reluctance. The war with France may have ended, but the seas continue to be dangerous."

"Of course." Julia felt like a pillow that burst and lost all its feathers. With that attitude, how would she convince him to take her along? She needed another plan.

∞

"Julia, Sir Drake is leaving."

William's skin crawled at the sharp tone in Lady Pembroke's shrill voice.

At her aunt's statement, Julia finished whatever she was saying to Susan before moving toward the door. Julia gave a brief flicker of annoyance at the interruption. But she masked it quickly and was politeness personified as she bade farewell to the baronet.

As soon as Sir Drake departed, Lady Pembroke excused herself, and Susan and Julia retreated a few steps away to finish their interrupted conversation.

"She is lovely, Sir Edward." Mrs. Ransome nodded toward Julia. "In fact, she is very similar to her mother's looks, if my memory serves."

"Aye, very much like her mother." The gruff emotion sounded odd coming from the admiral.

Sir Edward inquired of the Ransome farm, and William lost track of their conversation as he continued to watch Julia. All evening, he had been unable to keep his attention from straying to her, especially since their private chat earlier.

Why, at her age, had she not yet married? Had she, too, harbored dreams that they might one day meet again and finish what they started?

She looked up, their eyes meeting. Embarrassment at getting caught staring at her prickled up the back of his neck. She dropped her eyes, but dimples appeared in her cheeks as a self-conscious smile overtook her full lips.

William forced his attention back to his mother and Admiral Witherington. A few moments later, Susan and Julia rejoined them.

"I am so sorry to make you wait, my dear." Susan gave her husband a coquettish glance.

Collin responded with a besotted look that made William wish he had his own conveyance back to their house.

As the others made their way downstairs, Admiral Witherington held William back.

"William, I've a favor to ask of you." Sir Edward's gaze followed Julia's progress down the stairs.

Uncertain but unwilling to deny his patron anything, William nodded. "Anything, sir."

"Tomorrow morning, I leave for London. I shall be there at least a month. In my absence, Julia will be dependent upon her aunt's guidance and chaperonage." The admiral scowled. "I am grateful Julia will have a companion, but I do not fully trust Lady Pembroke to look after Julia's best interests."

William could not imagine Julia being dependent upon anyone, but kept his opinion to himself.

"I ask that you watch over her—I do not mean that you must become responsible for her, just that she knows your services are available should she need anything. And that you will contact me immediately if you suspect anything amiss."

In the twenty years he had known Admiral Witherington, the man had asked William to risk his life more times than he could remember. He had never balked at anything the admiral had commanded him to do. But no mission, no battle, had threatened William's peace of mind like this request.

He swallowed hard. "Aye, sir. I shall look out for her."

Sir Edward clasped his shoulder. "Good man. I knew I could depend on you."

The way Julia closed her eyes and sighed when they joined everyone in the foyer told William she knew what her father had asked of him.

He took his leave of her quickly, frustrated at the lack of discipline he'd had over his thoughts tonight. He followed the others out the front door as the enormous clock in the entry hall struck midnight.

"What a wonderful evening." Susan yawned behind her hand and settled into Collin's side.

William squeezed in between his mother and sister—both of whom yawned frequently and leaned against his shoulders.

Susan waved her lace fan lazily in the warm night air. "I do not think I have ever had such an excellent meal. Although with the time and effort Julia put into planning the menu, I really did not expect anything less than perfection—Julia would not have it any other way."

"It was Miss Witherington, then, and not her aunt who did everything?" Collin asked, surprise evident through the gravelly fatigue in his voice.

"Yes. 'Twas all Julia's doing. That is why she and I have not seen much of each other this week."

"Oh." Collin's wide grin shone in the darkness. "And I thought that was because of me."

Susan snuggled closer to her husband. "A happy chance."

William wondered how far they were from the Yates's townhouse and if he had enough energy remaining to walk the rest of the way.

In the quiet that fell, the memory of his first sight of Julia this night haunted him. Tonight it had almost seemed as if she would be amenable to William renewing his suit. But if there were any truth to the gossip around town, Julia would soon be receiving a proposal of marriage from her cousin.

While he hated to think of her married to the baronet, perhaps that would be better for her. William's life, his first and primary commitment, was the navy. When the Peace of Amiens ended in 1803 and he had gone back to sea, he'd sworn he would never let himself get caught up with affairs on land again. Duty and honor, hollow though they made his heart feel, would be his lifelong companions.

Chapter Thirteen

Hints of grayish pink touched the eastern horizon. The sound of movement outside Julia's door caught her attention, and she stepped into the hall. She smiled at her father as he tried to move quietly from his room to the stairs. He gave her a frank, approving glance, then extended his hand to her.

With her hand clasped in his, Julia could almost pretend this was one of their regular early morning breakfasts and not his leave-taking.

"I thought I told you not to rise early to see me off."

"You did. Shall I be court-martialed for disobeying a direct order, sir?"

Her father stifled his guffaw and raised her hand to kiss the back of it. "Ah, my daughter, how I shall miss these times together while I am in London."

Emotion choked Julia's throat. "I shall miss these times as well, Papa. You must write often to tell me of everything you accomplish while you are there."

Creighton, bleary-eyed and still settling his black coat around his shoulders, greeted them at the ground-floor landing. "G'morning, Admiral Sir Edward, sir, Miss Witherington. The coach will be here at five bells, sir."

Sir Edward checked his pocket watch against the hall clock chiming six o'clock. Julia's stomach twisted. Half an hour and her father would depart for a month—perhaps longer. The sick feeling returned— the disappointment from all the times he had left her standing at the dock in Kingston when *Indomitable* put out to sea after his brief and infrequent visits during her childhood. But this time he would be less than a hundred miles away, a distance a letter could traverse in only two days—one, if sent express.

She took two pieces of toast and strawberry preserves while her father tucked into the plate of eggs, sausages, and black pudding Creighton set before him. Though he performed his duty well, her father's former steward appeared beyond fatigue. Had he gotten any sleep last night? She would insist he take the remainder of the day off. He retreated to stand beside the fireplace, eyes heavy, posture stiff as if braced against the rolling of the sea.

"I think last night proved quite the success." Admiral Witherington spooned the soft yolk of his eggs onto his toast.

"Yes, I believe nearly everyone enjoyed himself." Julia rose to pour more coffee. Creighton started, his eyes trying to focus out of their former glassy state, but she silenced his protest with one look. "I believe, however," she turned back to her father, "one of our number did not find the evening quite to his liking."

Sir Edward did not look up from his plate, but amused lines danced around his eyes and mouth.

"Papa—what did you say to Sir Drake after dinner?"

The corners of his mouth twitched, despoiling his stern expression. "All I did was ask the man about Marchwood and the farms and mills. 'Twas he who brought up the topic of the press-gangs taking all of his workers. If the Marchwood mills turned out woolen of a quality the navy could use, perhaps he might not have had to sell three of them."

Julia's cup clattered against her saucer. "He has sold three of the textile mills? How do you know?"

"From a former subordinate who bought them. He seemed to think Pembroke in dire need of funds, as he was willing to accept a very low price."

"Was the loss of men to work the Marchwood holdings so severe?"

"I wondered the same, so I looked into the matter. For all his claims of press-gangs, I found very few had operated in the area—and those who did found men eager to volunteer for paid service, because many who worked for Pembroke had lost their employment. When I made further inquiry, I discovered the reason behind the reduced workforce and sold mills: Pembroke is in debt—deeply in debt. Even after selling off the mills, he mortgaged all the Marchwood land, and yet even that did not bring in enough to satisfy all his creditors."

"But how….?" Julia could not believe what she was hearing. Although she'd never given her Pembroke heritage much thought, the knowledge of how close Sir Drake might be to losing the estate where her mother had grown up made her ill. If she were to face losing Tierra Dulce—a chill trickled down her spine.

"Gambling." Sir Edward spat out the word as if it tasted foul. "He had not been left much. But his father, the general, was a good, honest, intelligent man who, according to local sources, had started to turn around Marchwood's fortunes. He had just paid off the lien against the land—the legacy he inherited from your grandfather—mere months before he died in glorious service to the Crown. Now, within two years, Sir Drake has sunk the estate lower than it has ever been before. Even your grandfather, with all his excesses, managed to pass it along intact."

"I had no idea."

"Nor would he want you to."

"Do you think my aunt knows?"

"I have no doubt she knows some of it. I am certain your cousin's visit to Portsmouth was not made from affection for his mother, but necessity."

Julia traced the rim of her coffee cup with the tip of her finger. "Do you think he hopes we will give him the money to pay off his debts?"

The admiral's scowl darkened. "Of that, I am not certain. I do know his creditors will soon be knocking on the door of Pembroke House here in Portsmouth. The sum of his debts would not harm us, but I cannot abide the thought of supporting a gambler—why, were he one of my crew, I'd have him hanged from the nearest yardarm."

The hall clock struck the half hour, nearly drowning out a business-like rap on the front door. Creighton started from his fatigued stupor and trudge-marched out of the dining room. Sir Edward finished the last bite of black pudding and rose, tossing his napkin on the table. Julia accompanied him to the foyer and greeted Admiral Hinds as her father shrugged into his coat, assisted by Creighton.

"If you need anything, contact Admiral Glover at the port Admiralty." Sir Edward kissed her forehead and then pressed a small brass key into her hand, lowering his voice to a whisper. "Keep a close eye on the household accounts—in my absence, your aunt might try to find a way to support her son." He gave her a significant look.

"I will, Papa." She closed her fist around the key. "And I will pray for your safe journey."

He caressed her cheek and looked as if he wanted to say something of import, but refrained. "I will write as soon as I arrive."

She stood on the front steps and waved as the hired coach rumbled down the cobblestone street. The sky glowed pink and golden in the east, and the warmth of the morning promised a deliciously hot day to come.

Creighton, a bit unsteady on his feet, stood in the open doorway.

"Thank you for making last night a memorable evening for our guests, Creighton."

"My pleasure, miss."

"And because of all your labors this week, I am hereby ordering you to take the day off and rest."

The butler cocked his head. "Ordering?"

"Aye. *Ordering.*"

"I see. So the chain of command is that when the admiral leaves it is the first lieutenant who takes command?"

Julia laughed at the way his lack of sleep allowed him to fall back into the easy rapport they'd built on the voyage from Jamaica nine months ago. "Whether I am captain or first lieutenant, I still outrank you," she pointed at him, "and disobeying a superior's order is an offense punishable by flogging or death—or have you been away from the sea so long you have forgotten the Articles of War?"

Creighton snapped to and knuckled his forehead. "Aye, aye—miss."

"Good, now that we understand each other—go. I do not want to see you until this time tomorrow morning."

She returned to the dining room for another cup of coffee before she faced returning to her room to review her tasks for the morning. Creighton followed her.

She poured the coffee and flavored it with milk and sugar. "Creighton," she said, taking a small sip, "I wonder if you might do me a favor?"

"Yes, of course. Anything you need, Miss Witherington."

"Go away. Go see your sister in Portsea or go down to the docks and practice tying rope into knots. I really do not care what you do as long as you are not doing it in my sight."

He knuckled his forehead again. "Aye, aye, Lieutenant Witherington." He gave her a saucy grin and bowed out of the room.

Julia rubbed her fatigue-gritted eyes. Returning to bed for a couple of hours might not be amiss. However, Lady Pembroke had left on Julia's desk, sometime before Julia retired last night, a list of the errands she wanted Julia to see to this morning—the post office, the apothecary, the stationer. Just thinking about it sank her further into weariness.

The hall clock chimed seven times. Julia finished her coffee and forced herself to climb the two flights of stairs to her room, where Nancy was making the bed.

Once dressed in an appropriate walking gown—or morning dress, she couldn't remember the difference—Julia returned downstairs to ask Elton to bring the carriage around in half an hour.

She entered her father's study and crossed to the bookshelf behind his desk. In the cabinet underneath, she opened the door and withdrew a small iron box—a precautionary device created for her father by a master ironmonger in the Navy. He'd kept it aboard his flagship to carry confidential orders and papers ever since the mutiny of the crew of a friend's ship.

With the key her father had given her earlier, she unlocked the box and removed the leather cash pouch and the bank record book. She laid the register flat on his desk and reviewed the most recent entries. Her allowance, the food for last night's dinner, the payment to the extra hands all summed neatly into a total balance.

She recorded the three guineas she took from the cash pouch for the household items she would purchase this morning, entered the new sum, returned the book and bag to the iron box, and locked it again. The key shone bright in the morning sun streaming through the window at her back. For now, she'd best hold on to it. She dropped it into her reticule and looked up at a tap on the door.

"Enter."

Her father's valet, filling in for Creighton, opened the door. "Elton is ready with the carriage, miss."

"Thank you, Jim."

✿❀✿

Several people were already in the post office when Julia alighted from the barouche a few minutes after eight o'clock. Most looked like household servants, but a tall man standing in the corner in deep conversation with the postmaster, their foreheads nearly touching, drew her recognition.

She turned to leave, hoping she could get out before Sir Drake looked around and saw her.

"Miss Witherington!" The clerk's loud voice silenced everyone in the place.

Her heart fell, and she stopped two steps from escape and looked over her shoulder. "Yes?"

"A letter arrived for you, miss, on that sloop from the West Indies."

The West Indies! All thought of Sir Drake fled at this news, and she rushed to the desk. The young clerk handed her a thick envelope. Eagerly she took it from him and turned it over to see the direction. Emotion clogged her throat and burned her eyes. Jerusha's meticulous, practiced hand would be recognizable to Julia anywhere—after all, Julia had taught Tierra Dulce's housekeeper to write.

The packet was thick enough to give her hope it might include a letter from Jeremiah as well. Temptation urged her to untie the twine that bound it together and break the seal, but with extreme effort she refrained.

"Good news from Jamaica, I hope."

Oh, how could she have forgotten Sir Drake's presence? "Yes—I hope so. Good morning, Sir Drake." She dipped a slight curtsey and turned to go…but then remembered Lady Pembroke's letter to Aunt Hedwig. She returned to the clerk and, doing her best to ignore her cousin, pulled the letter from her reticule—and something else fell with a sharp report on the counter.

A flash of bright brass caught her eye, but before she could reach for it, Sir Drake's hand covered the key. He lifted it between thumb and forefinger to examine it. "I have never seen such a fine piece of engraving as this." He held it so the flat, scalloped butt of the key caught the light from the front windows. "Was it crafted by a local smith?"

Julia's fingers itched to grab the key from his hand. "Aye, Mr. Chubb, formerly of the Royal Navy."

Drake gave her what he probably thought was a seductive smile. "Aren't most of the men in Portsmouth 'formerly of the Royal Navy'?"

Swallowing a retort, she completed her business with the clerk, and then held her hand out, palm up, toward Drake. "May I please have that back?"

He reached forward and, just as he was about to put the key in her palm, snatched it back. "It must be valuable, this key. Perhaps it is the key to Miss Julia's personal diary. No, too large for that. Ah, it is the key to the chest where she keeps the letters from a secret lover."

Julia's jaw ached from the pressure of her clenched teeth.

"It must be important, else she would not be carrying it with her," he mumbled, as if to himself. "I shall strike you a deal, Miss Witherington. Allow me to walk you to your next destination, and I shall there return the key to you."

She had a choice between acquiescence and creating a scene. She dropped her hand to her side. "Very well then, I have business at—" the bank was nearest, just across the street, but she could not conduct her business there with him dogging her steps—"the stationer."

Drake's triumph seemed to melt into disappointment at her rapid capitulation. Her stomach roiled, and she wished she had not indulged in the fourth cup of coffee this morning. Outside, she raised her parasol and tried using it to keep her face shielded from him—but the sun came from the opposite side. Like Susan, he talked without expecting much in the way of an answer, and in the few minutes it took Julia to walk to Collier's Papergoods, she'd grown sick of his slightly peevish tone.

At last, she threw open the wood-and-glass door and, before her eyes adjusted to the dim interior, turned and extended her hand, palm up.

Once again he almost put the key in her hand before snatching it away, smiling. "I must know what it is a key to before I give it back."

"It is a family heirloom," Julia temporized. If he found out it was the key that protected her father's wealth, the deeds to the house here and Tierra Dulce, paperwork on cargo ships he was in the process of purchasing...

"Oh, come now, my dear, surely you can tell your old cousin Drake."

Julia bit the inside of her cheek to keep from flying at him, ready to rake any flesh she could reach with her fingernails. "Sorry. No. Now, may I please have my key back?"

Drake tapped the engraved end against his chin as though weighing her request.

"I do believe the lady has asked for the return of a piece of her property." A man's voice reverberated behind Julia, and she started. The shop had been so quiet, she hadn't realized any other customers were in the place. She knew the voice, and a brief thrill shivered down her spine.

William Ransome came to stand at Julia's side, one brow raised in an expression very similar to the one her father wore just before he exploded in anger. Finally, the weight of the key landed in her palm, and she quickly wrapped her fingers around it.

Drake looked from Julia to William and back. "Miss Witherington, I hope I may have the pleasure of calling on you this week."

"I am never certain of my schedule from one day to the next, Sir Drake. But you are more than welcome to come by any day and leave your card if I am not in."

Her answer did not please him, but before William—and the shopkeeper—he could say no more. "I'll take my leave of you, then."

She hardly had time to bend her knees before Drake was out the door. Julia watched him go with satisfaction and then turned to thank William, only to see the back of his tan coat disappear through the door.

She wasn't sure exactly what had just happened, but she did know she owed William Ransome a debt of gratitude. Somehow, that thought did not bother her as it might have a week ago.

Chapter Fourteen

William adjusted his hat lower over his brow to try to conceal his eyes and avoid making eye contact with anyone, but the narrow brim of the civilian hat did little to shield him.

Why of all days should he find himself out of paper and low on ink? And why had the need to come to Julia Witherington's defense felt anything but a duty to his admiral?

He walked without knowing his heading or destination—merely driven by the urge to be near the water and ships. At the main gate, the two marine guards challenged his entry into the dock yard until he produced his letter of commission—the identification he never went anywhere without.

Looming in the distance above the three massive storehouses stood the triple masts of a ship. His pulse quickened at the sight, and he made his way through the dockyard, drawn ever closer toward the oaken masterpiece. As he cleared the buildings, he saw the two rows of gun ports and hastened his steps. Workers swarmed over the ship like crows on a carcass; he spotted someone nearby who looked to be in charge.

"Are you the dockmaster?" William hardly took his eyes off the ship. If only the workers did not obscure her so...

The crusty seaman eyed William's civilian clothing. "Aye. And just who might ye be?"

William drew himself to full attention. "Captain William Ransome. What ship is this?"

The dockmaster hastily rearranged his expression and knuckled his forehead. "Sorry, sir. No offense, sir. This here is *Alexandra,* seventy-four."

William nearly cried out with joy. He'd found her!

"She be under the command of..." The master flipped through the pages tangled in his hands. "The command of...ah, I see she's your ship, sir?"

"Aye, that she is."

"We're making goodly progress on her, sir. A finer ship I never seen. Your carpenter were a fair hand with the repairs, if I may say so, sir."

"You may, and I will pass along the compliment." William shaded his eyes to take in the full sight of his beloved home. "Do not let me keep you from your duties, Master...?"

"O'Reilley, sir." The man knuckled his forehead again. "If ye wish, there's a good place for viewing the work just there by the smithy."

"Thank you. Carry on, Master O'Reilley." William found a barrel that made a makeshift seat in the shade of the blacksmith shop, out of the way of the scurrying dockyard crew, where he could drink in the magnificence of his ship. Never before had he seen her out of the water, but the familiar lines, the patched and reworked hull, the place in the quarterdeck gunwale where a cannonball had missed taking off Ned's leg by mere inches, were all welcomed sights. He wanted to run his hands along the curving bow planks. He wanted to stroll the decks and feel the sway of the ocean below his feet. He wanted to sleep in his cabin, to have dinner with his officers. In short, he wanted life to return to normal.

These last days spent almost constantly in female company had addled his brain and muddied his once crystal-clear logic. He'd given more time to thinking about Julia Witherington—the curve of her neck where it met her shoulder, the perfect mahogany color of her hair, the boorishness of her cousin—than he had in praying for his crew, preparing for the voyage, and keeping abreast of all the newest advances in naval science.

Although each board the carpenters tore loose from his ship felt to William like a piece of his flesh, staying here and watching them dismantle her was preferable to returning to the Yateses' home, where Susan would no doubt have heard of the incident this morning and want to know why William had been so rude as to leave without speaking to Julia.

What had Julia and Pembroke been carrying on about back there? He'd seen the merest flash of a brass key as Pembroke had dropped the item into her hand. How had Pembroke come by the trinket, and why had Julia been so anxious to retrieve it?

He must stop himself thinking about Julia as anything other than his admiral's daughter. After all, he would be gone in a month, leaving Julia behind again. He couldn't go through the months of agonizing over her this time as he had before.

❦

Several hours later, eight bells chimed and reverberated louder than the smiths' hammers through the yard. The sun blazed straight overhead, eliminating all but the smallest sliver of shade beside the building. William's stomach growled.

He rose and stretched his back, cramped from hours sitting propped against a brick wall. If he did not want Collin to eat without him, he would have to hasten his return.

Now that he knew *Alexandra*'s berthing, he would pay regular visits. And maybe his constant vigil would encourage Master O'Reilley to spur the men on to have her ready early.

The walk from Collin's home to High Street had been pleasant early this morning; now, however, the noon sun beat down on William as he quick-marched a reverse path through Portsmouth, the land canting upward like a ship climbing a wave. He paused twice to mop at the sweat running down his face and then pressed on.

He had just reached the stoop outside the Yateses' home when the front door flew open.

"William, thank God. Susan, he has returned!" Collin's freckles stood out in sharp contrast to his unusually pale face. "I was about to find a marine brigade to muster and send out in search of you."

William stopped on the top step, consternated. "I apologize for my long absence—I had no idea anyone would worry as to my whereabouts."

"Oh, thank the good Lord you are unharmed." Mrs. Ransome pushed Collin out of her way, rushed out the door, and threw her arms around William. "When I heard...I was so worried."

William, hands hovering stiffly at his sides, looked at Collin over his mother's head, trying to figure out what had happened to create such a fuss. Susan and Charlotte joined Collin at the door, looking equally worried.

Mrs. Ransome stepped back. "You are well? Not injured?"

"I am perfectly well, I assure you." William straightened his coat and removed his hat. "Except for being heated nearly to exhaustion from walking in the sun this last hour." He wiped his dripping forehead with a handkerchief.

"How can we be so unpardonable?" Susan grabbed his sleeve and pulled him into the house, pushing Collin out of her way too. "Go up to the sitting room—there is a nice cross breeze—and I will have Ella bring you a cold tray for your dinner." She rushed off toward the kitchen.

William shrugged out of his coat and loosened his neckcloth. Dawling appeared and took the discarded articles before William could toss them on a side chair.

"Shall I have a bath sent up for you, sir?" Dawling took great care to fold the coat a particular way before draping it over his beefy forearm.

"A few buckets of cold water would be a luxury, Dawling. I thank you."

"Aye, aye, Cap'n." Dawling grinned cheekily along with the naval phrase he'd been told not to use, and disappeared the same direction Susan had gone.

"We shall await you in the sitting room, William." His mother touched his cheek, concern still palpable.

William was ready to get out of the black leather boots making his legs sweat from calf to ankle. He looked at Collin over his shoulder as they climbed the stairs. "May I inquire as to the nature of the harm that supposedly befell me while I was out this morning?"

Collin, whose natural ruddiness slowly returned, laughed. "I should have known it was much ado about nothing. After you left this morning, Susan decided she needed even more ribbon and trim for her hats and went into High Street. Apparently while there, she heard a few other ladies talking about an altercation they had witnessed in the stationer's shop."

William groaned. Of course someone had witnessed this morning's scene. "Altercation?"

"Aye, that's what she called it. The ladies thought Sir Drake must have challenged you because you both exited so swiftly. She came home and informed your mother and sister, and they have all been at wits' end with concern, imagining you lying dead in a field with no one to weep over your bloody corpse." Collin snorted. "As if you could not take a macaroni like him, blindfolded and with your cutlass in your left hand. Of which I assured them repeatedly."

"Ah. Thus the reason for your pasty coloration and the greeting you gave upon my return." William turned on the landing and looked at Collin over his shoulder.

"All show for Susan, I assure you." Collin shoved him and followed him up the second flight of stairs.

"My dear fellow, I know full well you are not so accomplished an actor. Come now, admit it. You gave weight to the possibility that peacock might have killed me in a duel."

"I did—you were not—he could not—oh, all right. Yes, I was concerned he might have gotten the better of you, but only by cheating or some other nefarious means."

Oh, how William missed being able to interact with a friend—an equal—like this. Although he and Ned had a good relationship, a friendship even, as first lieutenant, Ned had to respect William's superior rank, constraining what the younger man could do or say in

William's presence. With Collin—a friend for more than twenty years and his equal in station—the isolation of his life lifted.

Collin followed him into his room. "Do tell me what happened."

William unbuttoned his waistcoat and untucked his muslin shirt, relieved to have the fabric away from his damp skin. "I had need of paper and ink this morning and paid a visit to Mr. Collier's shop. Before I could complete my business, the door opened and in walked Miss Witherington and the macaroni—as you have quite aptly named him. Apparently he had taken an item from her, and she was anxious to retrieve it. He tried to hold it for ransom, and I did the only thing a man of honor could have done."

"You insisted he give it to her."

"Naturally. He did. He asked if he could call on her, she evaded the question with a suitably vague response, and he left the shop. Thinking I could discourage any further gossip about Miss Witherington and me, I left the shop as well—and made certain I walked the opposite direction of the baronet."

"And that was the end of the encounter?" Collin availed himself of the seat under the open window.

"Aye. I walked to the dockyard, found my ship, and spent several pleasant hours watching the crew tear her to pieces." He looked through the pile of correspondence Dawling had left on his desk. Familiar handwriting caught his attention.

"I will leave you to it, then. The dinner things will be set out in the sitting room, but take your time. Susan is expecting a few callers, so the afternoon should be free for us to review charts and warrants." Collin stepped aside to admit Dawling, gave a jaunty salute, and disappeared.

Water splashed onto the rug over the rim of the hipbath Dawling heaved into the room. He grunted as he set it down on the floor in front of the empty fireplace. Now would probably not be the best time to explain that one usually brought the tub first and then returned with buckets of water to fill it.

"There y'are, Cap'n—sir. Cook believes a cold-water bath is bad for the health, so she insisted on adding one bucket of hot water to it."

William dunked his hand into the water, which was by no means cold, but still cooler than his skin. "Then she would be highly upset to learn we have, on occasion, been forced to bathe with sea water, would she not?"

"She were right livid about it when I said so, sir."

William sank into the desk chair while Dawling dug out soap and towels and set out clothes. William popped the seal on his middle brother's letter. He skimmed the page, full of James's latest adventures and the news he was to be sent to India.

The cool bath worked to soothe his body and mind. He stood, dried off, and dressed, shrugging into the new green swallow-tailed coat the tailor had sent up this morning.

A soft, feminine voice wafted through the open window.

Susan. Collin seemed to be quite happy with her. His friend never seemed distracted by the fact he had a wife, nor had his marriage impeded his dedication to the navy or his ship and crew. And whenever he returned to port, he had a warm hearth of his own and a loving wife to welcome him.

But William had seen in just a few days the grief Susan suffered when Collin was out at sea—and Collin had only been on an escort mission, not in battle. William had seen the same haunted expression in his mother's eyes his entire childhood as she prayed for his father's safety. If William loved a woman, he would respect her too much to put her through such pain.

Yet to hope, to anticipate, to rejoice in the knowledge that someone awaited his return from sea; to have children and see how they'd grown each time his ship dropped anchor in port; to build a future and a home with a woman he loved...what man did not dream of these things?

A knock on the door startled him out of his reverie. "Enter."

"William?" Collin stuck his flaxen head around the door. "Susan wanted to know if you plan to come down or if she should have a tray sent up."

Oh, to have someone other than his steward worry about whether he ate properly. William frowned. Did Dawling care if he ate properly?

"Aye, I'm coming."

"Good. Ah, Dawling." Collin swung the door open wide so Dawling could enter past him. "Mrs. Yates asked me to remind you to sponge Captain Ransome's formal black for this evening."

"This evening?" William shared a frown with Dawling and both turned toward Collin.

"Dinner. She has invited a few people." He cuffed William's shoulder. "Sorry."

He pushed Julia's image from his mind, annoyed that every time he thought of marriage, her dancing green eyes and dimples came into sharp focus. He would not let his attraction to her coerce him into making a decision they might both regret later.

Chapter Fifteen

J ulia worked on the knotted ribbon at her throat as she climbed the stairs. Nancy took over when Julia got to her room, and then she took Julia's hat and spencer. When Nancy turned toward the wardrobe, her mouth dropped open as if she'd just seen a mouse run across the room.

"Leave us."

Julia spun around at her aunt's sharp voice.

Nancy dropped the bonnet and jacket on the end of the bed, curtsied, and scurried out the door.

"Aunt Augusta?" Julia's thoughts whirled, but she masked all emotion. "Is anything wrong?"

"Is anything wrong?" Augusta repeated, closing the door. "Did you think I would not hear of your behavior? Do you know from whom I heard it? Lady Fairfax called on me and told me of the scene you caused this morning in the paper shop."

Never before had she seen her aunt truly angry. "*I* caused a scene?" She moved behind her desk and set her reticule atop it. "If the baroness is your only source of the information, I should not wonder at its inaccuracy."

Augusta's indignation faltered. "So you deny, then, that you made a spectacle of yourself and my son this morning?"

"I did not purpose to create a spectacle, no."

The umbrage that had faded flamed back to life. "What do you mean? Was there an argument between the two of you during which you involved that sailor or not?"

"Again, I did not set out to involve anyone in anything, ma'am." Julia narrowed her eyes. "I was going about my own business—and yours—this morning when Sir Drake approached me and took... took something that belonged to me." Her gaze dropped to her reticule on the desk, then snapped back up to her aunt. "All I did was ask him to return it. He declined and told me he would do so only if I allowed him to escort me to my next stop. I agreed; and at the stationer's, I once again asked for the return of...my item. He refused. I was about to ask again when Captain Ransome—who happened to be in the shop—intervened on my behalf, as any other gentleman would have done."

Julia's emphasis on the word *gentleman,* especially in use to describe William, seemed to make Augusta's blood boil. "How could you expose Drake, your own cousin, to the derision of not just that man—a common sailor—but everyone else in Portsmouth? And you dare use the word *gentleman* when referring to a sailor?"

"Yes, ma'am, I do."

"A true gentleman would know when to keep to his own business and not interfere with the flirtations of another man. I do hope you apologized to Sir Drake."

Shock numbed Julia's body. "Apologize? I have done nothing for which I am sorry."

"Nothing?" Aunt Augusta's voice rose in pitch and volume. She took a deep breath before continuing. "Lady Fairfax said that my son was so offended he called the captain out. Pistols at noon on Portsdown Hill."

All strength left Julia, and she sank into the desk chair. "Duel? I cannot believe it. There were no heated words between them." She gained her feet and crossed to the window, her palms pressed to her cheeks. They had left in opposite directions, and no other words were spoken between them. Had they met again afterward? Why would they duel over so minor an incident?

Julia hurried to the bed and snatched up her hat. "I must call on Susan immediately to see what she has heard."

"I insist you do no such thing." Augusta crossed her arms and guarded the closed door. "Whether or not they dueled is something we will learn from my son in due course. But this incident has shown me that you have been suffered to run wild since you arrived here to your own detriment. This is not Jamaica, where you may do as you please, miss."

"I beg you pardon?" Julia stared, disbelieving, at her aunt.

"Yes, you may well begin by begging my pardon. I have been given the task of ensuring your place in society, a task I am going to begin to take much more seriously. You will call upon whom I deem fit. You will accept callers only if I am here to decide if the person is worthy to be received. You will drop the acquaintance of anyone not of our rank in society—especially those Yates people. From now on, all errands in town will be seen to by one of the household staff. You will behave as a proper English lady. My son wishes to court you, and I have given my consent."

Julia stood still a moment, mouth slightly agape in stunned disbelief. "Not call—ma'am, you cannot be serious!"

Augusta squared her shoulders. "I am deadly serious. You seem to have forgotten that you are not yet married, therefore you are still under your elders' authority. In the absence of your father, that responsibility falls to me."

Julia gave a bitter laugh. "My thirtieth birthday is in five weeks—at which time, I plan to purchase passage and return to Jamaica."

"I find it unlikely that will happen. Until your father's return, you must obey any rule I see fit to impose upon you. And I will know whether or not you have obeyed me."

Who did Augusta Pembroke think she was, telling Julia whom she could see and what she could do? Julia's spirit warred with her deeply held belief that her elders deserved to be honored and obeyed. Well, her aunt may be her elder, but she was not her parent. "Very well then. For the next five weeks, I will abide by your rules."

Augusta's face took on a triumphant gleam. "You will find that it will not be as bad as you think—in fact, I believe you will find the company of better society much more to your liking. Now, let us put this little incident behind us. I shall expect you for dinner at six o'clock."

Julia stared at the door long after her aunt left the room. Weakness spread from her chest out to her limbs, and she sank onto the rug, hugging her knees. The sickly sweetness in her aunt's voice as she'd departed left Julia feeling cold despite the heat of the summer's day.

No calls...accept Sir Drake's suit...

Though Augusta had feigned friendliness there at the end, the seriousness of her tone could not be denied. Julia was not certain exactly how her aunt intended to see this punishment enacted but had no doubt she would see it done. If only her father had not gone today—if only the call from the lordships of the Admiralty had come a month hence.

In five weeks, Julia would have access to her inheritance—not that she needed it in addition to the sum she'd put by from her monthly allowance. She would purchase passage home and put all this behind her.

Lady Pembroke's words rang in her head. Her aunt plotted something. But nothing she could do in five weeks could not be undone immediately thereafter with Sir Edward's help.

She had to get word to Susan. The next weeks would go easier if Julia seemed to capitulate to her aunt's demands, but she did not want her friends to think ill of her for ignoring them. Five weeks was not forever. Then Julia would make good on her promise to herself and go home.

The drawer where she kept her stationery was empty. Where—oh, yes, she'd left her writing case in the study. She pressed her ear to her door. When she heard nothing, she ventured out and let out a relieved breath. No sign of her aunt. She would write Susan and—

She stopped halfway down the stairs. What if her aunt had the idea to monitor her mail? Which of the household staff could Julia bring into her confidence? She must have some way of communicating with the outside world while under house arrest.

She reached the study—odd, but she did not recall the door being closed earlier. No sooner did she touch the knob, but the door swung open.

Julia gasped.

Augusta gasped.

Suspicion made the hair on the back of Julia's neck tingle. "What are you doing in my father's library?"

Color flooded back into her aunt's face. She held up a slim volume of poetry. "Just borrowing a book."

"Oh." Julia stepped out of her way. As soon as her aunt disappeared into the sitting room, Julia entered the library and closed the door. She looked around the room. Nothing seemed out of place—except...had she pushed her father's chair out of the way this morning?

She went around the desk to investigate. The cabinet door—she knew she'd closed it completely when she took the money out this morning.

Heart thudding against her ribs, she dropped to her knees and threw open the cupboard. The strongbox was still there, though shoved in lengthwise, which had kept the door from closing all the way. If her aunt knew about the box—

Julia jumped up and ran across the room, stopped, retrieved a handful of stationery, and returned to her room in haste. If her aunt knew about the chest, she might suspect that Sir Edward had given Julia the key.

Her reticule still sat where she'd dropped it on her desk. She picked it up and shook all the contents out onto the blotter. The key hit the desktop with a thunk. Her heart slowed to a more normal pace.

From the jewel box atop her dresser, she retrieved a long gold necklace—a gift from Michael upon their fifteenth birthday. Taking the brass key in hand, she threaded the chain through the filigree. She secured the clasp behind her neck and dropped the key inside the front of her dress. That would do for now, but she needed a more secure way to hide the chest. Julia hoped her aunt would not stoop to stealing, but she would not put it past Sir Drake.

She would send it to Susan. But until Creighton returned tomorrow, she couldn't do anything.

A thick envelope on the desk caught her eye. The letters from Tierra Dulce. Though aching with the need to do something—anything—she forced herself to settle down on the window seat and read the missives: Jeremiah's full of reports about the crops and income, and Jerusha's brimming with news about the families on and around Tierra Dulce.

She let the pages fall to her lap and stared out toward the horizon. Why had she agreed to come to England?

〰〰

After a night filled with strange and disturbing dreams, Julia rose feeling unrested and stiff. Nancy offered a hot bath or cold compresses. Julia declined, but she did allow the maid to brush the snarls from her hair and secure it in a long plait.

"Nancy, how long has it been since you have seen your family?"

The maid's eyes glowed. "I see them on Sunday every week. Just after you leave for the grand fancy church, my brother comes in the wagon—to the back of course, miss—to fetch me home. The service in our parish starts late so as all the farmers can finish their morning's work before they come."

"How would you like to go to them a day early?"

"Miss?" Nancy's hands stilled from braiding.

"I have no engagements today, and I am perfectly capable of dressing myself for church tomorrow—although I shall have to settle for a simple hairstyle."

"I—but miss, how—?"

"Elton will drive you. Do you not think it shall be great fun to surprise your family with not only an early arrival, but arriving in the admiral's barouche driven by so handsome a young man as Elton?"

Nancy's hazel eyes sparkled, making her look closer to her real age of five-and-twenty than her work-worn countenance usually conveyed. "Yes, miss! When?"

"Send Creighton to me, and we shall arrange it."

Nancy tied off Julia's braid and rushed from the room, not even pausing for one of her unnecessary curtsies. Julia took the note she'd composed to Susan last night from her desk. Elton fancied one of the Yateses' kitchen maids. If Creighton thought Elton completely trustworthy, Julia might be able to maintain a line of communication with her friend after all.

Creighton knocked lightly and entered at Julia's summons. "You asked to see me, miss?"

She pinned her father's former steward with her most direct gaze. "Creighton, I need to know that I can place my full trust and confidence in you."

Consternation tinged with offense flooded his face. "Of course, miss."

"I do not mean to question your integrity. I need to make certain that, should I entrust secrets to you, Lady Pembroke will not learn of them."

He made no immediate answer, but still seemed slightly offended by her words.

"It is not mutiny of which I speak," she teased, although levity was far from her mind. "Consider it reconnaissance or espionage." She took a deep breath, knowing what she risked for both of them. "Lady Pembroke has forbidden me from communicating with anyone she deems unworthy, including my friend, Mrs. Yates, and anyone else connected to the Royal Navy."

Although Julia would never have considered writing a letter to any man other than her father, the Tierra Dulce steward, or Jeremiah, the implied censure of naval officers would insult Creighton's pride.

Creighton's shoulders squared more, if possible. "I believe Elton is friendly with a maid in the Yateses' employ, miss. I am certain he would be willing to carry messages for you."

"And he has your full trust?"

"Aye. He is loyal to the admiral and thus to you, miss."

Julia tried to imagine what her aunt might do to gain information.

"He would not be tempted by the offer of money in exchange for secrets?"

Disgust darkened Creighton's features. "He knows the Articles of War as well as I, miss. He would never turn traitor."

Julia allowed a touch of amusement at Creighton's vehemence to crack through her worry. "We are not at sea. The Articles do not apply."

His brows raised in surprise. "You think Admiral Sir Edward Witherington would not hold each of us accountable to upholding the law of the sea? And that he would not enforce the punishments therein? Our service and obedience extends to our commander's daughter."

"And what of Lady Pembroke? Does she not also garner your obedience?"

The butler's gaze dropped to the carpet. "Miss, the law of the sea requires men to be obedient only to their superior officers. Passengers are afforded respect but not obedience or loyalty."

More cheer than she'd felt in the past twenty-four hours flooded Julia, driving out the bleak cold that had overwhelmed her since last night. It pleased her to know that Creighton thought so highly of her to give her the deference due a naval officer. She swallowed back the lump in her throat. Her bursting into tears of gratitude might make him reconsider.

"Very well, then. I have told Nancy I shall have Elton drive her home this morning. I want him to stop at the Yateses' home on his return. I need to send Susan something."

Chapter Sixteen

The quiet of the townhouse permeated William's being. He sipped his coffee and turned the page of the *Times,* not caring much about the week-old news from London, but reveling in the peace of having the dining room to himself this fine Saturday morning. He'd awoken before dawn, unsettling dreams driving him from bed to read the Bible and spend time in prayer.

Images from the dream—Julia Witherington being pursued through dark streets until apprehended by a figure draped in a black cloak—made William's heart clench again. He had not had the dream in years, but Julia had occupied much of his attention of late. Surely that was the reason the disturbing dream returned.

He shook the paper to straighten its drooping pages and tried to snap his mind to attention as well. No more distractions. No more complications.

"I know William will agree with me." Susan's voice echoed from the tiled hall seconds before she and a disgruntled Collin entered the dining room. The look Collin gave him told William not to agree with anything his friend's wife said.

She pulled out the chair beside him and sat sideways on it, facing him. "William, you are aware Julia Witherington is my dearest friend in all the world."

"I am acquainted with that fact, aye."

"You also will recall that I know your entire history with my friend. So you will understand it is with love and not a misguided sense of interference—" she shot a scathing look at her husband—"that I ask this."

So much for no Julia Witherington–related distractions. William started formulating an excuse as to why he could not interfere with Sir Edward's domestic affairs.

"I believe Julia is in danger."

His stomach dropped like a ship cresting a surge. Even Collin's snort of derision could not break through William's dread. "Danger?" he repeated, hoping his voice sounded more normal to them than to his own ears.

"Yes. I believe her aunt is going to try to force Julia into accepting a proposal of marriage from that awful Pembroke man."

The waves of fear started to ease, and William regained control of his thoughts. Hundreds of men jumped at his least word. Taking command of his mind should be as easy.

"If she has no one to act on her behalf, if she believes no one is on her side, she might give in and marry a man who wants her only for her wealth and will never love her."

The memory of seeing Julia ogled by the wolfish baronet brought the need to protect her flooding back into William's chest.

"If you were to offer your services for anything she might need while her father is away, it might be just the buoy she needs to stay afloat and weather this storm."

Susan's deliberate use of nautical terms did not escape William's notice. He had already given his word to Sir Edward, but how was he supposed to make good on that promise without increasing the gossip already running rampant in Portsmouth? "And exactly what services am I supposed to offer?"

Susan shrugged. "I am not sure—whatever she needs. At the very least, one of you—" she included Collin, who now sat at the head of the table with a heaping plate of food—"should write to Admiral Witherington to let him know we are concerned for her welfare."

Collin's fork hit the table none too softly. "We do not know that anything has happened—the admiral has not been gone but one day. And

Miss Witherington will likely write to the admiral herself should any-thing untoward occur. He would not appreciate our interference."

William's gut urged him to give in to Susan's plan, but the logical part of his mind sided with Collin. He was saved from the necessity of responding when Fawkes entered.

"Pardon, sirs, ma'am." His cloudy blue eyes fixed on Susan. "A young man begs your indulgence in the hall, Mrs. Yates."

Collin frowned. "A young man?"

"I believe he is in the employ of Admiral Witherington, sir."

Susan leapt from her seat, bumping William's shoulder in her haste. Collin followed her; however, although curious, William kept his place.

Moments later, they returned, Collin carrying an iron chest engraved with a large scrolled *W*, Susan breaking the seal on a note. "It is from Julia." Her smile beamed, then faded. "Her aunt has insisted she break off socializing with anyone connected to the navy." She cast a self-righteous glance at Collin and William. "The chest contains some very impor-tant papers of her father's along with other items she wishes to be kept safe until the admiral's return. She asks that we keep it with us, hidden, until that time. She currently holds the only key, but fears someone may devise a way to break into the box." Susan turned the page over. "She believes she can trust her butler and driver—the young man who came—to carry messages between us."

The image of a bright brass key passing from Sir Drake's hand to Julia's flashed in William's memory. No wonder she had been so anxious to regain it. The chest reminded him of a purser's strongbox, where the money for pay and ship's stores was kept.

"Collin—hide it under our bed." Susan pressed her hand to her heart. "Bless her ingenuity for finding an avenue of communication. I pray the two servants can indeed be trusted."

Collin moved the chest from table to floor with a grunt. "Both served Admiral Witherington on his ship before he hauled down his colors. If anyone can be trusted, it is those two." He returned his focus to his breakfast.

"Elton—the admiral's driver—will return at three o'clock tomorrow to retrieve any messages we wish to send." Susan refolded the note and slipped it into her sleeve at her left wrist. "So, William, you can send word to her that way."

"No." Collin's years of experience as a commander came out in the single syllable.

Susan's expression grew stony. "I do believe I was speaking to William, not you."

Being broadsided by three French frigates would be preferable to sitting at this table at this moment in time. William prayed his mother and sister would not choose this morning to begin taking an early breakfast.

Collin wiped his mouth and braced his hands against the edge of the table as if readying for a storm. "Madam, I would ask that you cease badgering our friend to take an action that would be not only impolitic but improper. If you would like to convey your sympathies and offer your prayers and services—and mine—to Miss Witherington, please do so. But do not try to further involve William in your schemes."

Rather than dissolve into tears and beg Collin's forgiveness, Susan's face flushed, and she stood, hands on hips. "How can you be so unfeeling?"

William took the lack of focus on himself as the opportunity to stretch canvas and sail for safer harbor. Susan's raised and Collin's soft-but-heated voices followed William into the hall, but soon he'd gained the solitude of his room. Once again, he wished they did not consider him so dear a friend they could do away with all sense of propriety in his presence.

The key had been to a strongbox containing important papers—most likely the deeds to the house here and the plantation—and possibly a large quantity of money as well. He applauded her wisdom at sending it to safety. Rumor circulated last night among Collin and Susan's dinner guests of Pembroke's losses at the Long Rooms since his arrival in Portsmouth.

He shook his head, trying to clear thoughts of people to whom he held no connection. He wrote a note for his mother and returned downstairs. No voices came from the dining room, but William would not go in. He left the note on the receiving table, situated his hat on his head, and left the townhouse, turning his steps to the dockyard. Fawkes had drawn out a rudimentary map for an alternate route with two benefits: a shorter distance and avoidance of High Street.

O'Reilley recognized William and toured him the length of the dock, pointing out the progress made.

Had it been only yesterday he'd seen his ship in a nearly whole state? Entire sections of the curved ribs now sat exposed like bones picked clean by scavengers. His innards twisted. *Alexandra* had been his home, her crew his family for nearly five years. Looking at her now, he felt like an orphan who'd just been turned out of the orphanage—with no home or family to call his own.

❧

Silence filled the house. Julia checked her appearance one last time before making her way down to the dining room. In Nancy's absence, she had pinned her plaited hair in a thick coil at the nape of her neck.

Lady Pembroke already sat at the dining table, her mouth drawn in a tight line.

"Sorry I am tardy, ma'am. I have given Nancy the day off and had forgotten the time it takes to arrange my own hair."

"Oh." Augusta's displeasure was replaced by confusion. "Why did you give your maid the day off?"

"My mother taught me long ago that granting servants a day off when unexpected keeps them happy." Julia added milk and sugar to her coffee and sat in the chair at Augusta's right.

Augusta set down the bite-marked toast and took a sip of coffee.

"What do you have planned for us today?" She had to keep her aunt believing she intended to obey all her rules rather than just abide by the letter of the law Aunt Augusta had laid down.

"Baroness Fairfax has invited us for tea at three o'clock."

"Very well. If it will not disturb you, I believe I shall practice my music today. I've not touched the pianoforte for nearly a month, and my fingers ache for the exercise."

"Fine." Augusta returned her attention to her breakfast.

"What dress should I wear to tea?" Julia tried to keep her expression as guileless as possible. "With Nancy gone, I am at a loss to know what is a morning dress and what is a ball gown."

"I believe your pale blue sarcenet silk will suffice." Still frowning, Augusta folded her napkin and stood. "I shall be in the sitting room should you need me."

Julia kept her smile to herself until she heard her aunt's footsteps on the stairs. The first part of her plan was working. Even if Aunt Augusta didn't believe her, at least she was no longer as angry as yesterday. Julia finished her breakfast and went up to the conservatory.

She sat at the piano and lost herself in some of her favorite pieces of music. Then she took up the violin—the instrument her mother had allowed her to learn with much reluctance, as it was not considered ladylike.

Though somewhat bored by spending the full day at her music, she managed to wile away the hours until time to dress.

Half an hour later, she met Aunt Augusta in the front parlor. The pale blue silk covered her up in an almost matronly manner, from the high lace collar to the ruffles at the wrist that flopped down to nearly cover her hands.

"Shall we go? I would hate to keep the baroness waiting." Julia smiled at her aunt's consternation and turned before she overplayed her role as the obedient niece.

❧

The rustle of footsteps in grass startled Charlotte. Quickly, she refolded the pages in her hand and stuffed them into her sleeve.

William's shadow fell over her. "May I join you?"

She nodded, nervousness increasing. Neither James nor Philip affected her like this. Both laughed and teased her, putting her at ease. All three of her brothers had been at sea most of her life, but Philip and James did seem to get home more often than William.

If William discovered her true reason for talking Mama into coming to Portsmouth...

"I apologize for my absences the last few days. I trust Susan has been seeing to your entertainment."

"I have met more of Portsmouth society than I ever imagined. Mrs. Yates has ever so many acquaintances in town."

William's expression finally eased into a chuckle. "Aye, she has never met a stranger, that one."

"Mama said you were going to the dockyard to see your ship this morning?"

"Yes. *Alexandra* has been stripped down to the bones."

Her nerves grew tauter as the hidden pages rubbed against her wrist. "Might I accompany you next time you go?"

"To the dockyard?" His forehead creased as his brows rose.

"Yes. I've long desired to see it. I have heard so much about Portsmouth, so much about the dockyard from you and James and Philip. I wish to see the place all three of you love so much." She swallowed hard and clasped her hand over her wrist to stop the letter from scratching so.

He frowned again. "I shall have to give it some thought. There is much that is rough and coarse about the dockyard. I do not know if you should be exposed to it."

"You think I have never heard coarse language or been around men with rough manners?" She needed to spend time with the common sailors, with those not of high rank, to get a better feel for their behavior, for their speech. He had to give in.

"I shall think about it."

❦

Drake turned his horse toward the less desirable part of town near the dockyard as darkness took hold in the streets. He had spent the day leaving calling cards at the homes of people his mother thought important. He'd also gathered intelligence while out, learning of the supposed duel between himself and Ransome yesterday.

He smirked. As if he would lower himself to dueling with a sailor.

But the key...a sick feeling returned to his stomach. When his mother had told him about finding the strongbox, about her suspicions of what it contained—coin, deeds, bank notes—the bright flash of the brass key as he'd returned it to Julia mocked him. And when his mother went back to find an alternative way to open the lock, the box had disappeared. Mother was coming too close to overplaying her hand and losing everything.

He entered the Long Rooms. Patrons at whist tables in the outer room greeted Drake as an old friend—several gentlemen he'd seen around town earlier—and he paused to speak as a way of seeing what stakes this room held. Too much silver and copper and not enough gold coin lay in small stacks at each man's elbow.

"May I say, Sir Drake," said Percy Fairfax, second son of the baron, "you are envied in your choice of lady. Many a man here has tried to gain the attentions of the fair Miss Witherington."

"Hear, hear," chimed in one of the pup's companions. "Why, she's a right old maid, but who could not desire her fortune?" The young dandy flushed red and quickly threw back the little brandy remaining in his snifter.

"I believe what St. Vincent means is that before her arrival, none of us expected her to be lovely in addition to heiress to a large fortune." Percy Fairfax nodded knowingly. "So, old chap, are the rumors true? Did you fight some rascal of a sailor on a point of honor yesterday? On the lady's behalf?"

Being the son of nobility gave the boy free rein with his insolence. Knowing how quickly gossip could spread in Portsmouth, Drake knew he needed to use this to his advantage. "No duel was fought. Just a matter of impertinent interference into a private conversation."

The young men clamored their congratulations. "When shall we raise a glass to wish you joy?" Fairfax asked.

Drake shrugged. "Perhaps soon." If his mother's plotting stayed between the two of them and did not reach Julia's ears.

The proprietor appeared. "Come, Sir Drake. Some serious players—" he eyed the young men with amused disdain—"wish for your company in the back room."

Drake inclined his head toward the pups. "Gentlemen, I bid you good night, then."

❦

Streaks of pinkish gray cracked the black of the eastern horizon when Drake stumbled out of the Long Rooms. His losses necessitated giving his letters to not just the devil who'd won each hand as if by some dark magic, but to the proprietor as well for the never-ending flow of fine brandy all evening. The sum of the IOUs would be nothing—a pittance—if he already controlled Julia Witherington's thirty thousand pounds.

First order of business—sleeping off the enormous quantity of alcohol he had imbibed. After that, he would call on his mother to concoct a plan for hastening the union with Julia.

Chapter Seventeen

The Windemeres' drawing room smelled of warm bodies, stale per-
fume, and the port being passed around by the footman. Julia's
back ached from the strain of holding her head high and ignoring the
looks and whispers her entrance had caused, but she was glad to be
out after four days under house arrest.

Though the room was filled with many of the same people who
attended the concert last week, an atmosphere of cold arrogance hung
heavy all around. The Windemeres apparently had no acquaintances
among the navy. She'd hoped for at least Mrs. Hinds's company to
make this evening bearable. After all, her aunt could not censure her
for associating with an admiral's wife.

As no one made room for her at their tables—and she was no card-
player, so felt the intentional slight no loss—she strolled the perimeter
of the room, smiling when smiled at but happy to be left alone. When
she drew near a table, the conversation ceased until she passed and
then continued in hushed whispers.

"Trying too hard…"

"On the shelf…"

"Desperate to marry the baronet…"

"Who would have her at her age…?"

"She is an absolute hoyden…"

"I'm sorry for poor Lady Pembroke, saddled with such a niece—"
Mrs. Windemere looked up in surprise and had the decency to blush
when she saw Julia standing there.

"Mrs. Windemere, I wish to beg your indulgence and see if I might gain your permission to take a turn at the pianoforte. You have such a magnificent instrument, it is a shame to see it idle." Julia tried to keep her irritation from her smile.

"Why, yes, of course, Miss Witherington," her hostess simpered. "I have often heard how well you play. It will be a pleasure for us to be so entertained."

Julia had just gained the bench and started the opening notes of a sonata when the drawing room doors opened and Sir Drake Pembroke was announced. To her great relief, her aunt immediately claimed Drake for her table. Focusing on the music, Julia was almost able to forget where she was—until she heard several excited voices behind her.

"You ask her—"

"No, you've been introduced before..."

She finished the last few measures of the piece and turned to face the young women clustered behind her. "What may I play for you ladies?"

"We wondered if you knew some country dances." The girl—one of the Fairfaxes if Julia remembered correctly—flushed bright red when Julia looked directly at her. "Mrs. Windemere, you see, has allowed us to move aside some of the tables for dancing, if you will play for us."

Glad to be of use to someone, Julia nodded and turned back to the keyboard. English country dances were among the first music her mother had insisted she learn to play as a child. She liked the swinging rhythm and happy melodies.

The dancers had just taken their positions when a shadow fell over her fingers. Julia glanced up. Sir Drake, looking darker and more brooding than ever in his black suit, leaned against the side of the Broadwood grand, his glass of port precariously poised over the exposed innards of the instrument.

"Good evening, Miss Witherington. I see the youngsters have kept you occupied since my arrival."

Her stomach churned in annoyance at his presumption that she would come to him as soon as he walked in the door had she no other employment. "I am only glad I can provide others with enjoyment this evening." She kept her eyes focused on her own fingers as they danced across the ivory and black keys.

"Surely some of the other young ladies play—perhaps we can encourage one of them to take a turn, and you and I can have a dance."

"No, thank you." She kept her voice light. "I am quite content where I am."

She sensed more than saw him stiffen.

"Then perhaps once the dancing has ended, I might persuade you to take a turn about the garden with me. It is quite a pleasant evening."

She shook her head. "I do not believe I shall feel like taking a turn about the garden later, but thank you, Sir Drake." Only when she looked up to give him as much of a smile as she could muster did she realize her aunt had joined him. Julia's fingers tripped over the keys creating a dissonance that reverberated like the palpitation of her heart at the mottled anger visible in Lady Pembroke's face.

Julia quickly righted her fingers and continued playing, but she knew she was in for another lecture as soon as they got into the carriage.

"Come, son." Aunt Augusta's voice was unnaturally high and strained. "We have need of a fourth." She stalked away from the pianoforte, Drake following in her wake like a great, black vulture.

❧

Drake did not know with whom he was more furious—Julia or his mother. He'd known wooing Julia would take time. But he'd hoped for some cooperation on her part; however, her coldness proved how difficult a task it would be. He'd broken horses wilder than Julia Witherington. All she needed was a firm hand, applied in just the right manner, and she would come to heel—but not if his mother continued to interfere.

He played his trump and won the hand, pulling a rare smile from his mother. Would Julia turn as cold and calculating as the women at the table with him? Would she lose the sparkle in her green eyes—the sparkle he'd seen directed at others but not at himself? Would she ever look at him with anything but disdain?

What did it matter if Julia liked him or not? He could find more pleasant company in the arms of Lady Margaret Everingham or even in someone like the Ransome chit. He need not depend on his wife to be agreeable—just on her money to be available.

He need not woo her; he need only marry her.

At midnight, the dancing and card games broke up as trays of supper were brought in by servants. Julia continued at the piano, shifting to more subtle, soft music; Drake found a quiet corner and motioned his mother to join him.

He swirled his brandy before taking a long drink. "I believe more drastic measures are necessary if I am to gain Miss Witherington's fortune before her birthday."

Something akin to light flickered in his mother's dark brown eyes. "Yes, courting does not seem to be working. There is a stratagem I have employed once…and gained myself a baronet. We can set the plan in motion day after tomorrow at the Fairfaxes' ball. The rumor mill is ripe, which is excellent, as my plan depends greatly upon spreading the word that you and Julia are engaged. We make no formal announcement at the ball, merely start the rumor."

A measure of hope, as warming as the brandy in his glass, started to burn in Drake's gut. "Go on."

His mother smiled, though the expression did nothing to alleviate the calculation in her dark eyes. "Friday morning, you will go to Saint Thomas's, present yourself to the rector, and give him a letter stating your intention to marry Julia. I shall provide you with a letter from the admiral expressing his permission." She gave him a sly wink. "Once the banns are read Sunday, there will be nothing she can do to stop the marriage. She has too much pride in her father's name to do anything that would bring it disgrace—such as refusing to marry you after a public announcement has been made. And no one will object to the banns. I am monitoring all post in and out of the house, so she should not be able to appeal to her father."

He dipped his head in pleasure. "Even should she manage to get a letter out of the house, it will not go beyond the post office, you have my assurance."

Augusta patted his arm. "My dear boy, I should have known you would have unplumbed depth of resource. In three weeks' time, you will be wed to Julia and can begin rebuilding the Pembroke holdings."

After taking a break for a bite of supper, Julia once again moved toward the piano. Though exhausted and wearied of playing, she could think of no other activity to fill the time until her aunt decided to leave.

"Miss Witherington."

She stopped at a touch on her sleeve and turned to face the girl who had asked her to play for the dancing. Now, however, the young woman appeared troubled. "Miss Fairfax?"

"I wonder—might you take a turn about the room with me?" Her light eyes implored Julia to agree.

"I will." Julia fell in step with the girl.

Miss Fairfax twisted a lace handkerchief in her hands, and they walked the length of the room in silence. When they reached the corner and turned, she finally spoke. "I was uncertain whether to say anything because I hate gossip; but I could not, in good conscience, keep what I heard to myself."

Defensiveness rose in Julia, ready to rebut any rumor about herself the girl might have heard, but she kept quiet.

"Just a little while ago, when I sat down to take some supper, I happened to find a seat near to where your aunt and cousin sat. They could not see me due to a large vase in the way, but I could hear them clearly." She glanced at Julia with tortured eyes. "I did not mean to eavesdrop, and I should have walked away as soon as I realized they were having a private conversation. But then I heard Sir Drake mention 'drastic measures' to gain your fortune."

Julia stumbled but righted herself immediately, fear and anger warring inside. "What else did you hear?"

"Lady Pembroke said they will start telling everyone at my mother's ball that you and Sir Drake are engaged. Then on Friday, he is to go to the church with a letter announcing your engagement so the banns can be posted."

Nausea threatened to fell Julia, but she refused to succumb. "I... thank you for reporting this to me." She stopped and touched Miss Fairfax's wrist. "Please, tell no one else."

Miss Fairfax covered Julia's hand with her own. "Have no fear. I would not have repeated it at all, except it directly involved you."

They continued to traverse the perimeter of the room. When Julia passed Lady Pembroke's table, she mustered the most pleasant expression she could and prayed the candlelight was dim enough to keep her aunt from seeing her clearly.

Their walk ended at the piano, and Miss Fairfax's friends once again entreated Julia to play. She could think of no excuse to give, so sat down at the instrument. The employment proved to be helpful, as it kept her occupied while her mind grappled with what Miss Fairfax had told her.

Her first inclination was to confront her aunt, to demand to know if Miss Fairfax's words were true. But as her fingers moved over the keys and the music started to calm her, assurance of the veracity of the girl's words drove away any uncertainty. She had never trusted her aunt's intentions, especially after the arrival of Sir Drake. She'd suspected all along her aunt meant Julia to marry the bounder—especially after learning from her father of the Pembrokes' financial situation.

At two o'clock in the morning, the party finally ended. Julia swallowed her disgust when Sir Drake took her hand in his and kissed her fingers in farewell, Lady Pembroke looking on with what appeared to be motherly pride.

Once in the privacy of the carriage, Lady Pembroke's pretense at pleasantness vanished. "I am highly disappointed in your behavior this evening, Julia."

"*My* behavior——?" Julia cut off the tirade of words begging to escape.

"My son has been nothing but kind toward you—he quite dotes upon you. And yet you sat there and humiliated him by cutting him publicly."

How did one look contrite when mutinous fury raged just below the surface? Julia dropped her gaze to her hands—fisted in her lap— and swallowed a few times. "I apologize, Aunt. As you have pointed out many times, I have not had much experience with good society. I did not mean to…bring any discomfort to Sir Drake." Her left eye started twitching.

Aunt Augusta released a long sigh. "You must rectify the situation at the ball Thursday evening. Drake, naturally, will request the first set, which will give you ample time to apologize to him."

*And for you to start your rumors…*but not if Julia thought of a solution first. "Yes. I shall see everything put to rights at the ball."

That response apparently satisfied her aunt, as Augusta began to enumerate the errands they must attend to on the morrow. Julia retreated into her own thoughts.

She could not allow Augusta and Drake to ruin her father's reputation. He was wealthy enough to leave the Royal Navy and live out the remainder of his life in luxurious comfort, but he would never again be happy if his honor was sullied by the appearance of breaking an engagement between Julia and Drake. She would not allow that to happen to him.

And she could not allow her aunt to manipulate her into marrying the blackguard.

At home, Julia dismissed Nancy, needing time to think, to pray, to plan. She spent most of the night between her desk—madly scrawling possibilities and then scratching them out—and pacing.

If her father were here, none of this would be happening. But with a mere day and a half until the ball, she had no time to get word to him. That she had not yet heard from him since his arrival in London surprised her. He'd promised to write—and before now had always been a prompt correspondent.

No, she must do this on her own. She stopped and sank onto the window seat, leaden with weariness. No solution presented itself, nothing she could do on her own to extricate herself from this horrible situation.

God, is there no one who can help me? I do not understand why this is happening or what I am supposed to do about it. I cannot fight them alone...

An idea started to form, rising from the turmoil of her mind like the pink dawn that climbed the sky outside. With renewed energy, she returned to the desk and pulled out a fresh piece of parchment. For the next hour, she wrote, scratched out, wrote more, considered, prayed, and planned.

Finally, with full morning light beaming through her windows, she sat back and wiped her ink-stained fingers. She read her notes carefully, looking for any flaws, any weaknesses.

It just might work.

She began a letter to Susan explaining—but stopped. No one else could be involved in this. If her plan failed, and it could, no one else need know what she was attempting. She tore the letter to bits and tossed the pieces in the hearth along with all but the last page of her notes. To ensure no one else learned of her idea, she lit them on fire and watched as they blackened and curled and disappeared into ash.

The mantel clock chimed six thirty. Her aunt would not rise until ten o'clock or later. Julia undressed and climbed in bed, clutching the plan to her chest in a viselike grip.

Chapter Eighteen

With his mother and Charlotte beside him, William waited behind a middle-aged couple, careful to stay far enough back to avoid the plumage swaying wildly from the woman's hair.

Beyond the enormous white feathers, the crowd of well-dressed guests surged and ebbed like the tide rolling into Spithead harbor during a summer thunderstorm. His nerves tensed just as they did every time one of the lookouts cried, "Sail, oh!" But this wasn't the sea, and these weren't French and Spanish ships lying in wait to blow him out of the water. He must secure the guns, loose the headsail, and make forward progress into these unknown social waters.

Behind them, he could hear Susan greeting acquaintances. Finally the couple before them finished their conversation with the baron, and William moved forward to greet their host.

"Captain William Ransome, is it not?" The baron extended his hand and shook William's vigorously.

"Lord Fairfax, thank you again for the honor of your invitation."

Fairfax waved his hand. "Tosh. We're honored by your presence."

"May I present my mother, Mrs. Maria Ransome, and my sister, Miss Charlotte Ransome."

The rotund man fawned over the ladies before he finally turned to pull his wife's attention from the couple before them. "Fanny, here is Captain William Ransome and his mother and sister."

The way Fairfax enunciated his name renewed the sense of dread William had entered with.

"My wife, Lady Fanny Fairfax."

William bowed to the equally rotund woman, whose large turban tried to make up for her lack of height. "My lady."

She simpered like a schoolgirl and tapped the buttons and braid across his chest with her folded fan. "Captain Ransome—what fun. Oh, we shall have an amusement tonight, shan't we? Miss Ransome, have you secured a partner for the opening set? No? There are many handsome young gentlemen here tonight who will clamber to dance with you, I am certain. And Captain, you must have a dance or two as well." A sly look entered the baroness's eyes. "Perhaps if Miss Witherington is not spoken for, you might engage her for the first set."

"Perhaps." Taking Charlotte's and his mother's arms, he started steering them away before Lady Fairfax could launch into the latest gossip. "Thank you again for the honor of the invitation."

"Oh, wait a moment, Captain." Lady Fairfax stopped him with her fan poking into his chest like a saber. "Percy, my dear, come here."

A lanky young man wove through the crowd. "Yes, Mother?"

"Percy, I wanted to introduce this delightful young woman—Miss Charlotte Ransome. Perhaps you and your sisters can take charge of her and make sure she meets all of your crowd."

The young man bowed with a flourish that set William's teeth on edge. But he nodded at Charlotte's questioning look and relinquished her arm to the baron's son.

"Captain, you will find many of the officers in the conservatory," the baroness said before turning her attention to Collin and Susan.

His mother's grip on his arm tightened as they maneuvered through the throng of guests. He caught a glimpse of Lady Pembroke through the crowd and steered his mother on a sharper angle to the wide-open doors of the blue and gold bedecked music room. The color scheme seemed made for the gathering of men in officers' uniforms. He inclined his head in greeting to Captain Mason but obeyed a wave over from Admiral Glover. He started to feel more at ease that no negative tales would reach his mother's ears in this company.

Mrs. Hinds and his mother had just fallen into conversation when William felt a tug on his sleeve. Susan's face looked anxious.

"What is it?" He looked around and saw Collin engaged in lively conversation with Captain Mason.

"I promise I am not trying to interfere or trying to pressure you into something you do not wish to do." She looked down at the fan she twisted in her fingers. "I know you have not yet secured a partner for the first set. I wondered if you would allow me to entreat you to ask Julia for it."

◌❧◌

Julia took another step back, allowing more people to pass between herself and her aunt. Lady Pembroke, caught up in conversation with Lady Dalrymple, did not notice the growing distance. A little bit more and Julia could blend into the crowd and slip away. She had no desire to be near her aunt when Sir Drake arrived. He would claim Julia for the first set, and her aunt's scheme would begin to see fulfillment. One more step back—

"Julia?" Although she had not raised her voice, Lady Pembroke's sharp tone carried over the noise.

Julia regained her aunt's side. "I do apologize, ma'am—the press of people is overwhelming."

The musicians started tuning their instruments, increasing the noise in the stifling room.

"I wonder where my son is. He promised he would be here for the first set." Lady Pembroke gave Lady Dalrymple a significant glance.

A twitter of voices surrounded them. Julia turned just as William Ransome, resplendent in his dress uniform, stopped and bowed. The people crowded around them all turned to watch in silence. Julia's heart pounded wildly.

"Miss Witherington, if you are not already engaged, I wonder if I might have the honor of your hand for the first set."

Her legs started to tremble. "I am not engaged, Captain Ransome, and the honor would be mine."

Lady Pembroke gasped behind her, but Julia merely curtsied to William, her stomach in knots and head spinning. The similarity to another ballroom, another dance, could not be denied.

"The first couples are taking their places." William extended a white-gloved hand. "Shall we?"

Julia's hand shook when she raised it to place in his. Her aunt's fury emanated like a raging fire at her back, but she did not turn to look. How had William known she needed him tonight?

The decision she'd come to this afternoon, after a day and a half of prayer and constant consideration, left her unsettled and anxious. But by making her own decision, Julia took her life and future back from the certain unhappiness marrying Sir Drake would bring.

She took her place opposite William and drank in his appearance. The deep indigo of his well-fitting uniform created a startling contrast to his eyes—eyes the same vibrant blue as the sun-kissed waters of the Caribbean. His short brown hair curled a bit about his forehead, ears, and collar, with slight touches of silver at his temples.

She followed him through the intricate pattern of the dance. Handsome. Wealthy. Highly respected by others both inside and outside of his profession. She swallowed hard and glanced at him. How was she going to ask? Now the time had come, she wasn't sure she could go through with it, wasn't sure she could risk her heart again.

She caught a glimpse of Sir Drake as she and William promenaded the length of the room hand in hand. If she married Sir Drake, he would not only receive her legacy but would also become heir to Tierra Dulce. Julia wasn't about to let him squander her father's fortune the way he had gambled away his own. It should go to someone more deserving. Someone her father respected and loved like a son.

"When does Admiral Witherington return from London?" William circled her around in a figure eight.

"Four weeks yet. He is gone only six days and greatly missed already."

She followed him easily through the allemande, weaving in and out of the other couples like fine needlepoint.

"But you should be accustomed to his being gone much longer periods of time. After all, he was at sea most of your childhood."

Two weeks ago, she might have resented him for reminding her of the years she'd lost—years William had been with her father. But tonight, the flood of enchantment in her heart every time he looked at her drowned out any former ill feelings for him. "Yes. But we have had almost a twelvemonth together since I have been in Portsmouth."

"Does he—" William paused when the pattern separated them.

They stood opposite one another as other couples promenaded between them. Her cheeks burned under his intense gaze like an inexperienced girl at her debut. She clenched her teeth and tried to control her rising anxiety, but her hand trembled when she reached out to place it in William's as they joined another couple in a circle.

"Does your father enjoy his duties?" William's grasp tightened.

"Enjoy being dry-docked? He finds pleasure in assigning commissions to deserving officers."

He laughed, a deep melodious sound that sent tingles up from their connected hands straight to her riotous heart. "No one could ever accuse you of not being diplomatic."

She turned and took his other hand. "And would you like giving up your life at sea for a career on land?"

The derisive sound that issued forth from him responded better than any words.

The dance once again separated them. *Lord, please help me to convince him.*

She'd made a mistake—she'd allowed herself to come to care for him again. If he declined to help her, she feared it might hurt deeper than before.

In her peripheral vision, she caught another glimpse of Sir Drake, now moving around the room as though trying to keep her constantly in view. She wasn't engaged for the next dance, but she couldn't give herself over to Pembroke. As the song ended, she looked around for escape.

William offered his arm. "My mother is here and wishes to renew her acquaintance with you, if you are so inclined."

Her breath hitched, and her chest tightened. She searched the room for her aunt, but the confusion of dancers and spectators blocked her aunt from sight.

"Yes, I should very much like to meet your mother again." She laid her hand on his arm and glided across the room—away from Sir Drake. Neither he nor Lady Pembroke would dare cause a scene in front of her father's friends and fellow officers without fear of word getting to Sir Edward in London.

The music room proved less crowded than the ballroom. Susan waved cheerfully when she saw Julia across the room. Their progress to her was impeded by several friends or admirers of her father who wanted to introduce themselves or be introduced to her.

Susan clasped her in a tight embrace. "Oh, my dear friend. How good it is to see you." She stepped back and held Julia by the forearms. "You are well?"

Julia nearly laughed with relief. "As well as I can be. I will see how things progress this evening."

"Miss Witherington."

Julia disengaged her arms from Susan and turned at William's voice.

"Here is my mother."

Julia returned the older woman's curtsey. "Mrs. Ransome, it is good to see you again. I trust you are enjoying your visit with your son."

"Miss Witherington, I am delighted." Mrs. Ransome beamed up at William. "This time together has been such a blessing." She returned her twinkling gaze to Julia. "William told us after your dinner that he met you for the first time when you were but a child."

"Did he tell you I was dressed in my brother's clothing and climbing to the top of the foremast to look for a French ship?" Julia's heart beat wildly at the smile William bestowed upon her. "He watched over me—made sure I did not fall to certain injury or death on the deck below."

Her eyes locked with his searching blue gaze. Memories of that first voyage to Jamaica flooded her. Every encounter she'd had with William had proven him to have been, even at fifteen, a man of honor—one who watched over and protected those younger or weaker than himself. A niggling of fear broke through her fervent haze. He had disappointed her once before in the name of honor. Would that same sense of honor keep him from agreeing to her plan?

Although the majority of guests stayed in the main room, the crowded conservatory soon became overheated. Julia fanned herself and wished she dared venture out of her safe haven for a breath of fresh air. But every so often, Sir Drake appeared at the doorway like a shark circling, waiting to attack.

"Miss Witherington."

She jumped at William's voice near her ear. "Would you care to take a turn about the garden?"

The garden. Of course. Where else would be more perfectly ironic than the garden? She nodded, not trusting her voice as anxiety wrapped its cold fingers around her throat, and took his arm.

Colored-glass lanterns cast an ethereal light on the wide path. Other couples meandered through the manicured shrubbery. More than one engagement would be formed this night.

She flicked her gaze at William and swallowed. "Do you look forward to your new posting in Jamaica?"

"I look forward to putting my crew out to sea as they deserve."

She smiled. "Being diplomatic?"

"No. Realistic. As you well know, the voyage is difficult."

"Indeed." The gravel bit through the thin soles of her kid dancing slippers. She'd gone soft since returning to England.

"Do you return to Jamaica soon?" William asked.

"I hope so." She couldn't catch her breath. She had to take the plunge. "May we find a bench and sit for a moment?"

He looked down at her in concern. "Are you unwell?"

Her heart hammered. "No. I'm perfectly well. I hoped to speak with you tonight, alone."

He motioned her toward a nearby bench within sight of the rest of the garden but far enough off the path no one should hear what she was about to say to him. She sat beside him for a moment but then sprang back to her feet and paced a circle around him. How to begin?

The directness of his gaze didn't make her task any easier. She stopped, staring at the flowering vine hanging from the branch over William's head. "When I was a girl, I always looked forward to receiving letters from my father. His tales of life at sea intrigued me. Your name appeared quite often in those missives. I know how highly he regards you. He looks upon you almost as a son." She'd gotten the words out without choking. This was so much harder than she'd imagined, and the setting was not helping matters any. *Business. Keep it strictly business.*

"I hope you do not think I have in any way attempted to take the place of your brother." William's soft voice drew her gaze down. Her anxiety started to melt at the frown that creased his handsome face.

"No, no, I do not think that." She tried to regulate her breathing. "You would be too polite to mention it, but I know you have noticed the tension between my aunt and me and that she desires me to marry— to marry Sir Drake Pembroke."

As the moment drew nearer, she started pacing again. "I have learned she plans for the banns to be read Sunday announcing that I am engaged to Sir Drake. Even though my father will not have given his blessing, once the banns are read—" She stopped and hugged her arms around her waist.

"Your father would not be able to decline his permission without doing great harm to your reputation as well as his." William rose and took up Julia's pacing.

"Exactly." She sank onto the bench, still warm where he'd occupied it. "That is why I wanted a private interview with you."

The colored lantern-light sparkled off the buttons and braid of his uniform as he moved back and forth in front of her, hands clasped behind his back, head bent, brow furrowed.

Lord, give me strength. "I—I wish to enter a business arrangement with you, Captain Ransome."

He turned on his heel to face her. "A business arrangement?"

Nodding, she tried to swallow the fear rising in the back of her throat. "Yes. My greatest desire is to return home—to Jamaica—and see to the running of Tierra Dulce. This is something I know Sir Drake will never allow should I marry him. Therefore, since my aunt insists on having my marriage banns published this week, I must find someone else to be my husband. That is why I wanted to speak to you tonight."

"Me?" He blanched.

Oh dear, he wasn't taking this well. "As I said, I wish to make this a business arrangement. You know that I will receive thirty thousand pounds upon my marriage. I am also my father's sole heir. He will allow me to live on the Jamaica plantation for the rest of my life. I know you have no desire to marry me, but if you will—only for a year—we can then ask for an annulment and you can keep the dowry for yourself and remain my father's legal heir."

He stared at her.

She dropped her gaze to her hands. She'd made a mess of it. Rambled on and on. Given him cause to think she'd lost her mind.

"Julia!"

Her head snapped up at the shrill voice. Close on her aunt's heels followed Sir Drake. Julia rose, regret clogging her throat. At least she'd tried coming up with an alternative solution. Tomorrow, she would send William a letter of apology for inconveniencing and embarrassing him.

"What do you think you are doing out here alone with *him*?" Lady Pembroke spat. "I should have known you weren't to be trusted, sir. All sailors are just alike. Not caring the least for a woman's reputation."

William drew himself up. "I apologize, Madam, if there has been any impropriety in my actions toward your niece."

Julia wasn't sure she could survive a lifetime of being pawed by Sir Drake Pembroke—and worse, of knowing he was gambling away her father's hard-earned fortune. Resigned, she rose and stepped forward.

"However," William continued. "I would appreciate it if you wouldn't speak to Julia in such a tone."

Her heart flipped. Had he meant to call her by her Christian name? She glanced up at him.

Lady Pembroke's mouth dropped open. "Insolent puppy! I am her guardian, and I may speak to her however I please."

"I am sorry, Lady Pembroke, but I cannot allow you to speak to my intended that way."

Chapter Nineteen

William's stomach sank faster than a hulled ship. What had he done?

"Your—intended?" Lady Pembroke gaped at him, an expression that shattered her carefully cultivated refinement.

Sir Drake grabbed Julia's arm and yanked her toward him. "She is *my* intended."

"Unhand her." William stepped between Julia and the baronet, reaching for the hilt of his cutlass that wasn't there. He fisted his hand instead. Oh, how he wanted Pembroke to refuse.

Sir Drake scowled, but Julia yanked her arm away from his grasp. William moved her directly behind him.

Drake did not back down. "You will remove yourself, sir. Julia is to marry me. Her father will sign the wedding articles when he returns from London."

William resisted the urge to pound the man's face to a pulp and to step away from the stench of alcohol on his breath. "Indeed? I find that fascinating, given the fact I have already received Admiral Witherington's permission and blessing to marry Julia." Sir Edward had given it twelve years ago when William asked for Julia's hand. He assumed it still stood.

Pembroke's expression turned smug. "But you are not yet legally wed. Banns must be read for three weeks before a marriage can take place. Objections can easily be raised."

"And why do you assume we will not marry by special license?"

William's stomach churned. When he'd stepped between Julia and her cousin, he hadn't thought through how complicated this "business arrangement" might become.

Pembroke raked his glance up and down William's uniform. "Because you are—"

"A post captain in the Royal Navy?" William scowled—an expression that made lower-ranked officers squirm.

Drake snorted with derision. "A man of obscure birth with no family name of consequence, no hereditary title, and no property."

Julia gasped. "Aunt—have you nothing to say?"

"Drake, that is quite enough." Lady Pembroke sounded anything but contrite. "Julia has apparently made her decision and we must capitulate to it. Come." She tugged on his sleeve.

Pembroke gave William one last glare and turned to slither off behind her.

William swallowed. That had been the easy part. Now he had to face Julia. He tugged at the waist of his coat and turned.

Julia's green eyes fixed on him in wide disbelief. "How can I ever thank you? When they came upon us—I—" She shook her head. "I was trying to reconcile myself to a life with *him*." She nodded the direction Pembroke had disappeared. She pressed her hands to her cheeks, then looked up at him and tried to smile. "I promise I will not be a burden to you. I will stay to my quarters as much as I can—"

"Your quarters?" Of what could she be thinking?

"Yes. Aboard *Alexandra*. Remember? One of the reasons for our business arrangement is so I can travel with you to Jamaica."

Lips pressed firmly together, he closed his eyes and expelled his breath. He'd forgotten about that part of the deal. A ship was no place for a woman.

Julia clasped her hands at her waist. "I know it has been a score of years, but you should remember I sail well. I don't get sick, even in the worst of storms; I know the schedule and the bells; I'm handy with a needle; and I can help teach and mind the younger boys."

"I don't—my cabin isn't—" The two-day voyage from Yarmouth

to Portsmouth with a commodore and his wife aboard had justified William's policy of no women allowed on his ship. But if they were to marry, he couldn't very well insist Julia find another means of transport to her island home. As a man of honor, he had to follow through on his tacit acceptance of the arrangement. "Would you be uncomfortable, being the only female aboard?"

"The only—" She clamped her mouth shut, then shook her head. "No. I am willing to sacrifice any comfort necessary to get back home."

"I will write to your father and make the arrangements." He cringed at the harsh edge to his voice. The poor woman had been through enough tonight; she didn't need his acrimony as well. He offered his arm. "Shall we return to the house?"

She slid her hand into the crook of his elbow and walked beside him in a silence that unsettled him. What would his men think? William was renowned throughout the fleet for his refusal to allow even a female cat aboard his vessel. Would his crew think him a hypocrite for marrying and bringing his wife aboard?

His *wife*. The word chilled him. Although Julia offered to request an annulment after one year, to William marriage was a lifetime commitment. He would be forever bound to her alone—his future in her emotional, illogical feminine hands.

Their meandering walk through the garden had taken them around the house and closest to the doors opening into the ballroom. He gave a curt bow to the couple they passed in the wide doorway. Then, like a sudden storm at sea, whispers swelled up and surrounded them as they entered the ballroom. Gossip of how the handsome, wealthy Captain Ransome had taken pity on poor Lady Pembroke's *spinster* niece by order of the admiral. Expressions of sorrow for Lady Pembroke being saddled with such a headstrong, obstinate niece who had refused several perfectly good offers of marriage in Jamaica and had snubbed Sir Drake Pembroke in public two nights ago. All in that inconvenient tone of voice seemingly private but meant to be overheard by the object of the secret.

William pressed his free hand over Julia's where it rested on his arm, and her fingers curled around his. She kept her eyes trained forward, her chin up, a pleasant expression on her attractive face. He admired her strength of character in ignoring the intentionally hurtful remarks. He could well imagine that the past nine months had been torture for a woman whose interest swayed more toward account books than the latest fashions.

Skirting the perimeter of the room to get back to the conservatory, he heard not only the whisperings about Julia but also speculations of his own wealth—most underestimated by half at least—and which rich young woman would capture his regard once he had fulfilled his duty to Admiral Witherington of attending Julia.

Several chaperones standing sentry nearby watched from behind their fans, no doubt waiting to see who would take *pity* on Julia and dance with her next.

As with a captured ship, he needed to run up his colors and claim his prize. He cleared his throat. "Julia, my dear," he said, his voice louder than necessary, pulse pounding in his ears, "shall we rejoin the others in the conservatory and tell them our news?"

She glanced at him in surprise, then over her shoulder at the unmistakable gasps and buzz of voices behind her. The older women whirled around to pretend they hadn't been listening.

Julia's cheeks flamed, but amusement danced in her green eyes. "Why, yes, W-William."

He nodded his approval and led her through the gaggle of intensely whispering women toward the music room.

The crowd ahead of them parted. "William, Miss Witherington— Susan has had me searching the house for you." Collin's smile came as a welcomed sight. "Come into the conservatory. Too stuffy out here." His friend looked about the room with a sniff. "You have to save us, William. Admiral Glover has had us under siege with stories of the West Indies."

"Is the admiral familiar with the Caribbean?" Julia asked, fatigue edging her voice. The bright candlelight gleamed in her emerald eyes.

William drew in a deep breath and tried to calm his heart, racing at the thought of telling his mother and friends of their engagement. "Aye, he claims to have been around the world three times."

"And loves to talk about it whenever he has a captive audience." Collin grimaced.

They followed Collin over to join Susan, who eyed them suspiciously.

"And where have you two been?"

Julia flushed and dropped her hand from William's arm. "For a turn about the garden."

"You have been gone quite some time."

"Where is my mother?" William looked around the room. She should be the first to hear of the engagement.

"Here I am, behind you, son." She excused herself from Mrs. Hinds and joined them. William steered his mother and friends to an unoccupied corner of the large room.

"Mother, Collin, Susan." He took a fortifying breath. "Miss Witherington and I have this evening entered into an engagement."

Tears sprang into Susan's eyes, and she threw her arms around Julia. Collin regarded William for a moment, shrugged, and then grinned and offered his hand. "Mason owes me twenty quid. What interest I could charge after twelve years!"

William shook Collin's hand and leaned over to accept his mother's kiss and congratulations. The warmth in her eyes expressed her genuine happiness for him more than words would ever convey.

Collin disengaged Julia from his wife, took Julia's hands, and kissed her cheeks. "Will you stay in Portsmouth, Miss Witherington? Susan will be so happy to have another captain's wife to keep company with."

"No, Captain Yates. I'll—" She turned an uncertain gaze upon William.

He shifted his weight and clasped his hands behind his back. "Julia will return to Jamaica to oversee her father's sugar plantation."

"Jamaica? The same destination as our convoy?" Collin let out a low whistle. "After all these years—"

"Ah, Miss Witherington, there you are." Lord Fairfax bustled through the crowd of sailors. "My daughter was just telling me she had the privilege of hearing you play at the Windemeres' card party earlier this week. Might you entertain us with a number?"

He took Julia's hand and led her to the cabinet piano on the opposite side of the room, brooking no opposition.

Not knowing what her aunt or Sir Drake might try, William followed, uneasy with the idea of letting Julia out of his sight.

Collin ambled after them. "I know I told you twelve years ago that I understood why you did not propose to Miss Witherington. I'm happy your feelings about marriage have changed." He shook his head. "But you should be court-martialed for making her wait all this time."

William shot his friend a withering look and took up sentry beside the instrument as Julia took her place at it. Collin stood beside him.

"My feelings on marriage have not changed," William whispered. However, having the questions of when and to whom settled did make him view it as a little less reprehensible.

"Then why?" Collin asked, standing below a wall sconce. He jumped when candle wax dripped onto his head.

"Because she asked." Oh, he shouldn't have said that.

"*She* asked?" Collin stifled his laughter. "Mason will—"

"Mason will say nothing because you will say nothing." William resisted the urge to rake his fingers through his hair.

"Mrs. Yates, will you play with me?" Julia handed a piece of music to Susan and nodded toward the harp standing nearby.

Susan blushed becomingly, accepted the music, and sat down at the instrument. What followed was the most divine music William had ever heard. Susan strummed the harp like an angel, accompanied by Julia on the pianoforte. That she could play the instrument was no doubt owing to her mother's concern with Julia's being a fashionable lady of society, even in the wilds of Jamaica.

He closed his eyes. The harmonious sound comforted him as much as a ship's deck rolling under his feet. The moment the song ended, everyone in the room applauded and begged for more.

Lord Fairfax set a brown case in front of Julia. She opened it and, eyes sparkling, withdrew a violin. Her cheeks pink with anticipation, she tuned it and crossed to the harp to pick out the next piece. Susan laid the sheet music on her stand, and Julia drew the bow across the strings. The object had been wrought by the hands of man, but the sound issuing forth came only from the grace of God.

William clasped his hands behind his back and relaxed. All eyes in the room rested upon the two women. A sense of pride swelled in his chest. His intended, his soon-to-be wife, commanded the room with her talent more easily than he commanded his crew. Her hair shone copper with threads of gold under the massive chandelier, ringlets bouncing and swaying at her temples and neck as she worked the bow over the strings. Her gown—ivory silk and dark blue velvet with gold thread— seemed to have been chosen for this room, for this company.

For him.

※

"Miss Ransome, might I interest you in taking a turn about the music room?" Percy Fairfax's eyes glittered.

Smiling, she rested her hand atop his arm. "I do believe I would enjoy that, Mr. Fairfax." She turned to invite Miss Fairfax to join them, but the lady's attention had been captured by one of Percy's friends.

The music that greeted Charlotte upon entry in the blue and gold wallpapered room was like nothing she had ever heard. Susan Yates sat at the harp, and beside her, Julia Witherington played the violin. William stood nearby, his expression wary and yet at the same time peaceful.

"Charlotte." Her mother appeared at her side. "Come, your brother has something he needs to say to you."

"Please excuse me, Mr. Fairfax."

The baron's son bowed. "Thank you for your company, Miss Ransome. Perhaps we might have another dance later."

"I would enjoy that, thank you." She bent her knees and turned to follow her mother to where her brother stood near the pianoforte. Her skin tingled. What did William need to say to her that their mother could not communicate? Had she done something terribly wrong this evening without knowing?

When she gained her brother's side, he took her hand, kissed the back of it, and tucked it under his elbow. Confused, she watched him as Julia and Susan finished their song and then refused to play another piece, insisting other ladies have a chance to exhibit.

A slight thrill of excitement shimmied down Charlotte's spine. Of all the guests tonight, Julia was the one she'd hoped to be able to spend some time with.

Although smiling, Miss Witherington had a drawn, fatigued look about her face. "Miss Ransome, what a pleasure it is to see you again."

"And you, Miss Witherington."

William cleared his throat. "Charlotte, Miss Witherington and I are to be married."

"Married?" A clap of thunder couldn't come as more of a surprise. "But they said—" She stopped, embarrassed at what she had been about to say. All evening, she'd heard nothing but gossip about Julia Witherington's impending marriage to her cousin, the fulsome baronet. She looked from William to Miss Witherington, and a sudden happiness filled her. "Congratulations—may I wish you joy?"

Affection filled William's blue eyes so like her own. He kissed her forehead. "Aye, you may, and thank you."

A sister. With three older brothers who took prodigious good care of her, even though she hardly saw them, the only thing lacking in Charlotte's life had been a sister. She looked at Miss Witherington again, and a tickle of tears blurred the edges of her vision. A sister. Finally. "When will you be married?"

William and Miss Witherington exchanged a long look. "Before my ship sails, as Miss Witherington will accompany me back to her home in Jamaica."

Would the surprises never end this night? "She will accompany you—on *your* ship? The ship you would not allow Mama and me to board two years ago?"

He looked down at his feet. "Aye, the very same. I will make it up to you by giving you a tour as soon as she comes out of dry dock."

"Oh yes, please!" Charlotte calmed herself. To be able to see the entire ship, to learn its layout before putting her plan into action—"I would very much like to see my brother's home from home."

Finally, the answers to her prayers seemed to be arriving tenfold. With William fitting out his ship for a transatlantic voyage while also preparing for a wedding, and then with the stir that having Miss Witherington aboard would cause—Mrs. Ransome as she would then be—Charlotte's plan might work better than she'd originally hoped.

⁂

The empty crystal decanter shattered with a resounding crash against the fireplace. "How could I have been so stupid as to follow your ill-conceived advice?"

"Calm yourself." Lady Pembroke sat on the edge of one of the ancient chairs in the dank sitting room of Pembroke House.

The brandy gone, Drake lifted a bottle of port, refilled his glass, and downed half of it. "How could you do something as idiotic as laying out the entire plan to Julia before it was put into action—to give a woman as intelligent as she two days to figure out a way to thwart us?"

Augusta stood, snatched the glass from his hand, and shoved him into a chair. "I do believe you've had quite enough to drink tonight." She removed the bottle and glass from his reach. "I do not know how that hoyden learned of our plan—though I am certain she must have, as the timing of her action cannot be coincidental. But if you will recall, we did speak of it in a public place. She has more allies than I suspected."

"What are we going to do?"

A sudden sting and sharp smack sent his head lolling back. He raised his hand to the cheek his mother had just slapped. "What was that for?"

"To make you stop whining." Augusta grabbed the glass and took a deep draught of the port. "You have never been denied anything you want. But with your ungoverned words and anger tonight, repairing the damage you've done is going to be difficult."

She paced the room, finishing the remainder of the drink. "We can only hope she does not throw me out of her house. I shall do what I can to remain in her good graces and see if I can discover a method to undo what has been done." She stopped, refilled the glass, and handed it to him. "Tomorrow, you need to visit the postmaster, as I'm certain both she and the captain will try to get letters through to the admiral."

"Yes, Mother."

"Julia Witherington's thirty thousand pounds and access to her father's estate is yours by right. And we must do whatever necessary to have it in our possession before month's end."

Chapter Twenty

The Yateses' barouche pulled to a stop in front of the Witheringtons' house. No lights burned upstairs, and only a dim glow defined the windows on the main level.

William leapt out and assisted Julia down.

Susan leaned through the door of the carriage. "Julia, don't forget—we shall be by for you at eleven tomorrow morning."

"I won't forget. And thank you for your kindness this evening. I don't know how I would have made it through." She squeezed her friend's hand.

"My dear Miss Witherington—Julia." Mrs. Ransome extended her hand to Julia with a warm smile. "I am so happy you will be join-ing our family. I wish we had more time to spend together before you leave the country."

"As do I, Mrs. Ransome."

"Well, we shall have all day tomorrow—you are staying for dinner, Julia. Did I tell you?" Susan grinned at her.

Only Susan. Julia smiled back. "I would be delighted."

Julia was finally able to bid them all goodnight and gratefully took William's arm to the open front door, which framed Creighton, stand-ing sentry with a lighted candle.

"Good evening, Miss Witherington." Creighton turned to William and raised his hand to salute, remembering himself when his arm was half-way up. His arm dropped back to his side. "Captain Ransome, sir."

"Creighton, is it not?"

This time, Creighton did knuckle his forehead. "Aye, sir."

"You served Admiral Witherington before he struck his colors."

"Aye, sir. Served Sir Edward as steward, sir."

Julia watched in fascination at the easy command in William's stance and voice and Creighton's immediate shift from butler to sailor.

"And where lie your loyalties?"

"To king and country, sir. To Sir Edward and the Royal Navy... and Miss Witherington, sir."

William again raised his brow in an expression so reminiscent of her father Julia nearly laughed.

"Very well, then." William looked at Julia then returned to Creighton. "Whatever Miss Witherington needs, she is to receive. I expect to receive word daily of Miss Witherington's continued good welfare. If I am needed, you are to send word. Are my orders clear?"

"Aye, aye, sir." Creighton's voice betrayed surprise that did not register in his solemn expression.

"Excellent. That will be all." William reached for the candle. Creighton saluted again and backed into the house.

She should have known William would see to her care with military precision and decisiveness. "Thank you."

"On days when you are to see Susan, your butler need not send a message. If Lady Pembroke or Sir Drake tries to waylay you or force you into any action or agreement, I am to be sent for immediately." He looked over his shoulder at the dark carriage. "My mother wishes to call upon Lady Pembroke."

Julia shook her head. "I think that is unwise. Perhaps you might explain—?"

"I will do my best to help her understand the situation." His expression softened. "Are you certain you do not wish to stay with the Yateses? I can remove myself to an inn."

She laid her hand on his forearm and gave it a light squeeze. "I shall survive, I promise. Captain Ransome, I—"

"We are to be married. I believe you should call me by my Christian name." He lifted her hand and held it loosely between them.

Her face burned and her entire arm tingled. "William. I must apologize to you." She searched his face—the face that was at once familiar and strange—for some revelation of his thoughts. "I would never have knowingly put you in the line of fire."

"I know. I am honored to have been the one there to offer protection." He raised her hand to his lips. "Until tomorrow, then."

The soft touch of his lips to the backs of her fingers nearly discomposed her. She swallowed hard. "Until tomorrow." She belatedly realized he tried to press the candleholder into her hand. She grasped it and remained on the stoop as he returned to the barouche. He turned at the carriage, nodded at her, and climbed in.

When the carriage rolled away, Julia entered the house and shut the door behind her. Creighton met her before she'd taken three steps, took the candle from her, and lit the tiered candelabra on the receiving table.

"Has my aunt retired already?" Strain pitched her voice higher than usual.

"She returned home a little while ago. Just before you arrived, she had me send Jim for an express messenger."

"To whom would she be sending an express at this hour?" Julia crossed her arms, hugging herself.

"I did not hear the name, but the message is being carried to London."

Julia hoped her aunt was trying to arrange accommodations there.

"Nancy awaits you upstairs. Shall I send Betsy up with a tub of hot water for your feet?"

"Only if she is still awake. I do not want you to disturb her sleep."

He bowed. "Yes, miss."

"Good night, Creighton."

"Good night, miss." He handed her the candle and disappeared down the dark hall.

Climbing the stairs seemed to take hours, her legs protesting every step.

In her room, she sank into the cushioned chair at the vanity table.

Nancy immediately started pulling pins from Julia's hair. Her scalp tingled and ached as the elaborate curls loosened and fell to hang down her back.

Doubts assailed her anew as Nancy combed out the tangles. Was marrying William the right step? God had never seemed more distant or silent than tonight, when she needed him most.

She climbed into bed and drew the quilt up to her chin. Three weeks from tomorrow and she would leave England, perhaps forever. She would board *Alexandra* as Mrs. William Ransome.

If William had never even let his mother and sister come on board when his ship was at anchor, what would his crew think of his bringing a woman—a *wife*—with them all the way across the Atlantic?

Lord, please let his men accept me. Let him have a good, strong, able crew that will make the voyage safe and fast.

Yawning, Julia tried to continue her prayer but drifted off to sleep, the last coherent thought a petition to God to give her a happy marriage with William Ransome. A happy *lifelong* marriage.

✦

William labored over the letter to Admiral Witherington, finally copying a clean draft as, outside his window, the morning star began to wane. Before putting his signature to the page, William reread it. Honest without being critical of Lady Pembroke, forthcoming without mentioning Julia's business arrangement. If the truth of that were to be revealed to the admiral, Julia must undertake the telling herself.

He sealed the letter and laid it atop the other correspondence bound for the post. More weary than after the most heated battle, he dropped into bed.

How would he break the news to his men? All of his officers had left Portsmouth to visit their families. When they returned next week, they would most likely hear rumors of the engagement from an innkeeper or tavern host. There was nothing for it. He would have to make the announcement to them their first morning—then do the same with the rest of the crew two days later. He pictured himself overlooking the quarterdeck, telling the crew Julia would sail with them. His imaginary crew reacted with indifference, but then, when his mind ran through it again, with consternation, followed by anger and then fury.

When he imagined them erupting into full-blown mutiny, he kicked off the blanket, dressed, and quietly made his way down to the kitchen. The scullery maid gave a startled squeak that alerted the cook to his presence. He was as surprised as she to find anyone stirring so early.

"Mornin', sir. Sommat I can get for ye?" the cook asked, wiping her hands of the meat she'd been butchering.

"Coffee." He cringed at the bark of command in his voice. "If you have any made, please."

"I can have it brewed in a trice, sir. Shall ye be in the dining room?"

"Yes—no. In Captain Yates's library."

"Yes, sir. Molly 'ere will bring it to ye."

"Thank you." He climbed the two flights of stairs and let himself into Collin's small but comfortable study. He sank into one of the chairs in front of the fireplace and stared at the empty grate, too many thoughts whirling in his mind to focus on just one. The coffee the girl brought up was better than he'd had at the ball last night but still needed plenty of sugar and milk to be palatable.

"I thought I heard you stirring."

He started at his mother's soft voice. Dressed in a simple gray gown, a mobcap covering her sandy hair, she entered the study and sat in the other chair.

"Good morning, Mother. I apologize if I disturbed your sleep."

"Sleep did not find me this night." Sadness edged her voice.

In the dim glow of the candle she had carried in, William was astonished to see tears collecting in her eyes.

"Mother?" He reached for her hand. "What is the matter?"

"Oh, William! I never meant—I cannot abide the thought you are marrying because of any pressure I have exerted on you over the years. Do anything but marry without love."

William moved to kneel beside her chair. "Do not fret so." His heart swelled with all of the emotions of his childhood when she began to stroke his hair. "How many years have I ignored your admonitions and pleadings that I find a wife?"

The question had the desired effect. She smiled before the tears could escape. "Then you do love her?"

"I—" He sat back on his heels. "I've never told you that I came within one breath of proposing to Julia twelve years ago."

Bewilderment now filled his mother's expression. "But you did not. Why?"

"Because I had nothing to recommend me. I could not in good conscience have tied her to a poor lieutenant with no prospects at a future."

"And you were too proud to accept her fortune."

"I told myself it was honor, not pride, but you are correct." He flicked at a piece of lint on his sleeve. "Pride stopped me from proposing to her then, and pride kept me from renewing my courtship once I had patronage and promotion and wealth."

"So what changed?"

"She needs me. And my admiral would wish it if he knew the situation."

"And what is the situation?"

He rose and crossed to the window beyond which dawn blossomed. He could not hide the truth from his mother. "Miss Witherington's aunt planned to force Miss—Julia to marry a man no woman should be saddled with. A man who would only bring her misery and who would squander everything Admiral Witherington has worked his entire life to gain."

He propped his forearm against the window frame, lack of sleep making his body heavy. "After we danced, as you know, we took a stroll in the garden. Julia explained her circumstance and her need to marry to protect herself and Admiral Witherington's fortune and properties." He turned to face his mother. "I could not refuse her— especially after we were accosted by her aunt and the baronet."

A slight smile pulled at his mother's lips. "William, dear, you did not say you love her, yet you must have some affection toward her, else you would not be willing to join your life to hers—and she to you."

"She did not ask for my love—what she has requested is the protection of my name. A 'business arrangement,' she called it. She asked we remain married one year, at which time she will request an annulment." He rubbed his eyes. "For this, I get to keep her dowry of thirty thousand pounds and become Admiral Witherington's heir."

Mrs. Ransome gasped. "And you agreed to this?"

"I had no time to consider the ramifications. Her aunt was upon us as soon as the words were out of Julia's mouth. When Pembroke clutched Julia's arm as if to drag her away, I acted without thought. She needed my protection. I gave it to her the only way I could."

Concern creased Mrs. Ransome's brow. "But you will take vows before God. 'Until *death* us do part.'"

"I know." He returned to the chair and melted into it. "Thus my lack of sleep."

"Can you help her without marrying her?"

"I cannot see how. If I simply take her back to Jamaica aboard *Alexandra,* now that the rumor of our engagement has spread, it would ruin her. Her father would waste no time in mustering the Channel Fleet to hunt me down and blow me out of the water. And if she is not legally wed, her fortune—and the admiral's—is still in danger of falling prey to the Pembrokes' schemes."

"But marriage? When your bride enters it with the plan of breaking the vows?"

He leaned forward and clasped his mother's hands. "You know as well as anyone how I have resisted marriage—railed against it at times. But I cannot imagine living out my days alone. Of any woman I have ever met, none other would make so fitting a wife for me as Julia Witherington."

"And the annulment?" Mrs. Ransome asked softly.

"There will be no annulment."

Chapter Twenty-One

After a night spent pacing her room, Julia still could not fathom what had happened. She was to be married to William Ransome, the only man she had ever loved.

But she could not love William. To do so would ruin everything. Her future consisted of becoming mistress of Tierra Dulce and living out the remainder of her years there, in peace. A year from now, he would walk away, and she needed to let him go with no regrets.

She collapsed into her desk chair, resting her head on her folded arms. But she wanted to be married to him. She wanted a child, someone she could give the love her mother had given her. A protégé to teach the running of the plantation. An heir to gain her father's attention and affection. A connection to William for when he went out to sea, and a guarantee he'd come back.

She wanted a real marriage. And she wanted it with William Ransome. But she would never tell him. She would never allow herself to become so vulnerable.

No. In twelve months, she would apply for an annulment and let William walk out of her life again and take her inheritance with him. Raising her head, she dipped the pen in ink and began a letter to her father to explain her actions.

A light tap sounded on the door.

"Yes?" She wiped her quill on the blotter.

Lady Pembroke entered. "Julia? I hoped we might talk."

Julia corked the ink bottle and motioned her aunt toward the chaise. "Please come in."

Augusta sat on the edge of the seat, hands clasped on her knees. "I wanted to apologize for my son's reprehensible behavior last night."

The contriteness in Augusta's tone didn't ring with honesty. Julia straightened the stack of stationery. "He did say quite a lot last night with the apparent intent of offending Captain Ransome. If I recall, you do not think much of my fiancé yourself."

The skin around Augusta's eyes tightened, but she maintained her expression of supplication. "When I said—I did not know then that you held him in high regard or that you were receiving his suit."

Guilt nibbled at Julia's ire. It had not been long ago that she held William in contempt. "I feel it should not matter if I esteemed him, but I am willing to overlook your insults. I am also willing to carry your apology to Captain Ransome. But I must ask you to desist from interfering in my affairs any further."

Tears welled in Augusta's eyes. "I only meant to act in your best interest. You are my niece—daughter of my husband's sister."

Could she possibly be telling the truth? Julia wanted to believe her, but experience told her not to give Augusta her full trust. "My father wished me to have a companion, so I will not ask you to leave. However, as I am now engaged, I will be responsible for my own schedule and for choosing with whom I am to spend my time."

"Yes, of course."

"And because I will be departing for Jamaica before my father's return, at that time, you will need to make other arrangements for your accommodation."

"I understand. To tell you the truth, I have been longing to see Marchwood again." Augusta dabbed her eyes with a handkerchief. "Perhaps, before you leave, you could make time to travel to your mother's home."

"I have seen it before. When I was a child, we lived there with my grandfather until my father took us to Jamaica, and we visited again last time I was in England." Julia tried to conjure an image of the Pembroke ancestral home, but only Tierra Dulce came to mind. "Maybe I should see it before I go. I know my mother would have wanted to visit if…" Julia swallowed a sudden welling of grief. *If she had lived to see her beloved England again.*

Augusta sniffed and smiled broadly. "Then we shall plan for it. In fact, we can time my removal with your visit. Elton can drive us and then bring you back."

"We shall see." The clock chimed the half hour. Julia stood. "If you will excuse me, Aunt, I must dress for an outing. I will be gone the rest of the day—and evening. I will not be home for dinner."

"Oh—well, I shall be dining out this evening, so that is no inconvenience." Augusta paused in the doorway. "Please do not think too ill of your poor cousin. He thought he was protecting you. That was the only reason for his vehemence yestereve."

Julia forced a smile. "Good day, Aunt." She shut the door as soon as her aunt stepped into the hall. She rubbed her eyes and then pulled the bell cord for Nancy. She prayed her aunt's apology was sincere, but she feared the woman only did it to try to ingratiate herself.

She vowed she would not let herself be vulnerable to her aunt's schemes and stratagems again. And Julia never broke her vows.

෴

Although Mrs. Ransome and Susan Yates conversed easily with Julia Witherington, Charlotte found herself mute, shy of this woman who had captured her brother's regard.

Or had she?

Something was going on, as she could tell from the considerable number of silent glances between Mama and William, William and Collin, and Collin and Susan over breakfast this morning whenever Miss Witherington's name entered the conversation. Did William love this woman, or was there another explanation for their sudden and unexpected engagement? Apparently everyone knew the truth. Everyone but Charlotte.

"It is so good to see you again." Susan hooked her arm through Julia's as the Yateses' carriage rolled away from the Witheringtons' massive house.

"It is good to once again be free to do as I choose." Miss Witherington gave Susan a look very much like the ones that had been passed around the breakfast table.

Being purposely left out of the secret annoyed Charlotte. She reconciled herself to being content with her own private affairs.

"Your gown last evening was exquisite." Susan squeezed her friend's hand once more and then let go of her.

The gown Miss Witherington wore last night—ivory and gold satin with a midnight-blue velvet overtunic sparkling with gold embroidery—had seemed a bit ostentatious on first glance, but the longer Charlotte had watched Miss Witherington, the more she'd seemed like an ancient queen, with all the other women in their safe, fashionable white as nothing more than ladies-in-waiting. Even now, dressed in a deep rose muslin, Julia stood out because of her choice not to wear white or another pale color.

"Thank you, Susan. The dressmaker my aunt brought in from London upon our arrival lived in Rome for the last five years. She brought some beautiful pieces of art that showed the colors worn by the ancient Romans. Then she showed us the fabrics she had brought back with her." Miss Witherington quirked the side of her mouth at Susan in a sardonic expression before turning back to Charlotte and Mama. "I know nothing of fashion. In Jamaica, I grew accustomed to dressing in bright colors, so I could not bear the idea of wearing naught but white for months on end."

At the mention of Jamaica, Charlotte's heart leapt. "What is it like— Jamaica?"

Miss Witherington's green eyes twinkled. "It is heaven on earth. Warm waters, sparkling sandy beaches, palm trees—air filled with hundreds of spices." She broke off, her gaze unfocused and distant.

"But what about hurricanes, pirates, yellow fever…?" The letters she kept hidden in the drawer of the wardrobe painted a much grimmer picture of life in the West Indies.

Miss Witherington met Charlotte's gaze with humor playing about her mouth. "Oh, there are occasional storms, and we do lose some of our cargo to pirates, but those problems cannot overshadow the joy of living there." She smiled, and Charlotte wanted to believe this version of life in Jamaica over the more dire images in the letters.

"You were quite young when you moved there, were you not?" Mama adjusted her parasol to better block the sun.

"Yes, ma'am—not yet to my eleventh birthday."

"And you have a brother, if I recall correctly." Mama cocked her head as she always did when facts escaped her.

"I had a brother—a twin brother—but he was lost at sea when we were fifteen."

The fear of losing William, Philip, or James resonated again in Charlotte's heart.

"He was in the navy?" Mama's pale cheeks hinted she, too, feared one of her sons meeting the same fate.

"Yes, ma'am. A midshipman aboard a sloop on the Caribbean station."

Miss Witherington's stoicism impressed Charlotte, whose own throat tightened with emotion. "Was it in battle, then?"

"Charlotte! It is not polite to pry into such matters." Mama never raised her voice above a whisper, but Charlotte cringed as if yelled at.

"I do apologize, Miss Witherington, I meant no disrespect."

"I am not offended. And please, you must call me Julia, as we are to be sisters."

Happiness—nay, joy—filled Charlotte until she thought she might not be able to breathe. *Sisters.*

"Michael's ship was attacked by pirates. All of the crew who were not killed in the battle were ransomed. We never received a ransom request, so we knew he had died trying to defend his ship and mates."

The way Julia told it, her brother could not have met a more glorious end. But to have been killed by pirates…a delicious thrill spilled down Charlotte's spine at the word. What a wild and untamed place the Caribbean was.

She could not wait to experience it for herself.

Chapter Twenty-Two

Julia stepped to the door of the shop, hoping to catch a breath of cooler air, while Susan told the merchant where the fabric should be delivered. Julia would have settled for a blue silk in the first shop, but Susan would not let her, as it was merely "good enough." Susan had taken them to three more warehouses, each being in succession her "favorite of all."

Susan's ability to negotiate with the merchants for the best price and delivery date impressed Julia. The woman would do well in the sugar market in Kingston, trying to get the highest price from the buyers, an annual task Julia dreaded.

"Just one more stop, ladies, and then we can return home, where tea will be ready for us."

In and out of the shops along High Street, Susan introduced Julia and the Ransome ladies to other officers' wives, ranging from middle-aged and more wealthy than Julia could imagine to young women barely into their twenties trying to live on half-pay while their husbands vied for assignment in the reduced fleet of ships. Julia sympathized with the unfortunate girls and their lot, trying to stretch ten guineas into a hundred to make a home for their husbands and, in most cases, children.

"Isn't there anything that can be done to help them?" Mrs. Ransome asked as Susan opened the door of a millinery shop. "Cannot all the officers wives' take up a collection to help out the poorest among them? To make sure their children are not going hungry?"

Susan glanced over her shoulder at the young woman they'd just exchanged pleasantries with. "Julia and I assist with the Naval Family Aid Society. 'Tis hard, now, with the war over and so many officers on half-pay and commanders disrated back down to lieutenant rank or worse. We are blessed that William and Collin have the admiral's patronage to further their careers."

"Yes, but they have had success throughout their years at sea, as have my other two sons. Even had they been turned out, they would still be able to live well." Mrs. Ransome fingered the stiff lace on the brim of a straw bonnet.

"Collin as well. Do you know, he told me that while he is on Caribbean station, he plans to investigate the possibility of buying land there? Can you imagine us owning land in the West Indies?"

"Only if you learn that those of us who live there do not refer to it as the 'West Indies.' Tell Collin that I shall be delighted to assist him in seeking out the best property. And I'll make certain it is within easy travel of Tierra Dulce."

Susan grinned. "Yes, that was my thought as well." Without warning, her face paled and she staggered.

Julia grabbed Susan's shoulders before she fell into a hat rack. "Are you unwell?"

After a few deep, gulping breaths, Susan managed to right herself. "Just the heat, I fear. If it gets hotter than this in your Jamaica, I do not know how you survive it."

"You'll learn to love it." Julia continued to hold Susan's shoulders until certain she could stand under her own power.

"I am certain I will."

Julia picked up a wide-brimmed bonnet piled high with silk flowers and set it on her head. "How do I look?"

Susan eyed her, mouth pursed. "You are my dearest friend in the world, Julia. But you are correct—you have no sense of fashion."

With a laugh, Julia took off the hat. She glanced over her shoulder and saw Mrs. Ransome and Charlotte on the other side of the store, examining the wide assortment of ribbons.

"You have shown more restraint this morning than I thought possible, Susan. I know you are bursting to hear what transpired last night."

The remaining vestiges of malaise in Susan's expression vanished, and she clasped Julia's forearm. "You could not speak in front of Mrs. Ransome or Charlotte, so I knew better than to plague you with questions."

In a low whisper, although she and Susan were quite alone, Julia recounted everything she could remember of her stroll through the garden with William—and the events thereafter. Several times, Susan covered her mouth to stifle a gasp.

"No wonder you were so quiet and withdrawn after you and William returned from the garden. If she were not your aunt, what words I would have to say about Lady Pembroke."

Julia absently picked up another hat to try on. "If she were not my aunt, I would not be in this predicament." She continued on to tell Susan about her exchange with Augusta this morning.

"Has she mentioned anything about the chest's being gone?"

"No. She has either not risked returning to look for it, or she knows I removed it because I suspected her." Julia turned to look in a mirror and grimaced at the sallow tone the orange bonnet gave her skin.

"What makes you believe she will not do whatever she can to interfere with your engagement to William? To find a way to force you into marrying Sir Drake?" Susan whispered.

"I hope I am too intelligent for that. I know she is not being completely honest with me, so I will have a hard time believing anything she tells me. But if you do not see or hear from me two days together, you might want to pay a call." Julia removed a lacy green chapeau and set the bonnet Susan handed her on her head. "I have written to my father and will be very much surprised if he does not write to her by express, forbidding her interference."

Susan cleared her throat. "Oh, Mrs. Ransome, what a lovely turban."

Julia turned to see the two Ransome women approaching.

William's mother held up the blue and burgundy silk-wrapped

headpiece. "Do you think so? Charlotte assures me it is the height of fashion and that it will compliment the gown I wore last evening."

"Charlotte is blessed with an eye for fashion," Susan assured the older woman. "Now, Mrs. Ransome, I could use your influence with your daughter-to-be."

Guilt dried Julia's mouth at Mrs. Ransome's beatific gaze.

"Only if it is something that will make dear Julia happy."

"You must help me convince *dear* Julia—now she is to be an old married woman like us—that she must purchase at least a gross of mobcaps." Susan thrust a stack of the frilly, white-muslin head coverings toward Julia.

Julia gaped at the symbols of both spinster- and matronhood and then laughed. "I will start wearing one of those when you do, Susan Yates, and not a day before."

Although she did not purchase one of the mobcaps, Julia did buy the small bonnet with a narrow straw brim and green-satin crown, which Susan said made her eyes positively glow. Julia's and Mrs. Ransome's bandboxes were added to the pile of packages on the floor of the barouche, leaving little room for their feet. Susan handed several items up into the seat beside the driver.

"Tea will be ready when we get home, and then we can take a rest." Susan fanned her flushed face vigorously. "And mayhap freshen ourselves before dinner."

Julia stifled a groan, her body aching, as she leaned against the plush seat. What she needed was a nice long swim in the cove, the warm Caribbean water rolling over her, rocking her like a baby in a cradle.

The rhythm of the carriage lulled her into a stupor and must have done the same to the others, as each remained silent the entire trip to the Yateses' home.

Julia could practically hear her bones creak when she climbed out and staggered through the front gate. She pulled up in surprise when a tall, burly man with a tangle of dark hair opened the door.

He lifted his hand toward his head, stopped, and then gave a jerky bow, as if unfamiliar with the action. "G'day, ma'am." He stood, hesitated again, then cleared his throat. "Ah, can—may I be of assistance wi' your parcels?"

"There are quite a few packages in the carriage, Mr....?" She raised her brows in question.

He knuckled his forehead. "Dawling, ma'am. Steward—er, valet, that is, to Captain Ransome."

Julia's stomach twisted. One of William's crew right here in Susan's home? His reaction to her would be a good indication of how the others might respond.

"Oh, wonderful. You've met Dawling." Susan stopped beside Julia on the stoop. "Dawling, this is Miss Witherington—Captain Ransome's fiancée."

The sailor's pock-scarred face broke into an enormous smile. "Miss Witherington, ma'am—miss." He knuckled his forehead again, while also executing another twitchy bow. "I'm right chuffed to meet you, ma'am—miss. If there be anything you need whilst you're here, you just call for me. Ol' Archie Dawling's your man."

Susan's tinkling laugh danced across the foyer. Inside the large entry hall, a young maid took their gloves and spencers.

"Have Agatha serve tea in the garden, please, Dawling." Susan called over her shoulder. "It's far too hot to stay indoors. Come, Mrs. Ransome, Julia, Charlotte."

"Poor fellow." Mrs. Ransome said with a slight frown. "William is so good to have kept him on—first as his steward, now as his valet. But he does seem to be learning quickly for someone who never apprenticed on a household staff." She turned to Julia. "He might make a decent servant yet. I am certain you will see to his continued training."

Julia swallowed hard. She did not like thinking of how things might be once she boarded William's ship. "I will do my best, ma'am."

Twenty minutes later, settled into a thick-cushioned rattan chair under the shade of an arbor in the back garden, Julia struggled to keep her eyes open. Mrs. Ransome, beneath the wide brim of her straw bonnet, seemed to have dozed off; Miss Ransome returned inside, claiming the need to write a letter. Susan fanned herself vigorously in spite of the breeze. Rather than being flushed with heat, Susan's cheeks looked too pale, her lips drawn in a tight line.

Julia frowned and leaned forward, grasping the arm of Susan's chair. "Are you quite all right?"

Susan patted her hand. "Just a bit peaky. Nothing a bit of a rest-up won't remedy. I still do not understand how you can bear heat worse than this. You must occasionally be scandalous and leave off wearing a spencer when going out in public."

"Jamaica is much warmer than this, but the ocean breeze makes it bearable. Most of the time, when not going in public, I've adopted the local way of dressing." Julia went on to describe the lightweight cotton blouses and skirts she wore around the plantation.

The kitchen maid arrived with the tea tray. Famished, Julia helped herself to a scone with clotted cream and jam, but she stopped after a few bites when she noticed Susan wasn't touching her tea or any of the pastries and looked paler than before.

She set her plate on the low table between their chairs. "Susan, I can see you aren't well." She kept her voice low so as not to awaken Mrs. Ransome and cause undue concern. "Shall I fetch Agatha and have her bring a cordial to you?"

Susan managed a weak smile and started to rise. "You are too good to me, dear Julia. If you will not take offense, I do believe I will retire to my room—"

Julia leapt out of her seat to catch Susan before her friend collapsed face-first on the ground. She eased herself and Susan down onto the grass, Susan's head cushioned on her lap, and reached for the silver bell on the tea tray.

Mrs. Ransome awoke with a slight gasp, knelt beside Julia, and waved a vial of salts beneath Susan's nose. Susan twitched and opened her eyes, embarrassment bringing color back to her face.

"I'm terribly sorry." Susan struggled to sit up, but Julia, larger and stronger, held her still.

"Never you mind about that." Julia smoothed her friend's now wild reddish-gold curls back from her face. "I just want to ensure you aren't ill."

Mrs. Ransome felt Susan's forehead, as if checking for fever. "My dear, this may seem like an indelicate question, so please forgive me. How far along is your pregnancy?"

Susan's eyes widened. "I am not...I cannot. Two years ago, after my last miscarriage, the doctor told me..."

Mrs. Ransome scrutinized her. "Doctors are not always right. I have been a midwife most of my life. I know when a woman is with child before she does in most cases."

"I—you—are you certain?" Julia asked Mrs. Ransome, nearly choking on a jumble of emotions.

"I have never yet been wrong. But Susan, you should go upstairs and rest now. All the heat and activity of this morning is not good for you."

Under mostly her own power and apologizing all the way, Susan made it to her bedchamber, assisted by Julia and Mrs. Ransome, followed by the housekeeper. Susan's maid took over her care once they arrived.

Assured her friend was well, Julia followed the housekeeper down the hall to Charlotte's room. Lace curtains billowed in the breeze, and bright splashes of silk fabric draped nearly every stationary piece of furniture. Julia smiled; the room was so like Susan.

A baby.

The fleeting thought that Julia might convince Susan to accompany Collin to Jamaica, then stay on at Tierra Dulce for a year or more, came back to haunt her. Never would Collin—nor Julia herself—allow Susan to sail in her condition.

"Julia, is Charlotte—?" Mrs. Ransome leaned her head into the room and frowned. "I wonder where that girl has gotten off to." Shaking her head, she left.

A washstand near a tall painted screen beckoned. Julia poured lilac-scented water into the basin and used the soft cloth to soothe her hot, sticky skin. She'd best enjoy this kind of luxury while she could. Such indulgences wouldn't be available on board ship.

The breeze wafting into the room did little to provide relief from the heat. Julia crossed to the large bed to lie down.

A baby. The fulfillment of Susan's greatest wishes and prayers.

Would it be a cherub of a little boy with his mother's blue eyes and ginger hair? Or a golden-crowned girl with Collin's brown eyes and dimples? If Susan and Collin were to have a son, and Julia and William a daughter—

She sat bolt upright. Allowing herself to continue that thought would only jeopardize her plan to remain distant. Although physically exhausted, she gave up trying to rest. She found her way downstairs and outside. The garden was large for a townhouse of this size, with a fountain surrounded by willows beyond the arbor where they had taken tea earlier. The manicured grass tickled her bare feet.

Looking over her shoulder to ensure no one from the house could see her, Julia lifted her skirts and stepped into the shallow pool surrounding the water-spouting swan. The cobblestone under her feet was nothing like the soft sand of her beach, but the cool water lapping about her ankles nearly brought tears of joy to her eyes.

She danced and splashed her way across and around the wide basin and laughed when she lost her footing and sat down hard in the water, feeling good for the first time in days.

Chapter Twenty-Three

Thank you, Dawling." William surrendered his hat and coat to his man. "Any correspondence I should know of?"

"Nothing of significance, sir." A smile played about the sailor's mouth.

William, hot and exhausted after his walk back from the dockyard, cared not if the steward held a secret from him. "Is Captain Yates in his library?"

"No, sir. Captain Yates has not yet returned from the port Admiralty. Miss Ransome is in there, writing letters. Mrs. Ransome and Mrs. Yates are resting." Dawling's eyes took on a sly gleam. "Miss Witherington, however, is in the garden."

How could he have forgotten Julia was to have spent the day with the women? "I can see you would like to say more, Dawling, so out with it."

"Oh, sir, if I may make so bold as to say, she is one of the loveliest ladies I've ever clapped eyes onto. Does she really see to the running of the admiral's sugar plantation?"

William frowned and loosened his cravat. "Where did you hear that?"

"All the servants here talk of it."

"Hmm." William took his handkerchief from the coat now folded over his steward's arm and swabbed the sweat from his face. "Thank you, Dawling. That will be all."

"Aye, aye, sir." Dawling saluted and disappeared through the service door.

William set his foot on the bottom step but then stopped. He wanted to review the charts, but he needed Collin to sit with him to plan their course, as Collin had sailed the waters to the southwest more recently. Additionally, he did not want to disturb his sister's letter writing.

Miss Witherington, however, is in the garden. The convoy's course was not the only one in need of plotting. With a sigh, he turned and exited the rear of the house. The hot July sun hung at half-mast in the west. How Julia could be out in this heat was beyond his fathoming. He frowned, not seeing her in one of the chairs under the arbor, and let his gaze sweep the confines of the yard. Perhaps she'd gone inside without Dawling's notice.

The splash of water caught his attention. Julia lay on the grass in the shade of dangling willow branches, her bare feet in the shallow pool under the fountain. She didn't stir, and when he drew closer, the reason became apparent: She was sound asleep.

He sank onto a nearby stone bench. She looked as if she'd gone for a swim—her dress wet and crumpled, her damp hair loose and curling about her cheeks.

A burning tingle crept across his skin that had nothing to do with the sun. In marrying Julia Witherington, he would be blessed with a wife who not only knew the naval life intimately but also was beautiful, intelligent, and strong—strong enough to withstand long separations and the anxiety they created.

Content and starting to relax for the first time since he'd dropped anchor in Spithead a fortnight ago, William shrugged out of his waistcoat, untucked his shirt, and removed his neckcloth.

The water arching out of the marble swan's mouth was too great a siren. He slipped out of his shoes and stockings, stepped into the pool, and lowered his head under the stream. His shirt and trousers were soaked nearly through by the time he felt human again, but after his long, hot walk, his dinner companions might thank him for his improvised bath.

He ran his fingers through his hair, doing his best to keep the water from dripping into his eyes. Wiping his face with the hem of his shirt, a slight noise, suspiciously like a gasp, caught his ear. He spun to face Julia.

Hot embarrassment crept up the back of his neck. The woman who moments before had looked so innocent and peaceful now sat up, her full bottom lip caught between her teeth in what looked like an attempt to keep from laughing. At him.

Pride writhed in his chest like a great sea-monster, swelling the heat up into his face. Swallowing hard and pushing the vainglory aside, he covered the short distance between them in a few steps, bowed in greeting…and shook like a dog, spraying her with water.

Julia's full, rich laughter conquered the beast of pride within him. "Is that your customary greeting, Captain Ransome?"

Julia's rosy cheeks tempted William's fingers, but he resisted touching her. She pulled her feet out of the water, moved back to lean against the tree, and covered her feet with her skirt.

"Only when caught standing in the middle of a fountain." He collapsed onto the grass beside her, stretching out on his back, hands pillowed behind his head. "Have you spoken with your aunt today?"

The smile melted from Julia's expression. "Lady Pembroke sends her apology for her son's behavior last night."

"And when will she be removing herself from your home?"

She made a soft, resigned sound in the back of her throat. "Father wished me to have a companion in his absence."

"But after everything—" He frowned, consternated at Julia's decision. "The strongbox…and she tried to isolate you from your friends…"

Julia's green eyes turned stormy. "I have spoken with her. She said she was only trying to act in my best interest."

"You cannot possibly believe her." If William had to remove Julia from her father's house to get her away from that harpy—

"No." She wrapped her arms around her knees and some of the sharpness left her expression. "But she is family, and I cannot throw her out in to the street when she has asked my forgiveness."

"Into the street? Come now, Julia. Why cannot she go and stay with that son of hers?"

Even with her mouth pinched and brows furrowed, Julia was beautiful. "The house is apparently in disrepair and under renovation. Those are no conditions for a woman to live in."

Pride in her compassion and frustration at her willfulness threatened to tear asunder his composure. "Very well. But please promise me you will take all due caution in your interactions with her and will not allow her to gain the weather gauge on you."

The dimples reappeared in her cheeks. "Aye, aye, sir."

The war inside him stilled at her smile.

She leaned her head back against the tree trunk. "I have no delusions that she is truly repentant and know she will do whatever she can to see her desires fulfilled."

"One of those desires being your union with her son?"

"Only as a means to her own ends. I have a feeling her motive for wanting the marriage is less about saving the Pembroke name and more about gaining a house in London, along with invitations to all the best events, participation in the intrigues of the courtiers, and a role in the passing and embellishment of the latest social gossip."

"Whereas intrigues and gossip hold no interest for you." He picked a piece of grass off the hem of Julia's skirt and wrapped it around his finger, trying not to lose himself in the refreshing emerald depths of her eyes. "Nor beaux, if the gossipmongers are to be believed."

Julia stared at the fountain, cheeks even pinker than before. "Beaux? I do not know what gossip you may have heard, sir, but beaux have been significantly lacking in my life for many years now."

"Indeed?" He rolled the grass blade between his fingers.

A saucy grin stole over her lips. "There was, of course, the governor's son. He asked for my hand upon our second meeting. I was only fifteen at the time, and my mother thought me too young. He was merely seventeen, and I thought him too young. Five years later when he asked again, I knew him too well to say yes."

William rolled onto his side and propped up on his elbow. "And was there no one else who captured your regard?"

"Only one. A sailor. Handsome, with blue eyes. Poor, but respected and admired by his peers. I had great hopes he would propose to me; but, alas, his feelings turned out to be different from mine." She kept her eyes pointedly away from him.

Hope surged in his chest—hope she might still love him. "Perhaps it wasn't that his feelings were different. Maybe he wanted to make something of himself, to prove himself worthy of a lady of quality like you."

Deep crimson flooded Julia's cheeks. "Then why did he not explain himself? Or renew his addresses when fortune and promotion raised him to a worthy rank?"

He sat up, bringing his face within inches of hers. "Because I convinced myself you would never be able to forgive me—that you no longer cared for me."

She finally turned to look at him, wide eyes searching his with an intensity that made him dig his toes into the grass. "For a while, for years in truth, I thought that was true as well." Her fingertips touched his cheek.

He swallowed hard, skin burning from the too-brief caress. The emotions vying for release would capsize him if he did not redirect the conversation. "I went to see the bishop this morning."

She dropped her gaze to her skirt. "You did?"

"Aye." He shifted position to put a few more inches between them. "I have secured the special license."

Julia closed her eyes, and a tear escaped down her cheek.

"What is this?" He dashed away the crystal droplet with his thumb.

"I am no better than my aunt and cousin."

He grasped her shoulders and turned her to face him. "Explain."

Her green eyes snapped to his at the command. "I have manipulated you into a decision with no thought to your wishes or desires—only my own."

William cupped her face in his hands. "Do not compare your actions to theirs. You were open and forthcoming with me about your reason for asking me to marry you. I would not have made an enemy of the Pembrokes if I did not wish to help you."

The trust that flooded Julia's gaze took William back twelve years to another garden, another moment when he stood on this same precipice. He leaned closer, tracing the contour of her lips with his eyes. One kiss and she would understand his heart—

"William! William!"

For the first time in his life, William hated Collin Yates.

৩৪৯৯৯

"What is wrong with me, letting my emotions show in such a way?" Julia tugged the comb through her snarled hair. Her heart still raced, thinking of how close she'd come to letting William kiss her. "I cannot, cannot, *cannot* allow that to happen again."

She plaited her hair and crossed to the window. The tendril limbs of the willow tree beside the fountain seemed to mock her as they danced and whispered her secret in the wind. She should never have agreed to spending the day here. To think she had actually hoped she would be able to spend time with William.

And who could have imagined that in a damp, loose-flowing white shirt, fawn trousers, and barefooted, he would be even more handsome—

No! She thrust the curtains closed and turned her back to the window. The lace drapes billowed in protest behind her. He admitted he'd agreed to her scheme only out of a wish to help her, not because he still harbored any affection for her. Yet why would he have been about to kiss her if he had no feelings for her?

Her love for William Ransome chafed her spirit—very much like her damp undergarments were starting to chafe her skin. Her valise sat on the floor in front of the wardrobe. She grabbed it and set it on the vanity table.

Something fluttered to the floor. Julia stooped to pick it up. A piece of paper, cramped writing covering both sides. Had it fallen out of her bag? She moved back toward the window for better light. No salutation—the writing started at the top of the page.

> I am writing this with much haste to get it out in the next packet, so forgive me if I seem abrupt. But I can no longer deny my feelings or hide them from you. I love you. I have no right to ask you to requite me. I am a pauper who hangs his hopes that a princess could deign to love him in return.

She smiled. It must be a page from one of Collin's old letters to Susan while they were courting. She really should set it aside, take it back to Susan…but curiosity about her friend's past led her eyes to the next paragraph.

> I wish I could be there to ask you this in person, but I do not know when I shall be able to return to England. So I must do the unthinkable and write it to you in a letter.
> My darling Charlotte, will you marry me—

Julia gasped and thrust the piece of paper behind her back. Charlotte? Alarmed, she glanced toward the door and then hurried back over to the—why had it been on the floor near the armoire? Uncertain, she carefully set the page where her valise had been and backed away from it. Sitting sideways in the vanity-table chair, she stared at the parchment.

Charlotte had a suitor. One who was, apparently, out of the country.

The crack of something hard hitting the floor made her jump. She quickly turned to face the mirror.

Charlotte entered, clutching a stack of stationery to her chest. She bent down to retrieve her dropped ink bottle.

Julia forced a smile for William's sister. "I am sorry you have had to give up your privacy for me, Charlotte."

"It is no bother—I volunteered to share." Charlotte stopped at the small desk, deposited the writing implements atop it, and crossed to the wardrobe.

"Do you find Portsmouth to your liking?" Julia asked, watching the younger woman in the reflection.

"Oh, yes." With her back turned, Charlotte rummaged in one of the armoire drawers. "There are ever so many more diversions in Portsmouth than in Gateacre or Liverpool. I never expected I would attend a formal dinner and a ball my first weeks in town."

"And you do not go to many balls at home?" Julia fidgeted with the clasp on her valise, still watching Charlotte in the mirror.

"A few every year, some dances in homes, but nothing akin to last night." Charlotte paused, looked at the floor, and stiffened.

Julia dragged her bag into her lap and began to sort through the items she'd packed as if searching for something. "Yes, last night's event was…memorable." From the corner of her eye, she caught the motion of Charlotte quickly bending, straightening, and then hastily stuffing the stray page into a muslin-wrapped packet which she then tucked into the wardrobe. The letter had been hidden in one of Charlotte's drawers…meaning her family most likely did not know of the proposal. Had Charlotte accepted?

She could think of nothing else to say, so she kept rifling through her packed toiletries and fresh undergarments. Charlotte returned to the desk to put away the stationery.

Julia turned to look at Charlotte when the silence between them grew too heavy, afraid she might blurt out her knowledge of the letter. "I do apologize. I am not nearly as vivacious and lively a companion as Susan. If we are to be sisters, we should take what time we have to get to know each other better."

Charlotte's shoulders seemed to lose some of their tension. "I agree."

"Then what may I tell you about myself you do not already know?" Talking about herself would get her mind off that letter—would keep her from probing for more information.

"I wondered, if I am not making too bold to ask, and if it is not too painful for you, if you would tell me about your brother."

Ah. Charlotte's intended must be a sailor, so it was no wonder she exhibited such interest in all things naval. If Julia opened up about her past, if they became close, perhaps Charlotte might confide in her. "He had no love for book-learning or numbers. But when we sailed to Jamaica, he reveled in working below decks as a powder monkey—"

Charlotte gasped. "Your father allowed your brother to perform such a dangerous task? I have heard that more boys are killed running the powder to the gun crews than any other assignment."

"We had no cause for the cannon to be run out, except for daily inspection and exercise. Father thought it would be good training for him, in preparation for becoming a midshipman. He did seem to learn and remember more from those weeks than the two years of studying we did before he signed onto his first ship."

Settling onto the chaise, Charlotte listened with rapt attention, appearing as though trying to memorize every detail Julia shared of her brother.

Julia moved from the vanity to sit on the cedar chest at the end of the bed, nearer the chaise. "For the three years Michael was on *Sparrow,* they had great success hunting down privateers. Because of that, they were assigned to a squadron with the assignment of hunting down one of the worst pirates the Caribbean has ever seen: Shaw. They captured one of Shaw's sloops and took it into Port Royal as a prize. Our father was en route to Jamaica, and Michael greatly looked forward to a week's leave to see us both—and Mother, of course."

Charlotte's blue eyes took on a sheen of excitement and anticipation. She leaned forward. "I am certain you were happy to see him as well."

"We did not have the chance. Just two days after *Sparrow* pulled out of Port Royal, Shaw attacked." Julia rubbed her arms as a sudden chill danced across her skin at the memory. "When Father arrived in Kingston and heard the news, he immediately put back out to sea, sending word express to Tierra Dulce of his intentions to hunt down Shaw and find Michael."

Charlotte wrapped her arms around her middle. "Did he? Did he find the pirate?"

Lost in the sensation that her brother wasn't dead—a feeling that had not left her in fifteen years—Julia shook her head. "No. Papa narrowly escaped court-martial for insubordination."

"What? The famous Admiral Sir Edward Witherington? They should have given him a commendation for taking such swift action."

Shaking off the bleak memories, Julia chuckled at Charlotte's appellation of her father as *famous*. "He was not yet an admiral, but a commodore with three other ships under his direct command—ships that had helped him guard a supply convoy from England. He risked provoking the wrath of the admiral of the Caribbean fleet by taking matters into his own hands." She stood and moved to the window. "He returned to Tierra Dulce for nearly a week—but he was riddled with grief, and being on land only made it worse. My mother lost all interest in the plantation after that."

"And your father?" Charlotte's voice came out thick.

Julia's own throat tightened, picturing her mother's sunken cheeks, hollow eyes. "He returned to the life he knew best: the sea. Being on *Indomitable,* being with his crew, was the best salve for his grief." She pressed her lips together and closed her eyes briefly. "And I believe that your brother—that William was a great comfort to him."

"As he had been for William when our father died. It reminds me of the passage of Scripture in which Saint Paul wrote that God has adopted us as his children. You are blessed to have a father who can exhibit such love and compassion for others."

Julia's breathing stopped. An old memory—older than those she'd just dredged up—nibbled the back of her mind. A year before Michael had gone to sea, they'd received a letter in which her father had written about, among others, William Ransome's successes in battle. Julia asked Michael if it bothered him, their father's always lauding the boys under his command.

What was it Michael had said? *"I am proud to be the son of a man who can love others the way God loves us—as sons."*

The door banged open, and they both jumped.

Susan burst into the room. "Julia, you must come immediately!"

"Are you unwell?" Julia moved faster than seemed possible, attaining Susan's side in an instant.

"It is Collin. Come, you must speak to him." Susan grabbed her hand and pulled her from the room.

Julia almost tripped twice running down the stairs behind her friend. "What is it? What's wrong?"

Susan strode into Collin's study. Collin leaned against the edge of his desk, thick arms folded across his chest, expression furious.

"Julia, you must convince him." Susan's voice contained a shrillness Julia had never heard before.

"I will not be swayed by either of you." Collin's voice had taken an opposite turn—gruff and low.

"Susan, please tell me—"

"Jamaica!" Susan threw her hands in the air. "Tell him—convince him that if it is safe for you to travel to Jamaica on board *your* husband's ship, it is perfectly safe for me to travel with *my* husband."

Oh, dear Lord, how did I get pulled into the middle of this? "Susan, I do not think I—"

"You have made the trip, Julia. You know what it is like. I am healthy as a stoat, and if need be, I can work hard."

Somehow, Julia found that hard to fathom. "I believe this is something for you and Collin to work out."

"Thank you, Miss Witherington." Collin shot a triumphant glance at his wife.

Susan, for her part, looked as if Julia had betrayed her. "But I thought you, if anyone, would see my point."

"Maybe I have painted a false picture of what life is like—both on the ship and in Jamaica. It is primitive—primitive and harsh under the best of circumstances. And in your cond—" Julia clapped her hand over her mouth, eyes widening, not knowing if Susan had yet informed her husband of her condition.

Collin's eyes snapped to Susan's face. "Condition? What condition?"

He surged to his feet and bounded to his wife, clasping her shoulders.

Susan's expression changed from hurt to rapturous in a flash. "I was saving that news to tell you after you agreed to take me with you. We're going to have a baby."

"We're—" Collin's mouth flapped open and closed a couple of times before he lifted his wife from the floor and spun around.

Julia slipped out the door and closed it behind her, happy to be out of the line of fire but saddened by the knowledge she would probably never see Collin and Susan's baby.

Chapter Twenty-Four

Drake chewed the end of his cigar as he worked on folding and tying the black cravat into an elaborate confection. After several minutes, he pinned it with one of the few pieces of family jewelry he had not yet sold off—a filigree pin set with a large ruby etched with the Pembroke coat of arms.

He shrugged into his plum, swallow-tailed jacket and looked at the combination of the color with the waistcoat—light green brocaded with gold—and tan trousers. He quite liked the effect. Although he loathed attending church, to save what might remain of his reputation, he must put forth the effort to appear unaffected by Julia Witherington's betrayal of his every intention.

Once he arrived at St. Thomas's Church, he walked toward the entrance with purpose, his silver-tipped cane punctuating his steps. He stopped among a throng of acquaintances near the gate to the churchyard, where he could observe the arrivals of the remainder of Portsmouth society.

His eyes narrowed when he recognized a tall man with dark hair. Ransome stood with a small group—including the very fetching Miss Charlotte Ransome—and although he conversed with them, Ransome appeared to be watching the arriving carriages for one in particular.

The Witherington barouche arrived with only a few minutes to spare before the bells would sound the beginning of liturgy. Ransome separated himself from his friends and approached the carriage. The sea captain visibly flinched and took a step back when Lady Pembroke stepped down from the conveyance with the assistance of a footman.

Drake's mother did her best to give the usurper a pleasant greeting, which was met by a terse bow. Insufferable social climber.

Augusta looked around the crowd, her gaze coming to rest on Drake for a brief moment. She strode toward the churchyard gate. Ransome offered his hand to Julia to assist her from the carriage. Drake did not remove his attention from them while he walked to the gate to meet his mother. The blush that covered Julia Witherington's cheeks as she gazed up at the sailor fueled the flame of Drake's desire to claim her inheritance for himself.

"Good morning, son," Augusta greeted.

"Good morning, Mother." He turned and offered his arm.

They entered the sanctuary, Drake deigning to speak to only those to whom his mother spoke, ignoring those she ignored.

He pressed his lips close to her ear. "Have you decided yet how we are going to regain the Witherington fortune?"

"I have a few ideas—the girl was off gallivanting with those navy people all day Friday, and yesterday she was at Lady Dalrymple's for most of the day, so I've had no chance to try to return myself to her good opinion."

The Pembroke pew sat three rows behind the pew Sir Edward had endowed, and Julia took advantage of her father's bench by inviting not just Ransome but also the others of his group to sit there with her.

The droning and wailing of the pipe organ drowned out all whispered conversations around them, but Drake had seen the curious and adoring looks cast at Julia and Ransome as the couple processed down the central aisle. From the twitter that rose up at their arrival, one would think this was their wedding, not another long, boring, Sunday morning service.

His mother leaned in close again. "I did, however, plant the idea that she accompany me to Marchwood before her wedding. Once she is there, we could find a way to ensure she stays…"

Drake glared at the mass of dark curls twined with gold ribbon three rows in front of him. White was Julia's most becoming color, and she looked as near to pretty this morning as he had ever seen her. Ransome leaned over to hear something she was saying.

A dagger of anger stabbed Drake's gut. How dare Ransome come in and take what rightfully belonged to him? What right had this sailor— a man, as Drake himself had so aptly pointed out Thursday evening, with no name of merit and no family connections at all—to claim the inheritance that would restore the preeminence of the Pembroke mills and farms, would raise Drake to the living he should enjoy as a baronet, would bring a lifetime of excessive income from the plantation to allow Drake to game and dally as much as he pleased?

Furious with determination, Drake lifted his gaze to the cross hanging over the altar. No matter what it took, he would have Julia Witherington's thirty thousand pounds.

∽⊱⊰∾

William willed his hand not to shake as he opened his prayer book and held it so Julia could follow along with him. He thought he had reconciled himself to their new status of being betrothed, yet his initial glimpse of her this morning struck him as if it had been their first introduction. The gentle lilt of her voice as she recited the prayers and responses to the Scriptures wove a tapestry around William's heart that both enraptured and frightened him.

The organ piped the introduction to a hymn, and William stood along with the rest of the congregation. Conscious of Julia at his side, he mouthed the words but allowed no sound to pass through his lips. He stole a glance at her and found her looking up at him, a puzzled expression on her face as she sang the sacred song with a strong, clear voice. Heat climbed the back of his neck into his face. He dropped his gaze to her hymnal and then returned his attention to the front of the chancel.

The service continued, almost beyond his notice. Focusing on the stained glass representations of scenes from the Bible finally cleared William's thinking enough to allow his soul to commune with God.

Since the ball Thursday, he had done little but worry—about his crew's reaction to Julia, about her presence on the voyage, about how his life would change, about his ability to be a good and godly husband. Sitting in the church, listening to the rector's soliloquy, William once again drew close to God and did as the apostle Peter bade, casting his cares upon the Lord.

Questions lingered in his mind, but the worries, the concerns, and the doubts no longer anchored his soul in their depths. Marrying Julia was the right course of action. A feeling of relief, a sense that God was pleased with his decision, lifted his spirits and cleared his mind.

When the service ended, William offered his right arm to Julia, his left to his mother. The shy smile Julia bestowed upon him seemed the final signal from God that all would be well.

"Captain Ransome, Miss Witherington, Mrs. Ransome." Admiral Glover flourished a bow to the ladies and then turned to William. "Captain, I wonder if I might have a moment of your time." The admiral indicated a more private setting with a jerk of his head.

"Aye, Admiral. Mother, Julia, please excuse me." He followed the small-statured admiral to a vacant spot near the rostrum and stood at attention even though neither he nor Glover was in uniform.

"Before Sir Edward departed for London, he commissioned me to give you this, should it become necessary." Admiral Glover extended a thick, twine-bound packet.

William accepted it and read his own name in Admiral Witherington's hand. He had received final orders before Sir Edward departed for London. What could the admiral have possibly left out? "Thank you, sir."

"Not at all." Admiral Glover smiled slyly. "I understand congratulations are in order—though not of surprise to anyone. I've always said it would be a lucky man to win the hand of Miss Julia Witherington."

"It is a blessing, to be sure, sir." William itched to cut the twine binding the packet and see—was it a letter of promotion?

"As you are marrying before her father returns, I believe I shall offer my services as a proxy to walk her down the aisle. Never married myself—too old for Miss Julia." Glover elbowed William and winked at him. "She is more like a dear niece to me, so never fear on that point."

William kept his expression neutral, though he remembered why he found Admiral Glover's company distasteful in private or large doses. "Aye, sir."

"Well, well. Come now, let us return to the ladies. Oh, and I would like to see you and Captain Yates at the port Admiralty Wednesday morning to review your course charts."

"Aye, aye, sir." William bowed in lieu of saluting and returned to his family and friends.

Collin quirked an eyebrow in question. William shook his head and slid the packet into his inside coat pocket.

"And have you not yet heard from your father?" Mrs. Hinds now stood beside Julia. "I received a note from my Frederick the day of the Fairfax ball—although only a few lines to let me know of their safe arrival. He expects they will be constantly occupied from dawn to midnight every day. So if your father has not written, he has most likely not had the time."

Julia smiled at the admiral's wife, but the slight crease between her brows remained.

"Oh, Captain Ransome." Mrs. Hinds beamed at him. "I wish you joy in your engagement to Miss Witherington."

William inclined his head, remembering her words at the concert nearly a fortnight ago. "Thank you, Mrs. Hinds. I trust if you have need of anything you will let me know; I will be honored to be of service to you."

Her smile added beauty to her otherwise plain features. "Thank you, Captain."

"I do apologize, but I see my aunt is nearing the door. I must give my farewells and depart with her." Julia accepted a hug from Susan before turning toward the back of the sanctuary.

William excused himself as well and offered Julia his arm. She hesitated a moment before taking it.

"My officers report back to me Thursday. Collin and Susan have asked me to invite them for dinner that evening. I hope you might join us so you can meet them."

"I would be delighted."

"I will let Susan know." He glanced at her, but the brim of her bonnet hid her eyes. "You have not heard from your father since his arrival in London?"

"No. But I am certain I shall receive a letter soon. He is an excellent correspondent."

"Yes. I have always found him to be so." William guided Julia through the throng of people crowding the door and squinted against the bright sunlight outside, the narrow brim of his hat providing no shade. "Whenever I did something for which my name appeared in the *Gazette* or that garnered the attention of the navy's rumor mill, I received a letter from Sir Edward—especially if word reached him I might not be performing up to his high expectations."

"My brother received many such letters as well—though his took much longer to arrive, certainly." She looked up to thank him when he opened the churchyard gate for her. "And what about your father? I do not know much of him, only that my father considered him a friend."

The snarl of carriages near the gate meant Julia would have a long wait, so he directed her into the flow of others strolling along the outside of the churchyard fence. "My father served yours as sailing master for nearly fifteen years—until the year before I went to sea, in fact. He counted Admiral Witherington as the truest of friends and a brother in spirit. When I was fourteen, Captain Witherington, as he was then, took me on as a midshipman. My father went to another ship, to try to gain patronage for James and Philip, though your father would have been willing to assist with their careers as well." William nodded at Lady Dalrymple when they passed her on the promenade in front of the church.

"How long was it until you saw your father again?" Julia asked, her voice soft with understanding.

William swallowed back all emotion. "I never saw him again. After our voyage to Jamaica, *Indomitable* was assigned to the Mediterranean, but my father's ship received orders for India. Our paths nearly crossed when I was sixteen. *Indomitable* had overtaken a convoy of ships bound for Brest and captured two prize vessels. I was assigned to command one of them back to Portsmouth and await *Indomitable's* return here. His ship had sailed out only hours before we made Spithead. But Mama and James and Philip were still here, so I was able to see them and tell them all about my first command."

"I am certain your father was quite thrilled by your accomplishment."

Fondness filled him. "Aye, that he was. I received a letter from him telling me how proud he was of me. It is one of my most prized possessions. A few days before my seventeenth birthday, I received two pieces of mail. One was from my mother, informing me I had a baby sister. The other was from the Admiralty, a notice that after his ship arrived in India, my father took ill with a fever and died."

"Oh." Julia stopped, her face raised to his, sympathy swimming in her emerald eyes. "Oh, William, I did not know—"

He patted her hand where it rested in the crook of his elbow. "Nor could you have known—and do not be concerned. I have faith I shall be reunited with him one day in heaven. Your father helped me see that. I believe he also felt the best way to honor my father's service to him was to take me under his personal care, to take my father's role of mentor, guide, strength, and support. Everything I have accomplished in the navy has been through an effort to try to make Sir Edward proud of me."

Julia's sympathetic softness vanished, replaced by a wariness William could not understand—until he recognized the two people walking toward them. Sir Drake and Lady Pembroke.

"Ah, Julia, Captain Ransome." Lady Pembroke simpered. "I am so glad we caught up to you. My son," she elbowed Sir Drake, "has something he wishes to say to you."

Drake's hooded eyes indicated otherwise. "Miss Witherington,

Captain Ransome, I—" Drake cast a glare at his mother, before turning a false smile back to them—"I behaved poorly toward you both
the other evening. I do hope you can forgive me."

Julia's fingers bit into William's arm, but she smiled at the miscre-
ant. "As I told your mother, I have forgotten the incident." She turned
her face up with an expectant look at William.

"I am willing to look beyond the encounter, as I understand you
felt you were only looking after Julia's interests." William pinned Pembroke with an unwavering glare. "Of course, Julia's interests are now
mine, so no further intervention should be necessary."

Pembroke's eyes narrowed, but he maintained his insolent posture. "Naturally."

"Oh, look, Julia." Lady Pembroke's breathy exclamation interrupted
the stare-down. "Our carriage has just rounded the corner. Come,
let us depart."

"Yes, Aunt." Julia's hand began to slip from William's arm, but he
clasped her fingers and turned around with her to walk a few paces
behind her aunt and cousin.

"I wrote your father of our engagement and sent it in Friday's post.
Although I am certain you shall receive a missive from him within the
next few days, I will contact you immediately when I receive a reply to
mine." He stopped a few feet back from where Pembroke was handing his mother into the coach.

Julia gave William a tired nod. "Thank you, Captain Ransome."

"William."

Her dimples finally reappeared. "William."

He raised her gloved hand and kissed it, then assisted her up into
the carriage. He watched it roll away, wishing he could devise a way
to get her away from the Pembrokes as soon as—

The answer struck him with the force of a cannon, creating a
quaver in his innards he had not felt since he first set foot on *Alexandra* as her captain.

"William."

He turned and waved at Collin, who descended the front steps of the church with Susan on one arm, Mrs. Ransome on the other, and Charlotte following closely behind, deep in conversation with Admiral Glover.

They returned to the Yateses' home and sat down to breakfast. William pushed his food about his plate, his mind occupied with prayer.

"Why so reserved, William?" His mother touched his arm. Her eyes twinkled as if she shared in a secret with him.

"I…" He looked around the table. Collin, Susan, and Charlotte all stared at him in expectation. "I have received the special license to marry Julia without banns being posted. But I believe I should marry her soon, rather than waiting until just before we sail."

Susan beamed at him. "I have not yet had time to discuss the plans for the wedding breakfast with Julia, but I believe we can have everything settled so you can get married next week."

"I had hoped we could marry even sooner than that—I do not trust her aunt and cousin and want to provide Julia the protection of my name so she is no longer vulnerable to them."

Susan shook her head. "One week, William. That is all I ask. Anyway, you will be busy enough these next several days—meetings at the port Admiralty, your crew returning, your ship coming out of dry dock…"

William looked to Collin for support, but Collin appeared lost in his own thoughts.

"Yes, William, wait a week. A woman's wedding should not be a rushed affair." His mother refilled his coffee.

"Very well. I shall visit the rector this week to set a wedding date for early next week."

Chapter Twenty-Five

Charlotte meandered down the dockyard, taking in the ships rocking gently at their moorings nearby and far away in Spithead Harbor, with the Isle of Wight a hazy lump beyond. Ships' boats scuttled back and forth from those just arrived, and all around her, dockhands bustled about, unloading goods, cargo, and officers.

At the nearest pier, a barge carrying a gaggle of midshipmen scraped to a stop. Charlotte glanced over her shoulder to ensure William was still engaged with the dockmaster before moving closer to watch the young men. They tossed their trunks—sea chests—onto the dock ahead of them, laughing and shoving as they debarked. Once out of the boat, the bigger boys hoisted the chests over their shoulders, bearing the weight with ease; the younger ones heaved them up in front with both hands and waddled forward, backs arched.

She strolled toward them, trying to discern their conversation. As soon as they spotted her, though, silence fell, and each touched the brim of his tall, round hat.

"Good morning." She smiled and inclined her head. "What ship are you from?"

"G'mornin', miss." The tallest boy touched his hat again. He was probably within a year of her own age. "We're from the *Hobarth*. Jus' paid off, and now we get to go home."

"'Course we'd 'ave been home sooner if we didn't have to stop in Plymouth on the way," another boy muttered.

"Welcome home, then. Godspeed." She nodded and strolled past them toward the end of the dock, ears keen for the accents, the words all around her.

"Look out!"

Something hard and heavy hit Charlotte's midsection. She flailed her arms against it as she crashed to the stone quay. Not two feet away, an explosion sent shards of wood and glass flying.

Charlotte could not breathe. Suffocation darkened her vision. The heavy object still lay atop her making movement—and breath—nearly impossible.

"Are you hurt, miss?"

The heaviness eased marginally, and the blackness receded. The object atop her resolved into a chiseled face, blond hair, and the most mesmerizing gray eyes she had ever seen.

"Miss? Can you hear me? Are you well?" Concern creased the broad brow.

"I…I cannot breathe."

"Do you think something is broken—a rib? Shall I send for a surgeon?" His panic would have made her laugh if she had access to air.

"Sir, *you*…are why…I cannot…breathe!"

"I—oh!" He pushed himself up and extended his hands. "I do apologize, miss. I meant no—but are you certain—?"

Charlotte drew in two gulps of air before taking the officer's hands and being hauled to her feet. One plain gold epaulette lay askew on his right shoulder.

"The cargo net was not adequately secured—" He waved his arm toward the wreckage of what had been a fine piece of furniture—exactly where Charlotte had been standing. A crane and ropes swung wildly overhead.

"I thank you, then, for saving my life, Lieutenant…?"

He doffed his pointed-brimmed hat. "Cochrane, miss. Ned Cochrane."

Charlotte wobbled; the lieutenant dropped his hat and grasped her arms to keep her from pitching over into the water. "Not the Lieutenant Ned Cochrane who served as first officer of *Alexandra?*"

He grew two inches and his chest swelled. "I still serve as first officer of *Alexandra*—or at least as soon as she comes out of dry dock." He picked up his hat, dusted it, and replaced it on his head. "But you have me at a disadvantage."

Charlotte flourished a curtsey. "I am Charlotte Ransome. It is very nice to make your acquaintance."

Lieutenant Cochrane lost all color in his face. "R-Ransome? You are the captain's—little sister." He groaned and covered his face with his hands. "I'm done for."

"Charlotte!"

She whirled around. The crowd of midshipmen from *Hobarth,* who'd turned to see the accident, parted to let William pass through—panic written clearly on his face.

"Charlotte." He clutched her shoulders. "You are unhurt? When I saw you and then the cargo—" His throat convulsed.

She reached up and patted his hands, hoping to stay them from strangling her when his shock wore off and he remembered she'd wandered away among the sailors as she had promised not to do.

"I am well, William. But not of my own doing. Come, you must thank the man who saved me."

In an instant, William collected himself, his expression once again neutral and inscrutable as usual. "Yes, I must—Cochrane?" The mask of composure dissolved into a broad smile. "By all that's—" He released Charlotte and greeted Ned Cochrane, first returning Cochrane's salute with a touch to the fore point of his own hat followed by a hearty handshake.

"Captain Ransome, sir." Ned's gaze shifted from William to Charlotte and back.

"I was just telling Lieutenant Cochrane how appreciative I am that he had the wherewithal and courage to save me from an ignominious end."

William looked at her askance and then smiled again. "Yes, Mr. Cochrane. Quite well done."

"Thank you, sir." Relief returned the ruddiness to Cochrane's cheeks.

He bent, fetched up his large sea chest, and tossed it over his shoulder onto his back with one smooth motion.

"But tell me—what brings you in three days early, and on a ship no less?" William ushered Cochrane toward the head of the pier. Just when Charlotte thought herself forgotten, her brother stopped. "Charlotte?" He held his hand toward her.

With a skipping step, she caught up and took his arm. He leaned down, his mouth near her ear. "We shall discuss this later."

The breath of his whisper sent goosebumps racing down the side of Charlotte's neck along with a shiver of fear. He could not ban her from returning to the docks with him, or all would be lost.

"I was in Plymouth," Cochrane said. "My sister married this spring, and they have moved my mother in with them—a very nice farm right outside the city."

William returned another officer's salute. "And how came you by passage on a ship returning from Mediterranean duty?"

"Well, sir, it seems *Hobarth*'s captain received word to put in at Plymouth instead of Spithead, but when he arrived, no one knew why. My sister's new husband has acquaintance among the workers at the dockyard there, and he informed me of the ship's arrival and planned departure. I knew I would enjoy the journey more on the water than overland, and after all, why pay for riding post when I could just stow my dunnage in with *Hobarth*'s first officer for a night?"

"Have you lodging? We can transport you wherever you are staying." William motioned Charlotte to precede him up the narrow stone steps at the head of the dock. Charlotte's heart thrilled at the idea of more time in the handsome lieutenant's company.

She tripped on the top step, horror-struck.

"Charlotte?" William caught her around the waist. "I knew you were not well. Here, take my arm again. That's it."

Guilt made speech impossible. One handsome officer, and her wayward heart forgot her promise—her commitment—to Henry.

"It's the Whitestone Inn for me, sir."

Charlotte turned her face away from Cochrane's direct, apprehensive gaze, angling her head so the brim of her bonnet hid her eyes.

"I see." Amusement laced William's voice. "Sister married well, so now all your eight pounds eight shillings once again land in your own pocket each month?"

"Yes. But Rebecca is beautiful; she was bound to catch the attention of the right sort. It was just a matter of timing."

William threaded Charlotte through the crowd with ease, his uniform the only necessity for clearing a path. "What manner of man is he? Does he treat her well?"

She regarded her brother. He frowned, a distant focus in his vibrant blue eyes. Did he think of his upcoming marriage? Would he ask the same questions about Henry when she revealed her own engagement?

"I am pleased to say it is a love match. His elder brother died—a fever or some such—and he inherited a very pretty estate. Farmland, but well maintained and productive. House not quite a manor and yet larger than a cottage. He dotes upon Becky. And she thinks of nothing other than his comfort." Cochrane sighed. "'Tis rather sickening, truth be told."

Charlotte laughed. When her closest friend fell in love, Charlotte had felt much the same of the way the couple billed and cooed when together. Had Charlotte been that way with Henry? A pang of longing wiped out the lingering guilt over her reaction to the lieutenant. She loved Henry, even though at this moment she could not conjure his image in her mind.

"And you, Ned? Any young lady use her wiles to snare you since last we met?"

Cochrane's face flamed scarlet. "No, sir. My three weeks away were exceedingly dull."

Recovered from her momentary lapse, Charlotte entered the conversation. "And what will you do to occupy your time in Portsmouth until Thursday, Lieutenant Cochrane?"

"Ah, Miss Ransome, many a sailor would answer your question

with plans of wild revelry and dissipation. But as first officer of *Alexandra,* serving under so esteemed a captain as your brother, I must act at all times with the utmost decorum and self-possession." His eyes twinkled with his grin. "I have many business matters to which I must attend before leaving on such a long assignment, miss. And I hope my captain will put me to work securing supplies and vendors for fitting out the ship."

"Of that you can be sure, Mr. Cochrane." They gained the rampart; William hailed Collin, and they convened at Collin's barouche. Once Cochrane's trunk was stowed under the driver's box, they set off from the dockyard toward High Street.

◈◈◈◈◈

Drake read the direction on the front of the two letters the postmaster handed him, tucked them in his coat pocket, pressed two guineas into the man's palm, and hurried out of the post office.

Several ladies squawked in protest when he whipped his horse into a gallop in the middle of High Street; Drake ignored them. A quarter hour later, he pulled the animal to a stop that nearly vaulted him from the saddle.

The front door slammed against the wall as he entered the house. He flung his hat and gloves toward the receiving table, scattering a few cards onto the floor. "Harry!"

The butler—also valet and houseman—slid on the tile rounding the corner from the back hall, hastily tying his neckcloth. "Sir, you're back earl—"

"Tend my horse immediately." Drake took the stairs two at a time. Upon gaining his library, he kicked the door closed behind him. The wall sconces rattled. Decrepit old place.

Removing the letters from the pocket, he shrugged out of his coat and tossed it over the back of one of the cracked leather armchairs. He opened the blinds over his desk and sat, placing the two pieces of correspondence side by side on the blotter.

Rolling up his sleeves, he lit the stump of a candle at his elbow. He took first the envelope, addressed to Admiral Sir Edward Witherington. He held it near the flame for a few seconds and then slid his penknife under the seal, careful to preserve the integrity of the mark pressed into the wax in case he should need to reseal it.

Monday, 8 August 1814

Dear Sir,

I hope this missive finds you well. In case you did not receive my last, I will once again take the opportunity to inform you that Miss Julia Witherington and I have come to an understanding and are to be married. I have reason to believe it better that we marry as soon as possible to forestall any undesirable circumstances. I beg your response to ascertain if this meets with your approval, thus the arrival by express.

I have visited *Alexandra*'s berth, and the work comes along apace to meet the designated launch date....

The remaining paragraph of the letter contained only drivel about reporting and admirals with whom Drake could not be bothered.

So, Ransome, you think to hasten the wedding? We shall see about that. He held the edge of the page to the candle flame and then dropped it onto the tarnished salver, watching the fire curl and blacken the parchment until only a few ashes remained.

He opened the second as carefully as the first.

1 Aug 1814, London

Dearest Julia,

Admiral Hinds and I arrived safely in London yesterday, so thank you for your prayers on our behalf. Lord Melville firmly believes our business shall be wrapped up in just four weeks, but I am not so hopeful....

A guarantee of four Admiral Witherington–free weeks. The rest of the letter was filled with details of the journey to London, the admiral's quarters, and more uninteresting information about people involved in naval circles. Drake burned it as well.

He unlocked the top desk drawer and withdrew a small lockbox. Something about this latest letter of Ransome's struck him as odd. He retrieved a letter also addressed to the admiral in the same hand as the one he'd burned.

He scanned it for the right passage.

> It is my honor to inform you that this night, your daughter and I have come to an understanding to become engaged to be married. I will seek a special license so we may marry before *Alexandra* leaves harbor. As you once expressed your approval of a match between Miss Witherington and me, I humbly seek your blessing on this engagement.

Dry. Formal. Cheerless. Not that Drake expected anything else from the stodgy captain, but the lack of emotion in the words registered false. He laid out the information as might be expected for a plan of battle, not a man in love expressing his joy over securing his bride.

Drake returned it to the box and removed another. He skimmed Julia's rather plain script until he came to the paragraph he sought.

> It will please you to learn that I have become engaged to marry Captain William Ransome. I know he has long been your favorite, and I pray it will bring you joy to hereafter call him your son. We plan to be married before his ship makes sail so I may return to Jamaica with him. I do hope you will be able to return for the wedding. I will write when a firm date is set.

Neither letter read as if written by a person still affected by the rush of emotion a love match should bring. And strange that Julia should write that she "became engaged" rather than accepted Captain Ransome's proposal of marriage. Wouldn't a woman in love want to express the details of the proposal to her loved ones? Especially since Ransome was the admiral's favorite?

The cold truth rained down upon him. Ransome had not been the instigator of the proposal. Julia, having somehow learned the Pembrokes' plan ahead of time, plotted her own course of action and convinced Captain Ransome to marry her.

Drake secured the letters in the box and the box in the drawer. Punching his arms into the sleeves of the coat, he hurled the door open. It hit the wall with a loud crack followed by a shower of debris and a cloud of dust as the plaster gave way. He hated this place and could not wait to raze it to the ground. Perhaps burn it as he had those letters. His boots echoed like marching soldiers down the stairs.

Although he held Lady Pembroke responsible for this complication, he needed to see her with all due haste. If the trust she put into the Portsmouth rumor mill was well founded, they could perhaps use this subtle evidence to their advantage. But as he was not as well versed in the starting and spreading of rumors, he would once again have to bring himself to rely on her. Hopefully this time she would not ruin everything.

◈◈◈

"How came you to be so far down that pier?" William regarded his sister with a careful eye, trying to discern the veracity of her words. He did not want to think her dishonest, but the entire length of her visit, he sensed she had something she was keeping to herself—a secret she was unwilling to reveal to anyone.

"I do apologize. I lost track of how far I wandered. I was only trying to discover the name of the ship that had just put in and was unloading." Charlotte's eyes met his with directness. "I did not mean to disobey you nor break my promise. But I found the bustle and activity so interesting it was hard not being a part of it."

William narrowed his eyes and remained very still, standing at attention beside the coffee table in the Yateses' front parlor. He had never met anyone with a guilty conscience who could abide a direct gaze and silence for long. Charlotte's focus never wavered. Her hands remained folded in her lap, her posture on the edge of her seat straight but comfortable.

Finally, he relaxed his stance, clasping his hands behind his back. "I accept your apology. You have been indulged at home, allowed freedom of movement. But Portsmouth is not Gateacre. I had good reason for eliciting your promise you would stay beside me and not wander alone through the dockyard. I would hope that my fellow officers are all honorable men, but I know they are not. And I know the men who serve below decks have even fewer claims to the title. Many of them have not seen a woman for months, or years even, and are seeking relief for their baser desires. I have no wish to see you hurt in any way."

"I understand. Next time—"

"No." William grimaced when his sister winced at the sharpness in his voice. "After what happened today—you were almost killed—I cannot risk taking you to the dockyard again."

She rose, still so small for a woman full-grown, and crossed to stand directly in front of him. "How am I to regain your trust if I cannot prove to you I can keep my word? When will I ever have the opportunity to witness the grandeur of the Royal Navy except to see it in action here and now? And, as you will be moving on to your ship as soon as it comes out of dry dock in three days, what other time will I have to spend with you except to dog your footsteps down at the docks?" Tears welled in her eyes.

Compassion flooded out the concern he'd carried with him since he turned from his conversation with Master O'Reilley and realized they had become separated. Seeing her nearly crushed to death by falling cargo—his heart climbed into his throat again just thinking of it. But she wanted to spend time with him. He might not see her again for years—and by then she would be married with children of her own…she would be a stranger. He arrived at the decision with great reluctance.

"Very well. But you must remain with me at all times. Or if not with me, with Captain Yates or Lieutenant Cochrane. Agreed?"

The dark curls framing Charlotte's face bobbed with the vigor of her nod. "I promise." She threw her arms around his waist, taking him by surprise. "Thank you, William."

He hesitated a moment, but then he wrapped his arms around her. "You're welcome." He kissed the top of her head and prayed he would not regret this decision.

Chapter Twenty-Six

The clatter of carriage wheels and horses' hooves drifted up through the open windows. Julia glanced at the clock over the fireplace and then at Creighton. "That sounds like it stopped here." She closed the household account ledger and crossed behind her father's desk. Through the verdure in the front garden, she had a clear view of the large coach but could not make out the crest on the door. "It did stop here. Come back when you can, and we shall finish the audit."

"Yes, Miss Witherington." Creighton bowed out of the room.

A one o'clock visit meant the caller was one of her aunt's closer acquaintances. Julia tucked the stack of receipts Creighton had given her into the front of the ledger and laid it on the desk. A loud knock resounded through the house. She strained to hear voices through the open study door—

"Yes, Lady MacDougall. This way, please."

Cold dread tingled on Julia's skin. Lady Hedwig MacDougall, her mother's aunt. How could she have gotten here from Scotland so quickly?

Footsteps on the stairs stirred Julia; she grabbed the ledger and fled up to her room. She had no desire to see the baroness before absolutely necessary. Aunt Augusta would want time alone with Lady MacDougall to fill her head with all of Julia's shortcomings and misdeeds, which should take most of the afternoon.

She slipped out of her room and padded on her toes halfway down the stairs to the turning to try to hear anything, but the voices were too soft. She crept the rest of the way down. Creighton came out of the admiral's study, a puzzled expression on his face—until he saw her. She motioned him to follow her upstairs, where they would be safe from any sudden opening of the sitting room door.

Creighton stopped at the threshold of Julia's room. Without Nancy or another woman present, coaxing him to come in so they could have the privacy of a closed door would be impossible. Julia sat at her desk and uncorked her ink bottle. "Is Elton back from town yet?"

"Yes, miss, I believe he arrived a quarter hour past."

"Good. I have another errand for him." She finished the brief note, reread it, nodded, signed and folded it, and sealed the flap by impressing the wax with the stamp of an intertwined, scrolled *TD*. She and Susan had agreed the Tierra Dulce stamp would be better employed for their private correspondence. Maybe she was overreacting to her great-aunt's visit, but she wanted someone outside this house to be aware more mischief might be afoot.

After Creighton departed to take the note to Elton, Julia paced her room. The condemned awaiting execution. Half an hour passed. An hour. Two. At a commotion downstairs, she cracked her bedroom door open to listen. The housekeeper delivering tea.

Tea? Julia's stomach rumbled. She'd breakfasted in the kitchen early this morning but had eaten nothing since. If she rang for Nancy, would Lady Pembroke hear it and be reminded of Julia's presence in the house?

Disgust coursed through her veins at her own fear—hiding like a fox in its den from the hounds baying in the distance. Staying in her bedroom would not hinder Augusta from coming for her whenever she pleased—but it did hinder Julia from finishing the review of the household accounts with Creighton.

She retrieved the ledger from her desk and softly made her way downstairs to her father's library—across the hall from the sitting room where Lady Pembroke and Lady MacDougall doubtless planned Julia's demise. She pulled the bell cord and set out the account book and receipts.

Creighton entered. "Are you ready to continue?"

Bless him for keeping his voice low. "Yes. But first I could do with some tea."

He nodded and departed silently, returning several minutes later with a tray laden with the cook's wonderful pastries—and with the housekeeper. Julia ate until sated, and then she carried her teacup to the desk, where she resumed the accounting of expenditures.

❧❦❧

At six o'clock, dressed in a gray silk gown that was embroidered about the wrists and hem in black, Julia entered the dining room, stomach churning.

"Come into the light, child." The words washed over Julia like a soft wave embracing the beach. Her mother's voice! No, a little lower, a little more raspy. "Let me have a look at you."

Julia moved from the shadowed doorway into the room, which was glowing yellow in the late afternoon light. She grabbed onto the back of the nearest chair to maintain her balance. The woman standing beside Lady Pembroke could have passed for Julia's mother—only her hair was white, her pale skin more lined.

She had always pictured her mother's Aunt Hedwig as a large, imposing woman. And yet here she stood, the very image of Eleanor Pembroke-Witherington, small and thin, her face sharp in its beauty.

Remembering herself, she released the chair and curtseyed. "Lady MacDougall, I am pleased to meet you at last. My mother spoke of you often."

The baroness came across the room and clasped Julia's hands. "My dear, you must call me Aunt Hedwig. No formality among family!" She stepped back to arm's length. "How like your mother you are. Her nose, her chin, and that hair! Though hers was a bit more titian, was it not?"

"Yes, my la—Aunt Hedwig." Her throat clogged around the words. Homesickness and longing for her mother might undo her—but she could not let that happen in front of Augusta Pembroke.

"But you have your father's eyes. I do believe it was those green eyes Eleanor first loved about Witherington."

If they didn't stop talking about her mother soon, Julia might disgrace herself by weeping. "What brings you to Portsmouth, Aunt Hedwig?"

"Augusta wrote me in London to share the news of your engagement."

Julia stiffened. So, Augusta had called Hedwig in as an ally in her campaign to coerce Julia into marrying Sir Drake.

"I had to come congratulate you myself—and to see you before you leave these shores for another twenty years."

Julia's gaze flickered unbidden toward Augusta. Lady Pembroke stood beyond Hedwig, eyes downcast, mouth pulled into a tight line. That cheered Julia a little. If Hedwig were in league with her, Augusta would not look so grim, as if fighting to keep a scowl from her face.

"I am happy you've come, my—Aunt Hedwig."

Over dinner, Lady MacDougall asked about Jamaica, a topic in which Augusta had never shown an interest. For the first time since returning to England, Julia could recall Jamaica and Tierra Dulce without a pang of grief for her mother.

At eight o'clock, Augusta stood and invited Lady MacDougall to join her in the sitting room for coffee. Julia rose as well, intending to join them.

"If I may be allowed an indulgence," Hedwig folded her napkin and placed it beside her plate. "I wish to retire for the evening. The journey from London has overtaxed me, I fear."

Augusta's expression was inscrutable—Julia could not tell if she was relieved or offended at her invitation's rejection.

"Aunt Hedwig, may I show you to your room?" Julia offered.

"Yes, my dear, that would be a delight." Hedwig swayed a bit when she stood. Julia clasped the older lady's elbow to steady her. Hedwig patted her cheek. "Such a sweet child."

The housekeeper had made up the other spare bedroom for Lady MacDougall—the room that her father had commissioned decorated with Julia's mother in mind. Hedwig exclaimed over the delicately carved furniture and Brussels lace curtains.

Augusta stood in the door, arms crossed. "We have been invited for tea with Lady Dalrymple tomorrow. Aunt Hedwig, we will be honored if you will attend us."

"Yes, my dear, that sounds lovely."

Julia returned to her room, her heart lightened. She finished balancing the household ledger. Then, just before bed, took up her father's prayer book and flipped through it until she found a section on gratitude.

The stories her mother had told about Aunt Hedwig over the years must have been exaggerated, and perhaps Hedwig had softened as she grew older.

જી.રી.રી.એ

In the morning, Julia sent another note to Susan, recanting her concerns over Lady MacDougall's presence. She was disappointed, though, that Lady MacDougall did not feel well enough to come down for breakfast. At half-past two, Aunt Hedwig came down, looking robust and rested.

As soon as they crossed the threshold into Lady Dalrymple's front parlor, Augusta's haughtiness transfigured into grating adulation—she praised everything from the décor to Lady Dalrymple's gown. With grace, the dowager viscountess received the flattery, though the corners of her mouth grew tighter the longer the fawning continued.

"And had you a pleasant stay in London, Lady MacDougall?" Lady Dalrymple cut off Augusta's remarks about the flower arrangement on the mantelpiece.

"Oh, ever so entertaining. Naturally, when one has status and means, any place can be made pleasant."

Augusta gave a grating, sycophantic laugh. "I really do not understand how everyone does not spend at least part of the Season in Town."

"I cannot speak for *everyone*," Lady Dalrymple enunciated, "but there are some who prefer the quiet of the country or a small town to the wild gaiety of London. Do you not agree, Miss Witherington?"

Julia nodded. "Oh, yes, my lady. I much prefer the quiet of the country to city life."

"You are fortunate to be returning to your home soon." Wistfulness infused Lady Dalrymple's voice. "I rarely return to Graysdown—the seat of the Dalrymple family for centuries. And when I do go, I do not overstay my welcome."

Julia regarded the dowager with curiosity. Never before had she spoken so openly—with such vulnerability or bitterness.

"But enough of that." Lady Dalrymple waved her hand as if shooing a fly. "Julia, how come the wedding preparations? Have you and the dashing Captain Ransome set a date yet?"

Julia chided her cheeks for growing hot. "No, my lady, no date is set yet. Our wedding is to be a simple affair—with our friends the Yateses to stand witness."

"Oh, no, my dear!" Lady Dalrymple reached over the low table between their chairs and tapped Julia's wrist with her fan. "You would deny all of Portsmouth the pleasure of witnessing the joining of the couple who have generated the most gossip this town has ever known?"

"But a large, public wedding? It would be unseemly." Not to mention an opportunity for the Pembrokes to try something underhanded.

"Of course, you are correct." Lady Dalrymple leaned forward and rested her hand on Julia's arm. "But I hope you might allow me the pleasure of holding your wedding breakfast here. You have become such the darling of Portsmouth society that they all want to wish you joy. And it will be a chance to bid you farewell. What say you?"

Julia opened her mouth but could not force a sound to escape. She took a deep breath and tried again. "Thank you for your generous offer, Lady Dalrymple. I—Mrs. Susan Yates has already begun planning a wedding breakfast for us in her home. We expected mostly naval officers and their wives to attend—"

"And they are all welcome here. Yes, even the captain's crew may come and have a glass of punch and piece of cake with the staff." She squeezed Julia's arm. "Think no more of it. I shall call on Mrs. Yates tomorrow morning, and the two of us will come to terms." Her one-brown-one-blue eyes twinkled. "You should know by now I am not to be denied my way, Miss Witherington."

۞

By the time she climbed into the coach to return home, Julia's head spun. Most of the conversation over tea had been Lady Dalrymple's account of her own wedding—the small private ceremony, the wedding breakfast, her trousseau, and the wedding trip to London. Julia had a hard time concentrating on the anecdotes, her mind wandering to the near future and wondering what her own wedding would be like.

"How kind of the viscountess to open her home for your breakfast." Aunt Hedwig touched the back of Julia's hand. "And how flattering that she holds you in such high esteem. And that she would be so magnanimous as to open her home to...more common folk and invite the captain's officers and crew."

Augusta's glance at Julia could have withered the most hardy sugar-cane. "If you but knew her as well as I, Hedwig, you would have recognized the look of pity she gave us when Julia mentioned those navy people. As if the granddaughter of a baronet should have to sink so low, marrying below her station. She must be seen as bringing her husband up in society instead of being dragged down to his level."

Hedwig clicked her tongue. "Now, Augusta, I know you have no love of military men, given it was service in the army that took your husband from you. But do recall that Julia's own father is a naval man, that it is her sphere of society into which she marries. Perhaps it might be said that Eleanor married beneath herself—God rest her soul—but Sir Edward did go on to make quite a large fortune in addition to receiving a knighthood."

Julia stared at her fists, trying to ignore the insult of both her parents from a woman who reminded her so of her mother.

"And who is to say that Captain—what's the boy's name?" Hedwig turned sparkling brown eyes onto Julia.

"Ransome."

"Yes, of course." Hedwig turned back to face Augusta. "Who is to say that this Ransome will not be as successful and singled out as Sir Edward?"

Augusta pursed her lips. Julia thought she understood her internal conflict—after all, if the Pembrokes' finances were as straitened as her father said, Augusta would do well to stay in Lady MacDougall's favor.

"Julia, I understand Augusta invited you to visit Marchwood with her before you leave for Jamaica."

"Yes, Aunt Hedwig." Though the idea of traveling anywhere with Augusta Pembroke was less appealing than falling into a vat of boiling sugar.

"I would love to see the estate again. I had the happiest childhood there and have only been back twice since I married the baron so many years ago." Hedwig sighed. "We shall all go—make a day of it. Perhaps Sir Drake can join us and show us the improvements he means to make, as well."

Improvements? Julia regarded Augusta from the corner of her eye, but Augusta showed no sign of distress. Maybe the house was in better condition than Julia imagined. If Lady MacDougall were there, Julia would go. It would have made her mother happy.

Chapter Twenty-Seven

At noon Thursday, all of *Alexandra*'s lieutenants sat around a table in the port Admiralty headquarters, discussing their activities and travels over the past three weeks.

William knocked on the table to gain their attention. "I am pleased to see each of you here and ready to get back to work. I have a few duties for you today, as well as an invitation to dinner tonight at the beginning of the second dogwatch—that's six o'clock in case you have forgotten over your long holiday."

The lieutenants guffawed.

"Mr. Blakeley, the warrant officers await without. Please ask them to come in."

"Aye, aye, sir." The youngest lieutenant rose and opened the door. General confusion filled the room as the purser, ship's master, boatswain, gunner, and carpenter filed in and filled the remaining free space in the small room. William waited until silence fell naturally.

"Men, at five o'clock tomorrow morning, *Alexandra* will be released from dry dock."

A cheer buffeted William's ears. He allowed himself a small smile. "A crew from the dockyard will move her to our assigned mooring. We shall take possession at eight o'clock and begin the task of fitting her out for the voyage to Jamaica."

Dread dropped into his stomach like an anchor. "Before I leave you, there is one more piece of news to impart." *Lord, give me strength.* William trusted the eleven men in the room with his life and knew them well—but not well enough to predict how they would react to his announcement. He scanned the expectant faces. "Before we sail, I am to be married."

After an infinite moment, Ned Cochrane's laugh broke the stunned silence…but his mirth quickly melted from his expression. "You are not joking?"

"No, Mr. Cochrane."

"The rumors be true then?" Boatswain Matthews asked with a sly grin.

"I do not know of which rumors you speak." Although William suspected. "I am engaged to marry Miss Julia Witherington. She will travel with us to Jamaica."

Cochrane stood. "Captain, on behalf of the men, may I wish you joy?" A hint of amusement laced his words. All of the others nodded.

No anger, no mutiny. Relieved, William cleared his throat. "Yes—thank you." He faltered for a moment, not knowing what else to say. "I must be off to the dockyard for a final inspection. Mr. Cochrane has your orders." He escaped and leaned against the closed door. The room erupted with voices. Above all, William heard his first officer.

"Gentlemen, the captain," Cochrane said as if making a toast.

"The captain," the other voices repeated.

"Oh, and if I may," Cochrane continued, "you all owe me five quid—not only is the captain marrying, but he's marrying Sir Edward's daughter, just as I said."

The rest of the men disagreed loudly with Ned's comment. William left before hearing more. Not the reaction he'd expected, but despite his officers' gambling—an offense, according to the Articles of War, punishable by whipping—it had gone well.

⊷⊶⊷⊶⊷

As soon as William's feet touched *Alexandra*'s quarterdeck, all anxiety over his officers' acceptance of Julia's presence aboard vanished.

The stillness of his ship jarred him—like an out-of-tune violin at a concert. But the brown aroma of new wood combined with the acrid smell of fresh paint and varnish whirled around him in a welcoming embrace. Above, the dockyard crew shouted and laughed as they trussed up the new sails and shrouds, the ropes whooshing and whirring through their stays and blocks.

Excitement scurried up William's spine. Fifteen days more, and he would put Portsmouth behind him.

Dockmaster O'Reilley showed him the finer points of the repairs and improvements. "Ah, and here's Boone."

William turned to see a small, raisinlike man.

"Cap'n Ransome, sir." Boone knuckled his forehead. William touched the tip of his hat in return salute. "Me missus heard tell you're to marry before ye leave, sir, an' suggested ye might be in need of a new bed, sir. Master O'Reilley tol' me you'd be here, sir, and per'aps ye might take a walk with me to me shop, as is. You'll be wanting your lady travelin' in comfort an' all, sir."

A dark cloud of William's former anxiety returned. "Thank you, Boone. I shall attend you directly, as soon as Mr. O'Reilley and I have completed the inspection."

The hammock maker nodded and departed. William charted his own course around the ship; O'Reilley followed in his wake, chattering like a gull. William ran his hand along *Alexandra*'s satiny wood and sinuous curves; a tingle shivered up his arm to his heart.

On a ship once again. No, not *a* ship—*his* ship. His home. His life's blood. Not the first ship he ever commanded, but something about this seventy-four gunner had worked its way into his very soul and become a part of him. During his service in the navy, he'd heard captains and admirals speak of their ships as they would a wife or lover. As a lieutenant he'd not understood the emotion behind their words. Now, standing on the highest deck of his ship and looking over her majestic size and elaborate design, he understood. Once he took vows with Julia, he would never be unfaithful to her. But *Alexandra* would always hold a piece of his heart.

Entering the great cabin, he removed his hat to keep it from knocking against the joists of the poop deck above. The worn place in the leather of the window seat running the width of the stern had been repaired, much to his disappointment—it had taken him more than a year to break it in just right.

Beyond the day cabin, the sleeping quarters appeared much larger than he recalled—devoid of his sea chest and hammock, furnished with only a sparkling black twelve-pounder cannon.

He eyed the iron rings on the beams above, from which he used to hang his simple canvas hammock. His stomach lurched. Why had Collin not reminded him he would need bedding suitable for Julia? Of course, he'd not seen Collin much since the engagement, as he'd spent most of his time at the port Admiralty or with Cochrane making a list of necessary supplies for the voyage.

"I had the boys put up these brackets." O'Reilley touched one of the four iron plates—two near the ceiling and two near the floor— bolted into the thick side wall. "In case yer missus should be wantin' a wardrobe. A couple o' sturdy ropes and it'll move nary an inch, even in the heaviest waves."

William's dark cloud exploded into a full storm, wiping out any feelings of joy over being reunited with his ship. He would be married. He could imagine himself happier about the situation if it were not for the knowledge Julia would be aboard his ship for six to eight weeks until they dropped anchor in Kingston harbor. What sort of disruption would her presence create? How would she cope with being the only woman surrounded day and night by more than seven hundred men?

No longer deriving any happiness from his longed-for *Alexandra*, he left the cabin and made a brisk tour of the rest of the ship. No need for thorough inspection today—over the next week, he and the officers would scour the ship from bow to stern looking for any signs of imperfection.

He left *Alexandra* and found Boone's stall in the dockyard market. He followed the hammock maker around the corner and up a side street to a graystone rowhouse. What should have been a front parlor had been invaded and conquered by piles of folded white canvas from floor to ceiling and hammocks and box beds hanging from closely spaced iron rings bolted into the ceiling beams.

William navigated the room with caution, his chest tightening from the close quarters created by the forest of canvas and rope.

"This is the one, sir." Boone shoved several limp hammocks out of the way to reveal a wide box bed draped with elaborately embroidered bed hangings. "It's not as large as a real bed, but wide enough for two to sleep comfortable-like."

"The work is exquisite."

Boone beamed. "Thank-ee, sir. Me missus and daughters done the work. She heard of the bed Lord Nelson, rest his soul, had on *Victory* and wanted to try her hand to recreate the like."

"How much?"

Boone named his price, which seemed low to William. Boone, however, acted surprised that William did not negotiate, but rather removed his money bag from his pocket and paid the full price. He added two shillings more in Boone's calloused, scarred palm. "Have it delivered to O'Reilley this afternoon."

"Aye, aye, Cap'n, sir!"

William squinted against the bright sun when he returned to the street. He oriented himself by the masts towering over the narrow gray houses and turned the direction that would take him to Harthorne Street. With a quick glance at his pocket watch, he hastened his step. Susan, Mother, and Charlotte would flay him and string him up on the nearest yardarm if he arrived later than four o'clock. That they thought everyone needed two hours to prepare for dinner reached beyond the boundaries of his understanding.

He opened the Yateses' front door just as the clock chimed. Dawling met him with an impudent grin.

"The ladies just started wondering where you were, sir. I must say, sir, what good it does my heart to see you in your uniform. Did you see her, sir? *Alexandra*, that is."

Dawling's enthusiasm brought William out from under the dark clouds. "Aye, she is magnificent once again. Straight and clean and with not a scratch on her."

Rapture filled Dawling's pockmarked face. "And when are we going to her, sir?"

"Tomorrow. I shall need to be at the dockyard at four thirty in the morning. I intend to be on her when they float her out from dry dock. We officially take possession at eight. The midshipmen are to arrive at noon. You may bring my sea chest during that time and are certain of finding a boat ready to transport you."

"Aye, aye, sir." The steward's grin nearly split his face. He knuckled his forehead and turned to leave, but then he stopped. "Ah, sir, I nearly forgot—Miss Charlotte picked up the post today whilst she was in town. I believe she put yours on your desk, sir."

"Thank you, Dawling." William tucked his hat under his arm and jogged upstairs. On the main floor, he stopped in the doorway of the sitting room. His mother and Susan looked up from their needlework. He bowed. "Ladies, as you requested, I have returned by four o'clock. And here I find you wiling away the hours with your sewing. I am astonished you have not yet retired to your rooms to prepare for dinner."

Susan returned her attention to the flimsy white fabric in her hands. "Do not be patronizing, William. If we did not give you a deadline, you would have spent all afternoon at the dockyard and been late for dinner with your own men."

"Come, sit for a moment, William." Smiling, his mother indicated the chair beside her. "Tell us of your ship and officers."

He did as bade, careful to limit his words to conveying only the facts of the meeting with his men and the beauty of his ship. He omitted the encounter with the hammock maker, disinclined to see their knowing smiles and exchanged glances.

At four thirty, Susan laid aside her workbasket. "I believe it is time I should be retiring to my room to dress."

No sooner had William stood than Collin appeared at the door, his face drawn—as it had been ever since the argument he and Susan had last week, the night Julia had dined here. "William, may I speak with you?"

"Of course." He followed his friend into the library.

Collin closed the door behind him, crossed to the fireplace, and sank into one of the club chairs, his expression pensive.

Disconcerted at seeing his usually cheerful friend so low, William sat, rested his elbows on his chair's arms, and pressed his fingertips together, waiting for Collin to speak.

"Susan is with child."

Perplexed, William said nothing. Collin had long expressed his hope, his prayers, that God would bless them with a child. Yet the flat, emotionless tone of his voice conveyed none of the excitement the announcement should bring.

Collin shifted in his seat until he leaned forward, elbows braced on his knees. "Last week she asked to go with me—with us—to Jamaica. She somehow got the notion in her head of an easy sail over, and that she would then stay with Julia at the plantation while you and I execute our commission in the Caribbean." He stared into the cold fireplace. "I told her no. She even tried to get Julia to convince me to let her go, but bless her, Julia saw the folly of the plan. If Susan should lose this baby too…" His voice trailed off, and he buried his face in his hands.

So that had been the subject of the argument last week and cause of Collin's subsequent graveness. William had no words for his friend, though he took comfort in the fact Julia showed such dispassionate logic.

Collin ran his fingers through his hair and then pressed his palms against the side of his head, face toward the rug. "She cannot come to sea with me. And I cannot bear the thought of leaving her at such a time. The doctor said after so many miscarriages, giving birth could threaten Susan's life. If she should…and I am on the far side of the ocean and cannot be here—" He gulped several breaths. "She has no family to speak of—an aunt who lives in London and a cousin or two in the north part of the country. She would be here all alone."

The resigned tone of Collin's voice forged a deep foreboding in

William's mind. With great effort, he remained silent, but he wanted to beg his friend to stop talking.

"I am resigning my commission." Collin straightened and looked at William.

"I see." Regret coursed through William, but he composed his expression with imperturbable detachment. He wished he could say he understood or that if he were in the same circumstance, he would come to the same decision. "And you are certain this is the course of action you wish to take?"

"Aye. Susan and I have spent many hours in prayer, and I am confident this is the right path." His eyes flickered as he searched William's face. "I would like for you to go with me to see Admiral Glover tomorrow."

"Of course I will go with you." William tried to infuse concurrence in his voice, but inside he railed against the injustice of the situation. Aside from keeping his ship and crew, William had most anticipated once again being stationed with Collin—something they had not enjoyed since midshipmen aboard *Indomitable*. His heart ached for the loss of his friend.

"Are you angry?"

"No, not angry. Disappointed."

Collin nodded. "I, as well. My heart and mind have been nearly split asunder with the agony of this choice. But I have had my adventure and made my fortune; I have fought many battles and seen most of the world. The war is blessedly over. My resignation will make room for another captain to have a ship. I need to attend to my family, and to do so, I must be here, not out at sea." He stood.

William rose and clasped hands with him. "I shall see you through this—and I know I will have the opportunity to see you whenever the Royal Navy calls me back to England. We shan't have to wonder when our paths will cross again as we have these last ten years."

"Thank you, William. We would have had great sport, chasing pirates throughout the tropics. I am depending on you to write often with the details of your exploits. And once the child is safely arrived,

Susan and I will come to Jamaica to visit you and Julia—and soon, too, so the child can be christened, and you and Julia named the god-parents."

"I would be honored. I know Julia will also, as she and Susan are thick as thieves."

"And a few years from now, perhaps we can come to an agreement on marriage articles between our son and your daughter—or your son and our daughter." Light rekindled in Collin's eyes. "Come now, Susan will be wondering why I have not yet come up to dress—as if it takes more than a few minutes!"

William laughed as warranted, but following Collin up the stairs, he allowed the humor to slide from his expression. *You and Julia.* Collin had twined the words together as if one unit. A verse from the book of Genesis burst into William's mind. *Therefore shall a man leave his father and his mother, and shall cleave unto his wife: and they shall be one flesh.*

He smiled at Collin at the second floor landing—hoping it looked more like amusement than discomfort—and continued to his quarters.

Charlotte's yelp startled him when he opened the door. She pressed her hand to her chest. "Oh, William. You scared me."

"I apologize—I did not expect you to be in my room." He raised his brows in question.

She motioned toward the desk. "I was just leaving your mail for you. I forgot about it when I came in earlier—Susan had a visitor, and she wished to introduce me."

"Ah." He started unbuttoning his uniform coat. "Thank you."

She grinned and pulled on his arm until he leaned down enough so she could kiss his cheek. "I cannot believe tonight is here. You and Julia are truly to leave soon."

"Aye, a fortnight for fitting out a ship is hardly any time at all."

"May I come to the dockyard tomorrow and see your ship?"

"I do not think that is a good idea. I will not have time to show you around, and everything will be in a state of confusion."

"Saturday, then?" Her tone was so hopeful, he could hardly bear it.

"We shall see." He shooed her out of the room. "Go and get yourself ready for dinner—you have only a little more than an hour."

His sister laughed. "You do realize it does not take that long to get dressed—some women must take a few hours because they cannot decide upon which dress to wear or how they want their hair arranged." She fluttered out the door.

William leaned against it, letting his head fall back until it made contact with the wood. *You and Julia…one flesh…leave his father and his mother; and shall cleave unto his wife…*Or leave his ship and the only family he had ever known.

Pain ground into his soul like grain crushed with a mortar and pestle. He wanted to follow God in all things, wanted his life to be a reflection of God's saving grace to his men. Yet in this instance, he railed against the responsibility God laid forth for a husband—to leave everything he loved for his wife.

Collin loved Susan; he had since the moment he first saw her. For twelve years, they cultivated and nurtured their love. The difficulty of separation, the tribulation of war, the agony of being unable to have children all acted as a forge, refining them into that *one flesh.*

Anxiety held William in its grip until he had only one course of action. *Almighty God, show me how to obey you in all your commands. Show me how to be a godly husband. Teach me to love Julia as Collin loves Susan.*

Chapter Twenty-Eight

Thank you, Creighton." Julia reached up and settled the gossa-
mer wrap about her shoulders. She took one last look at herself
in the mirror. The dress she'd worn the night of her father's dinner
party glowed golden and bronze in the light streaming in through the
narrow windows surrounding the front door.

She shook her head, setting the curls clustered about her temples
and ears to bouncing. "I should not have chosen this dress. They will
think I have too high an opinion of myself and will dislike me."

"Now, miss, you look lovely, and they will take it that you are
honoring them by dressing so fine." Horses' hooves clopped to a stop
outside. "Here's the carriage for you, so let's hear no more about it.
They will admire and esteem you as everyone else who knows you
does." Creighton cast his gaze up toward the first floor. "Well, almost
everyone."

"Cheeky!" Julia clicked her tongue.

Smiling, Creighton opened the door for her.

She stepped forward but then hastily retreated. An enormous man
dressed in a livid green coat with a wild shock of brown hair blocked
her exit.

Creighton stepped between them. "May I help you?" Julia had always
thought Creighton a tall man—taller by several inches than her father—
yet compared to the man he faced, he looked like a young boy.

"Evenin'." The man touched the rim of his tan hat. "This the resi-
dence of Admiral Witherington?"

"It is. He is not receiving callers today."

"Ain't here for no call, laddie. I been told around town a lady's staying here wot's related to a gennelmun I got business with." He eyed Julia over Creighton's shoulder.

Creighton shifted to try to block his view. "Lady Pembroke is also not receiving callers."

"Wot 'bout the pretty?" The man jerked his bulbous chin toward Julia. "She accepting callers?"

She stepped forward. "What is your business here, sir?"

The man looked over his shoulder as the Yateses' barouche pulled to a stop behind his high-flyer gig at the front gate. He spat on the step before turning back to them.

Julia grabbed Creighton's elbow to keep him from exploding at the man.

"I come to see if a certain *Sir* Drake Pembroke—" he sneered the title—"is here. I been watching the comings and goings at his house and ain't seen hide nor hair of him. Thought per'aps he might've come to stay with his relations, seeing as his losses been piling up mighty heavy in recent days."

Disgusted, Julia let go of Creighton's arm and inched around him. "How much does he owe you?"

"Not me, miss, my employer is the one he's owing. You see, the dandy baronet took out a mortgage on that fancy house o' his in the country—and most of the land and mills, as well—for the tidy sum of twenty thousand pounds. Up till recent, he's barely been paying the interest, see?"

A sick knot twisted Julia's stomach. No wonder he was so anxious to get his hands on her legacy. "He is not here. I have not seen him since Tuesday afternoon."

Green Coat took a card from his pocket. Creighton snatched it before the man could get his hand near Julia. The ruffian laughed. "If you see 'im afore I do, tell 'im if he don't pay in full by Monday—being the fifteenth—my boss will call in the note on that fine, big estate and sell it for a pretty profit, I don't mind to say. Tell 'im my boss is tired of waiting, and if Pembroke can't come up with the twenty thousand for the note and the five thousand for the interest, my boss will see him put in jail. G'day to you now."

"Insolent blackguard!" Creighton hissed, watching the debt collector swagger down the walk to the gig.

Julia wrapped the shawl tightly around her, suddenly chilled. Papa told her Sir Drake had mortgaged the estate, but she could not fathom so great a debt—nor why he would continue to compound it.

"Come, miss, you'd best be off." Creighton escorted her to the barouche where the Yateses' stable boy sat watching the gig drive away, fear clear in his eyes.

Creighton handed her up. "I know it is not my place to tell you what you ought to do, miss. But you should get Captain Ransome to see you home tonight. I do not feel easy about this man, that he will just leave things be."

"I share your concern, Creighton, and I was already thinking along those lines."

The butler nodded. "Drive on," he said to the young man in the box.

Twenty-five thousand pounds! More than most people saw in a lifetime. Yes, she and her father could spare the amount without straitening or retrenching much of their own lifestyle and without causing irreparable injury to their fortune. But this was only one collector—there must be more.

To lose her mother's ancestral home to creditors! What if she purchased the note on Marchwood from this money changer?

Julia checked her thoughts. She did not have nearly that much in her personal account, and she would not take the money from her father's nor the plantation's accounts. If only her dowry were not promised to William.

Had he ever considered purchasing an estate in England?

❦

"William, do stop pacing. You are going to wear out that beautiful rug Collin brought back from India."

He did as Susan bade, moving to stand in front of the fireplace, feet braced, hands clasped behind his back. Julia said she would be here at five thirty—the hands on the clock stood at almost five forty-five. Finally, just as it began its quarterly chime, footsteps sounded on the stairs. He arrived at the parlor door as it opened. Julia, white-faced and grave, entered and thanked Dawling.

Concern replaced William's former annoyance. "Has something happened? Your aunt or your cousin—have they…?"

She shook her head and took his proffered arm. "No. They have done nothing—other than Lady Pembroke insulting me, you, my father, the Royal Navy, and everyone connected with it."

"Julia! At last." Susan swept toward them.

"I shall speak to you of it after dinner," Julia whispered.

Though displeased with her answer, William had no choice but to relinquish her to Susan when Dawling reappeared at the door. "Sir, might I have a word?"

Frowning, William joined him. "What is it?"

"Ben—the driver—says he saw an unsavory character at the Witheringtons' front door talking with Miss Witherington when he went to fetch her. Said looked to him like he was not welcome."

Disgruntled with this news—something *had* happened and she did not immediately tell him?—William thanked Dawling and sent him back to man the front door with Fawkes. His vexation must have shown in his expression, for when he returned to Julia's side, her brows knitted together and worry filled her eyes.

He took a calming breath and relaxed his face and stance. She had said she would speak to him after dinner of whatever had happened. He would let her have her way—for now.

At the top of the hour, the six lieutenants arrived and were shown up to the front parlor by a beaming Dawling—who seemed to lack nothing but his own uniform to complete his joy.

As the door closed behind the steward, the lieutenants lined up by seniority. William offered his arm to Julia to convey her to the other side of the room and was surprised to feel her hand trembling when she rested it in the crook of his elbow. Her disquiet served to ease his.

He stopped before them. "Miss Julia Witherington, may I present the officers of His Majesty's Ship *Alexandra.*"

She curtseyed low, as if being presented to royalty. "I am honored to meet you, and I look forward to knowing you better in the coming weeks."

Cochrane's smile nearly reached both ears. "First Lieutenant Ned Cochrane, Miss Witherington. And may I say what joy you are bringing to our crew, to see our captain happily settled with a wife?"

Over Julia's head, William scowled at him; Cochrane's smile broadened.

"Patrick O'Rourke. Blessings be on you and the captain, Miss Witherington."

"Angus Campbell. I wish you joy, Miss Witherington—and the captain." The third lieutenant gave William a furtive glance.

"Horatio Eastwick, miss. It is a great honor to meet the daughter of Admiral Sir Edward Witherington. I had the privilege of serving under him on *Indomitable* when I was just a midshipman." William's fourth lieutenant had come to him on recommendation from Sir Edward.

"Eamon Jackson, miss, but everybody calls me Jack." The winning smile Jackson gave Julia made him a favorite of any woman he chanced upon.

At the end of the row, the sixth and youngest lieutenant blushed to the roots of his curly blond hair—which was in need of cutting. The lad shifted nervously from foot to foot. "R-Robert Blakeley. It's a great honor, Miss Witherington."

Julia smiled at the most junior officer, and he nearly toppled over. William swallowed his amusement. No need to embarrass him more. He introduced the officers to the others, and they all went downstairs to dinner.

At the table, Julia sat between Cochrane and O'Rourke, but all the lieutenants soon followed Ned's example of telling embellished tales of their adventures at sea—many of which William questioned to himself based on his own recollection of the events. They listened with rapt attention and interest when she spoke of her life on the plantation.

Was it his imagination, or did Charlotte laugh a little more at Cochrane's stories, affix her gaze on him longer? Wonderful—now William had his sister's romantic sensibilities to add to his troubles. While in person, manner, beliefs, and address, he could not object to Ned as a suitor for Charlotte, the difference in their fortunes was substantial. Although Ned had garnered a large share of *Alexandra*'s prize money over the years he'd served on her—and the total was significant—nearly all of his earnings had gone to support his mother and provide a dowry for his sister.

Although in that light, Ned presented the ideal candidate as a suitor—he had always put his family obligations before his own personal desires. And with the task of hunting pirates set before them, the potential for much more prize money was great—practically guaranteed.

But no firm date had been given for their return to England. They could be gone for years—what hope would they have of ever being reunited?

He supposed he could send for Charlotte—and their mother, of course—to come out next year and stay with Julia at Tierra Dulce. He could arrange for leave.

What was he thinking? Ned and Charlotte were strangers—she a pretty girl and Ned a man women fawned over. Naturally, they would show some initial attraction toward each other, but when the first blush wore off—or when Ned met another pretty girl—it would soon be forgotten.

He shook off his sobering thoughts and looked across the table at Julia. Although quiet and more serious than usual, she took part in the conversations around her, laughed when expected, and in general, impressed and delighted all six lieutenants. By the time Susan rose to invite the ladies to join her in the parlor for coffee, even Blakeley vied for her attention with softly spoken stories of his experiences at sea.

William rose with the men as the women departed the dining room.

"We shall be up shortly, my dear." Collin walked to the door with Susan and bent to receive a kiss on the cheek.

She ran a finger along his embellished epaulette and tapped the crown-and-anchor insignia on it that marked Collin's years of service. "No need to hurry. I am certain your toasts need saying and," she winked at William, "you have other matters to discuss."

Collin closed the door behind her and looked about the room in surprise. "What are you all still doing on your feet? Sit. Relax."

All six lieutenants glanced at William. "They stand because their superior officer and host is still on his feet, Captain Yates."

"Tosh. On *Auspicious*, we are not so formal among our fellow officers." He motioned for Fawkes and Dawling to refill the glasses.

William nodded at Cochrane, and the lieutenants all took their seats again as Collin returned to his place at the head of the table. After observing the traditional toasts, Collin raised his glass once more.

"Gentlemen, to Captain William Ransome. My best friend since we were first posted together as lads more than a score of years ago. May God bless him in all his endeavors. May he have fair winds at his stern and open seas at his bow. May his ship never fail him and his crew always support him. And may he always—*always*—return home to those who love him. To William."

William nearly choked on the hearty lump in his throat.

His officers raised their glasses. "Captain Ransome."

He lifted his in salute and pretended to drink, not daring to look at Collin, knowing he would not be able to repress his disconsolation at losing his friend if he did. Finally, after what seemed an eternity, he got the weather gauge on his inner turmoil and raised his glass again.

"Gentlemen, our host, Captain Collin Yates. The truest friend any man could ever hope for. May the friendship, kindness, brotherhood, love, and loyalty he has always given me follow him throughout his life. May he always have comfort and happiness at home and adventures and fortuity abroad. And may he discover the greatest joy of all in the arrival of his first child—and may God bless him with many more to follow. To Collin." Seeing Collin in the same extreme distress to hide his feelings cheered William a bit.

"Captain Yates," the officers saluted with their glasses.

Collin recovered faster than William had. "So, officers of *Alexandra*, what are your thoughts on your captain's intended?"

As usual, Cochrane spoke first. "She is more lovely than I expected, sir. Well versed on many subjects. And seems as though she will be an excellent passenger."

The others concurred.

"She knows enough of regulations and seafaring to have passed for lieutenancy," Jack added. "When I told her which question I had been unable to answer at my first examination, she said the answer as if it were something every lady should know."

"She will not send us to the big cabin for her parasol or to fetch her hat when it blows across the deck." A high compliment from Blakeley, who'd regaled them over the years about his previous captain's demanding wife.

"Of course, one always heard Admiral Sir Edward Witherington's daughter spoken of with only the highest praise," Eastwick said. "And she has far outstripped any fair description or compliment I have ever heard."

"She is lovely." Campbell blushed and kept his eyes cast down at the glass in his hands. "But seems sturdy enough to make the voyage with little complaint."

"Sir," O'Rourke turned to William. "Will she be happy alone on the ship?"

Loud laughter went up around the table.

"Alone?"

"Are you daft, man?"

"And shall we be invisible?"

O'Rourke scowled, the thin scar under his right eye going white. "What I mean is, there will be no other women aboard for her to keep company with, sir."

The raillery died away.

William raised his brows. "Are you suggesting we should hire on some women crew members to keep her company?"

Even O'Rourke had to smile at the absurdity of the idea. "No, sir. I just wondered why she is not bringing a maid or a companion along for company. She will have nothing to do and no one to speak to."

Collin snorted. "I like that, William. Your lieutenants have such respect for you, they think your wife will not want to speak to you."

O'Rourke flushed nearly purple. "No, sir! I meant no disrespect—"

William raised his hand and smiled at the young man. "I know, Patrick. I do take your meaning, and I commend you highly for being concerned for Miss Witherington's welfare and happiness. I share your concern and will speak to her and see if she wishes a traveling companion." Even as he said it, the thought of having to accommodate another woman rankled. *Another* woman aboard his ship! Thank goodness both Julia and Collin had already told Susan she could not go…but whom might she choose? He had never seen her with another female companion aside from her aunt—he shuddered. Frightening though the thought might be, no real concern rose in that quarter.

"Well, men, I believe we have deprived the ladies of our company long enough." Collin stood; William and his lieutenants did likewise and followed their host up to the parlor.

The gravity of the four women in the parlor immediately stifled William's good humor. Susan nudged Julia. "You must tell him. Coffee and conversation can wait."

The other men's mirth vanished, and they looked from William to Julia in great wonder. Julia's distressed gaze met his. He crossed to her and extended his hand. She took it, and once again hers trembled.

"Mrs. Yates, please excuse us for a moment." He inclined his head to Susan and led Julia across the hall. He took a candle from a sconce in the hall and lit several in the sitting room. He released Julia's hand only after securing the door behind them to ensure their privacy. No one in the house would care that they had no chaperone.

"What has happened?"

She wrapped her arms around her middle and paced away from him, the entire length of the room, and returned before speaking. "A man, a debt collector, came to the house today looking for Sir Drake."

"You have waited to tell me this until now? And only at Susan's prompting?" Keeping his voice neutral, removing all the simmering anger from it, nearly proved his undoing. She had told the women, who could offer no assistance nor protection—

"I planned to speak to you when an opportune moment arrived." Julia's green eyes flashed in the dim light. "He did nothing, merely left his card to give Sir Drake." She shivered. "But I do not believe it is the last we will see of him."

"Yes, he will most likely watch your house as well as Pembroke's. I will see you home tonight. Julia, I—" He took a fortifying breath that did nothing to fortify him. "I wish us to be married as soon as possible."

"I agree. In fact, I had already planned to speak to you of it tonight."

"Does early next week suit?"

A half-smile brought a dimple to Julia's left cheek, and she rested her hand on his arm. "It suits me, but I shall have to check with Susan to see if it suits her and Lady Dalrymple."

His arm tingled under her touch. "I shall arrange it and let you know the day as soon as it is settled." He raised her hand to kiss the backs of her fingers.

Julia's smile faded, her eyes following her hand to his lips. The few candles he'd lit heated the room to an extraordinary temperature. He released her hand and opened the door.

"We had best return to the others." He motioned her to exit ahead of him.

"Yes. We'd best." She floated out of the room, her gown glowing like an ember.

He snuffed the candles and joined her in the hall, shaking off a strange light-headedness. "Was there anything else this debt collector said to you?"

Julia frowned at him in confusion until comprehension dawned. "I asked him how much Sir Drake owed him. He said his employer holds a twenty thousand pound mortgage on Marchwood—the house and much of the grounds—and will be calling for full payment Monday unless Sir Drake can pay it and five thousand in interest by then. He also said Sir Drake has been losing quite a bit in recent days. No doubt gambling to try to win enough to pay this creditor. But how much more is he incurring?"

Aghast at such a sum, William stared at her for a moment.

"If I had the money, I would purchase the mortgage note myself—not to save Sir Drake, mind you, but out of respect for my mother's childhood home."

He trailed her into the parlor. Purchase Marchwood estate? The admiral had spoken of it as good farming country—good for raising sheep—and several mills were attached to the property. And according to Sir Edward, it lay only a couple hours' drive from Portsmouth. He could put good men to work and provide himself with an additional source of income—himself and Julia. Collin and Susan could stay there when they wished to escape Portsmouth.

Purchase Marchwood estate. To what better use could he put Julia's bridal legacy?

Chapter Twenty-Nine

*A*lexandra hardly moved at her mooring, but the faint motion of the harbor waves rocking the ship from side to side brought William to his knees. He knelt in his sleeping cabin, now half-filled with the hanging box-bed, overwhelmed by joy.

"Thank you, almighty Father, for bestowing upon your servant the answer to my prayer. Bless this ship and continue to bless her crew. Make me a captain worthy of them and guide me with your omnipotent hand to earn their trust and loyalty."

"Captain." Cochrane stopped short at the door.

"And, Lord, please teach my first officer how to knock. Amen." William stood. "Yes, Mr. Cochrane?"

"Sir, the midshipmen are gathered on the dock, ready to come aboard. Dawling is with them."

"Excellent." William shrugged into his uniform coat and buttoned it, striding out of his cabin onto the sunny, sparkling quarterdeck. "All hands!"

The lieutenants and warrant officers gathered around him.

"Launch boats and go pick up our little gentlemen. Ned, take the crew logbook with you so we have an accurate accounting of whom we are bringing aboard. Remember, only those who formerly served aboard *Alexandra* may sign on now. After the crew return next week, if we are short in any positions, we will sign on new mids or sailors at that time."

"Aye, aye, sir." Ned touched the fore point of his hat.

William repeated the gesture. "Mr. Ingleby, you are with me."

The ship's master knuckled his forehead. "Aye, aye, Cap'n."

As soon as three of the cutters were in the water and pulling toward the dock, William and Ingleby turned their attention to inspecting the helm, binnacle, and wheel housing, passing the next hour examining each peg, nail, and piece of metal or wood.

"Hoy, the *Alexandra*!"

William left the helm and went to the waist entry port. "Who goes?"

Cochrane saluted. "First Lieutenant Cochrane for *Alexandra*, sir. Request to come aboard."

William's smile claimed half his mouth before he could stop it. "Permission to come aboard granted. Midshipmen may enter by the main deck entry port, stow their dunnage, and report to me on the quarterdeck."

"Aye, aye, Captain." Each of the six young men in Cochrane's boat touched the flat, round brims of their hats, grinning like schoolboys on holiday. The second boat arrived with six more midshipmen, and William gave them the same orders. Twelve midshipmen—meaning four more would have to be found next week.

The warrant officers, in the smallest boat, arrived last and hurried up the accommodation ladder to rig the bosun's chair to haul William's trunk and furniture.

He followed the men into his cabin and tried not to notice their knowing glances at the sight of the fancy, large bed. Dawling came to the day cabin as soon as he stowed his dunnage in his own quarters. William dismissed the other sailors.

"Report."

"I seen the minister this morning. He said he can marry you on Tuesday morning, so I did as you said and saw to the arranging of it."

William's collar chafed against the sudden sweat on the back of his neck. "Very well."

"And then I went to see about posting your letter. I seen the express rider there, ready to go, but the clerk said I must pass the letter through him. But then, sir—you remember how that one time you pointed out that Pembroke fellow to me?—well, sir, I saw him talking to the post-master, and it looked like Pembroke was giving him money."

The perspiration turned to shards of ice on William's skin. "You saw money change hands between Pembroke and the postmaster?"

"I can't say for sure and certain, sir, but it appeared so to me. So I told the clerk I would watch him frank the letter and then I would carry it out to the express rider, who had already gone outside. The clerk figured I was wise to him, so he franked the letter and I gave it to the rider, and I watched him put it in his pouch and ride off on the road to London."

William stared out the stern windows at another ship moored a hundred yards away. No wonder neither he nor Julia had heard from the admiral. Pembroke had bribed the postmaster to intercept their letters.

How could he marry Julia without the admiral's knowledge? How could he *not* marry her and leave her unprotected from the rest of her relatives?

"Sir?"

"Thank you, Dawling. That is all—wait. Is my writing desk in my sea chest?"

"Yes, sir." Dawling made to move into the sleeping quarters.

"Never mind. I will get it myself. Report to Lieutenant Cochrane; he will have duties for you."

"Aye, aye, sir."

William unlocked and opened his flat-topped trunk. The past three weeks had made quite an improvement in Dawling's skills—if Dawling had indeed packed the neat, orderly trunk on his own. He found the mahogany box with ease, closed the lid of the chest, and placed the writing desk atop it—opening it out to expose the leather-covered writing surface. He withdrew paper from the large compartment under the top of the writing surface and sat on the floor beside his sea chest.

He would have to proceed with the wedding and beg Sir Edward's forgiveness later.

‾‾‾‾

"Miss Witherington?"

Julia looked up from her book. "Yes, Creighton?"

"There's a young man, a midshipman, at the door who wishes to speak to you. He will not tell me his name or purpose."

She marked her place in the thick, new novel, purchased just this morning and meant to be kept to read on the long voyage. In the entry foyer stood a young man, no older than sixteen or seventeen, dressed in a midshipman's uniform, perusing the trinkets her father had bought through the years in various ports of call, displayed on a narrow table.

He snapped to attention when she cleared her throat. "Afternoon, Miss Witherington. Cap'n Ransome asked me to deliver this to you and to carry back any message in response."

She masked her amusement with raised brows and angling her head askance. "And whom do I have the honor of receiving?"

He flushed dark red. "Sorry, miss. Josiah Gibson. I'm a midshipman aboard the *Alexandra*." He fumbled with his tall, round black hat.

"Thank you, Mr. Gibson." She took the folded note from the lad and slid her thumb under the seal.

> My dear Miss Witherington,
>
> If you are agreeable, I have fixed Tuesday as the day for us to be married at the Church of Saint Thomas at nine o'clock in the morning. I have sent an express to London to inform your father. I will leave it to you to inform Susan and Collin.
>
> Please send word with Mr. Gibson to let me know if after Tuesday I may address you as my dear Mrs. Ransome.
>
> Yours faithfully,
> Wm. Ransome

Skin feeling too tight and hot, she refolded the note and turned. "Creighton, please take Mr. Gibson to the kitchen for some refreshment. I'll be in the library."

The butler nodded and ushered the boy through the door at the end of the hall. Julia returned to her father's study and helped herself to parchment, pen, and ink from his desk.

She dashed off a note to William and took it down to the kitchen. Midshipman Gibson—was he the one the lieutenants had spoken of as the extraordinary singer?—tried to stand and leave his refreshments barely touched. Julia insisted he stay until he finished the shortbread and cider, plying him with questions about his duties and what the officers and captain of *Alexandra* were doing today.

She walked with him to the front door and had Creighton pay the hackney driver for the extra time he had been made to wait.

Creighton returned. "I take it the note was not ill news?"

"No. The opposite. I am to be married Tuesday. You are the first to know."

"Once again, I wish you joy, miss."

"Thank you. Have Elton bring Father's barouche around. I must go see Mrs. Yates."

"Yes, miss."

She sighed, looking up the wide, dark wood stairs. "And I suppose I should tell Lady Pembroke and Lady MacDougall."

Creighton cocked a brow and shook his head in a better-you-than-me gesture and left her to go fetch Elton. Julia stared up the stairs. At least one of the women would be happy for her.

The door of the sitting room stood open. Both women looked up from their needlework when Julia cleared her throat.

"To what do we owe this…honor?" Augusta's eyebrows raised nearly to her dark hair.

"I have come, ma'am, to let you know that my wedding date has been set—for Tuesday morning." Julia swallowed hard. "If you would like to attend, you would be welcome."

The two ladies exchanged glances. Julia backed toward the door.

Lady MacDougall's smile crinkled her porcelain skin. "We must celebrate. Will you not stay and take tea with us?"

"Thank you, my lady, but I must decline. I am on my way out to make a call. I will most likely not be back for dinner." Susan would insist Julia stay. "Please excuse me."

Entering her own room, she startled Nancy, who turned from putting folded underthings into a drawer in the wardrobe. "Quickly, Nancy, I must change into something suitable for tea or dinner. I have two calls I must make this afternoon and need to appear presentable."

Fifteen minutes later, dressed in a twilight blue gown embellished with Greek-key design in silver, hair down as she preferred, Julia returned downstairs.

"Afternoon, miss." Elton touched his hat as he offered his assistance to hand her up into the barouche. "Where to?"

"Lady Dalrymple's first. That will be a short call."

But Lady Dalrymple's butler informed them her ladyship was not in when they arrived at the massive, ancient stone manor. Julia left a card and directed Elton to turn the horses toward the Yateses' home.

☙❦❧

"Sir, Mr. Gibson's returned."

William looked up from the purser's account book when Dawling entered the cabin. "Thank you. Please show him in. Mr. Holt, you are excused for now. We will continue this shortly." He longed to remove his coat but tried to ignore the stifling heat coming in short puffs through the open stern windows.

Midshipman Gibson entered, removed his hat, and stood at attention.

"Did you see Miss Witherington?"

"Aye, sir."

William crossed his arms. "Describe her to me." He wouldn't put it past Lady Pembroke to have locked Julia away in her room and have a housemaid dress in one of Julia's frocks—

"Er, well," Gibson sputtered. "She's about so tall," he held his hand up level with his own nose, "with dark hair…oh, and green eyes."

That could pass as a description of her. "And what did she say to you?"

"She asked me whom she was addressing, and then she told the butler to take me to the kitchen for a refreshment—and I had no thought other than water. But the cook, sir, she wouldn't rest without I ate some shortbread and cider. And then Miss Witherington came down to the kitchen—aye, sir she came to the kitchen as if she does it all the time—and gave me this for you." He extended his hand.

William took the folded packet. The outside bore *Captain Sir William Ransome, HMS Alexandra* in a hand he didn't recognize. He'd expected it to be more flowing and artistic, not plain and angular, each letter formed clearly but without exaggerated tails or flourishes, the way his mother and sister wrote.

He cleared his throat. "Did she say anything else?"

Gibson shook his head, his sandy curls dancing about his cheeks and collar. The lad needed his hair trimmed. William would see all the officers were properly groomed before Julia—before Admiral Glover made inspection next week.

"Thank you, Mr. Gibson. Please see Mr. Cochrane for your duty assignment."

"Aye, aye, Cap'n." The midshipman nodded and exited, the door closing behind him with a soft click.

William sat on his sea chest and popped the wax seal, impressed with an intertwined, script *TD*.

> My dear Captain Ransome,
>
> Tuesday is an agreeable day for you to begin addressing me as your dear Mrs. Ransome. As soon as I finish writing and send Mr. Gibson back to you, I will call upon Susan and Collin to let them know of the date and let Susan fly into a whirl of panic as she will now only have Saturday and Monday for the final preparations for the wedding breakfast.
>
> I do hope your letter reaches my father. I fear none of mine have. I know our marriage will please him, but I still wish

to have his blessing. Please let me know with all due haste if you receive word from him.

Yours faithfully,
Julia Witherington

He slipped the letter into the front cover of his Bible and exited the cabin. He joined Cochrane on the quarterdeck, where the first officer supervised the arrival of cargo.

"Ned, did Holt see you about the butcher and grocer estimates?" William leaned over the gunwale to watch the progress of the boat carrying the rest of his furniture.

"Aye, sir." Cochrane yelled an order at a midshipman rigging the bosun's chair. He nodded when the teen jumped-to, and then he returned his attention to William. "I ran into a young man on the docks earlier. Lad by the name of Charles Lott. Scrawny for fifteen, but seemed to know what he was about when I put questions to him."

"You would recommend him for midshipman on *Alexandra* from one meeting?" William raised a brow. Ned was known for being a stern but fair taskmaster with the youngsters who were hoping to become officers.

Ned thought for a moment, watching the crew scurry about the deck. "Aye, sir. I believe he'll be a good addition, either to *Alexandra* or to *Audacious.*"

"See to it then. I will also need you to acquaint yourself with the Witheringtons' butler so when the time comes, you can arrange for Miss Witherington's dunnage to be brought aboard."

"Aye, aye, sir." Cochrane's voice took on a teasing lilt.

William scowled at him and then turned his attention to the hired men in the boat below as they secured ropes around the pieces of the long table for his dining cabin—the table at which he would dine with Julia every day for the next two months. That thought brought a smile he couldn't stop.

❦

"Miss Witherington, welcome." Fawkes threw the door open wide. "I believe you know how to find the parlor. Rheumatism." He bent to tap his knee. "Now that young Dawling is gone, I must speak to Captain Yates about an apprentice."

"Thank you, Fawkes." Julia handed over her hat and gloves to the wizened butler.

Elton turned to go back to the carriage. Julia turned. "Elton, I hope you realize I intend you to stay here and wait for me. I do not know how long I will be."

Delight beamed from his eyes. "Thank you, er, yes, Miss Witherington."

Julia trotted upstairs, eager to see Susan, but stopped short when she arrived on the main level. Voices floated out of the parlor—Susan's and another woman's. She stopped, adjusted the mother-of-pearl combs in her hair, and was pleased she had changed into a gown fitting to be seen in company.

She stepped into the open doorway and knocked.

"Julia!" Susan leapt from her seat, flew across the room, and nearly knocked Julia over with the force of her embrace. "Lady Dalrymple just told me—we've been planning the breakfast, you see!" Susan grabbed Julia by the hand and dragged her into the room.

On the table between Susan and Lady Dalrymple lay several pieces of paper covered in Susan's enthusiastic scrawl.

"How—"

"I am to blame, Miss Witherington." Lady Dalrymple stood. "My nephew is sextant at Saint Thomas's. He knew I wished to be alerted of your wedding date and came to see me this morning after Captain Ransome's man left."

"I can hardly stand it—Tuesday!" Susan gripped Julia's arm. "Only four days from now."

Laughing, Julia sank into a free chair at the table. "I cannot express my gratitude to the two of you for arranging the wedding. I have so much to do to prepare to leave—packing and readying my business affairs."

"I shall come tomorrow and help you." Susan alighted on the edge of her seat and nearly vibrated with excitement.

"Does Lady Pembroke know of the date?" Lady Dalrymple asked. The distaste in her voice startled Julia.

"Yes, I told her before I came here."

Lady Dalrymple beamed. "Good. I shall call on her and see how she is bearing it." The dowager viscountess pressed her hand to Julia's cheek. "You have no idea how much your presence in Portsmouth has delighted me these past months, my dear. Nor how I detest being taken in by the likes of that Sir Drake Pembroke. To think I believed him a gentleman deserving of your affection and Captain Ransome not worthy of your attention. How wrong I was. But all is as it should be now, and I could not be more pleased."

Susan walked Lady Dalrymple out and then returned. "Come, Julia, let us move across the hall, where we may be more comfortable." She took up the scattered pages and stacked them neatly. "What a charming woman Lady Dalrymple is. I never realized how delightful she could be until she called on me earlier in the week to say she wanted your wedding breakfast to be at her home."

"Nor did I."

"My dressmaker told me this morning—she was here to let out the waists in a few frocks—that your gown for the wedding is nearly finished. I shall send word for her to come tomorrow to fit it to you."

"Susan, what shall I do when I leave Portsmouth and no longer have someone to plan my days for me?" Julia teased.

Tears pooled in Susan's eyes. "Oh, don't say that! I cannot bear to think of your leaving so soon."

Contrite, Julia sat beside her friend on the sofa. "Now, Susan. What was it you read to me the other day? 'True friends of the heart can never be parted no matter how much distance separates them.'"

Dabbing her eyes with a handkerchief, Susan nodded. "Do not mind my outburst. Tears come whether I will or not these days. Besides, Collin says that after the baby comes and is strong enough, we will go to Jamaica to visit you. And perhaps by then," Susan smiled through her tears, "you will have a child of your own."

Julia blanched, all of her misgivings and confusion over the nature of her marriage to William returning. She forced a smile. "We shall see what God wills."

Chapter Thirty

Creighton knocked on Julia's door. "A Mr. Kennedy to see you, miss."

She tossed the armful of dresses onto her bed. "How did he arrive, Creighton?"

"Hack cab." His expression grew grave at the sight of the open trunk on Julia's floor.

She patted his arm as she passed him. "Father will return before too long. Of course, I could ask Captain Ransome if he knows of anyone looking for a steward."

Interest kindled in his eyes, then faded. "Thank you, miss, but I cannot leave the admiral."

This morning's midshipman appeared somewhat younger than yesterday's, with dark hair and eyes, and a short, stocky build. He knuckled his forehead and handed William's note to Julia with a toothy grin.

She couldn't help but smile back. "Go with Creighton for some refreshment. My response will be ready shortly."

"Thank you, miss." Kennedy knuckled his forehead again and disappeared behind Creighton.

Julia opened the missive as she ambled to her father's study.

13 August 1814
HMS *Alexandra*

My dear Miss Witherington,

As promised, here is my midshipman to bring word of your continued safety and happiness. The mids now consider this to be the highest of duties, once they heard of your cook's shortbread from Gibson.

Today will be a busy day as we sign on our crew and marines. I shall conduct Sunday services aboard *Alexandra* tomorrow, so I will not see you before Tuesday. I remain,

Yours faithfully,
Wm. Ransome

She wrote a quick reply and took it to the kitchen. Kennedy proved more open and talkative than Gibson and even had Creighton laughing over his stories of his and his fellow midshipmen's antics on their last voyage.

No sooner had Kennedy departed than Susan arrived as promised to spend the morning helping Julia pack—or at least get a good start on it in preparation for leaving in a fortnight.

Susan insisted Julia take all her gowns back to Jamaica. "Do you want the people thinking the wife of Captain William Ransome does not dress befitting her husband's wealth and rank?".

Julia acquiesced, though worried about the amount of luggage— the large trunk, which had fit all of her gowns and personal possessions on the voyage to England, would be needed along with a smaller chest and two valises. Additionally, she had enough books to fill at least one crate, and she really would like to take her banana-wood desk and chair back with her.

At two o'clock, they left to go back to Susan's house to meet the dressmaker. The lavender silk gown was rather plainer than Julia had expected. But perhaps simplicity was better.

She turned when she saw Susan assist the dressmaker to lift something out of the box—something white.

"You did not think, did you, that after the fuss I made over finding just the right color silk, I would allow you to marry in such a plain style? Close your eyes. I do not want you to see this until it is on you."

Julia did as bade, moving her arms and head when instructed.

When they finished pushing and prodding her, silence descended.

"Susan?"

"Yes—I do apologize."

Hands on Julia's shoulders turned her around.

"Open your eyes."

Standing facing the full-length mirror, Julia lost the capacity to breathe—the overdress was made completely of ivory lace, hand netted with thread fine as spiders' silk, revealing a few inches of the lavender silk at the hem in the front and cascading into a train behind. A dark purple velvet ribbon wove through the lace at the ribband and at the neck, where it gathered into a narrow ruff at the base of Julia's throat. The long sleeves also revealed the silk at her wrists.

Tears burned her eyes. "Susan, where did the lace come from?"

"It was my mother's—from the gown she married in. You are taller than she, but as the skirts were so much wider thirty years ago, there was plenty."

"Oh, I cannot—Susan, no—"

"Hush. My aunt wanted me to have everything new when Collin and I got married. In fact, I had forgotten until recently I had this in the bottom of my keepsake trunk. I can think of no better use than to make my dearest friend the most beautiful bride Britain has ever seen." Susan frowned slightly. "But tell me—do you like it?"

Julia cleared her throat. "It is the most exquisite garment I have ever laid eyes upon." She met Susan's gaze in the mirror.

Susan beamed. "You shall wear your hair down. William cannot keep his eyes off you when it is loose." She handed Julia a flimsy package wrapped in paper.

Julia untied the twine and unfolded the paper to reveal more of the lace.

"Rather than your wearing your veil from a bonnet, we shall make a wreath of white roses and lilac from my garden for your hair."

They argued about whether she would wear her hair up or down, wear a bonnet or a wreath of flowers, while the dressmaker nipped and pinned a few places to make alterations. After the woman left and

Julia was back in her day dress, she and Susan collapsed into the twin chairs that flanked the fireplace.

"I shall hold this dress in trust, Susan." Julia promised. "Should you have a daughter, I will return it to you to be made over for her—in whatever the style is when she is old enough to marry."

Susan's hands rested on her slightly thickened waist. "Collin says he does not care if the child is a boy or girl, but I know he wants a son because we cannot depend upon having any other children, if indeed we do have this one."

"We will have none of that talk, if you please." Julia hit Susan's knee with an embroidered pillow. "You must be confident; you must have faith in God's blessing."

"You are so good for me, Julia." She glanced at the clock on the mantel. "Oh, look at the time. I told Mrs. Ransome we would join them for tea at four o'clock."

Over tea, Mrs. Ransome acquiesced to Susan's and Charlotte's cajoling to tell stories of William as a child. Listening to his mother speak of him with such love evident in her voice, Julia sank into melancholy, thinking of her own childhood and how sad her mother had always been, waiting for a letter or a visit from her husband.

"Julia, are you quite all right?" Mrs. Ransome asked, interrupting her own story.

Overwrought from the day's extreme of emotions, Julia surprised herself and the other three women in the room by bursting into tears. She fumbled with her sleeve for a handkerchief before remembering she'd left it on the dressing table in Susan's room.

Mrs. Ransome moved to sit beside Julia on the settee and offered her own handkerchief.

"I am...sorry...your story. I was just thinking...my mother—" A fresh wave of sobs overwhelmed her, and she could not continue.

Mrs. Ransome pulled Julia into her arms. "There now, child. It is hard to lose one's mother at such a young age. Susan has told me how dear she was to you. Though I could never assume to take her place, I hope you will allow me to consider you a daughter of my heart—and that you will look on me as your mother."

Grief welled up and threatened to drown her. "I was such a disappointment. She wanted me to be a lady, to keep out of the business of the plantation. She wanted to see me married, to see her grandchildren…"

"Oh, my darling girl, do not let regrets hover as a cloud over you. I am certain your mother was very proud of you and all your accomplishments." Mrs. Ransome took the handkerchief back and wiped Julia's cheeks. "Come, now. No more tears. You will soon learn the Ransome family is one of happiness and joy. You will be sister to Charlotte and James and Philip; they will not allow you to know anything but happiness in our family. And, of course, there is dear William." She dropped her voice to a whisper hardly audible to even Julia. "You respect each other now, but I pray the two of you will soon find love and real happiness with each other."

She should not have been surprised that William told his mother the whole story of their engagement, but she was surprised that though Mrs. Ransome knew the truth, William's mother still treated her like a beloved daughter.

Charlotte came to kneel in front of her and took Julia's free hand in hers. "I have already told you how much I have always longed for a sister. And I know Mama prayed for many years for more than one daughter. You are the answer to that prayer, Julia."

Through the tears still blurring her vision, Julia regarded William's sister. The young woman sat here and listened to her mother call another woman "daughter," watched her hold and comfort another woman. And yet rather than jealousy, Charlotte joined wholeheartedly into the sentiment, happy to see her mother loving someone else.

Had William felt as Julia did now when her father took him under his care, treating him as a son? If Michael had lived, he would never have been jealous over sharing his father's affection with someone else. He would have been like Charlotte—would have seen William as an adopted brother, someone to bring more love and joy to his own life.

Oh, how she desired to see her father—to be able to apologize to him. To say she finally understood him, the man whose affections she'd chased her entire life. The man she might not see again for a very, very long time.

⊙≈≈≈⊙

"Thank you, Mr. Kennedy. That will be all."

"Aye, aye, sir." The teen saluted and exited the cabin.

William shrugged out of his coat and carried Julia's note to the leather-covered seat under the stern windows. Leaning his shoulder against the frame of the open window, he slid his thumb under the *TD*-imprinted wax seal and unfolded the parchment.

> My dear Captain Ransome,
>
> All is well. Susan is to call this morning to help me begin to pack so I shall be prepared for removal from England. Then we shall return to her home to meet with her dressmaker. I look forward to seeing your mother and sister while I am there.
>
> Naturally, I am disappointed I will not see you tomorrow at church, but as Lord Nelson so aptly said, "England expects that every man will do his duty."
>
> Yours faithfully,
> Julia

William tucked the note into the front of his Bible. He was marrying a woman who could not only quote Lord Nelson but who understood the importance and the honor of doing one's duty even when it called for sacrifices at home. God could not have blessed him with a more suitable wife; he would endeavor to do everything in his power to see to his duty of being a good husband as well.

Cochrane returned to the ship shortly after midnight with the last boatload of sailors. William dismissed them to hang their hammocks and get a few hours' sleep.

"Mr. Cochrane, the crew is to be piped up, hammocks stowed by seven bells in the morning watch as usual. No duties assigned before that time. At eight bells, they are to be assembled on the quarterdeck for Sunday prayers."

Cochrane, with dark circles under his eyes, black neckcloth askew, nodded. "Aye, sir."

William longed to rub the gritty exhaustion from his own eyes. "Who is officer of the watch now?"

"Blakeley, sir."

"He and his watch are to be on light duty tomorrow, as they have worked all day alongside everyone else with no respite."

"Aye, sir."

"How many sailors returned?"

"Five hundred fifty."

"And the marine contingent? Was Sergeant Ryken reassigned to us?"

"Yes, sir. He has already filled out his number to the required one hundred twenty-five and signed them on in good order."

"And the missing midshipmen—none of them came today?"

Cochrane shook his head wearily. "No, sir."

"So we need four mids and sixty-four sailors. Monday, we shall put a notice up at the port Admiralty, and the end of next week, we will fulfill our capacity."

"Aye, sir."

"And Dr. Wells?"

"No, sir. Though he did send word. He has returned to Yorkshire and taken up his practice there. He has, however, recommended a Dr. Hawthorne to us." Cochrane fished a letter from his pocket.

"Please see to contacting Dr. Hawthorne. Have him come Monday morning at eleven."

"Aye, sir."

"I believe everything else can wait until tomorrow."

"Yes, sir."

"Good. Dismissed."

Cochrane saluted and exited the cabin. William started peeling layers of his uniform off as soon as his first lieutenant's back turned. Dawling entered before the door could latch. The burly seaman bustled around the room, taking clothing as William removed it, straightening up, and dousing the lamps.

After dismissing Dawling and climbing into his old hammock, William lay awake, picturing himself telling the crew of his impending marriage and of Julia's presence on board. Though the officers had borne it well, the crew might not be so understanding. Most believed in the long-held superstitions that had once ruled the seas. Their belief that women brought bad luck to a ship and its crew could create any number of problems—from disorderly conduct to mutiny.

Staring at the oaken boards above him, he mentally rehearsed the words he would give to the crew after prayers in the morning. But his mind strayed into vivid imaginings of the sailors' reactions to the news.

The time between the bells, although only half an hour, dragged interminably. He prayed for sleep to come, yet each time he nearly drifted off, a new vision of the crew taking the news badly startled him awake. Would the night never end?

When three bells chimed at five thirty, he started out of a restless doze. He lit the lamp at his desk and opened his small, worn leather Bible. Reading in the book of Acts of Paul's shipwreck did nothing to increase his ease, so he turned to the Psalms instead. Still, he found no solace in the words.

He closed the book and touched it to his forehead. *Lord God, you have directed my path thus far. Father, please give me the appropriate words to tell the crew, and grant me wisdom for the day ahead.*

Feeling calmer than he had all night, William rose, washed his face, and shaved before Dawling appeared at four bells. William ignored the breakfast tray, visions of the crew mutinying still too vivid in his imagination.

He shrugged into the uniform coat Dawling held up for him. The morning ritual lulled him into a moderate sense of normalcy. He closed his eyes. His life would never be *normal* again.

"Everything all right, sir?" Dawling glanced meaningfully at the tray of untouched eggs, sausages, and black pudding.

"Fine." William turned away from the sight of the food, stomach churning. "Just not hungry."

Scowling, Dawling retreated with the tray.

William tucked his prayer book into his pocket and exited the cabin onto the quarterdeck. He climbed the stairs to take his position on the starboard side of the poop deck. As the bells chimed off the remainder of the morning watch, the crew began to fill the quarterdeck and forecastle, and by the time the midshipman of the watch sounded eight bells, eight o'clock and beginning of the forenoon watch, the six lieutenants had joined him.

Hands clasped behind him, William leaned forward, a slight breeze ruffling his hair between hat and collar. "Good morning, crew of the *Alexandra*."

The crew saluted and shouted their good-morning back, and everyone removed his hat.

William quoted from Habakkuk, the beginning of morning prayers as outlined in the prayer book. He paused, and the lapping of the harbor against the ship filled his ears. After praying, he opened his prayer book to read the passage from the Old Testament, a Psalm, and selections from an epistle and one of the Gospels, interspersed with responsive passages calling for the crew to answer. The voices of his men raised in praise to God and the words of the Scripture lifted William, buoying him with the knowledge of God's presence and ultimate control.

He reached the end of the service, secure in the knowledge all would be well. "Praise ye the Lord."

"The Lord's name be praised," the crew responded.

Returning his hat to his head, William glanced over his crew as they gazed at him expectantly, waiting to be released to duty or breakfast. "Before I dismiss you, I must make an announcement. Lieutenant Cochrane will be arranging accommodations for a guest...for a lady who will travel with us to Jamaica."

The men who'd just repeated the words from the prayer book now muttered in a manner unfit for Christian society. Cochrane called the crew to attention.

Now came the true test of the men who'd served under him for more than two years. William fisted his hands. "On Tuesday morning, I will marry Miss Julia Witherington who will—"

The crew erupted into cheers. Cochrane stood by, beaming his delight. William could not find his voice to call the men to order. How could he have doubted them?

Chapter Thirty-One

Julia, will you ~~will~~ join us in the sitting room?" Lady MacDougall asked as they entered the house after the church service.

Julia set her reticule and her father's prayer book on a side table and joined her aunts. She returned Lady MacDougall's smile.

"Augusta and I have been talking about the visit to Marchwood. If you are to go before you are married, that leaves us only tomorrow."

Her stomach lurched. Day after tomorrow, she would be married. To William.

"I know you have graciously allowed me to stay until your departure from England." Augusta sat on the edge of the white brocade settee. "But I thought it might be best if I were to leave tomorrow instead. That way, your husband will not think my presence an intrusion."

Julia opened her mouth to tell them he was now living on his ship, a situation that would not change with their marriage, but bit back the words. The last person she wanted to reveal the true nature of the arrangement to was Augusta Pembroke. "If you feel you must go, I will ask the housekeeper to help you arrange the packing of your belongings."

"Which brings me to my point, dear." Hedwig paused to cough into her handkerchief. "Augusta told me she has a few business matters to attend tomorrow morning before she can leave. It is a four-hour drive to Marchwood from Portsmouth. If we do not leave until late morning, that will not give you time enough to properly see the house and grounds."

Unless they left very early in the morning, Hedwig was correct. There would be no time to see Marchwood and still return to Portsmouth by a reasonable hour. "Then perhaps I'd best not go—or at least postpone my visit until after the wedding."

Hedwig drew in a deep breath, which sent her into another coughing fit.

"Are you unwell, Aunt?" Julia moved to sit beside her on the chaise. "Shall I ring for the housekeeper to bring you some tea?"

"Oh, I am quite all right. Just a cough that comes when the wind kicks up as it did today." She patted Julia's hand. "Now, what I was going to suggest is that you and I take the drive out to Marchwood this afternoon. We can stay the night. Then your driver can bring Augusta tomorrow, and he can return you to Portsmouth by the afternoon."

"I..." Uncertainty grappled with her interest in seeing Marchwood.

"It would give us a chance to know one another better." Hedwig cocked her head to the side the same way Julia's mother had when trying to convince Julia of something.

How could she deny her? "Of course, Aunt Hedwig. I shall need time to pack a bag and...see to some other necessities. But I shall go with you this afternoon."

"There is a reputable inn at Bishop's Waltham. If you leave within the hour, you would arrive in time to take tea there and have them send a messenger to Marchwood of your arrival." Augusta directed her smile toward Lady MacDougall, her ready agreement with the plan a bit suspicious.

"Oh, that would be lovely." Hedwig beamed. "Julia, do you think you could be ready to leave in an hour?"

Her heart wrenched, torn between wanting to find out what Augusta was up to and wanting to please Hedwig. "Yes, I believe I can be."

Hedwig stood, coughing delicately. "Then we'd best begin preparations."

Julia jogged up the stairs to her room. Tossing the reticule and prayer book onto the bed, she immediately sat down and started a note to Susan, informing her of the change of plans. Of course, she wasn't certain how she would get it to Susan, with both Creighton and Elton not working today.

She'd have to ask Susan to get word to William so he would not worry about her absence tomorrow.

After stamping the note with the Tierra Dulce seal, she thought for a moment and then wrote another note that she folded and sealed around it—a note to Creighton so he also would not worry and so he would pay careful attention to Lady Pembroke's actions. Quietly as she could, she sneaked down the hall to the service stairs and climbed the two flights to the servants' quarters. Creighton's room was the first and largest. She felt odd entering his private domain, but once inside, she was not surprised to see everything squared away with naval precision.

The floorboards creaked behind Julia. She whirled around, but saw no one. Just the house groaning with the day's heat.

She left the note for Creighton on the small table that served as his desk and then slipped back down to her room. She packed a few toiletries, undergarments, and a day dress in her small valise and was ready to leave when one of Lady MacDougall's footmen knocked on her door a few minutes later.

Julia wanted to call him back as soon as he disappeared down the hall with her valise. This was a foolhardy venture. She couldn't trust Aunt Augusta here on her own, could she? What if Augusta and Drake tried something in her absence?

"But what could they do?" Julia asked her empty room. The strongbox was safe with Susan and Collin. Certainly there were valuables in the house, but they would not be so stupid as to try to outright steal—would they?

Commotion out in the hallway caught her attention—the two footmen with Hedwig's trunks.

Hedwig stopped at Julia's open door. "Are you ready to go, dear?"

Go or stay? It was only one night. What harm could come of that? "Yes, I am."

CRRRC

"All well with Miss Witherington?" Ned touched the fore-point of his hat.

William returned the salute, watching as the launch carrying Collin back to shore rowed away from *Alexandra*. "Aye. Captain Yates reported she was in good spirits at church this morning." He looked toward the horizon. "Sunset. Have the drummer beat to quarters for inspection."

"Aye, aye, sir." Ned relayed the orders. The marine drummer began his tattoo, and the officers and crew sprang into action, converging on their battle stations.

William checked his watch once everyone had gained his place. "Too slow, Mr. Cochrane. We shall have to work on that before we leave harbor."

"Aye, aye, Captain."

William walked about the quarterdeck before descending to the main deck to inspect each gun crew. When convinced each of the men on *Alexandra* remembered his station and position, he returned to the quarterdeck. "Division officers, release your divisions."

"Dismissed!" resounded throughout the ship. The crew retrieved their hammocks from where they were stuffed into the netting and decamped below deck. William dismissed the midshipmen to their navigation lesson with the ship's master and the officers to the wardroom.

Dawling met him in the dining cabin, a dinner tray on the table. The weeks at the Yateses' had improved Dawling's skills almost miraculously—especially his cooking.

After devouring the beef and potatoes, William withdrew to his desk to take up the stack of applications he had received from those seeking midshipman positions. He would receive many more once they posted the openings tomorrow, and he wanted to ensure he chose the best.

At ten o'clock, two hours into the first watch and eyes gritty and head beginning to ache, William doused the candle and retired for the night. Phantom ships and cannon fire from long-finished battles haunted his dreams, and he climbed out of the hammock well before dawn, still exhausted.

He received the report from the officer of the night watch, then returned to the issue of personnel. Several times, he caught himself nodding off. This was no good. He left the cabin and took a brisk stroll about the ship. The light was not yet full, but the day promised to be a scorcher.

"Cap'n Ransome, sir!"

He spun at the boatswain's call. "Yes, Matthews?"

The small man's bare feet pounded the decking as he ran toward William. He paused to gulp in a few breaths. "Sir, a boat come up. There be a man on it who insist to speak to you—he says he needs to see you about Miss Witherington."

"Show me." He jogged behind the warrant officer to the other side of the ship, crewmen scurrying to move out of his way.

At the waist entry port, William leaned over to see a jolly boat bearing Creighton. His innards twisted with hurricane force.

"Permission to come aboard, Captain?" Creighton shouted.

"Permission granted." William stood stock-still as the admiral's former steward climbed the accommodation ladder. Creighton snapped to attention and knuckled his forehead as soon as he gained the deck.

"Come with me." William spun on his heel and hastened to his cabin. He closed the door behind them and circled to the head of the dining table. "Speak."

"Captain Ransome, sir." Creighton saluted again. "You told me that should anything happen—" The butler swallowed hard, panic rolling off him in surges. "Sir, Miss Witherington has disappeared."

Dread knotted around William's heart. "Explain."

"When I returned to the house this morning, Miss Witherington was gone."

William clenched his hands together behind his back, his facade of calm about to shatter. "You are certain she was not still sleeping?"

"No sir. I arrived for duty at five o'clock. I…" He flushed deeply. "Sir, because of your concern, I asked the cook to peek into Miss Witherington's room, just to make sure all was well. She wasn't there, sir. Her bed was not slept in." His voice quavered, and he took a deep breath. "Sir, Lady MacDougall's carriage is also gone. I fear Miss Witherington may have gone somewhere with the baroness."

"Marchwood." William's mood blackened. He'd kept his concerns over her aunt's invitation to visit the Pembroke home to himself. He had not thought she would be naive enough to go before she had the protection of his name.

"I do not wish to believe the worst about anyone, sir, but I believe Lady MacDougall might not have the best intentions toward Miss Witherington."

William nodded. "I believe you are correct, Creighton." He stepped to the door and opened it. The marine guard saluted. "Pass word for Mr. Cochrane." He went into his sleeping quarters and strapped on his cutlass and pistol before returning to the dining cabin.

Cochrane entered, surprise overtaking his bleary eyes at the sight of Creighton and of William armed. "You sent for me—"

"Ned, something has happened to Julia. I am going after her. The ship is yours until I return."

Chapter Thirty-Two

Charlotte jerked awake, a scream strangled in her throat. The pounding came again followed by footsteps running down the stairs. Pink shards of light needled through the lace curtains. The sun wasn't even fully awake yet, so why all the noise?

Men's voices reverberated through the house—and one of them sounded like William. She rolled out of the bed, thrust her arms into the sleeves of her dressing gown, and tied it as she sprinted from her room and started downstairs. She pressed her back to the wall out of Collin's way. He rushed up from the foyer, taking the stairs three at a time.

Concerned, Charlotte bolted downstairs. William paced the front foyer, his face stony with anger.

"What is it?" she breathed.

William's expression never changed. "Julia is missing. I need Collin's help to go after her."

"What can I do?" Charlotte grasped William's wrist. Julia in trouble?

He gently extracted his arm from her grip and turned away, rubbing his eyes. "Nothing—nothing but pray for her safe return."

A hand settled on Charlotte's shoulder, and she looked around into her mother's soft eyes.

"Yes, William. We will pray." Mama's calm voice had an edge to it. "But should not the authorities be made aware also?"

William paced the length of the hall. "No. This is my fault—my fault for delaying the wedding. My fault for leaving her in harm's way. My fault for not going to London myself to see her father—for not taking her to her father."

Mama left Charlotte and planted herself in front of William. When he stopped, she rested her hands on the gold epaulettes on his shoulders. "William, you cannot blame yourself. Do you know for certain what has happened to her?"

"She has been duped by those aunts of hers—from what her butler told me, it sounds as if Julia agreed to go to the Pembroke estate with Lady MacDougall yesterday."

"But she had planned this visit. It is probably nothing to worry about."

"Something does not sit right, Mother. The plans suddenly changed, yet Julia did not let anyone else know? Why would she and Lady Mac-Dougall leave a day early without Lady Pembroke? It makes no sense. I know they are plotting a way to get their hands on Sir Edward's money." He banged his fist against his leg. "This is all my fault."

Charlotte thought about the circumstances for a moment. "Julia said Lady MacDougall reminded her very much of her mother. Do you think she is capable of such duplicity?"

"If she is at all like Lady Pembroke, yes." William resumed pacing. "If anything happens to her, I will never forgive myself."

Mama stepped in his path again. "You cannot blame yourself for the actions of others. You had no way of knowing that something like this would happen." She raised her hand to stop him from speaking. "No. I do not believe even you thought her relatives capable of such deeds. I am confident no harm will come to her. Lady Pembroke might be prone to maliciousness, but I do not believe even she would want to see any physical harm come to Julia. There would be no benefit to it."

For a moment, William stood ramrod straight, face stony, eyes searching their mother's face. Finally, his expression eased, the lines around his eyes diminishing. "Knowing you will be praying for her gives me confidence we will find her and return her safely to your protection, Mother."

All three turned as Collin forged down the stairs, buttoning his uniform coat, his sword slapping his leg and the stair railing balusters. Susan, stricken and pale, followed, Collin's hat clutched in her arms.

Charlotte, Mama, and Susan followed the two captains to the door, Charlotte in the lead. She stopped short on the threshold. A man she vaguely recognized stood on the front walk.

"Creighton, return home," William commanded. "You must act as though you are ignorant of anything amiss."

The Witheringtons' butler saluted. "Aye, aye, sir."

"Also, you must serve Lady Pembroke as if nothing has happened."

"Yes, sir." Creighton ran down the walk to an unsaddled horse and took off at a gallop.

Collin turned and kissed Susan's forehead. "Everything will be well, my love. Pray for us."

She nodded, tears streaming down both cheeks. "I will. Give Julia all my best love when you find her."

Collin's mask of determination slipped into a slight smile. "I believe I shall give that task over to William, if you do not mind."

Susan gave a weepy laugh. "I do not mind at all."

Halfway to the street, William turned. "Charlotte?"

Her heart pounded at the sudden notice. "Yes?"

"Go to the port Admiralty. Find Admiral Glover. Explain to him that Sir Drake Pembroke bribed the postmaster to divert all correspondence to and from Admiral Witherington. Get Admiral Glover to go to the post office with you to see how many letters have arrived from the admiral and what has become of them."

Excitement at the assignment overrode the fear that had held Charlotte in its grasp since she'd awoken. "Yes, William."

He fitted his hat to his head and touched the fore point of it. "Ladies, next time we see you will be when we bring Julia home."

⌘⌘⌘

The pounding, pounding, pounding beneath him was enough to drive a man daft. Drake's head throbbed in rhythm with the horse's hooves. The darkness barely lessened as the sun made its way over the horizon behind the threatening gray clouds. Only the chill wind and intermittent rain slapping his face kept him alert and focused on reaching his destination.

Two hours ago, he'd stumbled back to the dingy room above the tavern where he'd been hiding out for the past week after a night of trying to earn back some of his losses at the tables. He'd been shocked nearly to soberness to discover a messenger from his mother waiting outside his door. The instructions in her note had almost knocked away the rest of the inebriation.

By the end of the week, he would be married to Julia Witherington, and her fortune would free him from his troubles.

How they had gotten Julia to agree, Drake did not want to imagine. He'd heard enough of his mother and aunt's scheming recently to know that whatever method they employed was better left unexplored.

After an hour's hard riding, he pulled up to the inn in Bishop's Waltham. Once he presented the innkeeper with one of the precious coins his mother had sent along with the note, the man was more than willing to answer Drake's questions.

"There was two ladies stopped by yesterday afternoon for tea—an older lady and a younger pretty mite. They had one of the lads run down to the big house at Marchwood to let them know to be ready for overnight visitors. But then the older lady let slip that they be heading for Scotland for the young woman's wedding."

"Thank you, my good man." Drake tossed the man another one of his few coins. Aunt Hedwig was following his mother's plan to the letter. He kicked the lathered horse into a trot. Fifteen minutes later, he pulled the blowing, sweat-flecked beast to a stop in front of the sprawling, two-hundred-year-old manse.

CRQRD

Julia yawned and walked the length of the hall to try to work the knots out of her back. The lumpy bed in her mother's old room had given her little rest, and doubts over the wisdom of this trip nibbled at her mind all night like a dozen ravenous mice.

Aunt Hedwig had taken to her bed as soon as they arrived last night, leaving Julia to explore on her own, though the long shadows cast by her candle had thrown an eerie pall over the vacant rooms.

The few servants were nowhere to be easily found this morning. The giant clock in the hall chimed eight times. She tried to calculate when she could anticipate Augusta's arrival. She hoped Augusta was even now leaving Portsmouth so she would arrive by noon. But the steady rain might slow her progress.

Julia stepped into another bedroom, the furniture ghostlike under white sheets. What little she'd seen of Marchwood last night was grand but colder than she remembered from childhood. Faces of angry-looking ancestors stared at her from ancient portraits on nearly every wall. And though everything was clean, an aura of neglect permeated the house.

If the house had been this cheerless when her mother was a child, it was no surprise she'd married at seventeen. Julia wrapped her shawl tighter around her shoulders.

"Julia?" Hedwig's voice pealed through the halls.

"Yes, coming." She hastened down the hall to her aunt's room. "You look like you're feeling better this morning."

Hedwig plumped a pillow and put it behind her as she sat up in the bed. "A good night's sleep was all I needed."

Julia puzzled over the gleam in Hedwig's eyes. "What...what a relief."

"Yes. Now, you and I must discuss our real reason for this visit to Marchwood. Sit. Your height is craning my neck."

With sudden trepidation, Julia sank into the straight-backed, wooden chair beside the bed. In this light, with no smile softening her mouth, Hedwig did not look much like Eleanor Witherington. "Our *real* reason?"

"We have something important to discuss now we are here. I came to Portsmouth in response to a letter from Augusta expressing her concern over your ill-judged engagement to a sailor." She shifted herself into a straighter position. "I have observed. And more to the point, I have listened. I can keep my silence no longer. It has come to my attention that this engagement of yours is not a love match as so many in that backward town are so willing to believe."

Invisible fingers tightened around Julia's throat.

"I hate to bring you pain, but I have learned that your Captain Ransome is not the man of honor that everyone believes him to be. No, let me finish. I have been told by a reputable source that he marries you only for your dowry, and that he has been duping your father for years, acting the part of son to him only to curry favor and gain promotion and prestige. And your father, bless him, is too daft—I believe that is the word that was used—to realize Ransome has been taking him in all these years."

A new understanding and a deep realization of her own stupidity for trusting Hedwig froze Julia's spirit. A year ago, this argument might have had the desired effect. But her rekindled relationship with her father and her growing knowledge of William let her see through this paltry attempt to turn her against him. "I thank you for your concern, ma'am, but I assure you that is not the case. Captain Ransome is a man of genuine honor, and he would no more dupe my father than turn spy for France."

The sympathetic simper vanished from Lady MacDougall's expression. "I did not want it to come to this, Julia, truly I did not. But you have given me no choice. You think what I said to be untrue. But what will others think should they hear it? What would Captain Ransome's fellow officers think should they know of his mercenary ways, marrying you only for your thirty thousand pounds?"

Icy dread wove throughout Julia's soul. *Oh, Father God, please do not let her do this...* "You would not dare—"

"Think of how it would affect his mother and his sister—she just came out into society, did she not?—if everyone knew William married you only to gain favor with the admiral?"

Hedwig leaned forward, her icy gaze now feverish. "And think of your father, Julia. If it should become widely known that he had his own daughter play the harlot with most of the Admiralty to gain favor and advantage for himself. Your father would be drummed out of all good society, and Captain Ransome denied any further advancement for being married to a loose woman. The Ransome family would be so tainted by association with you that Miss Ransome would never secure a good marriage, no matter the amount her brothers have settled upon her."

Julia gasped at the ugly insinuation and covered her mouth with a clammy hand, afraid she might be physically ill.

With a mad glint in her brown eyes, Hedwig thrust a piece of paper at Julia. "I have taken the liberty of composing a letter breaking your engagement. Tonight, this letter, copied over in your hand, will go to Captain Ransome; otherwise, all of Portsmouth will begin to believe you a paramour, Captain Ransome a mercenary, and your father a daft old man who prostitutes his daughter for his own advancement."

Tears of disbelief, of umbrage, of impotent rage clouded Julia's vision. She stumbled from the room. She would never have believed her aunt—her own relation—could be so cruel. The words swarmed and stung her mind like angry wasps. She could not believe anyone could be so barbarous, so spiteful, as to consider ruining the future happiness of so many people simply because Augusta and Drake had not achieved their own ends.

She fumbled through the house back to her room, closed the door, leaned against it, and slid to the floor. *Lord God, how could I have been so blind? I so wanted to believe that Hedwig was just like my mother that I never suspected she might be lying to me, might be in league with Augusta. I know I have gotten myself into this mess, so it is my task to get myself out of it. But I cannot. This is beyond my wits and strength, Lord. Please help me.*

Chapter Thirty-Three

Charlotte trotted to keep up with Admiral Glover, whose angry pace cut through the early morning crowd of shoppers on the street like a scythe through wheat. He looked over his shoulder and then slowed when he realized she was having a hard time keeping up, as were the two marines half-marching, half-running behind her.

When they reached the post office, Charlotte stopped with a gasp.

"What is it?" Admiral Glover looked around as if expecting to leap into battle.

Charlotte leaned close. "That's Lady Pembroke, Miss Witherington's aunt."

Lady Pembroke stepped down from a fancy barouche. "Elton, I will be in High Street for about an hour."

"Yes, my lady." The driver touched the brim of his hat, hopped back up in his seat, and drove away.

Charlotte quickly slipped into the post office, Admiral Glover close behind. She had briefed the admiral on everything William had told her. Hopefully now they would start getting some real answers.

"Lady Pembroke!" Baroness Fairfax greeted in a tone so high, Charlotte was relieved the windows did not shatter.

"Lady Fairfax." Julia's aunt looked less than pleased to see the baroness.

"Augusta, I commend you for how well you are holding up. If it were one of my sons—well, I would be absolutely out of my head with anger." Lady Fairfax made no point of keeping her voice low. Charlotte ducked behind the few other patrons to move closer yet stay out of Lady Pembroke's sight.

Lady Pembroke's face contorted as if she weren't quite sure how to react. "Holding up? Why, whatever could you mean?"

Lady Fairfax took Julia's aunt by the arm and pulled her toward the front window—closer to Charlotte. "My dear, it is all over Portsmouth. No one wanted to believe it, but it came from such a reliable source."

"I beg you, my lady, please tell me of what you are speaking." Panic laced Lady Pembroke's voice. Charlotte hardly breathed, straining to hear.

"Why, the word about town is that your son has abducted Miss Witherington and is taking her off to Scotland to force her to marry him. What with the debt collectors hanging about his front door at all hours of the day and night, it's no wonder he's been driven to such drastic measures." The baroness patted Lady Pembroke's arm. "You must be relieved that Captain Ransome set out after them so promptly."

Lady Pembroke looked like she was about to be sick.

"I see I have distressed you by speaking of it. You have my solemn oath that I shall not say another word to anyone on the subject." Rather than look sympathetic, the baroness gleamed, no doubt elated at the idea of spreading this story further.

"You—" Lady Pembroke took a gasping breath. "You said you heard this from a *reputable* source?"

"Yes. Lady Dalrymple had the telling of it—how he had the housemaid slip laudanum into dear Julia's coffee and then absconded with her when she was too weakened to resist him. It's a good thing Captain Ransome discovered the plot so quickly and was able to go after her. Why, he will most likely be back with her today with luck and good providence, and neither of them need worry about her reputation being soiled at all."

Lady Pembroke pressed her lips together. "If you will excuse me, my lady, I just remembered another urgent errand I must see to."

"But—did not you come in to post a letter?"

"It can wait." Augusta stuffed crumpled paper back into her reticule and rushed out the door.

Charlotte silently clapped her hands together and wended her way back to Admiral Glover. With a promise she'd tell him what she heard later, he marched toward the postmaster's office.

A clerk stopped him.

"I am here to see the postmaster. Please get him for me immediately." Though no taller than Charlotte, Admiral Glover's commanding presence—and possibly the amount of gold braid on his uniform—seemed to intimidate the clerk.

"Yes, sir. I'll get him right now."

The admiral turned and cast a wink over his shoulder at Charlotte. She grinned. He might be crusty, but he was a fountain of information. And she found his stories humorous, even though William called him an old windbag.

The postmaster came out, his round belly barely contained in his canary waistcoat. "What can I do for you, Admiral?"

"Might we have a private word, good sir?"

"Private?"

"Yes. It is about business dealings you have had with a certain Sir Drake Pembroke."

All color drained from the man's face. "S-Sir Drake?" He muttered several curses under his breath. "I knew this would come to no good."

Charlotte followed them to the door of the back room. The postmaster sank into a creaky chair at an overflowing desk and dropped his head into his hands.

"Then you do admit to knowing Sir Drake Pembroke?" Admiral Glover leaned his shoulder against a tall cabinet.

"Aye. He offered me money to divert a few letters to him. More money than I make in six months."

"To whom were the letters addressed?" Charlotte asked, stepping into the room.

The postmaster's head snapped up. "And just who might you be?"

"She is a party concerned." Admiral Glover's position never changed, but the bark in his voice made it seem he had just snapped to attention—and it certainly got the postmaster's attention. "Now, please answer her question."

"Letters to Admiral Witherington, Miss Witherington, or Captain Ransome." The portly man groaned.

"Very well then. Charlotte, my dear," Admiral Glover kept his eyes trained on the criminal in their midst, "please go outside and ask the marines to come in and arrest this man."

"Marines? But I've done nothing against the Royal Navy!"

"So you think stealing the post of two distinguished naval officers not a crime against the Royal Navy?"

A bit shaken by the heat in Admiral Glover's voice, Charlotte quickly retreated from the building and sent the guards in as requested. The red-coated marines escorted the manacled man out, and Admiral Glover offered his arm to Charlotte to see her home.

Susan met her on the front steps of the house. As soon as Admiral Glover relinquished Charlotte's arm and bade them good morning, Susan pounced. "So, what did you learn?"

"The postmaster had indeed been taking payment from Sir Drake. The admiral has placed him—the postmaster—under arrest for corrupting the good name of his office. He had no letters now, but he admitted he had given letters addressed to Admiral Witherington and the admiral's letters addressed to Julia over to Sir Drake."

"The knave!"

"But that is not all. I overheard Lady Fairfax telling Lady Pembroke that she heard Sir Drake abducted Julia, and William had gone after them to rescue her."

"Oh, good gracious!" Susan clapped her hands to her cheeks. "Abducted? Do you really think he abducted her? Wait—what am I saying? Lady Fairfax has never been known for her accuracy. Yet..." She took Charlotte's arm. "No matter. William will put everything to rights when he finds them. Come. Your mother awaits within.

We are having an early breakfast. We simply could not wait until ten o'clock, because our morning started so early."

Once they all sat at the dining room table, Charlotte repeated what she had told Susan and then continued her story. "I am certain Lady Fairfax, despite giving her 'solemn oath,' intends to broadcast the story far and wide."

"Good. Though I do not hold with gossip, perhaps justice will be served in this debacle." Susan stood and crossed to the sideboard to refill her plate.

"I wish we had some way of knowing if William and Collin have arrived at Marchwood yet." Mama lifted her fork but set it back on her plate.

"Shall I go over the calculations again, Mama? If it is a four hour drive by carriage, and a carriage travels at approximately five miles per hour—"

"Please." Susan stopped eating long enough to hold one hand up. "Stop. No arithmetic at the breakfast table. It made my head spin enough earlier when you told us all of the variables and calculations. You sounded just like Collin and William when they are engrossed in their maps discussing routes and distances and speeds." Susan shuddered. "Just tell us what time they should have arrived and when they will return."

"According to my calculations, they should be arriving at Marchwood shortly. Unless—"

"Charlotte." Mama's soft voice carried a tone of warning.

All three women started at a rap on the front door.

"Who could that be at this time of morning?" Susan sprang from her chair. Charlotte ran after her out into the entry hall—and halted and dropped into a deep curtsey beside Susan.

"Lady Dalrymple, what an honor." Susan sounded breathless, as if she had just run up a few flights of stairs.

"No, it is not. It is an imposition. Why, I imagine you have not even sat down to breakfast yet, and here I am knocking at your door." Lady Dalrymple's toothy smile sparkled in the morning light. "I see your guilty smile, Mrs. Yates. Come, let me impose upon your hospitality for a bite of breakfast, and I shall pay for it with information."

Susan grinned and swept her arm toward the dining room door. "Come. Breakfast is just now served, and we have more food than we three can eat. I am anxious to know what you have heard about what has happened this morning."

At Lady Dalrymple's request, Charlotte recounted the morning's experiences.

"Yes, that would explain why Augusta nearly ran out into the street in front of my carriage. I invited her to ride with me awhile. After all, I am the one who broadcast the news that Sir Drake kidnapped Julia."

Charlotte laughed; Susan and Mama gasped.

"But how did you learn of it?" Susan's hand trembled, and she set her coffee cup down. "We only know because Julia's butler informed William very early this morning."

"Julia's girl, Nancy, once served as an upstairs maid in my country house. She was a gentle, kind creature, and I knew Julia would treat her well. When Nancy arrived at the Witherington house this morning—she goes to see her family out near Fareham on Sundays—she discovered Julia had not slept in her bed last night. Being suspicious because I told her to be so, she peeked into Lady Pembroke's room. Augusta was still sleeping, but Nancy found a letter in Julia's hand on Augusta's dresser. Though I am certain it nearly gave her the apoplexy, Nancy absconded with the letter." The dowager viscountess pulled folded pages from her reticule and handed it to Susan.

"The outside note is to Creighton." Susan unfolded it. "She says she agreed to go to Marchwood with Lady MacDougall a day early, but instructs him to let us know and to keep watch on Lady Pembroke in her absence."

Charlotte took the first note, and Susan turned her attention to the one inside. "This one is to me."

Dear Susan,

I might be the grandest fool in the world, but I am going

to Marchwood with Lady MacDougall a day early to have time to see the grounds and estate. If you have not heard from me by five o'clock in the evening Monday, it might be best for you to alert Captain Ransome that something is amiss. I hope and pray that Lady MacDougall is nothing like Augusta Pembroke, but I cannot bring myself to fully trust her.

The page crumpled in Susan's fist. "Oh, Julia! For a woman so intelligent to have so little sense!"

"But, my lady, how did you know William had gone after her before now?" Mama asked. "Except for Charlotte, we have seen no one."

Lady Dalrymple laughed. "How do you suppose Nancy got out to my house in time to relate her tale, and with ample time for me to be among the first in High Street? Julia's butler, in an effort to calm Nancy, assured her *Cap'n* Ransome would handle everything, and he had their driver bring her out to my house armed with this evidence. I knew what Augusta Pembroke was up to the moment I read it, and set my own plan into motion. And I feel no guilt over embellishing the tale to cast aspersions on Drake Pembroke's already soiled reputation."

"Thank the Lord for your swift action, my lady," Mama breathed.

"Yes, and for Julia's wonderfully loyal servants." Susan nibbled on a piece of toast.

"It really is too bad word cannot now reach the admiral in time for him to come for the wedding," Lady Dalrymple remarked. "I assume, if the captain and Julia return today, the wedding will still take place tomorrow as planned."

"I hope so." Mama's enunciation emphasized her softly spoken words. "The sooner they wed, the better I will feel."

"She is truly blessed to be gaining a mother like you, Mrs. Ransome." Lady Dalrymple inclined her head toward Mama. "I can see from Charlotte here and the good reports I have heard of your son that your children have never lacked for love and affection from you."

Mama blushed. "Thank you, my lady."

"I also hope you might allow me the honor of inviting Charlotte to come stay with me for a few weeks. I have a great liking for collecting young people around me. Then I can host a dance in Miss Charlotte Ransome's honor next week, before her brother and new sister leave—we will wait to plan a more formal ball later."

Charlotte's heart pounded. An event in *her* honor given by a viscountess? Most young women of the *ton* in London were never distinguished in such a way. And what a send-off it would be as well. She begged Mama with her eyes to say yes.

Mama beamed. "I could wish no greater distinction for Charlotte. Naturally, if she wishes, I wholeheartedly consent to her staying with you."

"Wonderful! It has been too long since I have had a young, eligible woman in the house. Miss Charlotte, you just wait and see if we do not have you well settled before Michaelmas."

Charlotte's excitement faded. Of course a ball in her honor would be so she could meet potential suitors. What would Henry think if he heard of her dancing and flirting the night away—as she had done at the Farifaxes' ball not a fortnight ago?

"Naturally, we shall have all of the officers from Captain Ransome's ship to attend—they should greatly enjoy it. And you must dance with all the lieutenants, Charlotte." Lady Dalrymple's eyes twinkled. "I hear they are all monstrously handsome."

"Charlotte has met them, my lady." Susan turned to her. "Charlotte, what think you of William's lieutenants? Are they handsome?"

"Yes, each is handsome in his own way." Especially the first lieutenant with the gray eyes she could spend eternity charting the depths of.

No! Her heart belonged to Henry. Besides, the less time she spent in the company of Ned Cochrane, the better. She could not afford to have him pay her any measure of attention. For when the time came, he could not recognize her. At the end of next week, Ned Cochrane must see her only as Charles Lott, midshipman.

Julia paced the bedroom, Lady MacDougall's ugly threats still ringing in her ears.

Her father and William had survived so much—bullets and cannon, shipwreck, fire, disease—yet if their honor were besmirched in such a way, everything they had fought for and gained in their lives would be as naught. No one would remember the lives they saved or the battles they won. All people would remember were the savage, malicious lies.

Julia cared little for her own reputation. In Jamaica, nothing said of her in Portsmouth would matter. But her father's and William's livelihoods depended greatly on what those in authority above them believed to be true.

She sank onto the musty chair beside the fireplace, where a small blaze made little progress in chasing away the chill of the rainy day. If she agreed to Lady MacDougall's plan, if she broke her engagement with William and married Sir Drake, William would be humiliated. She would be casting off all her dearest friends. Susan might forgive her, but never again would they be as close as sisters. And Mrs. Ransome—pain seared Julia's soul at the disappointment she would cause that dear lady.

Her father's face floated before her mind's eye, mottled with rage. She'd only seen him that furious once, when she was a child and he'd had one of *Indomitable*'s crew flogged; but if she turned her back on William, she had no doubt she would see that expression again.

Yet how could she not accede to the demands? If she did not do as bidden, the results would be no better. Her reputation would be soiled worse as a reputed harlot than it would be as a fickle woman who jilted one man to marry another. Her father would lose his position. William, if he were not also drummed out of the navy, would most likely never again regain the respect he now garnered. The rumors would chase Charlotte Ransome all the way back to Gateacre, and as Lady MacDougall threatened, Charlotte would never make a good marriage. And what of William's brothers, also captains in the Royal Navy, whose progress depended greatly on reputation?

Lord God, please, show me what to do. I cannot make this decision by myself. It is not only I alone who must suffer regardless of the choice I make. So many lives will be affected.

If only she'd stayed in Jamaica. If only she'd never come to this horrid place.

Her mother's gentle voice and sweet smile infiltrated her thoughts, bringing the burn of tears to her eyes. Why had her mother never forewarned her that people—her own relatives—could be so cruel and spiteful?

She wished she could cut off all emotion and rely solely on reason to make her choice. Yet the idea that she might never see William and Susan and other friends again nearly drowned her with waves of sorrow and regret.

Honor. Love. The two were inexorably entwined. If she chose love, she would bring dishonor; if she chose honor, she would lose those she loved.

After what seemed hours, though the sun had hardly moved in the sky, a knock at the door interrupted her agony.

"Yes?" Her voice sounded shredded, just like her heart.

A servant entered. "Lady MacDougall requests your presence immediately, miss."

A tear escaped Julia's eye, but she dashed it away. A decision must be made, and she had only a gallows' walk in which to make it.

Chapter Thirty-Four

Drake lounged on the window seat in Aunt Hedwig's bedroom, though he did not understand why the woman was not up and dressed on this important day.

"She will agree. Mark my words." Hedwig looked up from her breakfast tray.

"How can you be certain? Everything Julia's done has defied logic."

"Only because you and your mother did not press the issue hard enough. What you've yet to learn is that when someone cares nothing of her own reputation—which is apparent for all to see in Julia, as it was in her mother—you must go further: You must go after those she loves most."

He picked at a worn spot on his coat sleeve. "Are you certain this is the only solution left to us? To force her into the decision?"

"She proved more stubborn than even I could have imagined. We are fortunate she did not do what her mother did and elope before a plan could be put into action. And I had such a suitor lined up for Eleanor. Second son of a Duke with a sickly older brother. The fortunes of the Pembroke family would have been ensured for generations. But no, Eleanor had to run off and marry a sailor."

Though the chill of the rainy day seeped around the windowpanes, Drake divested himself of the ratty jacket and threw it to the other end of the seat.

"Are you pouting?" Hedwig laughed. "You are upset that she did not come to you willingly, that she did not submit to your fumbling attempts at wooing her."

Irritation festered in the pit of his stomach, but he could not risk raising Hedwig's ire against himself. He wondered what, if any, spirits were in the house; he needed a stiff drink to settle his nerves. Since nothing in this room could answer, he stalked to the fireplace and stoked the blaze. "What man wishes to become a husband only by force and duplicity?"

Hedwig cackled louder. "Fool! If you had not wasted what little your father had restored to the Pembroke estate, imbecile though he may have been, you would not be in this position." Her spite-filled laughter subsided. "Drake, once you are certain of a Pembroke heir on the way, you can leave Julia here and go and do as you please in London. I understand you have already taken to paramour Lady Margaret Everingham. Once you are wed, your debts are paid, and your lineage is secure, you can take as many mistresses as you please with all the freedom of the security that marriage brings."

A soft knock was immediately followed by a servant opening the door. Julia, ghostly pale, entered the bedchamber. She balked upon seeing Drake and then closed her eyes as if the sight of him made her head ache.

He grunted and folded his arms. Even the idea of being able to set her aside in a few months did not offset his disgust of marrying someone who found the mere sight of him distasteful.

Aunt Hedwig continued eating. "Ah, Julia. Please come in."

On stiff legs, Julia came a few steps into the room. The servant closed the door; Julia flinched at the sound of the latch clicking into place.

"Drake, you have not greeted your cousin." At their aunt's hard look, Drake bowed. Julia's green eyes swept over him before she executed an ignoble curtsey.

Though it pained him, he offered his arm. "I am happy to see you, Julia. Come, sit with me."

She stared at his arm for a moment before settling her hand on it. He escorted her to the window seat, eschewing the two hard wooden chairs nearer the bed. She dropped his arm and her hand disappeared under her shawl as she perched on the edge of the cushion.

"May I say you are looking well, dear cousin?" He nearly choked on the compliment. She looked like she was about to be ill all over the Italian-made carpet. He regained his seat and leaned against the pillows he'd piled there earlier.

She answered only with a brief nod.

"Had you a pleasant journey to Marchwood?"

Again, a single movement of her head to indicate assent.

"Though the day is drear, cousin, I should love to take you about the house so you can see all Marchwood has to offer."

"Now, Drake, let us not be moving ahead of the issues at hand." Hedwig finally set aside her tray. She dabbed her mouth with a lace handkerchief, adjusted her frilly mobcap over her hair, and resituated herself against the pillows. "Well, Julia, you have had an hour to consider the proposal put before you. What say you?"

Julia's neck strained as she swallowed. Drake studied the outline of her profile. Really, she was not all that unattractive. If she were to soften toward him, they might have an amicable marriage.

"Lady MacDougall, I have spent the time since our last interview praying about the decision you have given me. Either choice I make will bring humiliation and pain to those I love." As if moved by some unseen hand, she rose and crossed to the opposite window. "I have not easily arrived at a decision. And before I tell you what I am going to do, there is something you should know."

She turned to face them both. "When Captain Ransome and I became engaged, I promised him that he would become sole heir to Tierra Dulce. If I jilt him, he may take legal action to claim this right." She visibly swallowed again. "And if my father is angry enough, he might agree and make William—Captain Ransome—his legal heir." She glanced from Hedwig to Drake. "As a man of honor, Drake, can you see the quandary this creates? Would you be willing to take me on so little promise as my thirty-thousand pound bridal legacy and nothing more?"

Drake's innards careened, alternating between panic and anticipation.

Without the promise of the fortune that would come from the sugar plantation upon the admiral's death, marrying Julia for an amount that hardly exceeded his own debts suddenly seemed less palatable. But what choice did he have? "Yes, Julia. I would still take you for as little as that."

Julia nodded and again turned to look out the window.

"Well?" Hedwig rasped, her hands fisted in her bedclothes. "What is your decision, child?"

Julia left the window and approached the bed. "Aunt Hedwig, I would like to have that letter, please."

Drake really needed a drink. Brandy, whisky, port, anything. In mere moments, his most pressing debts would be covered, with a little left over to use as a stake to win his way back into the comfortable lifestyle he deserved.

Hedwig beamed and took the folded parchment from under her pillow. "I knew you would come to see things as we do, Julia. Tomorrow, we shall all depart for Scotland, and we shall see the end of this nasty business."

Julia took the letter, unfolded it, her hand trembling as she read it. Though she probably did not even realize it, she edged toward the warmth of the fireplace.

Drake stood, preparing to receive his sentence with aplomb.

Julia stopped with her back to the fireplace and finished reading the letter. Her hands slowly ceased trembling. Drake's started.

Julia refolded the letter. "Very well then."

"I knew you would make the right decision." Hedwig threw back the bedclothes and made to rise.

Drake reached to adjust his coat's lapels and remembered he'd removed it. He settled for straightening his waistcoat.

"I was not certain I was making the right decision until I came in here." Julia ran her fingers along the crease in the paper. "But after our conversation, I am certain I received the answer to my prayers for clarity." Grasping the parchment with both hands, she ripped it in two and tossed it into the flames.

Drake could only stare. What decision had Julia made?

Aunt Hedwig gasped and flew from the bed, the breakfast tray crashing to the floor. She grabbed Julia's arms. "How dare you defy me!"

"How dare I *defy* you? My dear Lady MacDougall, in all of your scheming have you considered how these rumors you plan to start will affect your own reputation? And Augusta's and Drake's? The aunt of a loose woman, relative of a man who would prostitute his daughter? And they would quickly discover that you started these rumors yourself."

Hedwig raised her hand as if to slap her. Drake grabbed her wrist, realization dawning. Julia had decided not to marry him. Wounded pride could not staunch the relief that flooded him.

Color returned to Julia's cheeks. "I will marry Captain Ransome."

"We will see about that!" Hedwig jerked her wrist from Drake's grip. "Drake, lock her in her room. Augusta has already started the work of spreading the word about Portsmouth that you have run away to elope with Drake. No matter what you do now, you have lost your sea captain and all those around him."

"That is how little you know about the real nature of love and honor, Lady MacDougall. Those who love me will never believe the lies you spread. The revelation of the truth, though it may be long in coming, will undo any damage your scheming and gossip create."

"Take her out of my room this instant! I cannot abide the sight of her."

A little frightened by Aunt Hedwig's rage, Drake grasped Julia's hand and dragged her into the hallway.

"You can still make things right, Drake," Julia panted as she ran to keep pace with his long strides. "Take me back to Portsmouth. Own up to everything that has been done. Help put it all to rights. You can redeem your honor, though your mother and aunt have done their best to bring you down with them."

"Honor? What is honor when I face debtor's prison? When the note on Marchwood will be foreclosed this week? When I face losing everything dearest to me? Have you no sense of honor, of pride in your family name?" He thrust Julia into her bedroom, not wanting to listen to her anymore; her words made everything murky.

Julia stumbled a few steps into the room before whirling to look at him, incredulity nearly dripping from her full lips. "My family name? *My* family name? I have more pride than you can imagine in the *Witherington* name, which is why I refuse to despoil it by marrying you."

Drake grabbed the key from the inside of the door, slammed it, and locked it from the outside. He curled his fist around the key until the metal bit into his palm. How dare she? Despoil the Witherington name by marrying him?

He punched the door frame—and immediately regretted it when pain shot up his arm.

She pounded the door. "You cannot keep me locked in here forever. William will come for me as soon as he learns I have not returned to Portsmouth."

"You can stay in there until you rot—or until you learn what's best for you."

"Drake, is this really what you want? Do you really want to wed someone who must be locked up and forced to agree?" A tinge of panic laced Julia's voice. "I always thought you a gentleman, a man who would hold honor high. I will help you—help you find a way, a legal way, of retrenching so you can repay your debts."

"Stop." He pressed his fists to his ears. "I will hear no more of your woman's wiles. And none of the servants will help you either, so don't bother asking. There will be a guard stationed below your window, so you need not try to escape."

"Drake—"

"No. No more." He ran down the hall, away from her confusing words. In the dining room, he grabbed the first decanter he came to. Without bothering to find a glass, he tossed the stopper across the room and drank long and deep.

CRRRD

The gables of Marchwood loomed closer. William prayed Julia was still here—that her aunt had not absconded with her to Scotland already. The innkeeper in Bishop's Waltham had given a good enough description of Sir Drake Pembroke to assure William the baronet was also here.

Finally, William pulled back on the reins and slowed the horse, coming to a full stop at the front of the stone manor. He dismounted and, with Collin beside him, climbed the steps. Both removed their hats and shook off as much water as they could.

Just as he was about to knock, the front door flung open, and something blue and mahogany slammed into his chest, shouting and flailing.

"Madam, please control—" Recognition set in. He grabbed her arms. "Julia! Are you all right?"

She stilled, though confusion still clouded her eyes. "William?" She reached up a shaking hand to touch him as if he were an apparition. "Oh, William!" She flung her arms around his neck.

He hugged her tightly, lifting her from the ground, never wanting to let her go again.

"I cannot believe you came. They told me—the gossip and lies they were going to spread."

"Shush." He stroked her silken hair. "You can give me a full report on our way back to Portsmouth."

"We must go, quickly. I picked the lock—they do not know I've escaped."

Though Julia tried to release herself, William did not let go. "No, we must end this, now. They cannot—"

Something hard touched the back of William's head. "Sir, I ask that you put the lady down and step away."

William released Julia and slowly turned. The barrel of a pistol hovered mere inches from his nose. He forced Julia behind him. "And just who, may I ask, are you to be making such a request?"

"I'm Constable of Bishop's Waltham. I was told yesterday by these good folk that they are hiding this lady away from an unwanted suitor who beat her. They said you might come and try to take her back." The man looked down at Julia, then turned back to William. "Thought you would just grab her and drag her back to Portsmouth, did you?"

"As you were, sir." Collin's bull-like build had never come in more handy than now. Though a large man himself, the constable did waver a bit when Collin moved between him and William.

Julia tried to pull away from William, but he wouldn't allow her to move out from behind him. "Sir," he addressed the constable, "perhaps Miss Witherington can clear things up a bit."

"Beg pardon, miss. But maybe you can tell me what is going on here. They—" with his pistol, he motioned over her shoulder toward Drake and Hedwig, who now stood in the doorway behind her, dressed as if for visiting—"told me they were rescuing you from him." He pointed the pistol at William again.

She shook her head. "No. No—that's not right. She—" she pointed at Hedwig, "my mother's aunt tricked me into leaving my father's home to try to force me to marry him," she waved her hand toward Drake.

The constable scratched his head with the muzzle of the pistol. "So—you did not want to come to Marchwood with them?" He jerked his head over his shoulder.

With the pistol now pointed away from him, William allowed Julia to come forward and stand beside him.

"Well, I did—when I thought I was just coming to see the home where my mother grew up. But I never intended to stay, which they were trying to make me do. They locked me up and were going to force me to stay here while they went about spreading malicious gossip about my character so that I would have no choice but to marry him."

"And this man helped you escape?" The constable nodded at William.

"No. She used her own ingenuity to escape by picking the lock and sneaking out." William's panic subsided enough to let pride take a foothold.

The constable frowned at Julia. "But he's the one who's rescuing you?" He waved the gun in William's direction again.

"Yes, sir." She looked up at William, a strange light flickering in her eyes. "He is rescuing me."

The constable lowered the pistol. "You say they detained you against your will?" His mouth drew up in a half smile. "Kidnapping, that is, then."

"I have no wish to bring charges against them." Julia leaned more heavily into William's side. He repositioned his arm around her waist to lend her better support.

"You may not, but I got a grievance with that man there."

William whirled. An enormous man in a violent green coat dismounted a horse, two pistols stuck into his waistband.

"It's the debt collector I told you about," Julia whispered.

"Mornin', miss. Pleasure to see you again." The ruffian tipped his hat to Julia as he passed. "Sir Drake Pembroke, I am here to collect a debt for my employer. If you cannot pay it, I will have to ask this good gennulmun here to throw you into jail until such a time as you can."

William turned just in time to see Pembroke leap from the porch and sprint toward the front gate.

"Oi!" the bill collector bellowed.

"Oh, no you don't!" Collin flew into action. Though shorter and heavier, Collin made short work of the distance and tackled Pembroke into the muddy gravel drive.

Lady MacDougall screamed and trotted down the driveway, where she proceeded to flail at Collin with her reticule. Julia gasped. William stifled a laugh. From years of experience in dealing with drunken crewmen, Collin had Pembroke completely subdued by the time the bill collector reached them and pulled Lady MacDougall away.

"Fleeing! Fleeing arrest! We have you now, sirrah." The constable joined the fray.

When the debt collector released Lady MacDougall, she once again started whacking Collin with her bag. Seated as he was on top of Pembroke's chest and arms, Collin deflected her blows with one arm and finally caught the lady's weapon with the other.

"It looks like he might need your assistance, William." Julia's face had regained the light he loved so much.

She took his hand and led him from the porch. "Come on. I don't think we'll want to miss this."

William shook himself from his thoughts and accompanied her down the drive. The rain had eased to a fine mist. He released Julia's hand only to restrain Lady MacDougall while the constable and the debt collector conferred.

After a few moments, the constable motioned for Collin to let Pembroke up. "It seems his papers are all in order. If you cannot pay him five thousand pounds now, I am commissioned to take you to the debtors' prison right here in Bishop's Waltham." He took hold of Pembroke's arm.

The debt collector grabbed the other arm despite the mud dripping from Pembroke's face and clothing. "And if you don't give up the twenty thousand for the mortgage note, my employer will foreclose on it as soon as I can get word back to him today."

William glanced at Julia and stepped forward. "About that twenty thousand pounds. As I know Sir Drake Pembroke is not in possession of the money, I would be interested in speaking to your employer about purchasing the note from him."

"After all this," the green-coated man extended his arms to take in the scene, "you're going to pay his debt?"

William shook his head. "No, not his debt. He will still be responsible for paying the five thousand in interest. I want to purchase the mortgage note on Marchwood so your employer does not have to go through the expense of a foreclosure. He would receive his twenty thousand, and I would become creditor on the title of the estate."

"And the fancy baronet 'ere still goes to jail?"

"Yes." William concluded the business by taking a card and arranging to meet with the man holding the note on Thursday. "Come, Julia, Collin. I believe our business here is completed."

With Julia in front of him and Collin at his side, William turned his horse south toward safe harbor.

Chapter Thirty-Five

Julia slowly awoke to the rhythm of the horse beneath her and William's strong arm about her waist steadying—anchoring—her. Her restless night and the comfort of William's arms had been more than enough to lull her into a deep sleep. Now, the clouds had subsided, and the sun was well beyond overhead, beginning to move behind them as they traveled southeast.

"Is that…?"

"Aye. Portsmouth just ahead." William's breath tickled her ear. "You have been asleep for a while. How do you feel?"

"Foolish—and stiff and sore. But nothing, I am certain, that cannot be cured by a good night's sleep."

"If Susan will let you out of her sight." Collin chuckled. "I would not be surprised to see her at the city gate waiting for the first glimpse of us."

Though Susan did not await them at the gate, the streets of Portsmouth seemed abnormally busy. They did not have to pass through High Street or near the dockyard, but Julia still felt an extraordinary number of eyes turned her direction as they made their way to Harthorne Street.

When they drew nearer the fashionable part of town, curtains rustled and were pushed aside for both men and women to look down upon them. A young boy came out of one house and ran far down the street into another. When Julia, William, and Collin approached, the front door flew open, and Mrs. Hinds ran out to meet them.

William pulled the horse to a stop.

"Miss Witherington! Captain Ransome, Captain Yates. I am relieved to see you. When I heard—but of course you must not let me detain you from those even more anxious for your return. Tomorrow—" She pressed her fingertips to her lips. "The wedding is still tomorrow, is it not?"

"Yes, ma'am." William's immediate and emphatic answer sent a shiver through Julia. He inclined his head and touched the fore point of his hat. "Good day, Mrs. Hinds."

A paradelike atmosphere greeted them on Harthorne Street— neighbors leaned from upper windows waving, calling greetings and well wishes.

They had not fully stopped in front of Collin's house when two midshipmen rushed out into the street to greet them.

"Kennedy, Gibson—why are you here?"

The teens snapped to attention at their captain's words and swept their hats off.

"Sir." Gibson's voice cracked. He cleared his throat. "Lieutenant Cochrane commissioned me to come and await word of your return."

William swung down and turned to help Julia, hands securely holding her waist. "And you, Mr. Kennedy?"

Julia's legs nearly gave out when her feet touched the ground, and only by holding on to William's wrists did she stay upright.

"Sir, Lieutenant Cochrane grew concerned we had not yet received word, so he sent me to inquire as to the delay. I arrived a few minutes before you. We were sitting on the steps, sir. We did not take the liberty of waiting inside."

William sighed, his expression weary with resignation. The front door banged open. Before Julia had gained her balance, William's steadying hands were replaced by Susan's arms in a hug so tight, pain shot through Julia's ribs.

Over Susan's ebullient chatter, William ordered the midshipmen back to *Alexandra*. "Tell Lieutenant Cochrane he is to continue in command until I return, which may be very late tonight."

Though her legs were stiff from the long ride, Julia made it to the front door under her own power—with Susan's arm tightly around her waist. At the door, Mrs. Ransome enfolded Julia in a hug that brought tears to Julia's eyes with the comfort and love it conveyed.

Mrs. Ransome dried Julia's tears with her own handkerchief. "There, there, my girl. Was it so terrible? You are here now, safe and sound among those friends who dearly love you."

The next greeting came as quite a shock as Lady Dalrymple hugged Julia. "I cannot help but feel somewhat responsible for this."

Charlotte hung shyly back from the commotion. Julia smiled and extended her hands. With a relieved smile, Charlotte rushed forward and hugged her. "I am so happy—but I knew all would be well."

With Charlotte on one side and Mrs. Ransome on the other, Julia climbed the stairs and collapsed into a chair in the sitting room. Against Mrs. Ransome's and Collin's protests, Susan drew up a footstool and sat at Julia's knee, clasping Julia's hand, as if afraid Julia might vanish if she let go.

Mrs. Ransome and Lady Dalrymple questioned William and Collin for above an hour on the details of their experience. They, in turn, questioned Lady Dalrymple and Charlotte.

Julia's mind drifted in and out of a drowsing state until shocked out of it upon hearing of Sir Drake's and the postmaster's treachery. William, standing sentry near the large windows, grew graver and graver.

Tea arrived, and Susan refused to allow Julia to serve herself, instead plying her with sandwiches and pastries. Once Julia ate a bite of watercress sandwich, her stomach remembered she had not eaten since dinner yesterday.

"Well." Susan rose, Julia's hand still clasped tightly in hers. "I believe it is time for everyone to have a rest before dinner. Julia, your driver should be arriving shortly with fresh clothing for you. William, I will brook no opposition. You are staying. My lady," she curtsied to Lady Dalrymple, "we would be honored if you would join us, though it shall be a humble affair."

"I should enjoy that above all else, Mrs. Yates; however, I am expecting guests of my own for dinner tonight and should have been home hours ago to prepare." Lady Dalrymple crossed to Julia and kissed her cheek. "I shall see you in the morning, and then we shall all reconvene at my house to celebrate your marriage."

In the flurry of Lady Dalrymple's leave-taking, William caught and held Julia's gaze. When he left the room alone, she slipped out and followed him across the hall to the front parlor. He took her hand, tucked it into the crook of his elbow, and walked the perimeter of the room with her, as if on a promenade in the park.

The silence, the absolute stillness of the room, alleviated the ringing in Julia's ears from the noise and clamor that had surrounded her since their arrival.

William's eyes focused on the floor in front of him, his face impassive. If he hadn't kept tight hold of her hand, she might think he had forgotten her very presence. Scrutinizing his profile, Julia's insides quivered at the realization of how little she truly knew of this man to whom she was about to bind her life—for a year.

"Why did you ask to purchase the note on Marchwood?" Though she spoke in a whisper, William flinched as though at a cannon's firing.

"Why? Because I have been unable to stop thinking of the possibility since you mentioned it the other night. Though I have had no desire to purchase an estate in England, it seems a reasonable investment."

"Will you foreclose on it?"

They made a full circuit of the room before he answered. "I do not know. I know Pembroke cannot afford to pay the note or the interest that will continue to grow beyond the five thousand he already owes."

"How—I hate to pry into your personal affairs—but are you well able to afford to part with such a sum as twenty thousand pounds?"

The corner of his mouth raised in a smile, though he still kept his focus on the floor before them. "After tomorrow, I can part with such a sum and still be ten thousand pounds the richer. And to what better use could your legacy be put than to secure the estate of your ancestors?"

She tried to swallow the lump of gratitude in her throat. "I meant for you to keep the legacy for yourself. Our agreement—"

"Our agreement was that we would marry, and I could have your legacy to do with as I please." He stopped, put his hands on her shoulders, and turned her to face him. "This is what pleases me."

The air in the room thinned until no matter how fast Julia breathed, she did not seem to gain enough to relieve her sudden lightheadedness.

"Julia…" His sky-blue eyes delved into hers. "I can no longer abide by the terms of our arrangement."

Her heart, so full of expectancy, nearly shattered. "What? Why? If I have said—"

He touched his fingertips to her lips. "I still wish to marry you. However, I cannot and will not agree to an annulment. If we marry, it is to be a lifelong commitment. I wish—" He drew in a shaky breath. "I wish us to have a genuine marriage."

"A genuine…?" Julia's knees buckled. William caught her around the waist and led her to a chair.

He knelt on the floor in front of her. "Julia, is there any reason you think we should not be happy together? Do you find something lacking in me, something that keeps you from feeling any regard for me as a husband?"

Julia's cheeks burned. "I…I am only concerned at how little I truly know you. Everything has happened so quickly." She dropped her gaze to her lap, overcome with shyness.

He kissed her palm and rose, drawing her to her feet. "I agree. Our courtship has been far too brief." His mouth quirked in a grin. "But eight weeks in cramped quarters should soon alleviate that, don't you agree?"

Still quivering from the soft warmth of his lips to her palm, Julia nodded. "Yes."

Looking as pleased as if he had negotiated the peace with France himself, William beamed. "Good. Now, as I do not want my bride falling asleep in her soup, I advise you do as Susan suggested and go rest before dinner." He led her out into the hall.

"And you? You have had less sleep than I."

"Do not fret, my dear. Losing one night's sleep to see to the downfall of an enemy is something to which I am quite accustomed." He kissed her forehead. "Besides, Collin has a sofa in his study that is quite comfortable for napping—if he has not already appropriated it."

Over dinner, the day's events continued to be discussed as each person remembered more details and offered them for comment and examination. The evening ended when William bade all farewell to return to his ship as duty demanded, insisting he could walk as the evening was still young.

"I should return home as well." Julia rose. "William, Elton can take you to the dockyard after delivering me home."

Within minutes, they were in the barouche, William seated across from her.

"I wish your father could be with us tomorrow."

"I too." Julia refused to let any more emotions get the better of her, but her throat filled with longing for her father, wishing he, not Admiral Glover, would walk her down the aisle and present her to William at the altar.

"I told my crew yesterday of our wedding." William launched into the story of making the announcement to his men.

Julia watched him under hooded eyes. He so rarely smiled, as he was doing now. Yet she knew he could be humorous. Like her father, he must have learned to hide everything behind an expressionless mask, never letting his true emotions show lest it compromise his authority.

When they reached the front door, Creighton threw it wide open. "Miss Witherington! I'm chuffed to see you back safe again."

She almost hugged the servant but did not want to discomfort him. "Thank you. I'm happy to be home. Is Lady Pembroke still here?"

Creighton's smile vanished. "No, miss. Elton dropped her and her dunnage off at the Pembroke house just before noon." Though he didn't say it, *good riddance* resounded in his tone.

"How shall I ever thank you for raising the alarm?"

He flushed like a schoolboy. "'Tweren't nothing, miss. Just happy I could get to Cap'n Ransome in time."

"It was well done, Creighton." William gave a quick nod. "I shall write to Admiral Witherington commending your actions."

"Thank you, sir." Creighton backed into the house. "Now, I believe I will excuse myself."

Heat tweaked Julia's face. She turned to look up at William; the intensity of his gaze put her at a loss for words.

His hands cupped her jaw, fingers twining in her hair. His lips touched hers with such tenderness, her knees buckled and she grabbed the front of his coat to stay upright. The kiss ended in a brief moment, followed by one on her forehead.

"Good night, my darling Julia."

"Good night." Her voice came out a whisper.

❧

Alexandra's bell rang two couplets of chimes. William slowly came to consciousness. Four bells. He opened his eyes. The gray light coming in through the window meant it was morning watch. Six o'clock. He stretched, his muscles painfully reminding him of the hours spent on horseback yesterday. Though not wanting to leave the comfort of his hammock, William rose and began his daily routine, trying not to think of how this day was different from any other.

Julia had agreed to truly become his wife, to put aside the notion of their marriage being a business arrangement. But the fact remained that three hours from now, his life would irrevocably change. No longer could he be concerned only for his own well-being and happiness.

Julia's joy and safety, indeed her very life, would now depend on him. He prayed he could live up to his responsibility.

Dawling entered as William pulled his shirt over his head.

"Breakfast, sir." Dawling's smile gleamed across the dim room. "A last meal, as it were, sir."

"Humph." William shook his head and sat down to the plate of eggs, sausage, and black pudding. "Have the lots been drawn?"

"Yes, sir, among the crew, anyway. Of the officers, Mr. Ingleby volunteered to stay."

"Good man. I'll see that he is rewarded for his sacrifice." And staying behind was truly a sacrifice on the part of the ship's master, who enjoyed a good feast and time ashore. William downed the food without tasting it. "You saw the baker yesterday?"

"Aye sir. He will bring the cake and treats to the ship at eleven o'clock as you requested. I have told Mr. Ingleby of the plan so he does not deny the boat approach."

Sooner than he thought possible, the shrill whistles of boatswain's mates piped up the hands. His innards quivered like a jellyfish. Dawling assisted him into his heavy dress coat, the gold braid and brass buttons dull in the dim light from the overcast sky outside.

After a quick inspection of the hands gathered on the quarterdeck, William released them to breakfast and called for the ship's boats to be made ready to ferry him, the lieutenants, and the warrant officers ashore.

Rather than leaving the deck, the crew came to order by division, each saluting as if rendering passing honors to the ship of a superior officer. The lieutenants and warrant officers lined the path to the waist entry port.

"Three cheers for the captain!" Boatswain Matthews called as William came across the quarterdeck.

The crew's cheers resounded in William's ears and gladdened his heart. He raised his hat in a sign of honor to his men and then descended the accommodation ladder to the waiting boat, followed by the officers. The trip to the dock seemed but a blink of an eye. Sailors and workers alike cheered for him as he passed through the docks, his officers following him like novitiates.

In their walk from the dockyard to Saint Thomas's Church, more well-wishers than William thought possible called their congratulations or joined and walked with them. The large church was nearly filled to capacity when William arrived—all faces bright with smiles as he made his way to the front of the chancel.

Collin met him in the nave, and William's officers abandoned him to take up their seats on the front row.

"Julia awaits with Susan and Admiral Glover in the vestibule."

William's heart pounded in his throat. The organ groaned and began to expel music William hoped was pleasing to Julia. To him it sounded like nothing more than the rumble of cannons in battle.

"Ready?" Collin asked.

"As I will ever be." William clenched his hands into fists to keep them from trembling.

Susan, dressed in a gown the color of the lilacs that graced his mother's garden each spring, joined them at the altar.

William forced himself to stand at attention rather than galloping down the aisle to meet Julia when she appeared. Though it was covered with a lace veil, she wore her hair loose in a riot of curls down her back, the way he liked it best. Her face glowed, eyes luminescent.

The vicar stepped forward. "Dearly beloved, we are gathered together here in the sight of God, and in the face of this congregation, to join together this man and this woman in holy Matrimony; which is an honorable estate, instituted of God in the time of man's innocency..."

William could not keep his eyes from Julia's, losing himself in their emerald depths.

"I require and charge you both, as ye will answer at the dreadful day of judgment when the secrets of all hearts shall be disclosed, that if either of you know any impediment, why ye may not be lawfully joined together in Matrimony, ye do now confess it."

Julia's eyes twinkled, and she smiled for the first time. William returned it, his pleasure in her almost more than he could bear.

"If any man do allege and declare any impediment, why they may not be coupled together in Matrimony, by God's Law, or the Laws of this Realm, let him now speak his objection."

The sound of a door slamming caused a rustling gasp in the crowd, but William thought nothing of the latecomer's arrival—until a man's voice reverberated throughout the silent sanctuary.

"I object."

Chapter Thirty-Six

Julia stifled a cry and, heart pounding, turned. The little light from the overcast sky outside that filtered in through the tall stained-glass windows sparkled on the epaulets and prodigious amount of gold braid adorning the uniform of the man who strode with purpose up the aisle toward them.

"Papa." Her heart rose into her throat and then dropped into her stomach. That her father had come fulfilled her greatest desire. That he objected to her marrying William extinguished the hope for a future that included what might become a happy marriage.

A fevered pitch of murmuring swept around them like a whirlwind. Never before had Julia seen such an expression on her father's face. She had known he would be unhappy he had not been consulted, his blessing not given before they proceeded with the wedding. But surely once they explained the circumstances, he would understand—would give his permission for the wedding to continue.

She trembled as he mounted the steps to join them, Admiral Glover moving quickly out of his way. Sir Edward turned his gaze upon William for a long moment. William stood at attention, his eyes forward, focused over Julia's head. Then Admiral Sir Edward Witherington turned to his daughter.

"Julia, you will wait in the vestibule."

She swallowed the desire to disobey him and forced her feet to carry her back toward the rear of the sanctuary.

"Captain Ransome, you will come with me."

She turned and looked over her shoulder to watch William follow her father through a door at the front of the chancel. Susan joined her and, arm around Julia's waist, escorted her through the doors to the vestibule.

"Once William explains everything—oh, Julia, you know your father cannot object. He loves William as a son. I should think there is no one else in the world he should wish you to marry."

Julia paced the small antechamber. Her father was here. He would see that all was put to right—would see to it that Julia was protected from any further threat. But could he truly ask her not to marry William?

Anguish wrapped around her chest and tightened until breathing came harder and harder. The door opened, and her father came through. Susan excused herself and returned to the sanctuary.

Upon seeing Julia, he must have recognized her affliction, for his face eased into a smile. "Come. Have you no greeting for your father?"

"I—" Restraining her grief, she moved into his open arms, the wool of his coat rough against her cheek.

"My daughter. Long have I desired to see this day. I could wish no finer man as your husband, as I told him twelve years ago."

Julia stepped back in surprise. "No—but why—?"

He rested his hands on her shoulders. "I have one question to put to you to settle this matter. Do you love him?"

She opened her mouth, but no words would issue forth.

Sir Edward sighed and pulled her back into his arms. "Dear, dear daughter. I love you more than life itself. If I were to see you unhappy in your choice of husband, knowing I could have prevented it, my inaction would be untenable and my misery absolute."

"I will be happy with him, Papa. He is a good man—the best man I know, aside from you."

"That is not what I asked you, Julia."

Her mind whirled, memories of William as a fifteen-year-old midshipman taking care of her, of the handsome young lieutenant who charmed her out of all good sense, of the captain who'd ridden through the night to come to her aid yesterday.

"Yes, Papa. I love him. I have loved him since I was ten years old."

He kissed her forehead. "Excellent. Because there is no other man I feel is worthy of your affection. Now, as to my objection to this wedding."

The glimmer of hope his reaction brought was snuffed by his last statement. "Objection? But I have confessed I love him. You said—"

His green eyes twinkled. "My objection is that I did not get to walk my daughter down the aisle and give her away to her husband. That is not an office I want Crispin Glover performing for me."

She laughed as he pulled her into another hug. But—she pushed away from him again. "How did you know to come—how did you find out? The post…?"

"I received an express from William early Monday morning. I rode all day yesterday and took only brief respite to ensure I arrived before the wedding." The left side of his mouth quirked up. "Not quite the naval precision timing I usually have, but it will give everyone more to talk about, aye?"

"You are incorrigible." She slipped her hand into the crook of his elbow, feeling for the first time in more than a year that everything in her life was wonderful.

Susan turned when the doors opened, her eyes glistening with tears. But as soon as she saw Julia's arm through her father's, she handed Julia her bouquet and preceded them down the aisle. The organist was a bit slower to catch on; however, before they were halfway to the front, heavenly music once again filled the church.

The rector looked somewhat confused and very frightened of Sir Edward. William beamed his pleasure at her, and she returned his smile.

"I—er—shall I—?" the rector stammered, unable to take his eyes off Sir Edward.

Sir Edward scowled, though his eyes still smiled. "Continue, man, continue."

"Er, yes. Right. Uh…" The service book trembled violently in the minister's hands. He took a deep breath and did his best to still it before continuing to read the ceremony. "William Robert Ransome, wilt thou have this woman to be thy wedded wife, to live together after God's ordinance in the holy estate of Matrimony? Wilt thou love her, comfort her, honor, and keep her in sickness and in health; and, forsaking all others, keep thee only unto her, so long as ye both shall live?"

William's tender gaze caressed Julia's face. "I will."

Her heart fluttered.

"Julia Edwina Witherington, wilt thou have this man to be thy wedded husband, to live together after God's ordinance in the holy estate of Matrimony? Wilt thou obey him, and serve him, love, honor, and keep him in sickness and in health; and, forsaking all others, keep thee only unto him, so long as ye both shall live?"

Obey him? Serve him? She searched the depths of the crystal blue eyes looking so intently into hers. He would never ask her to do anything that would bring her pain or harm. Yes, she would obey him, knowing he meant any request only for her good. He would protect her, had already proven so, time and again. Serving him was the least she could do to repay him.

His dark brows began to draw together and she realized she had not spoken. "I will."

The rector released a sigh of relief. "Who giveth this woman to be married to this man?"

"I, her father, do." Sir Edward cupped Julia's cheeks in his hands and kissed her forehead. He then took Julia's right hand and placed it in the rector's before stepping back to take the seat made for him by the shifting down of William's officers.

The minister placed Julia's hand into William's. "Repeat after me…"

William pledged his troth, followed by Julia, her voice gaining strength with each word of the vows.

"Have you a ring?" the rector asked.

William turned. Collin withdrew a ring from the watch pocket of his waistcoat and laid it upon the rector's book. The rector prayed a blessing over it and presented the ring to William. Taking her quavering left hand, he slid the ring—a thin gold band set with a large emerald surrounded by small diamonds—onto her finger. "With this ring I thee wed, with my body I thee worship, and with all my worldly goods I thee endow: in the name of the Father, and of the Son, and of the Holy Ghost. Amen."

He raised her hand and kissed the back of it before they both turned to kneel. The rest of the prayers and Scriptures were read, the sermon on the duties of the husband and wife given, communion shared by Julia and William, and the ceremony concluded with a prayer.

After kneeling so long before the altar, Julia was grateful for William's support when she stood.

"Well, kiss her then!" A male voice called from the direction of William's officers.

Julia let slip a nervous laugh. Redness climbed up William's neck into his face. He raised his left hand and touched a curl at her temple, leaned forward, and kissed her.

When her knees gave out, his arm clasped her waist and hugged her to him. The kiss ended, and she buried her face in his shoulder, completely disoriented and filled with too many feelings to even know what they were.

The officers of *Alexandra* and every other man in uniform in the church *huzzahed* three times.

Knowing she could not continue to hide in William's uniform, she released him and turned to receive a hug and kiss from Susan. The organ bellowed out a raucous toccata as William took her hand and led her from the church.

Outside awaited one of the fanciest carriages Julia had ever seen. Standing beside it, in full formal livery, Elton swept off his hat and bowed low before opening the door for them.

William assisted her up into the large, open-topped carriage.

"Lady Dalrymple told me I was to drive you down through High Street and to the dockyard so all those who couldn't come to the wedding could see you and wish you joy." Elton secured the door behind William.

"Oh, no, Elton—" She implored William with her gaze.

He nodded and patted her hand. "After the wedding breakfast, you may drive us to the dockyard, Elton, so that I may take Julia out to see *Alexandra*. But not now."

"Aye, aye, sir." Elton knuckled his forehead before returning his tall, feathered hat to his head and climbing up into the box. "To Lady Dalrymple's it is, then."

७५१५७

"May I ask you to stand and join me."

William dragged his gaze away from Julia, who sat serene amid the flurry of Charlotte and Susan's animated conversation. Around him, everyone pressed in at Sir Edward's request. William extended his hand to Julia and brought her back to his side.

Sir Edward raised his crystal goblet. "To my beloved daughter and her husband. May they never know sorrow, but enjoy health and prosperity. May they never be faced with great trials, but if they are, may they find wisdom and counsel one with the other. May Julia find comfort in the knowledge that her husband fulfills his honor through duty to king and country. And may William be supported in the fulfillment of his honor and duty by the loyalty and prayers of his wife. Ladies and gentlemen, the bride and groom."

"The bride and groom," the crowd around them repeated and raised their glasses.

"Now, William, I understand that Admiral Glover has taken an office upon himself that I wished myself to do." At Sir Edward's scathing glance, Admiral Glover made a deep bow.

"Most humble apologies, sir." Admiral Glover's smirk was anything but contrite.

"May I assume you are carrying it with you?" Sir Edward set down his glass and extended his hand.

In the silence surrounding them, William's pulse thudded loudly in his ears. "Aye, sir." He, too, set down his champagne, and then he reached into his coat pocket and removed the packet Admiral Glover had given him. Heat rose up the back of his neck—a mix of pleasure and pride and humility.

"Very good." Admiral Witherington unfolded the pages and patted his pockets. "I do not appear to have my spectacles with me. Well, no matter." He raised the papers over his head. "What I have here are the orders officially raising Captain William Ransome to the rank of Commodore. When he arrives in the Caribbean, he shall take over command of Jamaica station."

A cheer went up around them. Julia's mouth dropped open before spreading into a wide smile. She hugged him tightly. "Why did you not tell me?"

He held her close so that she could not see the embarrassment creeping into his face. "So much has happened since I learned this news, it slipped my mind."

"Slipped your mind?" She pulled away and then raised up on her toes to kiss him. "No matter. But next time you are promoted, please tell me personally."

"I promise." He kissed her again and then released her. Collin and the other officers present crowded around to congratulate him and offer him their advice.

The continual press of the assembly set William on edge, remembering why he despised public functions so greatly. Julia received the attention with an admirable aplomb that increased his pride in knowing that regardless of where they went, he could always depend on her to part the social waters and afford him smooth sailing.

Finally, the crowd began to disperse. William dismissed the officers to go back to *Alexandra* to prepare the crew to receive Julia.

Lady Dalrymple approached them. "You should be honored by the number of people who turned out today," she said, taking one of each of their hands in her own. "Never have I seen a couple so universally celebrated as you. All of Portsmouth will remember this as the happiest—and most eventful—wedding ever. Thank you for letting me have some little part of it."

"No, it is we who must thank you for so graciously opening your home to us, my lady." Julia inclined her head.

"Captain Ransome, I understand you wish to take Julia to see your ship. My carriage is at your disposal, and Julia, your father has relinquished the services of his driver for today, so Elton will take you wherever you please."

"Thank you, my lady."

After the viscountess moved away to see to other guests, William turned to Julia. "Shall we go? I should like to present my crew to you and show you the only home I can offer—humble as it is."

The sparkling green of her eyes matched the ring he had placed on her finger two hours ago. "Yes."

Alexandra rose and fell on the choppy harbor. Matthews, who had been leaning over the gunwale railing, turned to yell over the deck, "Captain coming up, Mr. Cochrane."

"Very good, Mr. Matthews. Bosun's mates, pipe 'all hands.'" Cochrane's voice carried to them on the high wind.

Julia's eyes danced with gleeful delight as she took in the aspect of the two gundecks and newly painted side of *Alexandra*—until she saw the men rigging the bosun's chair.

"William, I've no need to be swung up. It has been a while since I have been on a ship, yes, but I believe I am still well able to climb up to the deck." Her expression turned saucy. "Or even the shrouds to the mast top, if need be."

The memory of their first encounter blazed clearly in his memory. "Aye, that I do not doubt. But no wife of mine will be doing any such climbing—"

Mutiny replaced her humor.

He sighed. "Unless she is properly dressed for it in a tunic and trousers. However, in the gown in which she was married, I would prefer she take advantage of the hospitality my crew offers." He caught the rope-and-plank swing and held it steady for her.

She laughed and settled herself onto the board seat. "I suppose I shall have to go see about having some appropriate attire made then."

William hastened up the accommodation ladder and reached the deck just as Cochrane assisted Julia from the bosun's chair. His crew, all standing at attention and dressed in their best, crowded the quarterdeck, the men eagerly craning for a better look at their captain's new wife.

He escorted her up to the poop deck, and the crew turned to face them. "Julia, I have the honor of presenting the officers and crew of His Majesty's Ship *Alexandra*." Looking out over his men, he raised his voice. "Men, I am pleased to introduce to you Mrs. Ransome, my wife."

The men cheered, but the pounding of William's heart drowned it out. His *wife*. He looked down at her in wonder. Hints of the ten-year-old Julia Witherington remained in the freckles across her nose and dimples in her cheeks. But standing beside him, Julia *Ransome* was his wife—the woman he had been falling in love with for the past twenty years.

He now understood—fully comprehended—Collin's decision to resign his commission and stay in England to be with Susan. William's ship, his career, his reputation—none of it mattered any longer. For, if asked, William himself would walk away from his crew, forsake his duty, and even sacrifice his own honor to provide for and protect Julia.

Love demanded nothing less.

Coming soon...Look for books 2 and 3 in Kaye Dacus's Ransome Trilogy

⟨⟨⟨⟩⟩⟩

Ransome's Crossing

To get to her secret fiancé in Jamaica, Charlotte Ransome disguises herself as a midshipman and joins the crew of one of the ships in the convoy led by her brother William. First Lieutenant Ned Cochrane had met his captain's younger sister briefly—just long enough to be sure she is the wife he's been praying for. But now he is about to leave for the Caribbean for at least a year.

An attack on the convoy gains Ned the promotion to commander he has long dreaded—especially once he discovers one of his midshipmen is actually Charlotte Ransome in disguise. After seeking the advice of Julia, William's bride, Ned decides to keep Charlotte's secret...and hopes to win her love. Charlotte will soon discover that losing her heart to Ned is not the greatest danger she'll face on this Atlantic crossing.

Ransome's Quest

The pirate El Salvador has haunted the waters of the Caribbean for almost ten years. When he snatched Charlotte Ransome, it was a case of mistaken identity. Now Charlotte's brother, whose reputation in battle is the stuff of legend, is searching for him with a dogged determination. But another rumor has reached El Salvador's ears: Julia Ransome has been kidnapped by Shaw—the violent and bloodthirsty savage feared by all other pirates and from whom El Salvador was trying to protect her.

When word reaches William of Julia's disappearance, his heart is torn—he cannot abandon the search for his sister, yet he must also rescue Julia. Ned Cochrane offers a solution: Ned will continue the search for Charlotte while William goes after Julia. William's quest will lead him to a greater understanding of faith and love as he must accept help from a sworn enemy and have faith that Julia's life is in God's hands.